LIVING

LISE GOLD

Cover design by Irvine Design

Edited by Claire Jarrett

All the art of living lies in a fine mingling of letting go and holding on.

— Henry Havelock Ellis

1

Ella buried her feet in the cold sand as the ocean washed over her toes. It was still dark, and the beach was deserted. She took a deep breath in a fruitless attempt to fight the nausea that was slowly spreading through her, then checked the time on her phone. It was 5:30 am. Not that it mattered, it wasn't like she had anywhere to go after this. That thought brought her on the verge of a panic attack, but she turned her attention back to the ocean anyway and faced it.

The current looked strong, the water making a loud whooshing noise each time it covered her feet, before retreating silently. That was a good thing, she supposed. Maybe the storm was a sign that today was the day. She'd already been here twice, and she'd managed to overcome her despair on both occasions, something inside her telling her that maybe tomorrow she'd feel better. But she hadn't felt better, and she knew nothing could take away the deep sadness inside her, the hole in her soul, that for some reason was only getting bigger, contrary to what her therapist had assured her would happen. She didn't feel whole anymore, and she didn't know how to be without Helena.

Her sister had always been the one to keep her grounded, and she'd been the only one able to make her laugh. Ella hadn't laughed in two years, since Helena died. She'd worked hard and had done what was expected of her. She'd gone through life on autopilot, putting on a smile when required. But she couldn't be in crowds anymore, and apart from a couple of appearances to promote her movies, she hadn't given a personal interview since before that night. It was a miracle she was still able to continue her career in the movie industry. Going out at her peak was probably for the best because if she didn't, there would be no career left if she carried on ignoring her fans and the people who mattered in Hollywood.

The second anniversary of Helena's death had seemed like a fitting date, two nights ago, when she drove around aimlessly, desperate to get away from her life. Playa del Rey Beach was the most peaceful place she'd been able to find then, and now, she knew it was her only way out. *The only way to see her again.*

Ella wobbled as her feet sank deeper into the wet sand. She was barely able to stand after washing down a couple of tranquilizers with half a bottle of vodka, the alcohol necessary in case she freaked out, lost her nerve and went back home, just like she had yesterday and the day before. Trying to fight the overwhelming nausea, she held onto her stomach and sank down on her knees. It wasn't enough to stop her from vomiting, and within seconds, the vodka shot out of her mouth, creating a pool in front of her. She hadn't eaten today. In fact, she couldn't remember having eaten much at all in the past few days. She didn't derive any joy from food anymore, or anything else for that matter.

A wave came up and washed the vomit away, tugging at her long, blonde hair, imploring her to venture into its depths. That would be her soon. *Washed away.* She grimaced at the sour taste in her mouth as she leaned forward and buried her head in her lap. Ella had thought about what would happen after she was gone, of course. The thought had all but consumed her. In a couple of hours from now, the director of her current movie would throw a tantrum on set, assuming she was late. He'd call her manager, who would then drive to her house, let himself in and realize Ella wasn't home. Would he call her mother? Did he even have her number? And if he did, would her mother be worried about her? Or would she just shake her head in disappointment at Ella's work-ethic and ignore the fact that she was missing? Ella wasn't sure. Even though they didn't speak anymore, she was fairly certain that her mother loved her, and that had been her only source of hesitation in her decision. She'd read somewhere that surviving a child was the worst thing that could happen to a person and her mother had already been through it once. She would be very, very rich though, after Ella was gone and perhaps that would be a small consolation. Her mother had always been about the money, and her talented daughters had been her way of obtaining it. As she got up again and stood there on the long, quiet beach, she realized she'd never felt so lonely in her life.

It was her birthday today, and it would have been Helena's birthday too. Her manager had arranged a party for her tonight, with tons of A-listers in just the hotspot of the moment. It was supposed to be her first private social gathering in two years. Private perhaps wasn't the right word, as she didn't know any of her guests well, and there had been no one she'd been looking forward to seeing or meeting.

The party would be talked about for years to come if they didn't find her in time, and even if the first beach goers found her in an hour, the news of her death on the day of her big party would certainly make for an amazing story, giving her invitees the chance to display their 'humanitarian' side and align themselves with mental-health charities in order to increase their appeal. That was how it worked in her business. Nothing was real.

The vodka gloom spread in the pit of her stomach and grew deeper, just as she'd expected. Then again, she knew that without it, she'd never have the courage to do what she was about to do. Carefully, she set one foot in front of the other and made her way into the water. The back of her long, white dress dragged behind her, the hem swirling wildly in the current. She thought she heard a voice but didn't look back, instead wading faster into the water, the level now reaching up to her knees. The last thing she wanted was to be 'saved' because the consequences of surviving would be unbearable. Even more paparazzi following her around, even more headlines.

'Ella Temperley attempts to drown herself on Playa del Rey Beach'. Or: *'Star of 'Born Naked' walks into the sea. Chasing headlines or cry for help?'* People she hardly knew would wrap an arm around her and ask her how she was holding up without any real concern while putting on their warmest smile for the paparazzi. Her mother would probably grab the opportunity to write another book, just like she had after Helena's death, spilling her most intimate secrets.

The voice behind her grew louder now, and there was no doubt that someone was calling her. Ella started wading as fast as she could but wasn't making much progress. It felt like running on a treadmill, and although it didn't seem like she was moving, the water reached up to her waist now. An imposing wave crashed against her and she was suddenly dragged down, the force of the ocean tumbling her around and making her lose her bearings. She didn't fight it for the first few seconds, disorientated and confused. Her first reaction was to swim back up, but she kept spinning and didn't know which way was up anymore. The real panic hit her when she realized that she wouldn't be able to take her next breath. She'd just breathed out when she was dragged back under, aware that there was no oxygen left in her lungs. Wasn't that the whole point? Wasn't this what she wanted? She scrambled around, desperately searching for the way up, her eyes wide open but unable to see anything. *Oh my God, I'm going to die.* Her heart was beating so fast and hard that she could feel her own pulse like a deep bass as she started flailing wildly, desperate to get some air. Her feet and hands reached up and down but the water was now so deep that she couldn't even find the ocean floor. Never in her life had she been so scared and never in her life had she wanted to live so badly. Right then, Ella knew she'd made the biggest and the last mistake of her life. The pain in her chest was excruciating and the darkness before her eyes turned to white as she had no choice but to give in to her screaming lungs and open her mouth, breathing in, liquid flooding her body causing what seemed like a never-ending stream of pain, panic and desperation. Her muscles spasmed, gave up, and she couldn't move. Then, her conscience faded into nothing.

2

Cam Saunders opened the sliding doors to her porch and stepped outside, wincing at the strong wind against her face. Deciding to ignore the weather, she stretched, grabbing one elbow behind her head, then switched to the other side before bending down and steadying her palms flat on the wooden surface that was covered with sand. She pushed her head between her knees as far as she could and looked in between her legs, feeling her long, lean limbs waking up. The longer strands of her shortish, dark hair were blowing into her eyes and she closed them for a moment, holding the position. It was still dark but as always, her alarm had gone off at six, and she was up and getting her gentle morning exercise in before teaching her first yoga class of the day.

It was a little too cold to do this outside today, with the November storm raging over the coast, but she liked the sea breeze and it always woke her up. Her favorite red hoody kept her warm but she knew she'd be sweating soon, despite the chill. Cam couldn't wait for the seasons to change. May was always the best time of the year, when the purple-flowered jacaranda trees were in bloom throughout LA and the beach started to fill up during the day. Unlike her neighbors, she didn't mind the spring-and-summer beach-goers in front of her house. In fact, it always cheered her up, seeing the locals excited about spring.

Hers being one of the few free-standing houses along one of the quieter beaches in LA, it was photographed a lot. And it looked picturesque, she had to admit, painted light blue with white windowsills and a bright blue door, wedged in between California palms. Built on the extension that separated the highway from the beach, it was a prime location. Several developers had been unsuccessful in their attempts to purchase it from her throughout the five years she'd lived there, and Cam knew she would never sell the house her mother had left her, no matter how much they offered her. Standing directly on the Pacific Coast highway, the house looked relatively small from the front entrance, but what it lacked in width, it made up for in length, stretching impressively along the beach, where the foundation was supported by sturdy stilts and the generous porch that overlooked the ocean.

She took a couple of deep, steady breaths, sinking into position, then slowly came back up again. Her eyes narrowed as she spotted a woman who was kneeling on the beach, bent forward. *What the hell is she doing?* She'd have brushed her off as a drunk partygoer on her way home if it hadn't been for the fact that she'd seen her the previous two mornings in exactly the same spot. It was a strange morning to sit there, with the storm blazing, and the woman didn't look like she'd just returned from an all-nighter. The long, white dress was way too romantic for the LA club scene, and as far as Cam could tell the woman wasn't wearing any shoes. *Is she sick?* She was holding on to her stomach, shaking heavily. *Jesus, she probably needs help.* Cam leaned over the railing in an attempt to get a better look at her, then decided something was off, so she walked down the porch steps to the beach.

"Hey lady, are you okay?" she yelled. The woman stood up without acknowledging her and started walking into the sea. Her long, blonde hair was furiously whipping in the strong gusts of wind and she looked almost ghostly in the dim light. "Hey!" Cam yelled again, picking up her pace now. Still no reaction, but the woman was wading into the ocean at an alarmingly fast pace now. "You're going to get yourself killed. This is no weather for swimming. The storm is dangerous, don't you get that?"

It was then that Cam realized what was happening, and she started running as fast as she could, taking off her hoodie in the process. She cursed as her toe hit a rock but ignored the pain and kept her eyes on the woman in case she went under. She was right at the spot where the current was at its strongest, and if she walked out any farther, Cam would be risking her own life by going out there to drag her back in. "Stop!" she yelled again, this time with panic in her voice. "Stop it, you fucking idiot!" Then the woman vanished as a wave hit her and pulled her under.

Cam ran into the water without even a moment's hesitation, her eyes fixated on the spot where she'd last seen her. It would still be too dark to see anything under the water, but she swam here almost every day and knew the direction of the currents. She sprinted farther in, heading right. *Where is she?* Cam dove in and swam farther out but didn't see any sign of the white dress. The waves were hitting her hard and she made sure to take a deep breath at every opportunity she got. It was hard to see anything at all with the salt water stinging her eyes. There was no point in screaming for help;

there was no one on the beach and her neighbors would still be fast asleep. They'd never hear her over the loud winds. Just as she was about to give up, to avoid drowning herself, Cam felt something against her arm and took hold of it. *A hand.* She dove under and grabbed the woman from the back, lifting her above the water before using the last of her energy to drag the lifeless body back to shore while fighting the relentless current.

Once they were safely on dry land, she slumped down on the sand, exhausted, and turned the woman on her back before pushing her head to the side. Water started seeping out of her mouth. *Oh God, I hope I'm not too late.* Cam turned the woman's head back up to face her, pinched her nose and forced five lungfuls of breath into her mouth. When there was no reaction, she applied thirty quick compressions, then put her ear against the woman's mouth and checked for any signs of breathing. There was nothing, so she tried it again, her hands shaking and her pulse racing with adrenaline. In the middle of her second breath, the woman's chest shot up and she coughed up water before taking in a deep breath first, then a shallower one. She turned on her side and broke out into a coughing fit, expelling the rest of the water from her lungs. Cam let out a sigh of relief and realized she was crying. She sat back and waited until the woman's breaths became steady and she finally opened her eyes, rolling onto her back again.

"Thank God," she muttered to herself as tears ran down her cheeks, burning her cold skin. "Can you hear me?"

The woman nodded. "Yeah." Her voice was weak and raspy.

"Good. I'm going to get you inside, get you warm and call 911, okay?" Cam studied the woman's face for the first time and frowned as she looked into her blue eyes. She looked familiar, but she was sure they'd never met before. Then it clicked. *Jesus, it's Ella Temperley.*

"Okay Ella," she continued when the woman didn't answer. "That's your name, right? Can you stand up? Help me get you inside?" Cam wanted to get Ella as far away from the shore as possible. Besides that, she needed her cell phone to call 911 and she couldn't leave Ella here by herself, in case she decided to repeat the attempt.

Ella sat up slowly and coughed some more before letting Cam help her up. Cam could feel her shaking uncontrollably as she supported her while they walked back to her house. Halfway, Ella collapsed back in the sand, leaving Cam no choice but to pick her up and carry her over her shoulder. Back inside, she brought Ella to the bathroom and turned on the shower while holding her up.

"Can you stand?"

"I think so," Ella mumbled in a weak voice.

"Is it okay if I take this off?" Cam tugged at the soaked dress.

Ella's teeth chattered as she nodded in bewilderment, her demeanor dazed whilst she stared at the floor. She raised her hands, allowing Cam to pull it off over her head, leaving her in her white lingerie. Then Cam stripped down to her underwear herself and pulled Ella under the shower with her to warm her up. She ran her hands through her hair, washing out most of the sand and grit from the beach. Ella stood there passively, trembling as Cam cleaned her up. She didn't bother with soap or shampoo, conscious that she had to get her to a hospital as soon as possible. A pool of mucky water mixed with sand and blood settled in the tub. Cam checked Ella for any wounds, then realized the blood was seeping from a gash on her own leg and her toe. She ignored it, figuring it wasn't serious enough to concern herself with right now. Sudden sobs echoed through the bathroom when Ella started crying, and Cam had no choice but to take her in her arms and hold her tight, stroking her back softly. Ella felt small, thin, weak and wounded, like a starved cat with nowhere else to go. Cam wasn't sure if it was appropriate to do this, but Ella clutched onto her in return, wrapping her arms around her waist while she rested her cheek against her shoulder.

Minutes passed as they stood there, still under the running water. By the time Cam turned off the shower, Ella had calmed a little. She dried her off and wrapped a robe around her before putting one on herself.

"Stay here while I call 911," she said as she settled Ella down on her couch and wrapped a blanket around her still shaking shoulders. Searching for her phone, she almost slipped on the floor where the water from their clothes and hair had settled into a small pool in the living room.

"Please don't call the emergency services. I'm fine." Ella looked up at her as if suddenly seeing her for the first time.

"You're not fine," Cam said, taking a couple of deep breaths in an attempt to calm down. Her limbs were aching from the swim, which she knew she'd been lucky to survive. Her left leg was still bleeding badly, leaving flecks of blood on the floor as she walked, but she couldn't remember hurting herself. She grabbed the first thing she could find – a long-sleeved cotton shirt that was draped over a chair – and tied it tight around her calf, hoping it would stop the bleeding. "You were trying to drown yourself and you're hypothermic." Cam walked into the bedroom and grabbed the comforter from her bed. It was the warmest thing she had in the house, so it would have to do. When she came back, Ella was sitting hunched on the couch. Cam wrapped the comforter around her while Ella's gaze darted from Cam to the sliding doors, then toward the front door. *Is she scared of me?*

"Hey, I'm not going to hurt you," she said as she reached for her phone on the dining table. "I'm just going to get you some help."

"No..." Ella waved her hands at Cam, barely strong enough to hold them up. "I know I'm not fine, okay? And I know how crazy this might sound but I just want to forget this ever happened so please don't." When Cam didn't answer, she raised her voice and started crying again. "I'm begging you, please don't call 911. No one can know, it's only going to make it worse for me."

"You really need to see a doctor; it would be very irresponsible of me not to at least drive you to the closest hospital. I could tell them it was an accident?" Cam suggested. "As long as I know you're fine and as long as you promise me you'll get help, I don't care what the tabloids write, I'll tell them whatever you want me to. Or I could take you to a private doctor? Do you have your own doctor?"

Ella cradled her head in her hands, her shoulders shaking in between deep breaths. "No one is going to believe it was an accident. If you call 911 or try to take me to a doctor I'll walk away right now," she sniffed. "I won't go." She stood up, but her legs gave way underneath her and she fell to the floor.

Cam ran toward her and helped her back on the couch. She felt a sharp stab of commiseration at seeing the vulnerable woman. Not going to the hospital was a really bad idea, but it was also clearly so important to Ella that she was willing to risk her health for it. But then she hadn't even cared about her life, let alone her health only thirty minutes ago, Cam reminded herself. She could imagine the circus surrounding a celebrity suicide attempt if it came out. The headlines, the tweets, the paparazzi following Ella everywhere she went, fighting over who got the saddest snapshot of the world-famous actress who had tried to drown herself… Ella seemed fine considering the circumstances; she was lucid and responsive. Cam knew there was a possible risk of Ella's hypothermia symptoms worsening, or that she might catch pneumonia from the dirty seawater that had been in her lungs, but if she ran away now in the state she was in, she'd probably get no help at all. And Cam couldn't exactly lock her up and call 911 against her will, could she? In that moment, she made a decision, hoping she wouldn't regret it, quietly promising herself she'd call the EMTs anyway if Ella got worse.

"Okay then. Stay here. Get some sleep, you must be exhausted." She searched for Ella's eyes. "But I'm going to wake you up every hour to check that you're alright and you have to eat something first." She hesitated. "I smelled alcohol on your breath. Did you take any drugs with that?"

"A valium and something else I had lying around. I'm not sure what they were, but they're supposed to calm me down. I thought it would help me…" Tears started rolling down Ella's cheeks again.

"Do you feel light-headed? Confused?" Cam asked, a frown of concern appearing between her brows.

"No, I think I'm fine."

"Are you sure? No dizzy spells?"

"Yeah, I'm sure. Just a little hazy," Ella assured her. "Thank you for letting me stay," she said in a whisper, relief washing over her face. "Thank you… What's your name?" For the first time, she looked up and locked her watery eyes with Cam's.

"Camila Saunders. Call me Cam."

"Thank you, Cam. You're very kind."

Cam limped over to the open kitchen and heated up a bowl of leftover soup in the microwave oven. When she came back, Ella was fast asleep. She put the bowl down on the table and pressed her ear against Ella's mouth to check her breathing while she placed two fingers on her neck to count her pulse. It seemed steady, so she pulled the comforter further over her and switched the thermostat up for the first time in years. Afraid to leave Ella alone in the living room, so near to the ocean, she got herself a blanket and sunk down in the chair next to her, setting her alarm for each hour in case she fell asleep herself. Her body felt numb, exhausted from fighting the waves. When she removed the shirt from her leg, she was relieved to see her calf had stopped bleeding, but the nail on her left big toe was missing. She shivered as she inspected it and carefully tried to wiggle it. It moved, so it wasn't broken, but she suspected she wouldn't be able to teach a yoga class in at least a week. With trembling hands, she messaged her studio manager Vanya to arrange a replacement for her 8 am yoga class. She'd understand something important had come up, as Cam never cancelled. Even if no one could replace her today, Vanya could always teach the class herself.

The sun was starting to come up now, tiny slivers of orange appearing on the horizon. Cam stared out over the water, hardly noticing she was silently crying again as the memories she still found hard to deal with came flooding back. Although it had been eleven years, the day two policemen showed up on her doorstep was still vivid in her mind. She also remembered her father's reaction like it was yesterday. He could hardly speak through the tears after she'd told him.

"Mom walked into the sea," was all she'd said, and in

that moment, he'd known enough, as if he'd been expecting it. It had been dawn too when her mother decided to take her own life, in the very same place Ella had chosen. She'd been hounded by mental health issues for as long as Cam could remember, and Cam somehow understood why she had done it here. This had been her home after she'd divorced her father a year before, and she'd always loved the sea. But why Ella had chosen that same spot, right in front of her house, was a mystery to her.

Cam remembered the headlines from two years ago, when Ella had lost her twin sister in an accident. To her, it had just been another story that barely registered before she went on with her day but to Ella, it must have still been very real and raw. Thoughts came and went as she cried, allowing herself to remember her mother's death again. It wasn't like she had a choice; this morning's dramatic events had violently dragged everything back to the surface. She wiped her tears when her alarm went off, reheated the soup and walked over to the couch, carefully stroking Ella's cheek.

"Hey, wake up. I need to know that you're okay." Ella stirred for a moment, then opened her eyes.

"I'm so tired. I need to sleep," she whispered.

"I know, but I still need you to sit up for a moment and talk to me." Cam walked around the couch and propped up the pillows, then pulled Ella up against the arm rest.

Ella finally complied. "I'm okay," she said.

"I just want to make sure." Cam handed her the bowl of soup. "Here, eat some of this. Just a couple of spoonfuls. Please." She watched as Ella ate some of the soup, then asked: "Where do you live?"

"Hollywood."

"Okay. Do you need to be somewhere today? Is anyone going to miss you?"

Ella nodded. "I'm supposed to be on set at nine, but they'll just have to do without me. I'm sure there are other scenes they can start with." Her voice sounded as fragile as she looked. Pale and small. Much smaller than she appeared in movies, Cam thought.

"I can't eat anymore, I'm so tired." Ella handed Cam the bowl and sunk back into the couch. She tugged the comforter under her chin and rolled onto her side before she closed her eyes again. Cam turned down the thermostat, opened the doors to the porch and continued to watch her for hours, waking her up now and then. Ella's hair dried while she slept, turning the wet streaks back into her iconic long, silky blonde locks.

3

When Ella finally woke up around midday, Cam had set the table on the porch. She was wearing yoga pants and a hoodie, and her dark, choppy pixie-cut hair was still wet from the two-minute shower she'd had, afraid to leave Ella alone for too long in case she'd venture toward the shore again.

"Do you want coffee?" she asked when Ella walked outside and sat down opposite her.

Ella winced against the sun and shielded her eyes with her hand, as if she hadn't seen daylight in weeks. "Yes, please." She gave her a polite smile, looking more than a little uncomfortable.

Cam poured coffee into a mug and pushed the almond milk toward her. "I don't have any sugar or normal milk in the house I'm afraid." She felt absurd talking about milk and sugar after what had happened and thought hard about what to say next. "Can I call someone? Parents? Boyfriend?" She hesitated when Ella didn't answer. "Your manager?"

Ella shook her head, her eyes fixed on her coffee cup. "No. I don't know his number by heart, but I'll let him know

I'm fine when I get home. I don't think he'll call the police just yet." She fingered the tie of the fluffy, white robe she was wearing. "Where's my dress?"

"I threw it away. You can take some of my clothes." Cam paused. "It was torn, and I didn't think you'd want to keep it since it would only remind you of..." she stopped herself, reluctant to say the words 'your attempted suicide' out loud. "This morning."

"You're right. I don't want it, I don't even know why I asked." Ella looked down at the plate with a toasted bagel and scrambled eggs Cam had made her, then took a sip of her freshly squeezed orange juice. "Are you not working today?"

"I'm off today," Cam lied, not wanting to add extra guilt on top of all the other stuff she was clearly going through. "How are you feeling?" She shook her head, internally cursing herself. "I mean, I imagine you don't feel great, but I mean health wise. Your chest?"

"I feel fine. You know, not great, but I think I'm okay." Ella took a bite of her eggs and chewed slowly. They ate in silence as the beach filled up with people. Runners, surfers, mothers with children and groups of teens skipping school. It wasn't a touristy strip of beach like Santa Monica or Venice Beach, but it was very popular with locals, even on weekdays.

"I haven't thanked you yet," Ella said, chewing her lip as she nervously fiddled with her napkin. "You saved my life and you risked your own. You could have drowned." A single tear trickled down her cheek. "I'm so sorry."

Cam gave her a sweet smile. "But I didn't drown, and you're still here too." She stirred almond milk through her coffee, a little taken aback when it hit her that this was Ella Temperley she was talking to. She'd always imagined her less timid. Of course, she wasn't feeling her best at the moment, but she wasn't putting on a show either, trying to convince her that she was doing great in order to get out of there. "I kind of expected you'd be angry with me. I assume you went in with the intention of ending your life and I hope you understand I couldn't let you do that." When Ella didn't reply, she focused on her breakfast and took a bite of her bagel. Cam wasn't hungry but she hoped it might encourage her to eat something.

"You're right, I did want to die," Ella said after a long silence. "Or at least I thought I did. But then all I could think of before I lost consciousness was how much I wanted to live. I've never felt such a strong craving for life as I did in that moment. I realized I'd made a terrible mistake, but by then it was too late, and I wasn't strong enough to fight anymore. I know you probably don't believe me, but I have no intention of trying that again, ever. I swear." She locked her eyes with Cam's. "I want to live and I want to be happy. I just need to figure out how."

Cam studied her. She didn't know what to believe. She didn't know Ella, and Ella didn't know her. Frankly, it wasn't her business. But something about the way Ella implored her with her eyes, nudged her toward believing that she was telling the truth. *Don't be fooled. She's an actress.*

"I'm glad to hear that. You still need professional help, though."

"I know."

"Do you have a therapist?" Cam didn't mean to be nosey, but Ella seemed open to talking to her and maybe that was what she needed right now.

Ella nodded. "I do but I haven't been completely honest with him. I have trouble trusting people. I suppose it defeats the whole point of therapy, lying to your therapist." She paused. "I was prescribed antidepressants last year, but they made me feel weird, so I stopped taking them after a couple of weeks. I guess I just expected to feel a little better eventually. I never did, it only got worse."

"You need to give them time to work," Cam said. "And if they don't work for you, there are other kinds you can switch to. Believe me, I've tried three different pills. They won't make you happy, but they can enable you to cope and help yourself." She took a sip of her coffee, once again, thinking back to the hardest year of her life. She was fine now and she'd moved on, but after last night even the smallest details came back, and she remembered the first time she'd broken down in therapy. "I had a very good therapist, years ago. She really helped me. I can give you her details if you'd like. She's not some hotshot therapist to the stars of course, but she made all the difference to me."

"Thank you. I'd like that." Ella pushed the scrambled eggs around on her plate, then forced herself to take another bite. "Why were you in therapy?"

"I lost my mother and I couldn't cope with it." Cam wondered why she was sharing intimate details with someone she didn't know. Despite being a very private person, she'd opened up to Ella without even giving it a second thought.

"I'm sorry."

"Yeah, me too. But it was a long time ago and I'm okay now. You'll be okay too, even though that may seem unthinkable right now." Ella nodded and stared out over the ocean. She had a faraway look in her eyes and Cam wondered what was going through her mind. "Why like that?" she asked. "Why walk into the ocean? And why here?"

"I like the ocean and I like it here," was Ella's simple reply. "I drove around for hours, three nights ago and I was drawn to this place. And it seemed..." she shook her head. "I know it sounds stupid and I see that now, but I thought it seemed like a fitting way to end my life. I didn't want to take an overdose or slit my wrists in the bathtub. I wanted to wash ashore."

Cam shifted in her seat as her expression grew dark. "Are you serious? Did you think dying like that would be romantic or something?" She tried to calm herself but the anger that suddenly welled up in her was too strong to fight. After her mother's death, she'd tortured herself by researching drowning online, as if she'd somehow find answers doing so. "Did you really think you'd look all pretty in your white dress once they found you? Let me tell you, you'd be far from pretty. And let me tell you something else, drowning is considered one of the worst ways to die."

"I know that. I wasn't exactly thinking clearly." Ella wiped away a tear, put down her fork and stood up. "I'm sorry, I shouldn't bother you any longer. I'll go home."

"No, wait... I'm sorry." Cam immediately regretted her outburst. Here was a woman who had been desperate enough to consider taking her own life and yet she was raising her voice at her. "I didn't mean to upset you, it's just that..."

"It's okay," Ella interrupted her. To Cam's surprise, she walked around the table and gave her a hug. She leaned over Cam, burying her face in her neck as she wrapped her arms around her. Cam stood up too and pulled her tight against her, closing her eyes. Ella's hair still carried a faint scent of salt water and that saddened her. "My sister Helena died," Ella then said out of nowhere. She let out a soft whimper as she started crying again. "I miss her so much."

"I know." Cam tightened her grip and they stood like that, holding each other for a while until Ella stepped back, wiped her cheeks and looked up at her through red-rimmed eyes.

"Thank you," she said in a soft voice. "I promise I won't do it again and I promise I'll work on getting better." She bit her lip and winced. "I lost my phone in the sea and I don't have any cash. I took an Uber here. Could you call me a cab? I can pay them when I reach my apartment."

"I'll drive you," Cam heard herself say. It was the least she could do to make up for her outburst and she wanted to make sure Ella got home safe, even though she had no idea what she would do as soon as she closed the door behind her.

"Okay." Ella looked down at Cam's swollen toe that was crusted with blood. "What happened to your...?" She covered her mouth with her hand. "Oh my God, did that happen this morning? Is it bad?"

"No, it's not and please don't worry about it. You have other things to deal with right now." Cam didn't mention the big gash on her leg that would most likely leave a scar for life. She rubbed Ella's shoulder. "Let me run you a bath and find you some clothes, then I'll take you home."

4

"Thank you again, for everything." Ella touched Cam's arm when they pulled up in front of the apartment complex where her penthouse was. She was wearing a pair of Cam's black yoga pants, her red hoodie and a pair of flip-flops that were way too big for her. "I'll wash these and bring them back to you," she said, gesturing to her outfit. She was a lot shorter than Cam, and she'd turned up the hem of her pants twice so she wouldn't fall over the excess material.

"Don't worry, I don't need them back." Cam put the car in park and turned to her, hesitating for a moment. "But if you ever want to talk or if you feel lonely, you know where to find me. You can always use the clothes as an excuse to come over." She scrolled through her phone and wrote down her old therapist's number on the notepad she kept in her car. "And here's Theresa's number. Just in case."

"Thanks. I think I'll give her a call, and I might take you up on your offer." Ella studied her intently then, her eyes shifting from Cam's face to her sporty attire. "I just realized I don't know anything about you. We've shared intimate details this morning, but I don't even know what you do for a living."

"I'm a yoga teacher."

"Oh." Ella gave her a smile. "Somehow, that doesn't surprise me. It suits you."

"Thank you, I like my job so yeah, I think it suits me too." Cam gestured to the luxurious, art deco-inspired white building on Franklin Avenue in Hollywood, shielded by a tall white fence. The front of the fence was lined with palm trees that obstructed the view of the windows. She guessed there would be a lush garden and a beautiful pool behind it. Or maybe Ella had her own private pool on the roof with a view over the Hollywood sign. "Will you be able to get in? I assume you lost your keys too?"

Ella held up her hand, wiggling her thumb. "The security guard and the doorman know me, and my thumbprint takes me into my apartment, so I'll be fine."

Cam rolled her eyes. "Of course. Who needs a key in a place like this?" Ella let out a chuckle and for the first time, Cam noticed a tiny spark in her expressive eyes. She was pretty, and Cam had no doubt that her delicate heart-shaped face and her big, blue eyes had won over many hearts throughout Ella's life. She was so charming when she smiled, and she probably didn't even know it. Ella pointed at Cam's bare foot. Cam hadn't been able to get into her slides with her swollen toe hurting more and more, and so she'd opted to wear only one while driving.

"I hope your toe heels quickly. It looks really painful." Then another thought hit her, and her eyes widened. "Oh my God. You won't be able to teach yoga like that. Can I offer you some kind of compensation? Surely you won't be able to work?"

"No, of course not. It's nothing, just a bruise," Cam assured her. "It will be fine in a couple of days."

Ella looked unconvinced as she nodded and cast another glance at Cam's foot. "Well, I'd invite you up for a coffee, but the place is a mess and I'm a little embarrassed. Keeping things tidy wasn't exactly my priority in the past week and I cancelled the cleaners because I wanted to be alone." Her expression turned serious. "Listen Cam, I feel really bad about what I did this morning. It feels strange now, like a dream, like it never happened." She closed her eyes and took a deep breath, trying desperately not to cry again but she felt the tears rising despite the effort.

"Don't," Cam said as she reached out and wiped a tear away "I don't want you to feel bad about anything at all." She paused, keeping her hand on Ella's cheek. "But it *did* happen, so please don't try to brush it under the carpet. Work hard on getting better, focus on yourself and talk about it because it really helps. You're not going to solve anything by ignoring it."

"You're right." Ella gave her arm another squeeze before she opened the door. "I hope I'll see you again."

"I'd like that. You know where to find me. Take care of yourself, will you?"

"I will." Ella nodded, and it hurt Cam to see a tear trickling down her face again. "I promise I'll try."

"Good. And you don't need to worry that I'll go to the press. I'm not like that."

"I know. You don't strike me as that kind of a person." Ella sighed before she got out of the car, as if saying goodbye was somehow hard. "Bye Cam."

"Bye Ella."

5

The floor was strewn with empty liquor bottles and Ella's clothes were everywhere. She kicked at a shoe as she made her way into the living room, then searched for her laptop underneath a heap of throws and pillows on the six-seater corner couch. She'd never cared much for the apartment she'd bought six months after Helena's death in an attempt to escape memories and with that, a little bit of the pain. She'd stored all her stuff in the basement of her house in Palm Springs that she was renting out now, and had started fresh. There were no photographs here, and very few personal things. It hadn't made a difference, and instead, she felt like she was living in a hotel.

The big picture windows framing the modern, open living space were hidden behind closed dark curtains. The realtor had been raving about the view over the Hollywood Hills when she'd first viewed the apartment, but she couldn't remember ever letting daylight in here because she'd felt more comfortable in the dark. The gray rubber-coated floors, and the mostly empty walls, seemed sterile and reminded her of hospital waiting rooms. The roof garden, adjacent to her luxurious bedroom, had a beautiful pool that she had never used, but the landscaper and the pool boy still came every other day, maintaining the grandeur of her surroundings. The huge flat-screen TV on the wall in front of the couch had been used often, though. Ella couldn't bear silence, so she only ever slept on the couch in front of it, never really watching anything before she dozed off for an hour or two at a time.

Today, when she'd woken up on Cam's couch, she'd been confused at first. She hadn't been in a real home in a while and it had been strange to see photographs on the walls and knickknacks scattered across the room. There was something very warm and calming about Cam and being in her presence had made Ella feel comfortable and safe. *If it wasn't for her...*

Ella closed her eyes and took a deep breath, trying to block out the flashbacks that kept replaying in her head. The burning pain in her chest, the panic, the overwhelming feeling of being paralyzed and the realization she was going to die... She wasn't worried Cam would go to the press because, even though Ella didn't know her, somehow, she trusted her. The ever-present feeling of gloom and the heavy emptiness had settled back in her core as soon as Cam had left, and loneliness took over again.

As much as she'd tried to avoid people in the past couple of years – at least outside of work – she'd found comfort in talking to Cam. She regretted not asking more questions now, and she wondered what her life was like. Sharing so many intimate details yet knowing nothing about the other person didn't seem right. She knew Cam was a yoga teacher and she knew she'd lost her mother, that was it. Perhaps their shared grief had been the reason they'd opened up to each other, or maybe it was simply easier to talk to someone who'd already seen her at her lowest.

There were several messages, she saw as she logged into her phone from her Mac, and most of them contained exclamation marks. Two were from the director of her latest film, telling her she was wasting everyone's time and money, four were from Tom White, her manager, asking her where the hell she was, and then there was a another one from Tom, letting her know he was worried now, and that he would call 911 if she didn't get back to him soon. She sent him a quick message, apologizing for not showing up on set without an explanation, and promising she'd be back tomorrow. Would she be back on set tomorrow? Ella wasn't sure if she could physically fake another day of smiles, politeness and interaction. The acting wasn't the problem; that was second nature to her. It was all the real stuff in between she had trouble dealing with. The small talk with her co-stars in their breaks, the practical jokes on set, and even the fifteen-minute meetings with her assistant each morning were getting close to unbearable. It took enormous effort to join in, to engage with people, but she couldn't ignore them either. Even the rare moments in which a real smile sometimes crept on her face didn't last long. It just felt wrong.

She'd kept working after Helena's death and her colleagues had left her alone for months, sensing she didn't want company. But now, with the best intentions, they were trying to engage her again and the fact that she couldn't even make small talk was painful and even embarrassing at times. She couldn't cancel on the movie; too many jobs depended on her and too much money had been spent already. Besides that, pulling out in the middle of a project was sure to ruin her career.

Ella messaged Raphael, her new assistant who she'd

been ignoring this week, and asked him to get her a new phone and send the housekeeper back in to her apartment tomorrow. Tom would call the director, so at least he wouldn't worry she'd been kidnapped or hurt. As it stood, Tom was the closest thing she had to a friend, and she didn't even like him very much.

She was reminded of the fact that it was her birthday when an automated pop-up message notified her that twelve thousand 'friends' had congratulated her on social media. Few people apart from Tom, her assistant, and the directors she worked with, had her private number and none of them had sent her a birthday message. Ella assumed they knew it would be a difficult day for her without her twin, but then why had Tom arranged a party tonight? Was he hoping he could replace memories of that tragic night two years ago by happy ones, just by throwing her some stupid party? Of course not. She was his meal ticket and he was just doing his job. He did it for all his clients and he did it well, making sure their special night was featured in all the magazines. He hadn't attempted it last year, knowing Ella was a mess, but apparently she'd been so good at hiding how bad her depression was, that he'd decided she was better now and that it was time for her to step back into the limelight.

She took a deep breath as a feeling of helplessness began to tighten in her chest again. She was still here, still alive, she reminded herself. And that was a start. She looked at the piece of paper Cam had given her, googled Theresa's practice, and decided to send her an email. After that, she would ask Tom to cancel the party. Everything else could wait.

6

"Overall, grief has five stages, but I'm sure you've already discussed them with your previous therapist," Theresa said, counting them out on her fingers. "Denial, anger, bargaining, depression and acceptance. Are you familiar with those?" She opened her notebook and crossed her legs, sinking back into her white leather Eames chair.

Ella was sitting in a similar chair, opposite Theresa in her cozy office downtown. The room was full of greenery and it was painted in soft yellow tones, giving the space a calm and cheerful atmosphere. Theresa was in her fifties, Ella guessed. Her hair was a natural looking blonde color, cut to shoulder length, showing a small amount of gray at her roots. She wore black slacks, a white silk blouse and her square glasses were black-rimmed, framing friendly, blue eyes. It had taken Ella two weeks to get an appointment and it would have taken a lot longer if her assistant hadn't called several times a day to check if a slot had become available.

Ella nodded. "Yes, I've been through that in my sessions with Dr Matthews."

"That's good. From what I gathered from our brief conversation, you seem to be stuck in your depression stage." Theresa gave her a warm smile. "And that's not abnormal in any way. A lot of people go through the same thing."

"Yes, we discussed that also," Ella said, silently wondering how Theresa could possibly make more of a difference than Dr Matthews. She did feel more at ease with her, though, so she decided to give her a chance.

"Well, it's good to hear we're all on the same page." Theresa clicked the back of her pen a couple of times. "I'm going to be honest with you, Ella. Your depression seems severe, but as your recent actions have proven, I'm sure you're aware of that. Since you've told me you've never suffered from depression before, we're going to work under the assumption that it is situational and indeed related to your sister's death. I know this might seem obvious to you but it's important that we establish this so I can treat you accordingly. I've picked up on intense sadness, emotional pain, the inability to engage in happy memories, avoidance of reminders..." She traced her pen down the notes she'd made. "Also detachment, social withdrawal, isolation, anxiety, numbness, lack of appetite, weight loss, trouble sleeping, physical symptoms such as migraine and sickness... And again, none of these reactions are abnormal in your situation. You were very close." She paused. "I think I can help you get back on your feet Ella, but I can only help you if you choose to actively work with me."

"I'll work with you." Ella swallowed hard. "I want to get better and I really just want to feel normal again but it just seems impossible to find anything close to a tiny bit of joy."

"I understand." Theresa tilted her head and locked her

eyes with Ella's. "What worries me most, of course, is your attempt to end your life. Do you regret being saved?"

"No." Ella shook her head frantically. "I even felt something close to happiness for a split second, when I realized that I was still alive. Relief, that's what I felt, and it was amazing. If only I could have held onto that feeling..." She took a moment and swallowed away her tears. "I don't want to die. I want to live."

"So you've had no further impulse to end your life since?"

"No."

Theresa nodded. "That's good, Ella. That's a start. A lot of people who come here still need to realize that." She paused for a moment. "As you probably know, I specialize in grief therapy, which has proven to be highly effective in cases of extreme mourning."

"Honestly, I didn't know you were a specialist in this field, someone just told me you were good," Ella said. "But I'd like to try working with you." She sniffed. "I'll try anything."

"Okay." Theresa handed her a tissue. "We're going to deal with your trauma first and then talk freely about your sister during our sessions, twice a week. Can you manage that around your busy filming schedule?"

Ella nodded. "I'll talk to the director. I'll tell him it's important and they'll just have to work around my appointments. We only have a month left on this project and I'll ask my manager to add a clause into the contract of the next movie I'm signed up for. I'm not sure if I should try to get out of that one and take some time off but I'm afraid I might go crazy if I'm not working."

"In my opinion, it's good to keep working if you feel you can handle it, and I'm glad you'll be able to fit in our appointments because it's important that you show up for every single session. We're going to talk about Helena a lot, and that will help with your detachment. We're also going to deal with emotions, and you should be aware that it's only going to get harder before it gets easier, okay?" Theresa looked at her intently. "The most important thing is that I need you to be honest with me, even if you're embarrassed or ashamed. If something is too difficult to say out loud, you can write it down on that notepad on the table next to you, but eventually, you'll have to verbalize it." She gave Ella a warm smile. "We're going to work through feelings, thoughts and memories and eventually that will result in a positive adjustment. I'm not a miracle worker though; *you* have to do the hard work. I'm only handing you the tools to do so."

"I know." Ella had heard it all before, but she still mustered a small smile.

"And I see here that you took antidepressants for a while." Theresa flicked through a file containing Ella's recent medical records. "What was the reason you stopped taking them?"

"I didn't like how they made me feel, physically," Ella said. "I had dizzy spells and I felt sick all the time."

"That can happen. I'm by no means saying they're essential; there's no guarantee with them and they're purely a vehicle to help you cope. But if you're open to it, I'd like to prescribe you a different SSRI and see how you react to that one. How do you feel about trying an alternative?"

Ella thought about it, then nodded. "I'll try it. Could you give me something to help me sleep, too?"

"I can do that, but they will be a lighter variety of the sleeping pills you had before. I don't want you to feel sedated while you're working through your feelings because the process is raw and you're supposed to feel it and embrace your emotions every step of the way." Theresa jotted something down before she turned back to Ella. "I'd like to see you again in three days' time but before you leave, we need to discuss ways for you to get your daily routine back because that's really important right now. We can start small, by tracking your meals, for example. As you mentioned you don't eat regularly, so you need to start thinking about getting back into a healthy, regular diet. I'd also advise to refrain from alcohol, at least in the coming months."

"Okay. I'll ask my assistant to fill up my fridge; I never have much in the house. The thought of cooking and eating makes me feel sick, but I promise I'll make an effort." Ella hesitated. "And I'll stop drinking too. I don't have a drinking problem, but I do often use it as a means to fall asleep so I probably drink more than I should."

"If you use alcohol as a means for anything other than occasional enjoyment, then technically, there is a problem," Theresa said. "So in your case, I think refraining from it would be for the best. I also think you should take care of the groceries yourself," she continued. "It's something to focus on besides work, even if you do it online. It's small routine things like these that can make a real difference. Indiscriminate jobs that don't suck you in too deep, distracting you from the healing process but get you back into life instead. As you're quite isolated, I'd also advise you go for a walk every day. It doesn't have to be long or far, just a short walk is fine. The point is that you get outside and do something active."

"Going outside isn't that easy for me." Ella bit her lip. "If I'm not in my car, I'm always afraid of being recognized. I used to have a bodyguard, but I let him go after I isolated myself more from the general public. I'd rather not hire a new one, it always felt like an invasion of privacy."

"Did you ever go for walks by yourself before your sister's death?" Theresa asked.

"Yes," Ella admitted. "Not often, but sometimes. To my local coffee place or a nearby restaurant. But I've moved since."

"Then this is just your anxiety playing up. Try to find a new favorite local coffee shop. If it gets too much, you can always call a cab home, or perhaps you have a driver who could pick you up?"

"I have a new assistant," Ella said. "I could always ask him to come with me. Protection isn't part of his job description, but I think I'd feel relatively safe with him and definitely more comfortable than with some muscle-bound guy in a suit who's breathing down my neck the whole time. Raphael seems nice, although I don't know him very well."

"Raphael it is, then." Theresa tore off a slip from her prescription pad. "These are for your new scripts. Besides eating three meals a day and the walking, I have some homework for you. I want you to write down three happy memories of Helena. We'll discuss them in our next session; you can book an appointment with Bree, my receptionist."

Ella winced at the mention of her homework, then nodded. "I will. Thanks, Theresa. I'll see you in three days."

7

Cam quickly flicked through the tabloids on Vanya's desk. Her best friend, who was also the manager of her yoga studio, was out on her lunch break, which gave her exactly twenty minutes to go through them. Cam always made fun of Vanya for reading them, so she didn't want to get busted.

Since the incident three months ago, she'd occasionally looked online too, but as usual, the big pile of fresh tabloids had been calling her from the other side of their small office, so here she was again, trying to find evidence that Ella Temperley was unharmed and hopefully getting her life back together.

She smiled when she finally found a picture of her in the second tabloid. It wasn't much; there was never much to report on Ella. She seemed to keep to herself, and apart from the occasional appearance to promote her latest movie, she clearly avoided parties and personal interviews. But the small picture of Ella with a handsome young man in a coffee shop in Hollywood was enough to put her at ease.

'WHO IS ELLA TEMPERLEY'S NEW MAN CRUSH?'

the headline said. There wasn't much information and the little that was written was probably made up. That didn't matter though; Cam wasn't interested in the gossip. Ella had put on a bit of weight, and her face had filled out. She looked a lot better than the morning Cam had dragged her out of the ocean, and she was even smiling in the picture. She frowned when she noticed Ella was wearing her red hoodie in the picture. It wasn't cool in any way, and Cam wasn't even sure if it had been clean when she'd given it to her. But it had always been her favorite hoody and for some reason, she'd wanted Ella to have it.

She'd thought of Ella a lot over the past months. Not obsessively in any way, but she'd always been in the back of her mind and Cam had asked herself more than once why she was still worried about her. Ella wasn't her responsibility and it was unlikely that they'd ever meet again. Cam closed the tabloid after staring at the picture for longer than necessary. She was just about to put it back down when the door was dramatically flung open.

"Forgot my wallet!" Vanya announced, before her gaze shifted to the tabloid in Cam's hands. "Hey, what's that?" A teasing smile appeared on her face as she crossed the office and snatched it away from Cam. "You of all people. You're the one who gives me constant shit for reading this 'crap', as you call it." Vanya crossed her arms, looking smug. Her lunchtime taco had clearly moved to the bottom of her list right now. "Well? Explain yourself, Cam Saunders. I'm waiting."

Cam shot her a goofy grin as she tried to come up with a valid excuse, the impatient tapping of Vanya's foot interrupting her concentration. "I was just ehm..." She paused. "It's not what you think."

"Bullshit. Is that why you didn't want to get lunch with

me? Huh? So you could stay here and secretly read my tabloids?" Vanya's smile widened; triumph written all over her face. "You look just like Greg when I walked into his den last night. I've never seen anyone click away from a website as quickly as he did."

"You caught Greg looking at porn?" Cam laughed, grateful for the distraction. "What was it exactly he was looking at?"

"Don't change the subject, I know what you're doing. Soft porn is one thing…" Vanya shrugged. "I'll admit; I checked his history and it was just a woman getting it on with a vibrator, nothing shocking. But you and tabloids? That's just downright dirty."

"I just needed to check something," Cam finally said, a little confused as to why Vanya was comparing tabloids to porn. Although she was technically telling the truth, she knew it wouldn't hold up. "But you're right. I *was* looking, I'll admit that."

"You don't need to admit anything, I caught you red-handed." Vanya grabbed her wallet from her desk and gestured to the door. "Now that I know about your guilty pleasure, you might as well come and get a taco with me. You can read your precious gossip over lunch when we get back." She pointed a finger at Cam. "But I'm not done with you yet."

"No, that would be wishful thinking." Cam chuckled and shook her head. "Sure. Let's go." Admitting defeat, she grabbed her phone and followed Vanya out of the office.

8

Ella looked at her walk-in closet, feeling accomplished. Everything was perfectly arranged; her socks and lingerie in the drawers, her jeans on a shelf, underneath her T-shirts and sweatshirts. The rails of hanging garments spanning three of the walls in the room were organized too; her dresses, skirts, blouses and blazers were even sorted by color. Her shoes were all on the top shelves, and the rolling steps were kept underneath the empty space where she'd just picked out a pair of sneakers. Her accessories were stored in containers, piled up in a corner of the room and she'd carefully placed her jewelry in a leather box in front of the tall mirror that came up from behind the modern, white dressing table next to the door. Her purses were still on the floor as she didn't know where to put them, but she made a mental note to order more storage boxes. It wasn't like she was out of space. She'd done it all herself this time, organizing it just the way she wanted it, and she even felt a little proud as she scanned the room, looking for something to wear.

Ella hadn't been able to sleep, and trying to refrain from

taking sleeping pills, she'd come in here and worked throughout the night. She hadn't really done this before; her assistants had always taken care of it, but she liked her own work much better, she decided. *Now, what to wear?* They weren't shooting today, and although Ella still didn't feel like venturing out, Theresa's urgent reminder was always in the back of her head, telling her to get dressed and do something, to make every day a 'normal' day. So, she'd had coffee, eaten breakfast and had enjoyed a shower, after working through her closet, and felt calm and collected now.

"Here we go again," she mumbled to herself as she automatically reached for the red hoodie Cam had given her. She'd worn it many times but hadn't washed it yet and she wondered why she felt the need to keep wearing it. There was something comforting about the worn-out garment that was frayed at the edges of the hood and ripped at the hem of the sleeves, that it almost felt like putting on a protective shield. Maybe it was the light smell of Cam's citrus scent that still lingered on the fabric or the way it felt soft against her skin, or maybe it was simply the fact that she didn't own any other casual pieces of clothing. Everything else in her closet was either uncomfortable or made her feel exposed in one way or another and that didn't help while she was trying to blend in.

The past six months with Theresa had been really hard, but it had been worth it. She was now at the point where she could talk about Helena without feeling the urge to burst into tears every time she said her name. Some days were easier than others, but all in all, she was feeling okay, and so she messaged her assistant to meet her at a local coffee shop instead of in front of her penthouse.

'Feeling brave again?' was his reply. She chuckled at that. Raphael was very aware of how private she was, and they'd

only met somewhere public on a handful of occasions, apart from their daily walks at 7 am. Their early morning strolls, during which they had their daily meetings, had become her new favorite pastime. It was easier when the city was still half asleep, and no one paid much attention to who was doing what. Over time, they'd settled into a comfortable companionship that had been branded as a romance by the paparazzi. Ella didn't care all that much about the unfounded gossip, and she didn't think Raphael did either. He'd never said anything to indicate that he was interested in her romantically and so she felt at ease around him.

Raphael worked for her five days a week and had the weekends off, unlike most celebrity assistants who were on call twenty-four seven. That didn't always coincide with Ella's own downtime, like today, but there was always something to do. Ella wasn't a diva and she wouldn't dream of asking him to do some of the things her fellow actors asked of their assistants, varying from midnight emergency condom or tampon-runs, to buying drugs, doing their kid's homework or have scripted conversations with their pets while they were away. No, Raphael was in her life to help her out with everyday practical stuff. He was in charge of her shooting schedule, he read her mail, paid her utilities, helped her with arranging travel, brought her lunch to her trailer when she needed time to go over her lines, booked appointments with hairdressers, beauticians, doctors, dentists, her manager, designers and stylists. He also liaised with her housekeeper, booked her drivers and took her calls when she couldn't. Ella didn't really need a full-time assistant, especially not now, but the studio required that she was reachable at all times, so she required someone who could take calls and pass on messages when she was having a bad day. Raphael was good at his job and Ella was finally starting to trust him. Besides, it wasn't like she could just walk into a grocery or drug store unrecognized. She'd tried it once years ago when her previous assistant had a day off and within no time, the drug store had turned into a circus and was more crowded than ever. She'd been a little scared then. People calling her name, touching her, tugging at her, waving cameras in her face in an attempt to get a selfie... That was another reason she'd picked Raphael out of the twelve people she'd interviewed. He was built like a linebacker, which was a stark contrast to his sweet, soft and playful character, and she knew there was a smaller chance of being harassed if he was with her.

"This is unusually spontaneous." Raphael chuckled when Ella arrived and sat down at the table opposite him.

"Unusual but necessary. I really do need to get out more," Ella clarified as she smiled at him. "Is that for me? Thank you." She took the coffee closest to her and looked around the coffee shop. She'd been here a couple of times in the middle of the day when it was quiet, but she'd never actually sat down at one of the tables. She felt exposed, despite her cap and shades, but there was also something liberating about sitting here amongst the locals.

"That's yours, yes. Skinny latte, no sugar." Raphael studied her intently. "How are you, Ella? You look well today."

"Thank you. I feel okay, actually." Ella's smile widened. "It's like the fog is lifting. I don't really know how else to put it. The sunshine felt nice on my walk here, and there was just so much to look at. Moms and dads were taking their kids to school, there were lots of runners, the guys from the bistro were putting the tables out and one of them even said good morning to me. Do you know what I mean?"

Raphael looked a little puzzled. "Yeah, it's a nice morning, although I'm not sure what you mean by fog. It's been sunny all week. And speaking of the weather, why are you wearing that again?" He pointed to Ella's worn hoodie and grimaced. "Aren't you really warm?"

Ella laughed. "A little. But I like it." She took a sip of her coffee and brooded over what she'd just said. Because it really did feel like a fog was lifting, as if everything was more outlined and clearer. Was this how she used to feel? She wasn't sure; she'd forgotten what it felt like to feel normal. "Anyway," she said, turning her attention back to Raphael. "Enough about me. How are you?" Again, Raphael shot her a confused glance and Ella felt guilty at the realization she'd actually never asked him that question before.

"I'm ehm... fine," he stammered. "I went to visit my sister last night; she's just had a baby."

"Congratulations. A boy or a girl?"

"A boy." Raphael grinned. "His name is Raphael, after me. I'm going to be his godfather."

"That's so sweet." Ella took his hand over the table and squeezed it. "You must be so proud."

"I am. His father's not in the picture so I want him to have a male role model, you know. Someone he can always come to if he's in trouble or needs advice. It's not going to be easy for him, growing up without a dad."

"No, it's not but he'll have you." Ella retracted her hand and decided to change the subject, sensing Raphael was a little nervous with how personal they were getting all of a sudden. "And you're a really great guy."

"Thank you." Raphael smiled and opened his phone, ready to make notes. "So, what do you need doing today?"

Ella opened the reminders app on her phone. "Right, let's see... Could you please pick up my scripts? It's the usual and they know you're coming." She narrowed her eyes and zoomed in on the list. "I've answered that fan mail you brought me. I've written everyone a short thank you; it's all piled up on my dining table, so if you could post those for me that would be great. As you know, I have a meeting with a local mental health charity, *LA Help* tomorrow, so I need you to arrange transport and come with me. I'm going to donate a new center in East LA, and I need help with that too once we've ironed out the details and I know exactly what it is they require. I'm happy to be hands-on with this but I'm due to be on set most days over the coming weeks, so I won't have much time to liaise with them while I'm filming. Other than that, my dry cleaning needs picking up and I'm out of sunblock. We're filming outside tomorrow, so I'll need something with a high factor. I don't like the ones they have on set. Also, our house..." She shook her head and corrected herself, trying not to think of Helena right now. "*My* house in Palm Springs... you said the tenants were moving away next month. I've changed my mind about renting it out again. I'd like to keep it free in case I'm ready to go back there, so if you could call the realtor and tell him the plans have changed, that would be great. I'll give Sid, the caretaker a call myself to let him know what's happening. Oh, and it's Neil Messenger's birthday tomorrow. You know, my co-star on the movie I'm currently working on."

Raphael chuckled. "I know who Neil Messenger is. Besides the fact that he's super famous, I've met him on set a couple of times."

"Of course, I forgot." Ella rolled her eyes. Although she had no problem remembering her lines, her brain still didn't seem to function the way it used to. "So yeah, like I said, it's his birthday and I think I should get him a present. Do you have any idea what a man in his mid-thirties, who already has everything, might like?"

Raphael thought about it for a moment while he finished his coffee. “Does he drink?”

“I don’t know,” Ella admitted. “We talk on set, but never about personal stuff. He’s asked me out a couple of times though, so I know he’s single.”

“Neil Messenger asked you out?” Raphael lowered his voice as he said it, a grin spreading across his face.

Ella sighed. “Yeah. He’s a nice guy but I’m not interested in him so needless to say, the present can’t be romantic in any way, let’s be clear about that.”

“Okay.” Raphael laughed at her candor. “How about socks?”

“Socks? Isn’t that a really weird present?”

“Sure, it’s weird but at least it’s not romantic or personal.” He googled something and handed his phone to Ella. “This sock brand is all the rage at the moment. They have really random things drawn on them, like sheep, assholes and bacon.”

Ella shot him an amused glance. “These are ridiculous. But you’re totally right. I’ve got a feeling Neil will appreciate them. So, which ones should I get?” They worked through the list of socks and chose ten of the most outrageous pairs. Ella was just about to order them when Raphael noticed people were looking at them.

“I think it’s time to go,” he said. “Get in my car, I’ll drive you home.”

“Yeah…” Ella stood up and saw five people gawking at her. The rest of the clientele was shooting her glances too, but at least they were being way more subtle about it. One girl held up her phone and took a picture of her, then other people followed. Soon phone cameras were clicking all around her. “Let’s go.” She smiled at the gawkers and waved at the staff before rushing out to get into Raphael's car. "At least we got twenty minutes in there."

"That's a positive way to look at it." Raphael started the car and drove off. "Do you want me to get Neil a birthday card too?"

"Yes please. Just get something you like. I'll be at home practicing lines and I'll have my phone on me in case you have any questions. Are you up for a walk later tonight since we didn't do it this morning?"

"Of course." Raphael parked the car in front of Ella's building. "Pick you up at nine?"

9

"You're doing well, Ella. It may seem like slow progress to you, but remember where you started from, and remember how you felt during our first session. You've really opened up and I can clearly see positive changes." Theresa looked at Ella over the rim of her glasses. "If you'd like, we could take our meetings down to once a week. If you prefer to stay on twice a week, that's fine of course. For now, I'm keeping your antidepressant script the same as it seems to be working for you, but I think we might try taking it down in another couple of months and see how that goes. Have you tried sleeping without the sleeping pills like we discussed?"

"Yeah I have, and I'm fine after long shooting days because I'm really tired. It's harder when I'm not working, so I still take half a tablet every now and then, but I've noticed I'm doing better too." Ella met Theresa's kind eyes. She was the polar opposite of her previous therapist, and although she knew their relationship was purely professional, Theresa somehow felt more like a friend to her now.

Crow's-feet appeared behind Theresa's black-rimmed

glasses as she smiled, telling Ella she had faith in her and assuring her that she was doing better. Ella did feel better; at least she thought she did. Lately, she'd been able to see the bigger picture more and more, and to think long-term instead of just dwelling on her pain.

"And I agree with you that I should try and get out more," she continued. "It's just that I don't have any friends. Any real friends, you know? I have over three-hundred phone numbers in my phone but only a handful of people have mine and honestly, I don't feel like spending time with any of them either."

"Then maybe you could try to venture out on your own with the goal to meet new people? It doesn't have to be a vacation, just push yourself to be a part of something. Saying that, I'm really pleased to hear you took on the charity work. You might meet people you click with if you're open to interaction. I know it's not easy for you because you're a public figure, but not everyone is an opportunist." Theresa brushed away a lock of hair from her pale face.

"You're right," Ella said. "The people at the charity have been really nice to me and I'm looking forward to getting their new center up and running. I'm also okay having lunch with the crew now during our breaks on set. I mean, I'm actually fine talking to them, I don't have to pretend so much anymore. I had a coffee with my assistant again yesterday, and our next meeting will be over lunch in a restaurant."

"That's good, that's really good." Theresa leaned forward and folded her hands in front of her. "So, what about Cam? You've mentioned her a lot during our sessions. Have you ever thought of looking her up again?"

Ella nodded and swallowed hard at the mention of Cam's name. Theresa was right, she'd mentioned her a lot;

probably more than necessary and she wasn't sure why. Today was the first time that Theresa had been the one to bring up Cam though, and now that she had, it somehow made her real, rather than a memory she was afraid of losing.

"I think about her all the time, and I'd really like to see her again," she admitted. "She hasn't gone to the press... Not that I expected her to," she added. "I got a good vibe from her." She hadn't mentioned that Cam was 'Camila', one of Theresa's former clients, and she was certain Theresa had been puzzled as to why a famous actress would drive forty minutes through heavy traffic to talk to *her* instead of going to one of the more costly 'wonder shrinks' in Hollywood. Even so, Theresa hadn't been star-struck when she'd walked in. She'd treated Ella like a normal person instead of trying to please her and although that should be expected from a therapist anyway, Ella's experience had taught her otherwise.

"You just said you'd really like to see her again," Theresa said, repeating Ella's statement. "When was the last time you felt like doing something of your own accord, just because you wanted to?"

Ella thought about that. "I guess it was a long time ago. Before Helena died, for sure." She smiled, knowing this was a good sign. "So, you think I should go and see her?"

"That's up to you."

"Sure." Ella bit her lip and sighed. Sometimes, she wished someone would just tell her what was best for her, instead of having to figure everything out on her own. "What if she doesn't want to see me?"

"Why do you think she wouldn't?"

"No reason." Ella leaned forward too, facing Theresa. Their session was almost over, and after this, she'd have two whole days off from shooting. Two very long days. Normally, she'd stay in bed and read scripts that her manager had sent her or practice her lines over and over until her voice went raspy, but maybe it was time for a change. "I think I feel drawn to Cam because she made me feel safe, and because she hasn't broken my trust, since she could have easily cashed in on the story. So yeah, I think I'll pay her a visit this week. Maybe I should have done it sooner, but I didn't feel ready to face her after what happened. I think I am now, though."

"That's great. Let's talk about that in our next session, then." Theresa smiled as she looked at her watch, seemingly pleased with the answer. "Well, our time is up for today."

"Thanks, Theresa." Ella stood up and grabbed her purse from the floor, feeling a strange sense of excitement. "I'll see you next week, have a good day."

10

"Now slowly open your eyes and move back into the here and now." Cam kept her voice soft in the dimly lit room, where twelve people lay before her, tired but completely relaxed after a heavy yoga session. "Move your eyeballs, your fingers, your toes. Become aware of your body, your breathing, this room, this moment and this day... Whatever's ahead, it's all going to be good." She waited for a couple of beats before she continued. "When you're ready, sit up slowly." Everyone started to stir, apart from one woman who was now fast asleep on her mat. Cam walked over to her and carefully touched her shoulder, waking her up.

"Oh God, I wasn't snoring, was I?" the woman whispered.

"Don't worry, you weren't." Cam gave her a reassuring wink, then walked back to her mat and sat down cross-legged in front of the group, placing her palms against each other in front of her chest. "Namaste." She bowed and smiled at her class. "Great work, guys. I'll see you all soon."

"Namaste," the group repeated after her. People stood up

and put their socks and shoes back on. The ones who had to go straight to work made their way to the dressing rooms to get changed. Others put on a casual hoody and went to the juice bar to grab a drink for their journey home. They all looked relaxed though, and that made Cam happy.

Her yoga studio in West Hollywood had received nothing but rave reviews since she'd opened it eight years ago at the age of twenty-seven, and the waiting list for the classes was now so long that she was contemplating opening another one downtown. She'd taken on four other yoga teachers because she didn't like turning people down, but the list just kept growing and there simply wasn't enough space to expand. She was proud of what she'd built; the building on Hancock Avenue wasn't big, but it housed two mirrored yoga studios, two comfortable dressing rooms with luxurious amenities, an amazing juice bar and a large yard at the back where some of the early morning classes took place when the weather was nice. There was also a small office that she shared with Vanya, who did an excellent job at running the business side of the studio so she could focus on her classes. Normally, Cam took some time off in between classes to hang with her bar staff over a fresh juice, check the schedules for next week or catch up with Vanya. She waited until everyone had left, put on her zip-up hoodie and was just about to close up when a blonde woman with a black cap and large, dark shades walked into the studio and locked the door behind her.

"Sorry, the last class just finished. Are you a new member? There's a space left in my afternoon class; we've had a cancellation so I can book you in if you want." Cam stopped in her stride when the woman took off her shades and instantly recognizable light blue eyes met hers.

"Hey," Ella said shyly, holding up an expensive looking

bag with a dry cleaner's logo on it. "I still had your clothes and I thought you might want them back."

"Ella... I didn't recognize you." Cam's face pulled into a big smile and to her surprise, her heart started racing. She hadn't expected to see Ella ever again. They came from different worlds and she'd assumed that Ella would want to leave that morning behind her, move on and forget all about it. She walked up to Ella and hesitated for a moment before she shook her head in disbelief and held out her arms. "Come here." Ella fell against her and wrapped her arms around Cam's waist. The hug affected Cam more than she ever could have anticipated. Just seeing Ella and knowing she was doing a little better brought tears to her eyes. The warmth and strength that Ella held her with was almost overwhelming and as if on cue, they both started crying, shaking in each other's arms. The emotional outburst came out of nowhere, and they chuckled in between sniffs, shocked at their own intense reaction.

"It's so good to see you again." Ella finally let go of Cam and wiped her tears.

"It's great to see you too." Cam took Ella's hands and glanced up at her. "You look so much better." She fell silent for a moment as her eyes got sucked into Ella's. The white around her irises was clear now instead of bloodshot, making the blue stand out even more. "How are you?"

"I'm coping," Ella said. "I'm not there yet, but I'm working on it."

"You're smiling, that's a start." Cam marveled at how beautiful Ella looked in her gym clothes, dressed down and incognito. She wondered if anyone had recognized her coming in. It was unlikely that her students would make a fuss about Ella being here, even if they had seen her. Cam's classes weren't cheap and most of her clientele were wealthy, in their thirties or older, and not the type to start fangirling on someone famous.

"I don't think anyone saw me coming in," Ella said as if reading her mind. "I've been extra careful; I didn't want to drag the paparazzi to your doorstep."

"Don't worry about that." Cam took the bag Ella handed her and gestured outside. "The back yard is closed at the moment, so we'll have it to ourselves if you want a coffee or a fresh juice?"

"Sure. I could really use a strong coffee. I only just woke up and I haven't had my caffeine fix yet."

"You just woke up, huh? You certainly don't look like it." Cam locked the door to the studio and led the way to her office. It was probably wiser to use her own coffee machine so they wouldn't have to wait by the juice bar as it tended to get busy there. "So, are you filming today?"

"I have the day off, but I'm meeting with my manager later. You?"

"I'm teaching another class at two but I'm free until then." Cam opened the door to her office and waved at Vanya as she put the dry cleaning bag behind her desk. "Hey there, sunshine."

"Hey." Vanya's eyes shifted from Cam to Ella and back. She didn't flinch, but Cam could see red blotches appearing on her face, spreading to her neck.

"Vanya, this is Ella. Ella, this is my friend Vanya, the manager of Pure Studio," Cam said, putting two cups under the coffee machine.

"Hi Ella, it's nice to meet you. Are you signing up today?" Vanya asked.

Ella shook her head and gestured to Cam. "No, I just came here to return some stuff to Cam. It's a nice place, you guys must be proud."

"All Cam's doing," Vanya said, her twenty-something bracelets clinking like wind chimes as she wiped a lock of long, dark hair away from her face. "I just make sure things run smoothly."

"Not true." Cam held up the almond milk and poured some in Ella's cup when she nodded. "Vanya's everything I'm not and I couldn't have done this without her. She lives and breathes Pure Studio. I just teach the classes." She handed one of the cups to Ella and grabbed a set of keys from her desk. "Sugar?"

"No thank you."

Cam chuckled. "That's a relief because we don't have any, at least not in here." She figured it would be best to get out of there as she didn't want Vanya to start asking awkward questions about how they'd met. "We're going into the yard," she said, casting her friend a smile over her shoulder. "I'll see you later."

"It wasn't hard to find me then, I take it?" Cam asked when they were seated on the lawn in the shade of a tall palm tree. She was grateful that the blinds facing the juice bar were down, so they had privacy in the yard. "I never told you where I worked."

Ella shrugged and took a sip of her coffee. "Honestly, I have no idea. My assistant looked you up yesterday. I went by your house, but you weren't there so I asked him to find out where you worked. I remembered your first name, knew where you lived and I knew you were a yoga instructor, so I guess it couldn't have been too hard for him." She paused, looking around the well-kept yard that was shielded by an ivy-covered brick wall on three sides. The dense lawn was mowed to perfection, and it looked so inviting that she felt like lying down on it. "I was surprised to find out you had your own studio. Most people would brag about that, but you just told me you taught yoga. It looks really cool, and this grass is just lush..." She took off her sneakers and her socks and let her feet sink into it.

Cam laughed. She was still barefoot herself after her class and she rarely wore anything else other than slides inside the studio. "Yeah, it's not cheap to maintain but people love the fact that it's so soft that they don't need yoga mats. We close the yard around noon. It's too warm to practice outside in the summer and anyway, the grass needs time to rest in between classes so we don't want to encourage people to take a nap on it, or have their lunch here." Her eyes fell on Ella's manicured feet, her nails painted a pastel shade of lilac. *God, even her feet are cute.* "It's really nice to see you again, Ella."

"Yeah, same here," Ella said in a soft voice. "I contacted the therapist you told me about. You were right, she's good. I felt a lot more at ease with her than I did with my previous one." She hesitated for a moment, clearly contemplating how much to share. "I've been taking antidepressants for almost five months now. It took a long time before I even noticed a slight difference, but I've been feeling better recently, and I've even been out in public with my assistant. I know it doesn't sound like much, but it felt really good and so I'm trying to get out of my apartment more and do other things besides working. The pain is still there, and I miss Helena like crazy, but the worst of the anxiety is gone, and I feel like I can cope again, you know?"

Cam nodded. "I know."

"And then," Ella continued, "this week, for the first time in years, I felt the need to see someone." She bit her lip nervously and Cam could see her cheeks flush. "I wanted to see *you*." She fell silent for a moment. "Theresa already knew about you because we'd talked about that morning in our sessions, and she was the one who kind of brought it up." Ella shifted her focus to her coffee and once again, it amazed Cam how shy the famous and on-screen-always-outgoing Ella Temperley was. "So here I am."

"I'm glad you came. I've thought about you a lot, wondering how you were doing." Without thinking, she reached out for Ella's hand. It felt warm in hers, and for a moment, it seemed completely natural to just hold it. Cam shook her head and retracted her hand as she realized what she was doing, but Ella held onto it for a moment longer before it slipped out of her grip.

"I've been wondering the same." Ella took another sip of her coffee and put the cup down in the grass. "I'm sorry for being half a year late with returning your stuff. I'm not sure why I'm here. I mean, apart from to thank you and to bring your clothes back. But I remember feeling at ease around you. For some reason I've been wearing your hoodie a lot and it gave me a weird sense of comfort, if that makes sense. It bothered me that I didn't really remember what you looked like. That whole week and especially that day, it's all a haze and now that I've seen you again, you're..." She looked up at Cam, trying not to get sucked too deep into her dark eyes because they did something to her that she couldn't quite understand. "You're..." Cam waited for Ella to finish but instead, she pulled her cap further over her head, hiding the blush that had crept up on her cheeks. "You're very nice," she finally said. "And I'd really like to meet up again sometime, unless you're busy or you don't want to. It's totally fine if you don't, I'll understand."

"Of course I'd like to see you again." Cam gave Ella a warm smile in an attempt to calm her. Something was clearly making her nervous. Maybe Ella just wasn't used to talking to people other than her staff and co-actors. "You can join us for the next yoga class if you can fit it in before your meeting? As I said, someone dropped out."

"No, not now, I have to meet my manager soon. I'd like to try it one day, though." Ella shifted her gaze to Cam's legs. She was wearing capri running tights that revealed a long scar on her left leg. Then she looked at Cam's foot. Half of her toenail had grown back but at a strange angle, creating a triangular scar on her toe.

"Oh God. Is that from...?" She reached out to touch the scar, trailing her finger along it. "I'm so, so sorry."

"Don't worry about it, it doesn't hurt at all and within a year, you won't be able to even see it." Cam placed her hand on top of Ella's that was resting on her leg. "Really, it's fine."

"But I'm still sorry." Ella seemed flustered as she stood up and handed Cam her empty cup. "I have to go. Thanks for the coffee." She shuffled nervously from one foot to the other, typing something into her phone. "Could I ehm... have your number?"

"Sure." Cam stood up too, took Ella's phone and added her number, noticing that Ella had saved her as 'Camila.' "You remember my name."

"Of course." Ella put her phone back in her purse. "It's an unusual name, at least for California."

"I suppose it is. My mother was Spanish."

"Oh, right. Your mother..." Ella's voice trailed away, her expression shifting as she recalled their conversation over breakfast that morning.

"Yeah. She was from Seville, but she grew up here." Cam had heard the slight tremble in Ella's voice and quickly changed the subject. "Anyway, my phone is in the office but if you call me or send me a message, I'll have your number too."

"Okay, I'll do that." Ella followed her back through the building and protested when Cam opened the front door for her and stepped outside. "Oh, you don't have to walk me to my car, I'll be fine."

"I know. But I want to." Cam cursed herself for being chivalrous. She wasn't trying to charm Ella, was she? Because Ella needed support, not someone who was going to look at her in any other way than a friendly one. She couldn't deny that seeing Ella again had excited her, though, and that her presence was doing unexpected things to her body.

Next to her black SUV, Ella scanned the parking lot for onlookers or photographers. When she didn't see anyone, she closed the distance between them and gave Cam another hug. Cam placed a hand on Ella's back, stroking her long blonde hair that fell down from underneath her cap. The scent of salt water had been replaced by coconut oil and her perfume was light and fruity. It felt really good to hold her. "Thanks for dropping by, Ella. I'd love to see you again."

"Me too. I'll call you." Ella got in her SUV and rolled down the tinted window. "Hey Cam? Your friend, Vanya..." She hesitated with an uncertain look in her eyes. "She doesn't know what happened, right? It's just that she didn't seem surprised to see me."

"No, she doesn't know." Cam leaned over the window, resting her elbow on the roof of the car as she gave Ella a reassuring smile. "I haven't told a soul and Vanya was just being professional." She chuckled. "That, or she genuinely didn't recognize you. She's got this amazing poker face that even I can't see through sometimes, but she did have a little excitement rash."

"Oh. Sorry, I didn't mean to assume you'd told her."

"That's okay. I'll make something up to feed her appetite for gossip." Cam took a step back and gave her a wave. "I'll see you soon, Ella."

"Yeah, I'll see you soon." Ella sat back in the driver's seat and watched Cam walk inside, still a little flushed from the hug. She was frustrated and thankful at the same time for all the things she hadn't said. Why had she left so abruptly? Her meeting wasn't until this afternoon, and Cam hadn't been in a hurry. There were so many things she'd wanted to ask but something had thrown her off her game entirely. She had no idea what she'd been expecting from their reunion; she hadn't even been sure if Cam would be there until the receptionist had shown her to her studio, and she certainly hadn't expected to feel so overwhelmed at seeing her again. It wasn't just the fact that everything had come flooding back. Ella couldn't deny that had played a big part in her emotional outburst, but she knew the main reason was the gratitude she felt toward Cam, for saving her life. Without her, she wouldn't be here now. Cam had been the same sweet and caring woman Ella remembered, yet she had seen her in a totally new light. She'd seen her at work and in charge, clearly doing what she loved most. She'd seen her through fresh eyes, unaffected by the deepest depths of her depression, a lethal hangover, a terrible headache and the horror of what had happened early that morning. And she'd seen that Cam was very, very attractive. Her dark hair was cut shortish, slightly longer at the front. The way it danced in front of her brown eyes and around her high cheekbones when she moved was playful, and her broad smile reflected that carefree side of her. She looked androgynous in a very cute way and the little dimple that appeared in her left cheek when she smiled hadn't gone unnoticed either. Her skin was sun-kissed and smooth and her body... Well, Ella could only guess what she looked like underneath the running tights and zip-up hoodie, but she'd seen enough to know that Cam was very much in shape.

It wasn't strange that she hadn't noticed her good looks last time, Ella thought, considering what a mess she'd been then. But it *was* strange that she was still shaking in her seat. People rarely affected her in that way. She'd met most A-listers in Hollywood at least once, and she'd mingled with media moguls and artists she admired but never had she been left shaking. *You're beautiful.* She'd almost said it. *Thank God I didn't.*

Ella closed the window, clamped her hands around the steering wheel and muttered a quiet curse. Cam's scent had thrown her the moment they'd embraced each other. It was the same fresh citrus scent she'd tried so desperately to hold onto when wearing Cam's hoodie, making sure she never applied any products herself. It wasn't the first time she'd felt instantly attracted to a woman and she suspected it wouldn't be the last, but it had been a long time since she'd felt this flutter in her core. *Is she gay?* Another flutter welled up at that thought, because her gut told her there was a good chance she was. She hadn't felt much at all since Helena died, not until today. She shook it off, as she always did, and it was then that she looked up and saw a man with an enormous lens in a car parked a little farther down.

"Asshole," she said out loud before letting out a long, frustrated sigh. How had she missed him? He wouldn't be able to see her through the tinted windows, but she guessed he'd been there all along, snapping pictures of her walking back to the car with Cam. Had he followed her all the way from home? If she got out of the car and confronted him, he'd surely make up some story about her being drunk and aggressive, and she wasn't going to give him that satisfaction. Right now, he had nothing but an actress walking out of a yoga studio, and there was no money in that.

Ella used to be good at playing them, at turning headlines into great PR for herself. Hell, she'd even had fun with it at times but now, she loathed the leeches for trying so desperately to document her misery and sell it to the highest bidder. Fighting the paps was a game you couldn't win though, and she knew that all too well. For a moment, she fantasized about crashing into his Mercedes but instead, she started the engine and drove off, pretending she hadn't seen him.

11

"What the hell was that?" Vanya gave Cam a good, long stare when she got back to the office and sat down behind her desk to check on her bookings and cancellations. Cam tried not to laugh at her friend who was unable to hide her overexcitement.

"What was what?" She ignored Vanya's dramatic outburst as she opened her calendar and her inbox. She needed time to come up with a credible excuse, but she couldn't think straight. Seeing Ella today had affected her in unexpected ways, and she felt a little funny inside.

"Seriously?" Vanya rolled her chair toward Cam, nudged her out of her faux concentration and gestured wildly toward the coffee machine where Cam and Ella had stood just over half an hour ago. "Are you seriously going to act like it's a perfectly normal thing that you waltz in here with Ella Temperley and make her a coffee? And I'm supposed to do what? Act like nothing happened? My God, if you'd told me I would have cleaned the machine because it was dirty!" she half-shouted, covering her face with her hands in sheer embarrassment.

Cam sighed and turned to Vanya. "So you recognized her?"

"Of course I fucking recognized her, she was right here in front of me, talking to me. Why didn't you tell me you knew her? You know I'm a fan and most importantly..." Vanya paused for effect. "Why did she bring you that dry cleaner's bag? With *your* clothes in it?" She huffed. "How could you keep this to yourself, Cam? You know how I love gossip and it doesn't get any bigger than this."

"Chill Vanya, it's no big deal. She's nice, that's all. I didn't sleep with her if that's what you're insinuating." Cam suddenly noticed the dry cleaner's bag was now next to Vanya's desk. "Hey, did you go through my stuff?"

Vanya threw her arms up in the air. "I'm sorry. I had to investigate, since you've clearly stopped sharing things with me," she said, her voice reflecting her hurt expression that was a little too overdone to pass for genuine.

"As I said, it's no big deal. We just met on the beach and got talking." Cam had been worried about this since the moment she'd introduced Ella to Vanya. Vanya was analytical and logical in her thinking. That made her an amazing manager, but also a very skilled interrogator. She just wouldn't let things go until she was presented with an explanation that made sense to her, and as an unfortunate side-effect of that, it was all but impossible to lie to Vanya. Not that Cam ever did. This was the first time, and although she felt a touch of guilt about it, the little white lie was nothing compared to Ella's secret, one that she swore she would take to her grave.

"Then why did she bring your clothes back?" Vanya continued, studying Cam closely for any signs of nervousness.

"Because it started raining and she got wet, so I lent her some of my clothes to go home in. Is that so unreasonable?" Cam knew to keep her explanations simple so Vanya couldn't poke holes in them.

"Really. So you swear you didn't sleep with her? I mean, I know she's straight, of course, and she probably has a boyfriend, but it's not like that ever stopped you before."

Cam rolled her eyes. "That only happened twice, Vanya, and I didn't know they were married, alright?" She stared right back at Vanya. She had no problem deflecting that accusation, because it was the truth.

"Whatever. So again, you swear you didn't sleep with her? Because you know that would be front-page news, right? Ella Temperley goes gay for local yoga teacher? Ella Temperley involved in steamy lesbian relationship? Ella Temperley..."

"Stop it, I swear I didn't sleep with her, okay?" Cam cut her off. She wasn't annoyed with Vanya; she would have been curious too if it was the other way around, but she wanted to put the subject to rest to protect Ella's privacy.

"Okay." Vanya pulled her mouth into a straight line and turned back to the spreadsheet on her screen, making it clear she was still a little hurt that she hadn't been informed right after Ella had left her house. Cam let out a soft sigh of relief, then tensed up once more when Vanya swiveled her chair around again, facing her. *Jesus. Why can't she just let it go?*

"When did this so-called random rainy encounter take place? When did you meet her?"

"Yesterday," Cam lied again, thanking her lucky stars it had actually rained the day before. "And I was going to tell you, but I was busy this morning."

"Oh." Vanya nodded, seemingly more accepting of the explanation now. She kept quiet for a minute or so as she brooded over it, then fired another arsenal of questions at Cam. "So, what did you guys talk about? What's she like? Are you going to meet up again? Can I come?"

12

"Tell me about your reunion with Cam," Theresa said, opening her notepad.

Ella sat back and smiled. "Cam..." She repeated her name and took her time to think about the question. It had been a week since they'd seen each other. In that time, Ella had spent long days on set, but she'd thought about her constantly in between scenes. She'd been very close to messaging her a couple of times, but she had no idea what to say. Would it seem too intimate if she asked Cam out for dinner? Would it seem too impersonal if she suggested they meet up for a coffee? Would going for a walk together be weird? What did people do if they wanted to make new friends? All those things that used to come naturally to Ella were a mystery to her now. She hadn't been herself for such a long time that she'd forgotten what it felt like. She second-guessed her every move, as if she was waiting for a script that would never come, and she'd forgotten how to just be. "It was nice but... very different from what I expected I suppose," she finally said.

"Different? In what way?"

"Different as in, it was way more emotional than I thought it would be. I cried when I first hugged her, and she did too. I… I don't know. It was just a little overwhelming. We had a coffee at her yoga studio, and we talked. I didn't stay long because…" Ella sighed. She'd never discussed her sexuality with anyone other than Helena and it was scary to say it out loud. So far, her sessions with Theresa had mostly revolved around Helena and her mother. "Because I felt attracted to her," she finally said. "And I was shocked, I guess, because I really hadn't seen it coming."

Theresa didn't flinch of course. She never did. Instead, she gave Ella a sweet smile and wrote something down on her notepad. Ella had asked to see what she wrote down once, and Theresa had shown her. It was nothing special, just a recap of what they'd discussed and some jargon she didn't understand but that Theresa was happy to explain. After that, the note-taking didn't bother her anymore.

"In what way did you feel attracted to her?" Theresa asked.

"Sexually," Ella said, lowering her voice to a near whisper as if she were sharing a dirty secret. She nervously picked at her fingernails. Theresa's gaze lowered to Ella's fidgety hands for a moment, then settled back on her eyes.

"Have you felt sexually attracted to women before?"

"Yes. I think I always have been." Ella's hands were trembling now as she spoke. *Why was it so scary to talk about this?* Theresa was her therapist, and what she told her would never leave this office. Deep down, Ella knew why she was terrified. Saying it out loud and discussing it with Theresa made it real, and that meant she'd have to deal with it at some point.

"Tell me about that."

"I ehm…" Ella took a moment to mentally dig through

her past. There were so many things she had buried. So many girls she'd pushed from her memory. "I think I knew when I was around fourteen or fifteen. I had a crush on a co-star. We were friends on set, but she was so much more to me." She shook her head. "Looking back now, I don't think it was just a girl-crush. I think I was in love with her. It went so deep that I sometimes cried myself to sleep because I didn't know what to do with myself. The feeling lasted for over a year, until she fell madly in love with a boy and wouldn't stop talking about him. It broke my heart."

"And after her?" Theresa asked.

"There were more after her. I've been attracted to other women over the years, but I've never acted on my feelings, even though I've always wanted to. It's been a while since I've felt this kind of attraction."

"And men? Have you ever felt anything for a man?"

Ella shrugged. "I had boyfriends when I was younger. My mother, and later, my new manager, set me up on dates sometimes. They said it was good for my image to have people speculating about romances with co-stars for my own popularity, or to promote a movie. But no, I've never been in love with a boy or more recently, with a man."

"Have you ever had sexual relations with a man?"

"Yes." Ella almost felt sick at the memory of the few times she'd had sex with a man. "I never enjoyed it, though. I wasn't forced in any way, don't get me wrong, but I've never physically wanted sex with men either." She cleared her throat. "I'm not sure why I did it. Maybe I was just trying really hard to be normal."

"Do you consider being homosexual abnormal?"

"No, but I think I did when I was younger. It was unusual to be a lesbian in Hollywood back when I was a teenager. Things have changed of course, but even now, gay actors and actresses don't get big mainstream roles, even if it's called acting for a reason."

"Is that the reason you've been discreet about this? Because of your career?"

"I don't know... I think so."

Theresa nodded. "And you've never discussed this with anyone?"

"I talked to Helena about it. She was also gay, only much braver than me. When we were toddlers we mostly worked on the same sets, starring in ads and TV shows, so we witnessed each other's crushes throughout the years and supported each other. She came out after she quit the movie industry. Not to the world, but to me and our mother, and to her friends." Ella felt tears well up when she thought of the late-night talks they used to have on the phone after Helena had moved away to study architecture in New York. She used to devour every word Helena told her about the girls she was dating, imagining herself doing the same one day. "I never had the courage to join her in coming out because my job was always my priority."

"And now? Is your job still your priority?"

"I think so. I don't really have anything else."

"Did your job make you happy before Helena's death?"

"I suppose so." Ella swallowed hard. Their conversation was taking a whole different turn from their usual sessions, and she hadn't expected to start re-evaluating her whole life today. "I don't know any better. I was never unhappy before, until Helena died, so I guess that means I didn't hate acting. I still don't hate it; I just don't feel things the way I used to feel them, and sometimes I'm afraid that makes me a bad actress. I'm very self-conscious now on set, and that's not a nice place to be in."

Theresa nodded. "Okay. We'll revisit that another time.

Let's go back to your meeting with Cam today because as you said, you did feel something and that's a great start. Have you agreed to meet up again?"

"Yes. I said I'd call her."

"And are you planning on doing that?"

Ella nodded and smiled. "It's all I can think of."

13

"That class was a bitch, Cam. I'm wiped out." Vanya sat down behind her desk and downed half a bottle of water before wiping the sweat off her forehead. "Now I need a shower and I didn't even bring a towel. This used to be easy, what happened to me?"

"What happened to you is that you haven't done a single class in three weeks. That's what happened." Cam looked at her with mock reproach. "You'll get back into it in no time, of course you're tired, you've been lazy, babe," she chastised her in a cheeky tone. "No wonder you feel tired instead of energized."

"Yeah well, I've been busy with work and the wedding preparations. It's stressing me out." Vanya rolled her eyes. "The wedding of course, not work."

"Relax. You still have ten weeks and the venue is booked, right?" Cam took a sip of her green juice. "Still no luck finding a wedding planner, then?"

"No." Vanya sighed. "All the planners who specialize in Indian-American weddings are fully booked and I wouldn't dare ask just any other wedding planner. They'd quit within the first week after meeting my mother-in-law. Nothing's ever good enough for her."

Cam laughed. "Let her take care of it then, if she's such an expert."

"Yeah right. And have fifteen-hundred guests that I don't know witnessing our vows? Five hundred is crazy enough as it is. I asked Greg to tell his mother to back off a little and believe me, he tried. But with his family paying for the wedding, it's not like we can exclude them. And my mum and dad aren't exactly helping either. They actually like his parents and told me to be more respectful toward his mom, can you believe that? I've been nothing but kind to that woman. I do everything for her as it is, and Sour-Face is still fucking ungrateful."

"Sour-Face? Is that what you call Greg's mom behind her back?"

"Of course I call her that, it makes total sense. Who else has a face like thunder and has been a pain in my ass ever since I met her?"

"Great name," Cam said after thinking it over. "It suits her." She rolled her chair toward Vanya's desk and put an arm around her shoulder. She felt for her, but it wasn't like Vanya hadn't known exactly what she was getting herself into. She'd been complaining about Greg's mother for years now, and even Cam, who had only met the woman twice, had witnessed first-hand that she was bossy and overbearing. With too much time on her hands, only one child, a husband who was never home and enough money to feed a small country, Sour-Face was not a pleasant person to be around.

"I know it's considered bad form to elope, but don't you just want to go to Vegas and get it over with?" Cam joked. "And then, she'll never speak to you again, you won't feel like you owe her anything and all your problems will be solved."

"I couldn't do that to Greg, he really wants a wedding with our family and friends." Vanya said it in all seriousness, as if she'd actually considered the idea. "I just wish I wouldn't have to worry about stuff like this." She sank further down in her chair and rested her head against Cam's shoulder. "But I love him, and he comes with the package I decided to accept."

"A very rich, powerful and opinionated package."

"Yeah well, it is what it is. I'm going to shut up about it now and get to work. I'll be looking at some potential venues for a new yoga studio downtown this afternoon. Once I've narrowed down the selection, we can have a look at the best options together when you have the time."

"Jesus, you sure don't beat around the bush, do you? I only told you about that idea last week." Cam turned around and rolled back to her desk when she heard her phone vibrate. She bit her lip, trying not to smile when she saw she had a message from Ella.

Hi, it's Ella. Are you busy tonight? Would you like to meet up and if so, do you know any discreet places in town? Cam didn't have to think twice about that. Even if she had plans, they'd be cancelled right about now.

No, I'm free. Would you like to come over for dinner at my house? It's very discreet . She winced as she sent it, wondering if it was too personal to invite Ella to her house, or that it might bring back bad memories. She finally let out the breath she was holding when her phone lit up again.

Dinner at yours sounds great! Is seven okay for you?

She swiftly typed a reply: *7 is perfect. I'll see you then.*

"Hey, I know that look. Who's that?"

"No one." Cam said a little too casually.

"Liar!" Vanya grinned as she stood up and leaned over Cam's shoulder to read the message. "Dinner at seven, huh? Do you have a date?" Cam was grateful she hadn't saved Ella's number yet, so there was no name above the messages.

"No, not a date. Just a new friend."

"A new friend as in Ella Temperley?" Vanya clapped her hands together when Cam was unable to hide her blush. "Ha! I knew there was something going on between you two! I told Greg yesterday and he was convinced I was making it up but..."

"You told Greg?" Cam's eyes widened. "Vanya, this is private, do you understand that? You can't tell anyone about this, and that includes your fiancé, okay?"

Vanya's grin vanished when she realized Cam was being serious. Cam rarely got upset. "I'm so sorry. I didn't realize... I didn't..." she stammered. "Well, I guess I just thought it was a fling and..."

"Even if it was a fling, which it is *not*," Cam said, articulating the last word, "Ella has a right to her privacy. She doesn't get much of it as it is, so you have to be careful about this. And once again, we're not dating and no, I haven't slept with her." She felt guilty when she saw Vanya's expression and took her hand. "Listen, I'm sorry I snapped, but this is important."

Vanya nodded, squeezing Cam's hand back. "I'm sorry. I won't say a word to anyone."

"Thank you." Cam stood up and gave her a hug. "I love you, Vanya, but I can't talk about this. Can we just go back to the subject of your wedding and your overbearing, bossy and rude soon-to-be mother-in-law?" She was relieved to see Vanya smile again.

"Please no. I think I might have to block it all out and let things take their course or I'll look ten years older on my wedding day." Vanya gestured to the two towels on a chair behind Cam's desk. "Can I borrow one of those? I need to freshen up before I meet with the realtor." Without waiting for an answer, she grabbed one of the towels, then started rooting through Cam's drawers.

"Sure, go ahead. There's also shower gel and shampoo in the..." Cam turned to find Vanya already holding them, along with her body lotion and her razor. "So that's how I go through my shampoo so quickly." She frowned. "And do you always use my razor?"

Vanya shot her an innocent look. "Sometimes. Just for my legs," she quickly added with a grin.

"Okay..." Cam paused. "That's a bit intrusive, don't you think? I hope you don't use my toothbrush too?" She gasped when she saw the top of her toothbrush sticking up from behind the towel but all she could do was shake her head and laugh. "Seriously, Vanya..." She held out her hand and waited for Vanya to hand it back to her. "Boundaries."

14

"Thank you for having me over," Ella said as she walked in and looked around Cam's beach house, studying the pictures on the walls and the souvenirs from Cam's travels. She felt as if she was seeing it all for the first time. The living room was decorated in neutral colors; mostly grays and whites, with hints of blue as a reference to the beach. The wooden floor was white-washed, partially covered by a big blue and white hand-knotted rug under the coffee table and the couch, which faced the porch and the ocean. The open kitchen had wooden fronted cabinets painted in a light gray, and a large cooking island that separated the kitchen area from the living area, with on one side four high, white modern barstools. One wall was covered in bookshelves with a selection of thrillers, cookbooks and yoga-related books. A cabinet underneath the shelves was full of plants and white orchids, and there were more orchids on the windowsill, facing the front of the house where the small drive was. Ella loved the off-white, floor-length linen curtains in the windows and on either side of the sliding doors that were open now, letting in the sea breeze. "I should have brought you a plant or something, but I didn't know what you liked, and I didn't know if you drank alcohol either since you told me you were a health freak."

"No need to bring anything, I'm just glad to see you. I have enough plants, believe me. I can barely remember to water them, and as far as alcohol goes, I have enough of that too." Cam laughed. "Vanya tends to drink the bulk of it though, when she comes over." She kept half an eye on the stove as Ella wandered around, taking in the room and the view.

"I love your house," Ella said, running a hand over a blue tapestry hanging on the wall. "I guess I didn't notice how great it was last time. I remember it feeling homey, just not so beautiful." She swallowed away the lump in her throat when she thought back to that morning but decided nothing was going to get to her tonight and so she put on a brave smile instead. "Your yoga studio must be doing pretty well if you can afford a place like this."

Cam chuckled at that. Ella clearly had no idea what the average salary of a yoga teacher was. Even if she owned five studios, there was no way she could afford a beachfront house in LA.

"It was my mom's. She bought it after she divorced my dad and left it to me in her will." Cam handed Ella two wineglasses and gestured toward the fridge, then started chopping tofu into squares on her cooking island. "Do you mind pouring us a glass of wine? Or do you prefer something else? Gin and tonic?" Then a thought struck her. "Or are you in a program or something? I'm so sorry, I forgot you were on medication. I have tea or coffee and I have some sparkling water too if you want to avoid caffeine."

"No, wine is fine," Ella reassured her as she walked toward the fridge, seemingly grateful for something to do. "I can have a glass or two as long as it's not too excessive. I didn't take you for a drinker though." Her eyes darted to Cam's toned stomach, exposed between the low-cut yoga pants and the crop top she was wearing underneath the open zip-up hoodie.

"I'm not really. But I like a drink while I cook and eat, and white wine is my choice of beverage." She took the full wineglass Ella handed her and smiled as she held it up in a toast. "Cheers Ella. Thanks for coming over." What she really wanted to say was: 'you look stunning', but that would have been inappropriate. Ella really did look stunning, though. She was dressed down in jeans, leather sandals and a black top with a tantalizingly low neckline, and Cam tried her best not to stare at her cleavage.

Ella took a sip of her wine while she watched Cam chop herbs and season the tofu. "What are you making?"

"Just some different things. I wasn't sure what you liked, or if you were vegan or vegetarian. I've got spicy tofu, steamed vegetables, a salad, brown rice and I'm going to grill an Asian marinated seabass." Cam gestured to the small grill on the porch.

"Sounds and smells amazing." Ella inhaled the scent of garlic and ginger coming from outside and felt something pretty close to happiness in that moment. "Are you vegetarian?" she asked. "I mean pescatarian," she corrected herself.

Cam shrugged. "I eat what I feel like, but I mostly eat vegetarian at home. It's something I've been doing for years. I don't really eat meat unless someone's made the effort of cooking if for me, but I'll eat fish now and then. I always make everything from scratch, and I use free-range and chemical-free produce. It's not hard; I love cooking, so I don't mind putting in the effort." She glanced up from her task and smiled when she met Ella's eyes. "Do you cook?"

Ella looked down, in slight embarrassment. "No. But only because I've never had to, so I wouldn't mind learning. Do you want help with something?"

"Sure." Cam pointed to a bowl with garlic and onions on the kitchen surface. "Chop one of each for me please." She took off her hoody and opened the sliding doors to the porch, letting in another waft of the grilled fish and the noise coming from the beach. "I'm sorry, I'll get into some decent clothes in a bit. It's just that I rarely have people over, so I forget to dress appropriately when I do."

"Don't bother, I don't mind." Ella felt color rise to her cheeks, unsure of how that sentence had come out. "You never have friends over?" she then asked, changing the subject while grabbing an onion and a garlic bulb.

"Not often. I throw a dinner for my team once a month, and Vanya tends to invite herself over." Cam laughed. "She usually shows up without warning. Her notions of privacy are completely opposite to mine; basically she doesn't believe in it. But other than that, I like my own company and besides, I usually get up around five or six to warm up, go for a swim and get some breakfast before I teach my first class, so I go to bed early." Cam wanted to ask Ella about her social life, but she had a feeling it was a sensitive subject. "You might want to go easy on the garlic in case you're filming an intimate scene tomorrow," she joked instead, pointing at the heap of garlic Ella had chopped into massive chunks.

Ella laughed. "Oh, did you mean you only needed one of these, not the whole thing?" She held up the only clove still intact. "I thought you meant the whole bulb."

Cam laughed too, pulled a freezer bag from one of the drawers and shoved most of the garlic into it before placing it in the freezer. "Don't worry, I'll use it another day."

Ella rolled her eyes in amusement. "I *am* actually filming an intimate scene tomorrow, so thanks for the heads-up. I'll make sure to bring extra gum."

"Oh yeah?" Cam grinned. "Who's your intimate scene with?"

"Neil Messenger."

"Really? He's quite the heartthrob, right?"

"Yeah, supposedly." Ella frowned. There was something in the way Cam had said it that indicated she wasn't the slightest bit interested in Neil Messenger, despite his reputation. "You don't sound like you're into him."

"Nope..." Cam threw the tofu into the frying pan and tossed it around before adding the herbs, chili, garlic and soy sauce. "I can see he's a pretty boy, sure, but I'm not into men, so I can't say I find him sexually attractive. Good for you, though."

Ella stared at her then. She didn't mean to, but the way Cam's bicep flexed when she shook the heavy pan aroused her no end. That, and the fact that she had basically just told her she was into women was a little too much to process. It threw her completely and she had no idea what to say next.

"Are you okay, Ella?" Cam's voice brought Ella back to their conversation.

"Ehm... yeah, I'm okay. Of course I'm okay." Ella started slaughtering the onion like her life depended on it, but it backfired when her eyes disagreed with the action. Tears started running down her face and it got even worse when she tried to wipe them with her onion-stained hands. "Fuck, it hurts. Is this normal?"

"Perfectly normal." Cam walked around the cooking island, laughing out loud, and Ella felt another surge of arousal when she reached out to wipe the tears off her cheeks before handing her a napkin. Cam's hands on her skin felt amazing and even after she'd stepped back, Ella could still feel the tingling sensation of her touch. "It's pretty clear that you've never chopped an onion before."

"No, I can't say I have, and I don't think I will again either. This is awful." Ella dabbed her eyes with the napkin, a little embarrassed. She ran her hands over her cheeks where Cam's fingers had been. "Have I ruined the onion too, now?" She looked at the uneven, roughly chopped pieces on the board.

"Not at all." Cam gestured to the porch. "But why don't you give your eyes a rest? Sit down on the porch, light the candles, relax and I'll bring everything out in fifteen minutes."

"You're an amazing cook." Ella tucked into the dishes with a big smile on her face. "This food is great, and it's so lovely out here." They were sitting opposite each other at Cam's porch table and had already discussed topics such as the movie industry, music and life in LA, and both found themselves laughing and teasing each other throughout their conversation as if they'd known each other for years.

"Thank you." Cam put her chopsticks down and sat back, taking a sip of her wine. Candlelight covered everything in a warm, soft glow, and if Cam had been delusional in anyway, the atmosphere on the porch could have passed for highly romantic, with the setting sun in the background. She hadn't changed clothes in the end. It wasn't like this was a date, and she didn't need to impress Ella. "So, do you have an early start tomorrow?"

"Eight," Ella said, helping herself to more fish from the plate in between them. "You?"

"Same. But as you know, I get up way before that to have my own private yoga session on the beach. Nothing too heavy, just a warm-up and stretch and maybe a little swim."

"That sounds lovely. Can I join you? I mean I'd pay you for a private yoga session of course. I know you're very in demand and..."

"Of course you can join me," Cam interrupted her. "But I don't want your money; my 6 am session isn't for sale."

"Awesome." Ella's grin widened. "It must be amazing to wake up here and be able to start your day like that. It's such a nice place. Did you redecorate it before you moved in?"

"Yeah, I did some work on it but not too much. Mainly cosmetic stuff. Some painting, new furniture, and I expanded this porch. To be completely honest, I wasn't sure how I'd feel living in my mother's old house, but I'd had tenants in here before and they'd changed it quite a bit over the years, so that helped a little."

"What did your mother do?" Ella bit her lip. "I'm sorry... do you mind me asking?"

"No, not at all. She was a TV producer, actually. The last show she worked on was *Beach Babes*." Cam chuckled. "You know, that silly dating program."

Ella's eyes widened. "That's so cool. I know *Beach Babes*. It used to be my guilty pleasure."

"Really?" Cam laughed even harder now. "It was so tacky, though."

"I know, but who doesn't love bad TV." Ella slammed a hand in front of her mouth. "I'm sorry, I didn't mean to insinuate that your mother worked on bad TV shows, it's just that..."

"Hey, it's fine. She was a good producer, actually. A very good producer of very bad TV shows. That particular show actually had mega high viewer ratings, and so did all the other crap she worked on."

"Were you close?"

Cam thought about that. "Yes and no. My mother had a lot of mental health issues. She was bipolar and suffered from severe anxiety. She loved me, and I loved her, but we rarely spent time together when I was younger. It was always all about her. Her career, her looks, her life... If she wasn't the center of attention, she wasn't happy, but she was great fun to be around when she was in a good mood. When she was in a bad mood, or when she stopped taking her medication for whatever reason, I made sure I stayed well out of her way." Cam pursed her lips with a faraway look in her eyes. "She was extremely vain and spent a lot of money on clothes and her appearance. I think her biggest fear was growing old and her looks fading, but maybe that's what working in the industry does to you. She had affairs with younger men and every time my father found out about them, she threatened to kill herself if he left her. My father was crazy about her, but there was only so much he could take, and in the end, he filed for divorce."

Ella's hand reached for Cam's over the table. "That must have been hard for you, growing up like that."

"It was what it was, but I didn't know any better. Kids are resilient that way, and I wasn't miserable or mistreated. In fact, I have many happy memories and I always knew she loved me." Cam felt the hairs on her arm rise at the touch of Ella's gentle hand covering hers.

Ella was silent for a moment as she looked into the living room where a framed picture of a stunning dark-haired woman stood on the bookshelf. "Is that her?" she asked, nodding in the direction of the picture.

"Yeah, that's her. Valentina Bandera. I got the slightly

less exotic surname Saunders, from my father," Cam joked, but Ella could see the pain in her eyes.

"You look like her," Ella said.

"We're very different."

"Of course, but your face is the same. Your bone structure and your eyes and your lips..." Ella felt her eyes drop down to Cam's mouth. "What happened to her?"

"She drowned herself." Cam tore her eyes from Ella and stared out over the ocean. "Right there." When she turned back to look at her, she almost regretted telling her the truth because Ella's face went pale in a split second. She didn't want to lie to her though; they'd been nothing but completely honest with each other so far.

"I'm so sorry," Ella whispered. "When I..." she closed her eyes for a moment and took a deep breath. "I can't imagine what that morning must have been like for you. I'm so sorry for forcing you to relive that."

"It wasn't easy, but it gave me a strange sense of consolation at the same time. Even though I wasn't able to save her, at least you're still here..." Cam managed to fight back her tears and took her time to pull herself together before she continued. "Her show was cancelled in the same year the divorce went through. She struggled equally with both, I guess. My father and I were worried that she would stop taking her medication if she lived on her own, but she wouldn't let me look after her either. She was depressed back then and wanted to be alone. I felt guilty for a long time. I told myself I should have been there for her, but she didn't want me around and I had to respect that. Eventually, Theresa made me see that there was nothing I could have done, and that I wasn't responsible for her. That's why I gave you her number. Because she really made a difference to me." She locked her eyes with Ella's. It was dark now and the light from the flickering candles was reflected in her gaze, making her big eyes stand out even more. Cam shivered again at the sight of her. *She's so beautiful.*

Ella stared down at her hand and pulled it back a little too sharply as if she only now realized, she'd been holding Cam's hand during their whole conversation. "I'm glad you gave me her number. She's made a difference to me too."

"That's great, I'm really happy to hear that. It's not always easy to find a therapist you click with." Cam took a sip of her wine. "Anyway, that's my story. If you don't mind sharing, what's yours? Are you close to your parents?" She remembered reading about Ella's mother. According to the tabloids, she was quite the stereotypical fame-obsessed Hollywood mom, currently estranged from her only child. But she didn't know Ella's situation and she didn't want to make assumptions.

"Can we talk about that next time?" Ella winced. "I'm sorry, but I don't want to talk about her tonight. It will only ruin my mood."

"Sure, no problem." Cam's heart skipped a beat at the realization that Ella wanted to meet up again. "I'm sorry, we don't ever have to talk about her if it makes you uncomfortable."

"Okay." Ella smiled as she took a last bite of the tofu that was left on her plate. "Thank you, Cam, for cooking for me. I know I probably should have taken you out for a lavish dinner in a fancy restaurant after everything you did for me, but it's so much nicer and private here and anyway, a dinner would never be enough to repay you for saving my life. Nothing would ever be sufficient to show my heartfelt gratitude so I'm not quite sure what to do next." She shrugged. "I want to give you something, but I haven't the slightest idea what."

Cam shook her head. "Ella, I don't want you to thank me or give me anything, I want you to be happy. And seeing you so much better, without that vacant look in your eyes, is more than I could have hoped for, so thank you for coming over. I really enjoy hanging out with you."

Ella smiled and Cam could have sworn she saw a blush on her cheeks. "I like hanging out with you too," she said. "We should do it more often."

"Hey, you have my number. Call me whenever you want." Cam said. "My guess is that your schedule is a little more complicated than mine."

"It's not too bad, actually." Ella refilled their wineglasses. "But only because I've ignored all offers in the past few months. I finish filming in a month, and I haven't got anything lined up after that. I know I need to get back into networking soon and go through the three-hundred something scripts I've been sent, but I've been working non-stop since I was a toddler, so my manager is in no position to pressure me."

"Good for you." Cam held up her glass in a toast. "So, what's on your to-do-list, now that you'll finally have some downtime?"

Ella winced when she realized how her next statement was going to sound, but the second glass of wine was going to her head, after six months of very little alcohol, and she liked that she could be straightforward with Cam.

"Actually, I have no idea." She laughed and continued in a self-deprecating tone. "I don't have any close friends, I don't have any hobbies, I'm still depressed and often sad apart from right now and quite frankly, it would be pretty stupid for me to have too much time on my hands. It's probably not the best time to take a step back from the little structure I have."

Cam sobered at her candid words. "Well… if you decide you like yoga tomorrow, you'll officially have a new hobby because I'll make sure you're there at least twice a week at six, and as far as friends go…" She gave Ella a sweet smile. "You'll always have me. And imagine how much time you'll have left between yoga and me to read all those scripts and decide on the ones you really want to do."

"It actually doesn't sound too bad when you put it like that." Ella stood up, not wanting to overstay her welcome. "I should really get home, I've got an early start. Let me do the dishes before I go."

Cam shook her head and took Ella's hands to stop her from cleaning up. She didn't want her to go just yet, but she assumed Ella was tired.

"It's a five-minute job. Please don't worry about it."

"Okay. But it's my turn next time. I had a lovely evening, Cam."

Cam walked her to the door, where they lingered for a moment. "Me too," she said. "How are you getting home? You're not driving, are you?"

"No, my driver is waiting outside."

"Of course, you have a driver," Cam said with a smirk, adding an exaggerated eye-roll for good measure.

Ella laughed and rolled her eyes dramatically too. "Of course I do." Then she noticed Cam's stare drop to her mouth and she subconsciously licked her lips. Fighting the urge to grab Cam's face and kiss her senseless, Ella gave her a quick hug and opened the door. "I'll see you tomorrow morning for our yoga session."

15

Ella tugged at the neckline of her top in the back of the car. *Why is it so warm in here?* Her hand felt clammy as she grabbed a bottle of water from the minibar and downed it, then took a deep breath. She knew there was nothing wrong with the car's AC; she'd been feeling like this all night, even outside on Cam's porch. Still on a high from the wonderful time she'd had, she realized it had been a long time since she'd felt this good, and she replayed their conversations as her driver navigated his way through LA.

Cam had known loss, just like her, and Cam's childhood hadn't exactly been conventional either. The more Ella found out about her, the more they seemed to have in common, even though on the surface they couldn't have been more different. The flutter she'd felt at Cam's every touch, no matter how casual, was nearly overwhelming, and she reached up to touch her cheek again where Cam's hand had been.

Desire was a strange thing, she thought as she rolled down the window and stared outside. The city lights, that normally made her anxious, seemed beautiful tonight, and suddenly she understood the LA charm portrayed in movies, and she understood why people loved it here. The plump, bearded palm trees, the different neighborhoods with their own identities, cultures and sub-cultures that somehow all seemed to blend into one, the old theatres on Broadway, the eclectic architecture, the Googie diners, the hordes of people queuing for their favorite taco truck in the big parking lots by the malls, the ruins of old film-sets, the neon lights, the bougainvillea, the mountains and the beach... And then there were the string of fancy hotels that all claimed to have been the favorite haunts of iconic movie stars at some point, the overflowing restaurants downtown where most staff were actors, waiting for their shot at fame, the young people hanging in front of liquor stores, dodging the cops whilst pre-drinking because the prices in the latest hot spots were extortionate... It was like seeing the city for the first time and when the Hollywood sign came into sight for a split second, she smiled, grateful to be a part of the magic. Yes, desire was a strange thing, but if desire could make her forget about Helena for a while, and if desire could make her feel alive again, she was happy to embrace it.

Ella was buzzing from the revelation that Cam was gay. The confession had changed everything, at least for her. It didn't mean that Cam was attracted to her of course, and it didn't mean anything would happen between them, but it was nice to have someone to fantasize about again after a very, very long time.

When Helena had told her about her first experience with a woman, Ella had immediately known she was also gay, and that she wanted to live that lifestyle too. She'd dreamed of being able to do just what she wanted one day, to live her life freely, but so far, apart from two ex-'boyfriends' she didn't care for, it had only been herself and her right hand.

"We're here," the driver said through the intercom, pulling Ella out of her thoughts.

"Thanks." Ella got out and handed him a tip through the window before waving a friendly goodbye.

Upstairs in her apartment, Ella kicked off her sandals and walked into her bedroom. She opened the sliding doors to her roof garden, which she'd barely used since moving in, and stepped out, inspecting the pool and the surrounding area filled with big plants and flower beds. The night was warm and breezy, and the terrace was lit up by the pool and the strings of white colored lights that twinkled in the palms surrounding the pool. Two comfortable lounge chairs were shaded by a large parasol, protecting the thick, navy blue covers from the sun and rain. The pool looked inviting and Ella dipped a toe in the water, testing the temperature. It was nice and she wanted to dive in, but a sudden surge of fear stopped her. She gasped as she balanced on the edge, suddenly terrified. *Fuck.* Slowly, she took two steps back and tried calming herself down. *No, no, no. Not now. I'm fine and even if I fall in, I'll be fine. I can swim. I won't drown, I'll live.* She retreated to one of the lounge chairs and lay down as she tried to steady her breathing. *You're fine, Ella. You'll be just fine.*

After a while, she was able to relax and open her eyes again. She forced herself to look at the water and imagined Cam in the pool. It helped. The vision of Cam sliding through the water morphed her fear into something far more pleasurable and the thought of her in a bikini took her mind away from her sudden panic. Her toned body, her mysterious, dark eyes, her wide smile... Ella wondered what it would feel like to kiss her, and to feel that body against her own. A soft moan escaped her mouth and she unbuttoned her jeans before slipping a hand inside. Sex had been the last thing on her mind since her depression had numbed her senses, and it had been over two years since she'd done this. She wasn't even sure if it still worked down there until she felt her own wetness on her fingertips. *Oh God.* Clearly, seeing Cam again had awoken her desire. Ella thought of her smile and her gentle touch as she traced her sex up and down, shuddering at her own touch. *Everything is definitely still working.* She closed her eyes and moved her fingers up to her clit, circling it fast until a warm heat started spreading from her core. *Cam.* Her body convulsed as she climaxed, and she marveled at the physical sensation that hit her much harder than expected.

Although she remembered what it had felt like before, the relaxation that took over her entire body was a pleasant surprise. Lying there, she let out a deep sigh and smiled, knowing she'd be able to sleep tonight.

16

"Morning sunshine." Cam's face lit up with a smile as she descended the steps to the beach and saw Ella waiting there in gray jersey shorts and a white T-shirt, her hair pulled up into a casual topknot. She looked sleepy and adorable. "Do you want to ask your driver if he'd like to join us? Or can I get him a coffee?"

Ella laughed. "I drove myself; I need to go to the set straight after." She looked at Cam, who was wearing a pair of gray, knee length yoga pants and a gray crop top and tried not to stare at her abs. "Also, can I just clarify something in case you think I'm a total asshole?" She kicked the sand in front of her and looked up at Cam. "The limo company I work with send me a different driver each time. There's like fifty of them and they're not allowed to interact with their clients. That's why I didn't offer him anything last night, he could get fired over it. You probably don't know these things and I don't want you to think of me as..."

"Hey, I'd never think of you that way," Cam said, rubbing a hand over Ella's shoulder. "You don't strike me as an asshole at all and I'm a pretty good judge of character." She looked Ella up and down, then stopped herself from saying anything she'd regret. "Anyway, shall we get started? Talking isn't going to get you out of this."

Ella's arms were burning as she stood in the downward dog, attempting to create a triangle with her body. Her hands were flat on the sand in front of her, and her head was between her shoulders as she looked at her knees. They had gone through a set of positions and stretches of various levels and intensity and she was now supposedly in a 'rest position'. If this was a gentle beginners' session, Ella didn't dare imagine what an actual class would be like because right now, everything hurt. Cam was next to her in the same position and turned her head to look at her.

"You're doing great," she said. "Stay like that. I'm just going to correct you a little." Cam got up, put a hand on Ella's back and gently pushed it, guiding her down and lowering her shoulders more. "That's right. Don't forget to breathe. Long and steady breaths." Her other hand pushed Ella's bent knees back, straightening her legs. Ella let out the breath she'd been holding. She felt so flustered from Cam touching her that she was afraid her legs might give way underneath her. Last night's private pleasuring session had brought back a whole array of sexual feelings that suddenly didn't seem to want to subside.

"Step in between your hands and look up, then put your other foot next to it and straighten your legs." Ella did as she was told, her fingertips still touching the ground. "Perfect. Now let's slowly roll up." Cam held Ella's waist as she rolled up until she was finally in a standing position. She let go of her as soon as she was upright.

Ella figured Cam didn't touch her any differently to how

she touched people in her class when she corrected them, but somehow, it felt so impactful that it was hard to ignore.

Pressing her palms together in front of her chest, Cam walked around her, made a small bowing gesture and said: "Namaste."

"Namaste," Ella repeated, doing the same as she kept her eyes locked with Cam's, whose dark features were framed by the rising sun now. How could she look so calm when Ella could barely breathe? "What does it mean?" she whispered.

"It means 'the divine in me bows to the divine in you'", Cam said, lowering her voice too.

Ella continued to stare at her. Was she imagining things or had the heat just turned up between them? *No, you're imagining things, Ella. Stop looking at her like that.*

"It's like a greeting or a thank you to the teacher and vice versa," Cam continued, still not shying away from their intense eye contact.

"In that case, thank you, teacher. I'm very grateful." Ella gave Cam a smile that could very well have passed for flirty. "I feel great. It was hard, but I feel like my body is awake now and I feel, I don't know... energized, I suppose."

"That's good. Did you enjoy it?"

Ella pursed her lips. "Yeah, I think I did. I mean, I feel like doing it again, and that's a good sign, right?"

"It is." Cam nodded toward the ocean. "I'm going for a quick swim. Do you want to come with me or...?" She winced. "I'm sorry, I almost forgot that..."

"No, it's fine," Ella assured her. "I'd rather not, but I'll make us a coffee while you go for a swim, how does that sound?"

"That sounds good." Ella could tell Cam felt a little self-conscious when she stripped off her yoga pants in front of her and handed them to her. She was now only wearing a pair of black bikini bottoms and her gray crop top. "Will you take these upstairs for me?"

"Sure." Ella watched Cam as she sprinted toward the shore. A longing to run with her tugged deep in her gut but the idea of going into the ocean terrified her. Cam's well-defined shoulder blades were flexing as she ran, and the bikini bottoms didn't cover much of her perky ass as her hips swayed from side to side. *Jesus. I'm now officially drooling over her.*

Ella had managed to pull herself together by the time Cam came back from her swim, but when she stepped under the shower, at the edge of the porch right in front of her, she had to summon every inch of willpower in order to tear her eyes away from her again. Cam shook out her hair, grabbed a towel, secured it around her waist and sat down at the table opposite Ella. Drops of water were still running down her face and her hair was slicked back, emphasizing her sculpted androgynous features.

"Oh yum, you made breakfast." Cam's eyes narrowed when she saw Ella staring at her with her mouth slightly agape. "Are you okay, Ella?"

"Yeah, yeah. I'm fine." Ella painted on a smile as she shuffled in her seat. "There's your coffee. I didn't know if you wanted anything else, so I toasted some bagels and sliced an avocado I found in the kitchen. I'm sorry if that's intrusive but I didn't think you'd mind."

"Not at all. Thank you, you didn't need to do that." Cam took a sip of her coffee. "Are you nervous about filming your intimate scene today?"

Ella rolled her eyes and laughed, the question finally distracting her from Cam's body a little. "It's no big deal; It's not like I've never done a sex scene before. I'm just happy I got some exercise in before I have to stand half-naked in front of fifty people with a heap of hot lights on me. It will be nice to get the sex scene over with. The first one was all about lust and this one is all about love, so I'll be shooting soppy glances at Neil all day." Ella transformed her features to form the most lovesick face in her repertoire and they both burst out laughing.

"That's impressive. Your loving look is very convincing." Cam cocked her head with a grin. "Now show me your lusty look."

"Seriously? You really want to see it?"

"I do." Cam grabbed half a bagel and topped it with slices of avocado, her face serious in a mocking way.

"Okay..." Ella ran a hand through her hair, slowly and seductively, then stood up from the chair and walked around the table. She leaned over Cam and looked down at her mouth, licking her lips before she parted them and lifted her gaze to meet Cam's eyes. She was breathing fast with a look in her eyes that promised she was going to kiss her any second.

Cam swallowed hard as she looked up at her. "Holy shit."

"Is that lusty enough for you?" Ella giggled but stayed there for a moment with her mouth close to Cam's before she moved away and sat back down, color washing over her face. She hid her trembling hands under the table and made sure she looked smug rather than how she felt, which was terrified. Being so physically close to Cam had made her head spin and her body react in explosively pleasant ways.

"Fuck, yeah." Cam looked like she had no idea what to say in the silence that followed. "You are a really, really good actress, Ella," she finally said when she found her voice again. "I mean, it's not even 7 am and I'm seriously turned on. I bet Neil Messenger's been pining after you ever since you guys filmed that lusty scene."

"Neil doesn't stand a chance." Ella picked up a bagel too. "I will however take the compliment that I've managed to turn you on."

"You should." Cam shifted in her chair, brushing her bare foot against Ella's leg by accident. For a split second, Ella saw something shift in her expression, and there it was. She'd felt it the previous night, if only for a brief moment, that strange thing between them. Some kind of sexual energy that momentarily surfaced and disappeared again when Ella stood up, taking the bagel with her.

"I need to go, or I'll be late," she said, taking one last sip of her coffee. "This was fun, thank you." Her face was bright red now.

"It was. Thanks for joining me." Cam followed Ella with her eyes as she ran down the steps. "Enjoy the smooching today," she yelled after her.

17

"How was your date?" Vanya immediately asked when Cam walked in and flung her sports bag in the corner of the office.

"Good morning, Vanya. It's nice to see you too. How are you today?" Cam answered with pointed sarcasm, although she couldn't help but laugh at her friend's unashamed directness.

"I'm fine, I'm always fine, you know that. So, how was it?"

"Vanya, I thought we'd agreed that I couldn't talk about this, and that you were going to respect my wishes."

"I do respect them, but I still want to know all the juicy details. It's Ella Temperley for God's sake!" Vanya threw her henna-covered hands in the air, her bracelets clinking against each other as she waved them imploringly. Cam sat down and realized the choice was made for her. Vanya's nosiness was an unstoppable force and there was no fighting it.

"Fine." She sighed. "It was nice. We had dinner and we talked."

"And?"

"And, nothing!" Cam started removing her sneakers and socks. "Ella's straight, it's common knowledge." She ignored the flutter in her belly that still hadn't settled since Ella's performance that morning. Deep down, she wasn't sure of anything anymore, and she couldn't stop thinking of the comment Ella had made about Neil Messenger. *'Neil doesn't stand a chance.'* She shook it off, telling herself to stop the wishful thinking. "Now, are you joining me for class or what?"

Vanya shook her head. "I'm way too busy."

"Nonsense, I just saw you click away from that gossip site on your laptop so come on. If I manage to wear you out, it might stop you from interrogating me for a couple of hours."

"Fine, fine." Vanya held up both hands, admitting defeat. "But don't work me too hard, remember we have those viewings this afternoon."

"This is nice." Vanya tucked into her salad four hours later. They were having a late lunch downtown after viewing the first two buildings on Vanya's shortlist. Cam wanted the second yoga studio to be close to the film studios to attract the people who worked there, and she'd gone through a rigorous selection process to find the best ones. "We never do this anymore, just you and me."

"What do you mean? You're always at my house." Cam looked bemused as she took a sip of her green juice.

"I know, but we never go out anymore, like we used to. Things are changing, and I'm getting old and boring."

"Hey, you're not old and boring. Your priorities have changed, that's all, it's perfectly normal. You love Greg so of course you want to stay home with him." Cam speared her fork through a piece of grilled pepper and pointed it at Vanya. "Wait a minute. Are you having some kind of impending-wedding-related crisis because you're about to get married?"

"Maybe." Vanya pursed her lips. "I just feel like I'm missing excitement in my life. You're hanging out with a celebrity, my sister's making movies in Mumbai, Greg just made CFO in his company and me..." Vanya stabbed at a tomato, looking a little defeated. "I'm about to get married and have kids and that will be that."

"I thought you wanted kids," Cam said.

"I do, but I always hoped I'd achieve something special before I settled down, something big..." Vanya caught herself. "I'm sorry, I didn't mean career wise because I love my job. I just expected to be really good in at least one thing, you know. At first, I thought it would be yoga, following that intense course we did at that resort in Goa, but even though I'm a qualified instructor now, I don't love it enough to practice every day. Then, I thought it would be cooking, but I have no talent whatsoever in the kitchen and then, my piano teacher suggested I try a different instrument the other day. Apparently, I'm so bad that the small fortune I'm paying him isn't enough to compensate for the suffering he's subjected to, having to listen to me once a week. And now, even my wedding will be mediocre if I don't find someone to help me out soon." She groaned. "Maybe I'll just get a tattoo on my face, at least I'll be known for going all the way with *something*." Cam leaned in and took Vanya's hand, stirred by her confession.

"Vanya, stop this. You're a fantastic person and the most loyal friend anyone could ever wish for. You're smart, funny, gorgeous, and I'm sure you'll be the best mother in the world one day. You're also brilliant at your job and your organizational skills are beyond awesome. You're already special and as far as the wedding's concerned, why don't you put those skills to even better use and plan it yourself?"

"Thank you for trying to make me feel better," Vanya said, squeezing her hand, "but with my family being Hindu and Greg's family being Christian, I just wouldn't know how to organize it all. There will have to be different ceremonies, dress changes, several DJ's and I'm not even talking about the food or the decorations."

Cam shook her head and tried not to laugh. "But what do *you* want, Vanya? What do *you and Greg* want? Surely the two people getting married should have a say in the matter. What about Greg? Is all that stuff important to him? I know it's not important to you."

"No, it isn't. Greg just wants a fun party." Vanya balled her hands into fists. "You know what? You're right. Neither of us is religious so why am I stressing about a church and a Hindu ceremony? We could just pay for the damn wedding ourselves and do it on a smaller scale. I don't even want a wedding at the Country Club. I've always wanted to get married in a vineyard. And I don't want to wear a wedding dress or a sari, I just want a pretty, bohemian-style dress. Neither of us wants to invite Greg's parents' friends from the Country Club or his father's contacts in the city or my distant relatives who I've never met before and we're not into haute cuisine either. We like tacos and my mom's home cooking."

"Then there's your answer to why you're stressed."

Vanya nodded in agreement and let out a frustrated sigh. "But surely it's too late to change things now? I can't just cancel on the Country Club? And how will I find another venue at such short notice?"

"You'll find something. You're good at this stuff. Besides,

I've never known you to do anything you don't want to so why start on the most important day of your life? Talk to Greg, see what he thinks and tell his mother to back off. Take some time off and focus on putting together your dream wedding. I'll get one of the bar staff to pick up most of your daily work while you're away and I'll try my best to take care of the rest."

"Really?" Vanya looked surprised by the proposition.

"Yes, really. In fact, I'm banning you from the office starting today." Cam looked at her firmly but with warmth in her eyes. "No, wait. Let's finish these viewings today before you go home and do what you need to do. I need your opinion, you're better at this than me."

"Thank you, Cam." Vanya seemed a little more relieved now. "I can't believe the idea never occurred to me; it makes complete sense."

"No problem. And let me know when you want to go out, I'm always available." Cam reached into her bag and opened a file containing the information packs on the two properties they'd already viewed. "Now, while I've still got you… what did you think of these?"

Vanya pointed at the picture of the first building. "This one might be too small. We could fit in two yoga studios, but then there won't be enough space for decent sized dressing rooms and a nice chill area."

"I agree." Cam held up the other pack. "What about this one?"

"I like it," Vanya said without hesitation. "But I'm not sure about the yard. That's why I wanted you to see it."

"Yeah, it's quite long and narrow." Cam liked how they always seemed to be aligned when it came to work. "But I'm not dismissing it yet, and I've got high hopes for the next one, with the roof terrace. That would be really cool, to have rooftop classes in the middle of the city."

"It looks like it's a great space," Vanya agreed. "The price, not so great. We'd have to increase the cost of membership if you wanted to go for that one."

"True. But if we..." Cam's voice trailed away as her phone lit up.

'*Hey! Thanks again for the yoga session this morning, still feel great . Love scene wrapped up successfully so I'm off tomorrow. Want to grab a coffee on your break? X Ella.*' She tried to hide her excitement as she typed a reply.

'*Coffee sounds perfect. Glad the love scene went well but not surprised.*' Cam contemplated finishing with something flirty. '*Looking forward to more lusty looks?' No*, she told herself. This was ridiculous, and she felt a little embarrassed for even considering the option. '*Looking forward to seeing you tomorrow* ', she finally typed. As soon as she'd sent it, another message came in.

'*Looking forward to seeing you too. X.*' Cam stood up quickly before Vanya had the chance to enquire about the sudden grin on her face and went inside to grab the check. Really? Why was she even contemplating flirting now? She shook her head as she handed over her credit card. Despite their playful interactions, Ella was likely to be straight, and even if she wasn't, she was probably nowhere near ready or willing to form any sort of relationship. *Don't flirt with her, it will never end well.*

18

"One latte with almond milk for you." Ella handed Cam the tall take-out coffee when they met in the parking lot in front of Cam's yoga studio. As if on cue, they both broke out into a big grin and shuffled on the spot, a little uncomfortable. Suddenly, the carefree tone of their messages was replaced by something that seemed closer to shyness.

Cam looked down at her hand when Ella's fingers brushed hers as she took the cup. *Did she do that on purpose?* "You're amazing, Ella. I needed this. What's yours?"

"Iced cinnamon latte. It's good, try it." Ella gave Cam her cup and she took a sip, conscious that her lips were folded around Ella's peach-colored lipstick marks on the straw.

"Not bad." Cam handed it back, her heart racing when Ella reached out and brushed a tiny bit of color from her lips. "Do you want to go for a walk? West Hollywood Park isn't far, and you seem to have your disguise nailed so it should be safe." She laughed and tapped the visor on Ella's white cap, wishing she could see her eyes that were hidden behind a pair of enormous black shades. Ella was wearing a cute lilac summer dress and white leather sandals, the color of the nail polish on her toes matching her dress. "You look nice by the way."

Ella shyly blushed at the compliment. "Thanks. So do you."

"Me?" Cam smiled. "I'm just wearing my workout gear."

"I know, I like it." Ella hesitated. "I hope you didn't mind me texting you again yesterday."

"No, not at all. As I told you, I love hanging out with you." Cam took a sip of her coffee. "What are you up to today? Any plans?"

"I was supposed to read scripts today but so far I've only had a shower and done some online shopping." Ella shrugged. "That's okay, though. I've gone from doing nothing to doing something in my free time, so it's a start." She shot Cam a smile. "Oh, and guess what? I did thirty minutes of yoga this morning too. I felt so good all day yesterday that I figured I should keep doing it."

"That's great, Ella. Does that mean I've turned you?"

Ella laughed. *If she only knew how loaded that question was.* "I gave you a lusty look, didn't I?" she joked, hiding behind her coffee cup.

Cam rolled her eyes and laughed too. "You know what I mean. Feel free to join me in the morning whenever you want. I'm there at six every day and I know it's a long drive so show up or don't show up, I'm easy."

"I will. Thanks again for the offer." As they chatted and walked, they passed shops, clubs and restaurants with rainbow flags hanging off the facades and crossed the rainbow-colored zebra crossings on Santa Monica Boulevard. Ella had never noticed them when driving here before, but she did today. It was nice to walk around and enjoy the city outside her own neighborhood again, and as far as she was aware, no one was trailing her. It had been too long since she'd walked through town, she decided, and she told herself she was going to do this more often. The traffic was lighter than during her usual rush-hour drives to set, but the park was busy, full of young moms with kids, couples, office workers on their lunch breaks and teenagers working on their laptops. They found a bench just inside the park with a nice view of the Pacific Design Center with its red, blue and green buildings vibrant against the clear sky.

"I'm sorry, I have to get this," Cam said as she unlocked her phone when it pinged. "Vanya's off for a week and I'm covering most of her responsibilities." She scrolled through the messages and send a couple of short replies, then put her phone away again. "Done." She smiled. "I have a cancellation for this afternoon if you're in the mood for some more yoga."

"Oh, I don't know if that's a good idea..." Ella looked doubtful. "Unfortunately, the luxury of making a fool of myself anonymously is not granted to me." She did however, like the idea of being able to stare at Cam for an hour with a legitimate excuse. "Besides, I don't have any yoga pants or a T-shirt with me anyway."

"Come on, my students don't judge and Vanya has a stash of spare clothes in the office you can borrow. I think you two are about the same size," Cam said, trying to convince her. "And you won't need shoes, we're all barefoot."

"I can't just borrow Vanya's clothes; I don't even know her."

"Oh, but she knows you and believe me, she'll be delighted to hear you wore them. In fact, she'll probably never wash them again." Cam laughed. "Okay, that sounded creepy. I promise you she's not a creep, just a big fan."

"Alright then," Ella said, giving up all pretense of hesitation. "I'll come. But only because I'm dying to see you in teacher-mode."

"Really?" Cam's grin spread. "In that case, I'll do my best to impress you." She cursed herself for making yet another flirty remark without thinking it through. She just couldn't seem to help herself when Ella was around.

"You don't need to impress me, Cam. I think the world of you already." Ella gave her a sweet smile and took her hand. "Okay, I'm going to make a dramatic statement now, but only because I need you to know this. I've never really given anyone a chance to get close to me, because I didn't know whether they were after me for my fame, or my money. You changed that. You changed everything after you risked your life for me and kept my secret. And here I am, sitting in a park drinking coffee with you, and I'm about to attend a group yoga class. That would have been unthinkable only a couple of months ago."

"It wasn't me. You did all the hard work. You battled for months to get out of the black hole you were in, and you may not be out yet but you're definitely climbing. So I don't want you to thank me or remind me, anyone would have done the same. Enjoy the fact that you're feeling better and don't overthink it. Look back in therapy, look forward in life and always try to live in the present. I'm sure Theresa told you that too."

Ella nodded. "Yeah, she did. The only advice she's ever given me. All the rest I've had to work out for myself. Why is it that therapists never just give you the answers?"

"It wouldn't work if they did." Cam shrugged. "Your thoughts have to be formed within you if you want to make a change, it's just how the human psyche works. No one knows what's best for you apart from you, and sometimes you need help to see it."

"I guess you're right." Ella took a sip from her coffee and reluctantly let go of Cam's hand.

"I read your sister died in a traffic accident," Cam said, sensing that Ella was a little more open to talking about it now.

"Yeah. It happened in New York, where she spent the last four years of her life. Helena was the only casualty on the bus, which carried thirty-five people that day. I was full of anger at the time because it was so unfair that she had to die while everyone else survived. I know it sounds horrible when I say it like that, and I don't wish death upon anyone, but that's how I felt for a long time. Talking about her death has helped me give it a place, though, and enabled me to move on from the anger and the hopelessness. I still feel like slamming my fist against a brick wall sometimes, but mostly, I'm stable and I can feel myself getting stronger each day." She turned to Cam. "You seem steady and happy, so therapy must have worked for you."

"It did, that's why I recommended Theresa to you. But time heals too." Cam paused. "All the art of living lies in a fine mingling of letting go and holding on. I'm not sure where I read that, but it always stuck with me."

"I like that." Ella gave her a curious look. "Have you always been a yoga teacher?"

"No. It never even crossed my mind when I was younger. I worked as a sales executive before this," Cam said.

"You?" Ella's eyes widened. She found it hard to believe that Cam had ever been a part of the corporate world. Everything about her screamed calm and Zen.

"Yes, me. I worked for a food manufacturer after I graduated in sales and marketing. It was fast food too, believe it or not." Cam gave her a small smile. "Loss can do strange things to people. It can make you question things you always accepted for what they were and sometimes that's good. I told you I suffered from depression too, after my mom died. I kept to myself and hated going to work. Maybe I'd never been happy in my job, I don't even remember. You just do what you're supposed to do, you know? After you graduate you find a job and you go to work every day, expecting it will get better as you climb the ladder." She glanced at Ella, then realized Ella probably had no idea what she was talking about. "I'm sorry, I forgot it hasn't been like that for you."

"No." Ella's voice was soft. "I understand what it's like to just do what you're supposed to do. To be on autopilot."

"Yeah, of course you do." Cam took a moment. "Anyway, life as I'd always known it suddenly seemed so pointless and empty back then, so I tried a yoga class one day, thinking it couldn't hurt. I thought maybe it would make me feel a little bit better, or at least a little more alive, and I figured it would be something to focus on. To be honest I didn't have much faith, but I was desperate for anything, and then it actually worked a little. I felt a physical difference after my first class and for the first time after my mom's death, I felt like I was moving forward. I started practicing at home and took three classes a week after that. Within two months, I'd even started eating better and natural because I could feel what my body craved. About half a year later I realized this was the life for me so I decided to sign up for a course to become a yoga teacher and as they say, the rest is history."

"That's brave," Ella said. "Making a big change like that when you already had a steady career."

Cam shrugged. "At the time I didn't know whether it was brave or stupid. I had to quit my job to attend the daily classes, so I got a bar job at night to pay the bills." She smiled. "After I got my teaching certificate, I went to Goa in India and signed up for a live-in six-month course to perfect my skills and that's where I met Vanya. She was an accountant at the time, also from LA, and we hit it off straight away. When we came back, I asked her to help me open my own yoga studio. I used money from my mom's inheritance and luckily, it all worked out fine."

"I have a feeling luck had nothing to do with it." Ella grinned as she tried to imagine Cam in sales. "What about your dad? Does he live in LA?"

Cam shook her head. "He moved to Boston with his new girlfriend a couple of years ago. We don't see each other much anymore, but we speak on the phone and I'm happy he's moved on and is all loved up. I like her." She looked at her watch. "Do you mind if we start walking back? I don't want to be late for my own class." Cam stood up and hooked her arm into Ella's as they headed for the exit. "So what about you? Did you always want to be an actress?"

"I was never really given a choice," Ella said, cherishing the touch of Cam's arm. "Our mom had Helena and me in commercials before we could walk, so I never knew any better. I grew up in Palm Springs. Mom used to be an actress herself, not a big name but she had steady work and managed to stay out of debt. She was on the brink of breaking through when we came along; the result of some drunken night with a stranger. The big role she'd been waiting for her whole life was given to someone else when they found out she was pregnant, and I don't think she ever forgave us for that, so she started making money from us instead." There was a spark of anger in Ella's eyes. "I know that sounds harsh, but you've never met my mom; she's *the* Hollywood mom through and through. Twins were popular in advertising back then and the agency she used had a lot of work for us. Diapers, clothing brands, toys… There were strict laws of course, as to how long a baby or a young child was allowed to be on set, but the thing was, the work never stopped even when the cameras stopped running. By the time we were four, she took us to acting and dance classes after shooting. I don't remember ever just having time to myself. The work just kept coming in and so she never gave us a break." She shrugged. "But you know, here I am now with a steady career in acting."

Cam tightened her grip on Ella's arm. "Jesus that sucks, it can't have been easy."

"Looking back, what our mother did was wrong," Ella said. "I would never rob any children of mine from their childhoods if I ever became a mother myself. But as you said – when you're a kid, you just accept it and it wasn't like I was miserable. I remember liking all the attention I got. When we were five, Helena and I got a role in a TV sitcom, playing the same child, so it was always either Helena or me on set. If my mother hadn't already figured out that cute, blonde twin girls were a goldmine in Hollywood, she did then. After that sitcom, which ran for five years, she drove us around to auditions, and we got another role playing the same kid. Helena and I hated being apart. We were home-schooled but never complained about that, as it at least allowed us to be together during study hours. By the time we were fifteen, we were on set most of the time and only hung out with adults." Ella looked up at Cam. "So no, it wasn't a choice, but I have a choice now. And the thing is, I like acting and I wouldn't know what else to do."

"Well, you're pretty damn good at it." They crossed the parking lot and Cam opened the door for Ella. She felt for her, knowing she'd never been able to make her own choices, but she also admired her for being such a decent and kind person, despite her crazy childhood. There was so much more she wanted to know about this woman who she found so captivating, but people were already walking into studio 1, so she decided to leave the rest of her questions for another time. "Come on, let's find you some clothes."

19

Ella lay down, feeling pleasantly tired. Cam had been right; the session they'd done on the beach really was just a stretch compared to this. It was the first time she'd done a group class in her life, and it felt amazing to be among other, normal people just doing the same, normal thing. She'd always done everything privately – private sports instructors, private tutors, private drivers – and she'd never realized how isolated she'd been until now. Just lying here next to the other students made her feel like she was part of something, and that was incredibly exciting.

She tried and failed to relax when Cam's voice sounded through the room telling them to close their eyes, images of Cam in the most appealing positions flooding her conscience. Her power and control, her grace and flexibility. Her muscles tensing and relaxing. It had been a pleasure to watch her, and to listen to her soothing voice. But the physical attraction was only a small part of the reason Ella loved spending time with her. Cam had been the first person in years to treat her like a normal person. She didn't walk on eggshells around Ella and she didn't try to please her all the time, like other people who constantly fawned over her did. She talked to her like an equal, like a friend. And they were friends, weren't they? Ella knew she was supposed to clear her mind but right now, there were just too many thoughts crowding in, interrupting her relaxation flow. She felt a presence close by, then heard Cam's voice as she kneeled down behind her.

"May I touch you?"

Ella nodded, barely suppressing a moan at the sultry voice and the hint of warm breath against her ear. She breathed deeply as Cam put one hand underneath her head and pulled it back a little, then placed the palm of her other hand in the middle of Ella's chest. Ella felt a delicious stretch in her neck and her shoulders, letting out a deep sigh when Cam withdrew her hand.

"Just keep breathing, slow and steady," she whispered. "Long, deep inhalations and exhalations."

Ella flushed. Had Cam noticed she'd stopped breathing the moment she'd put her hands on her? The group lay there for another couple of minutes, Cam now helping others with their technique. By the time the sound of a soft bell rang to indicate that the class was over, Ella felt more relaxed than she had in a long time. Slowly, she sat up and looked around her as others gathered their mats and water bottles.

"Did you enjoy the class?" A woman next to her asked.

"Yeah, it was great." Ella smiled at her. "I think I might put myself on the waiting list."

"You should." The woman rolled up her mat. "I've got three children and you wouldn't believe the difference yoga has made to my mental state, trying to juggle a full-time job and a family. I used to be so angry all the time, I honestly thought I was going to have a breakdown, but yoga's taught me how to finally relax."

"I can see why. Cam seems like a great teacher."

"She's the best in town, I'll vouch for that. Well, I hope I see you again, then. Have a nice day." The woman waved at Ella as she left, and Ella waved back at her. Other people were standing up and leaving, some giving her a smile and a short greeting, as if acknowledging her as one of them now. No one had asked for her autograph or a picture and no one had stared. They hadn't even whispered amongst each other. It had just been a nice class with nice people who didn't want anything from her and couldn't care less whether she was famous or not. She'd never experienced anything like it, and was painfully aware of how much she'd been missing. She got up too and put on Vanya's hoodie.

"Thanks," she said to Cam when she came up to her.

"No problem, I'm glad you enjoyed it. Do you think you'd like to do it again?"

"Yeah." Ella felt another surge of arousal as she looked at Cam's toned arms and shoulders. She folded her arms, afraid that she might reach out to touch her if she didn't. "I'm going to sign up. I know it might take a while until a space becomes available, but in the meantime, I'll come and join you for early morning sessions on the beach. That way I might be able to keep up better next time."

"Nonsense, you did well." Cam patted her on the back. "You really did. I was watching you in the mirror and you're naturally flexible. You seem pretty strong too, I can tell you used to work out a lot." She shook her head. "Not that any of that matters; the aim of yoga isn't to be the best, it's to feel your best."

"Well, I feel pretty good right now." Ella grabbed the borrowed mat and started rolling it up, in urgent need of distraction. She only hoped that Cam assumed the color that had risen to her cheeks came from the exercise and not from looking at her sweaty and smoking hot body. "I'd better get going," she said. "I'll wash Vanya's clothes and bring them back. Call me if you want to meet up."

"I will. I'll call you soon."

20

"Vanya, what are you doing here? You're supposed to be off." Cam spun her chair around to face her friend, who stood in the doorway of her office, wide-eyed.

"Never mind, I'm here on personal business." Vanya held up her phone as she crossed the room. "Jason from the juice bar just sent me this. I thought you should see it before people start talking about you, so I came right over."

"What? What's wrong?" Cam took the phone off her and was surprised to see a picture of herself and Ella with a message from Jason underneath that said: '*Great marketing! Was this your idea, Vanya? And more importantly – is it true?!!*' The screenshot of a magazine spread showed Ella hugging Cam in the parking lot in front of her yoga studio. There was another picture, taken while they were walking close together and another one with them sitting on the bench in West Hollywood Park showing Ella holding Cam's hand during their conversation. The pictures were accompanied by a ridiculously speculative article and the caption: *ELLA TEMPERLEY SEEN COZYING UP TO YOGA TEACHER.*

They weren't intimate, of course. They hadn't been intimate. But yes, there was definitely something about the pictures that suggested there was something between them. Maybe it was the way Ella looked at her, or the way she looked at Ella. Or maybe it was their body language, the way they leaned into each other as they walked.

"What the fuck?" she mumbled as she started reading it, then changed her mind. "How?" She handed Vanya her phone back. "I never saw any paparazzi hanging about."

"Isn't that the point? That you don't see them?" Vanya started reading the article now, most likely for the tenth time. She was clearly fascinated. "So? Is it true?"

"Is what true?"

"That she's cozying up to you." Vanya continued without waiting for an answer. "They're mentioning your name and the name of the studio. That's great marketing for sure, Jason wasn't wrong about that."

"They're lying and you shouldn't read that crap. Neither should Jason. They probably took hundreds of pictures and picked the most suggestive ones." Cam rubbed her temples. "This is so intrusive, how dare they?"

"You have to admit that the two of you look pretty close, though." Vanya then googled Cam's name and sure enough, more articles came up. "Oh my God, there's more. They're all using the same picture, I think they've just copied them over."

"Stop reading it, Vanya." Cam took the phone and put it in Vanya's purse that was still dangling from her arm. "They're all lies and it's a problem. There's nothing great about this, it will escalate." She sat back down and sighed. "Ella took a group class here, which is a big deal for her. She was really excited but now she won't be able to come back for months because we'll likely have photographers lurking around the building."

“Ella took a class here?” Vanya rolled her eyes. “Trust me to take some time off and my favorite actress rocks up again. When did this happen?”

“Two days ago. She borrowed some of your clothes but she’ll give them back to me next time I see her.” Cam tilted her head to one side as she watched red blobs appear on Vanya’s face. “You’re suffering from excitement rash again,” she stated, noting it was spreading to her neck now. “Jesus, it’s even worse than when Greg proposed to you.”

Vanya nodded dreamily as she sat down in her chair and scratched her neck. “I can’t believe she wore my clothes.” Her eyes widened again. “I hope you at least gave her something nice to wear? Not that pair of old jersey yoga pants?”

“I don’t know. I just grabbed something.” Cam bit her lip. “Anyway, that’s not exactly our biggest problem here. What do we do? Do we need to get security for the parking lot? Register our clients’ license plates? That’s going to be a big job.” Vanya crossed her arms as she did her best to calm herself and get back into problem solving mode. Cam could almost hear her analytic brain whirring inside her head.

“I don’t think there’s any point,” she said after a long silence. “They could set up on the sidewalk or even sit at the café next door. With those lenses, it wouldn’t make a difference whether we secure the parking lot or not. Besides, they’re only after Ella, and potentially you. We don’t have any other famous clients we need to protect, apart from that woman who’s married to one of the LA Rams quarterbacks and a couple of ex-presenters and they’ll probably jump at the opportunity to get back in the spotlight.” She winced. “If you ask me, there’s nothing we can do apart from wait it out until people get bored with the story. That is, if it’s not true, as you say. And I believe you of course,” she quickly added when Cam gave her a warning look. “But honestly, it seems to be the story of the year so far and it's spreading like a virus. It's long from over yet."

"Fuck." Cam buried her face in her hands. "Okay, let me talk to Ella, see what she thinks we should do. I'm sure she'll have plenty of experience with unfounded gossip." She unlocked her phone, groaning when she saw she had countless messages about the article, including one from her father. Deciding to ignore them all for now, she sent Ella a message: '*What are you up to?*'

21

"You want me to do what?" Ella stared at Tom White, her manager, in disbelief. She'd been called in for an emergency meeting after a long day of shooting and was now sitting opposite Tom at his enormous desk in his office downtown. The walls were covered in photographs of actors and actresses he'd represented, with the exception of the wall behind his desk, which was solely dedicated to Ella. She hated being confronted with the cheesy shots of herself in the most ridiculous poses, but she'd learned to ignore them over the years.

Tom put on his most persuasive tone. "It's nothing, just a little lunch date to get people speculating. It's good to be talked about, Ella. You need to start getting out there and getting photographed again, it's time. And let's face it, Tyler Kane isn't exactly offensive to look at. He's in the top five of all the 'hottest men' lists and he's been trending for months. Who knows? You might actually like him."

"I'm not going to like him because he's an idiot." Ella shook her head and grimaced in disgust. "Last time I saw him he was wearing a diamanté eye-patch just to look badass. I mean, that doesn't make any sense. Why can't I just have lunch with someone I actually want to spend time with so at least I'll have fun," she argued, thinking of Cam. "We could go somewhere public, if that's so important?"

"It's not just that." Tom sat back and folded his hands in front of him, the way he did when he meant business. "Apart from your assistant, you haven't been seen out with a man in a while, Ella. It's been what… three years, since you dated Justin?"

Ella arched a brow, a little confused now. "What has that got to do with anything?"

"Well… people might start speculating if you're spending more time with your yoga instructor than with Hollywood's most eligible bachelors." He nodded toward the magazine on the corner of his desk. "This was published today." Ella picked it up and opened the pages Tom had marked with a sticky note.

"Bastards," she whispered. "Why do they have to drag *her* into this?" She studied the picture of her and Cam, both with a coffee, walking back from the park to the yoga studio and felt a pang of anger rise in her chest. Ella had no idea her privacy had been invaded. She'd had a really great time and knowing that there had been someone spying on them made her feel a little sick. There was also a picture of them on the bench, in which Ella was holding Cam's hand, and one of them that had been taken weeks ago, when Ella had first visited Cam at work. In the latter, they were hugging in the parking lot. Ella couldn't help but smile at it because if she was being entirely honest with herself, they looked cute together.

"What's so funny?" Tom studied her. "I mean, sure, I can see how it's funny to you. You with a woman… it's ridiculous, I know, but I'll tell you something, Ella. It's not funny to me because I've had more phone calls about your sexuality than I have about movie roles today and it certainly won't be funny to you either when you're out of work."

"That's a bit harsh, don't you think?" Ella crossed her legs, leaned in and looked him straight in the eyes. "Are you saying my career would be over if I were gay? Because I can assure you that there are a lot of gay actors out there that are doing just fine for themselves. We're not in the Middle Ages anymore, Tom."

"No need to tell me that." Tom cocked his head. "But none of those gay actors are of your caliber. They don't get scripts thrown their way on a daily basis and they don't get to choose whatever they want to do and who they want to work with. Do you even realize the incredibly lucky position you're in?"

Ella thought about that as she fiddled with her phone. Sure, she was in the best position an actress could possibly be and she knew all too well how lucky she was. Still, what good was it to have all this fame and money if she couldn't live an honest life, ever. If she couldn't date who she wanted to date.

"Listen, I know you've had a very rough couple of years, and I don't want to put any pressure on you," Tom continued. "But you've only accepted a handful of invites to events since twenty-sixteen and it's important to be talked about, Ella. It's important to be talked about in a good way. It's time for you to get back out there and network. Make friends." He lifted his hands and made quote marks at the word 'friends'. "You seem a little more like yourself now, and maybe it will do you good to hang out with people again, and when I say people, I mean other celebrities. Have some fun, go to parties, drink Champagne, laugh for the camera, show them that pretty smile." He scratched his perfectly trimmed beard and sighed when she didn't answer. "I care about you Ella, and I want you to be happy."

And you want your bank account to be happy. Ella was glad she hadn't said it out loud. Tom *was* a friend, in a weird way. He'd always been there for her, but in this case, his intentions were questionable as she was his biggest source of income. A message from Cam came in on her phone and she smiled.

'What are you up to?'

'I'm coming your way tonight if you're home,' she replied.

'Great. I'll be there with pizza, waiting for you . See you at 7?'

"Ella? Are you even listening to me?" Tom rolled his eyes when he realized he'd lost her attention.

"Yeah, sorry." Ella stood up. "I have to go. Set up lunch with Tyler, whatever. Just let me know when and where and I'll be there. Can't promise I'll want to do it again, though."

Tom's eyes lit up at her response. "Okay, sure. I'll arrange something for this week." He stood up too before Ella got the chance to escape. "Wait, we're not done yet. I've emailed you some more scripts. Have you read them yet? You'll be done filming soon and you need to pick your next project. I've shortlisted the ones I think would be best for you."

"Thanks." Ella gave him a friendly pat on his shoulder. "I've been a little distracted, but I'll take a look at them this week and get back to you, okay?" She didn't wait for an answer as she hurried out of the door. "Bye Tom, have a great day!"

22

"Are you a psychic or my dream woman?" Ella joked as she stepped into Cam's living room. Candles were burning in deep ceramic dishes, and a light breeze was blowing into the room. The couch was covered in blankets and fluffy pillows, and Cam had pulled it toward the sliding porch doors, bringing the atmosphere of the house's beach-side location inside the room. There was a delicious smell of pizza in the kitchen and best of all there was Cam, standing behind the cooking island in a skimpy outfit, consisting of knee-length yoga pants and a crop top.

Ella had dressed up a little before she came over. She'd thought long and hard about what to wear before selecting a pair of tailored black shorts, black sandals and a white satin top that was low enough to draw attention to her cleavage but not quite bold enough to hint that she was trying to get Cam's attention. Her hair was left loose, and she'd used a minimum amount of make-up, sticking with only a little mascara to enhance her blue eyes.

Cam pointed at Ella and laughed uncomfortably, barely able to keep her gaze off of her. "Believe me, if you were into women, you'd be on the very top of my list." Her laugh faded when she saw heat rise to Ella's cheeks. "I'm sorry, I didn't mean it like that but the article... I'm sure you've seen it and..."

"No, it's fine, I..." Ella bit her lip. "Let's just say I'm honored to be on the top of your list." She walked over to the fridge and poured herself and Cam a glass of wine. For some strange reason, she felt at home in the cozy beach house where she'd had the worst morning of her life only seven months ago. She lingered by the fridge as she put the bottle back and took a sip of her wine, then pushed the other glass in Cam's direction. "And yes, I read the article too," she continued, letting out a nervous chuckle. "My manager shoved it in my face actually, before suggesting I go on a date with Tyler Kane." She shuffled on the spot and rolled her eyes, looking a little nervous. "He's worried this exposé might affect my career and thinks a diversion tactic would be our best option."

"Shit... I'm so sorry, Ella." Cam took a large gulp of her drink too and placed her elbows on the cooking island, facing Ella. "If I'd known this would happen, I wouldn't have..." she paused. "Actually, you know what? I didn't do anything, and neither did you. It's all bullshit, so why am I defending myself? Is this what you go through every time you go out in public?"

"Welcome to my world." Ella gave her a small smile. "And yes, it's BS, but you have to admit, the pictures do look pretty cozy."

"They do," Cam agreed. "I totally would have believed it but for the fact that I knew it was me who was involved."

"There you go." Ella's smile faded. "It's only going to get worse from here on in, and I want you to know that I'm so, so sorry that you got sucked up in this. It's not fair on you.

If you don't want to see me for a while, I'll understand and..."

"No!" Cam didn't mean to raise her voice, but the thought of not seeing Ella because of some ridiculous lie seemed beyond stupid. "I don't care. I mean, I do; it's disgusting but I'm not the victim here, you are. So, if you don't want to see *me*, that's fine, but if you do, then we'll figure out a way to deal with this." She took a long gulp of her wine. "I can only begin to imagine how it feels now when your personal life is constantly being invaded."

Ella shrugged as if it wasn't a big deal. "I usually ignore magazines and online shit. My manager only gets involved when things threaten to spiral out of control, and I guess now is the time."

"Yeah but still... Tyler Kane." Cam stretched her mouth into a straight line and gritted her teeth. "Unless you like him, of course. In that case, I won't say a bad word about him. I obviously don't even know him personally, and it's totally unfair to judge someone by the same kind of gossip I've just been subjected to myself... but still, he seems kind of full of himself." Cam had no idea why she was rambling on all of a sudden, but she had a feeling it might have something to do with a little thing called jealousy. The thought of Ella going on a date with the seemingly self-absorbed ladies' man made her stomach drop, and she tried her hardest to push the vision from her mind's eye.

"No, I don't like him." Ella laughed. "I'm not attracted to him in the slightest, and honestly, I'd still rather be photographed with you than with him, but until I figure out what to do, I'll go along with Tom's plan, just to make them back off the rumors surrounding us."

Their conversation was interrupted by the sound of the oven timer ringing, letting Cam know the pizza was ready.

Ella watched Cam take it out and place it on the island. It smelled divine. *She's sweet, trustworthy, she's incredibly sexy, and she can cook.* "I never asked you why on earth you were single," Ella said then, genuinely puzzled. "I didn't even know for sure if you were gay until you told me. Although I did have a feeling, you were."

"Oh... How did you guess?" Cam did her best to sound casual as she cut the homemade pizza into triangles before placing them on a big plate. Had it really been that obvious? She felt frustrated for clearly not having been able to hide her attraction to Ella.

"I don't know, just a feeling I had when I saw you, that first day after... you know... When I met you in your yoga studio." Ella swallowed hard and shook her head. "Never mind, maybe I imagined it."

"No, please continue," Cam said. "I want to know." Her heart thumped in her throat as she sprinkled rocket over the goat cheese and grilled vegetable pizza, then drizzled chili oil over the slices in an attempt to distract herself from the crazy conversation that had come out of nowhere. When she looked up, Ella's fingers were tapping the wooden surface of the cooking island, giving away her nerves.

"Okay." Ella took a deep breath as her eyes locked with Cam's. "Just a vibe I got from you." She kept her gaze fixed, letting her know she wasn't scared to talk. "An energy."

"So it's obvious that I find you attractive..."

Ella shook her head. "I didn't know that until now, but I'm glad you told me."

Cam looked caught out as she stopped fussing over the rocket leaves and pushed the plate with the pizza to the side. "I don't want anything from you, Ella. I like our friendship, and I don't want you to feel uncomfortable around me. I'm sorry if I made you feel that way."

"I'm not uncomfortable at all," Ella answered honestly. "You make me feel great, and you get me like no one else does. I... I like it when you look at me the way you sometimes do." Ella realized she was tapping her fingers, and she stopped herself then. She could see Cam's eyes darkening, first with confusion, and then with something else, something Ella hadn't seen before, desire.

"Have you ever felt anything for a woman?"

Ella nodded slowly. "Five, six times," she said, lowering her voice. "But I've never been involved with a woman." She saw Cam frown in even more surprise. Her lips looked so good when she pursed them, the way she was doing now. Her upper lip curled upwards just a tiny bit, making her mouth almost irresistible, and at that moment, Ella was dying to kiss her. She was terrified of the consequences, though. Cam was the only real friend she had, and she was the only person who made her feel normal and gave her some stability. She couldn't risk losing that.

Cam was silent for what seemed like forever, studying Ella as she took another sip of her wine. Ella knew she sensed her hesitation, and she watched her take a deep breath as if trying to compose herself.

"How long have you known?" she finally asked. "How long have you known that you were gay?"

Ella shrugged. "Forever, I guess."

Again, Cam gave her another surprised look. Ella kind of expected some speech about being true to oneself, but instead, Cam's expression softened.

"Jesus, that must have been so hard for you, pretending to be someone you're not all your life... Does your family know? Your manager?"

"No. I don't really have any family, apart from my mother, who I don't speak to and my manager has no idea;

that's why he's sending me on that ridiculous date. I'm only going so they'll back off on us a little. I really have no interest in men."

Cam walked around the island and took Ella's hand. "As long as you don't do this for me. I'm a nobody, they'll have forgotten about me in a matter of days. And what you just told me stays between us, of course." She looked at Ella, her eyes dropping to her lips again. "But doesn't this drive you crazy? And doesn't the fact that your manager wants to send you on a fake date make you furious? You don't have to go, you know."

"I know, but it's better if I do. I'm really enjoying spending time with you, and I don't want to drag you into this circus. It gets crazy, with photographers following you around, blocking your way, waiting for you the moment you walk out of your front door... I don't want you to suffer just because you hang out with me. So, it's better if I give them another storyline." Ella bit her lip. "I don't want to lose you as a friend. I haven't felt this comfortable around someone in a long time. Not since..." Her voice trailed away.

"Hey, you're not going to lose me." Cam put her arms around Ella and pulled her into a tight embrace. "I don't care about any of that stuff. I just want you to be happy." Ella sighed as she melted into Cam and buried her face against her chest. Her familiar citrus scent flooded her senses. The butterflies were back again, and there were millions this time.

"You say that now, but you have no idea how bad it can get. I'm basically media poison just by association." Ella stepped out of the embrace, needing some distance to cool down. "Anyway, are you going to tell me why you're single or what? Because I find it hard to believe that someone like you doesn't have an amazing girlfriend."

Cam smiled. "Flattery is clearly your strong point."

"It's not flattery, it's the truth."

"Okay…" Cam thought about it for a while. It was a question she never asked herself. She was happy with her own company, and she wasn't looking for love. "I guess I've never met the right person. I've been in relationships; two long-term ones and two shorter ones. The shorter ones ended abruptly as neither of them told me they were married." She chuckled. "To men, I might add."

"Ouch." Ella winced. "Clients?"

"Yeah. I stopped dating private clients after the second drama when the woman's husband busted us whilst we were out on a date. Clearly, I hadn't learned my lesson after the first. Let's just say I walked out and never looked back. I hate dishonesty."

"I get that. And the long-term ones?" Ella asked.

"My last real relationship ended not long after I resigned from my sales job and decided I wanted to become a yoga teacher. I guess my girlfriend at the time saw us as some kind of power couple and was hoping for a big house, a flashy car and vacations in the Bahamas. When she realized I'd be a struggling new business owner, teaching yoga for the rest of my life, she broke up with me, saying our goals weren't aligned anymore."

"That's ridiculous."

"Yeah well, I never really struggled in the end, and my business is booming, so it's her loss." Cam shrugged. "And my first long-term relationship simply faded. We were young when we met, and as we grew up, we became different people. We separated amicably, but it's not like we're still friends. She moved to San Francisco, and I stayed here. We're not in contact anymore."

"So you've been more or less single for a long time now," Ella concluded.

"I guess you could say that. I date sometimes, and it's not like I have trouble meeting women, but I like my life. I'm busy, and I'm happy. I'm open to love, but I'm not looking for it, and if I can't see it going anywhere, I don't waste my time." Cam picked up the pizza and beckoned Ella to follow her to the couch. "I'd ask you why you're single, but I guess I already know the answer to that now." She sat down and waited for Ella to sit down next to her. "Ever thought of coming out?"

Ella winced at that. "I've thought about it, but it scares me. My job is about all I have right now, and I don't want to risk jeopardizing my career. Besides, it's not the same as coming out to your family. I have to come out to the whole world." She took a slice of pizza and leaned back. "But needless to say, I think about it all the time. I told Theresa too."

"You've hidden it well," Cam said. "I would have never thought you were into women. Not at first anyway."

"Not at first..." Ella repeated. "And now? Now that you know me better?"

"I don't know." Cam hesitated. "I guess I've noticed something. This..." Their eyes locked, and there it was again; that electrifying tension. "Never mind, I don't really know what I was trying to say." She cleared her throat and looked away. "Thank you for telling me. I'm here for you if you want to talk about it."

"Thank you." Ella let out a long sigh. It felt liberating to tell someone other than her therapist. She wasn't sure if it was easier to talk to Cam because she felt so comfortable around her, or because coming out to her therapist had opened her up more. Either way, the feeling of relief made her feel lighter already, but at the same time, the 'something' Cam mentioned had stirred a longing in her that did crazy things to her body. "When did you come out?" she asked.

"When I was twelve, I think." Cam took a bite of her pizza. "Or I might have been thirteen, I don't remember. It wasn't exactly a memorable moment, my parents were very relaxed, and my mother had been involved with a woman when she was younger, so she didn't even blink. They simply asked me if I preferred girls one day and I answered that I did. I'm sure they knew long before I realized it."

"That's sweet." Ella moaned as she took a bite of her pizza too. "Mmm... you're an amazing cook." She studied the slice that was covered in goat cheese, grilled asparagus, red peppers and tomatoes. "It even tastes healthy."

"It is healthy." Cam kept her eyes fixed on the pizza slice in her hand, conscious of how close together they were sitting. "Did your sister know you were gay?" she asked, remembering Ella had told her how close they were.

"Yes, Helena knew. In fact, she was gay, too. I only told her after she came out to me. The whole world found out about her sexuality last year when our mother wrote a 'tell-all' book about her and included chapters from her diary. It was a horrible thing to do; I'm surprised you haven't heard about it."

"I didn't know that. I usually don't read gossip, just because it doesn't interest me at all. Is that why you don't speak to your mother anymore?"

Ella nodded. "It was the final straw. Our relationship was already rusty after I'd fired her as my manager seven years ago because she kept making decisions behind my back and stealing from me. I'm not an unreasonable person, and despite our differences, I would have given her whatever she wanted on top of her already hefty salary and commissions if she'd just asked for it instead of lying to me. But the book she wrote about Helena was a really low blow. Diaries are diaries for a reason. Helena chose to live a private life in the end, and so when mom saw the opportunity to make cash over my dead sister's dignity, I decided I'd had enough of her. I don't even know how she got hold of the diaries. Helena kept them under her bed in our house in Palm Springs so she must have talked her way in there and stolen them."

"Jesus."

"Yeah. I started reading the book when it came out, but I stopped halfway. When I got to the diary sections, especially the ones where Helena wrote her first thoughts on having feelings for a woman – it was like reading my own thoughts and knowing it was public made me really anxious. Of course, mom had left out the parts that reflected badly on herself."

"So, you haven't spoken to her since?"

"No, and I don't intend to." Ella helped herself to another slice of pizza, her face stern and indifferent. She'd learned to switch off all emotions when it came to her mother. "I heard she moved out of LA a while ago, but I have no idea where she went. I'm just glad she's gone..." She winced. "I'm sorry, that's not fair to say considering your mom..."

"Don't worry about it." Cam gave her a smile. "You don't have to watch what you say around me. I don't know your mom. I don't even know you very well, but if her being out of the picture makes life better for you, then I'm all for it."

"I know we don't know each other that well," Ella said. "But I'd like to get to know you better. There's so much I'm curious about."

Cam held up her hands and smiled. "Hey, I'm an open

book, and I've got all night. Fire away, ask me anything you want."

Cam couldn't sleep after Ella had left. It was almost 2 am and she was still staring at the ceiling, thoughts and regrets filling her head. She shouldn't have admitted she was attracted to Ella, but she'd been completely thrown by her confession. She'd hardly been able to look at her when they were sitting on the couch together because each time she did, her breath caught, and she felt drawn to Ella's mouth like she had no control over it. Their brief conversation, insinuating there was something between them, had evoked fantasies she was better off having alone, and she'd quickly batted the thoughts away right there and then. A little innocent flirting was one thing, but this was a whole different ballgame.

She felt protective toward Ella in a way she never had over anyone before. Maybe because she'd saved her or maybe because Ella simply didn't have anyone else to look out for her and she didn't want to risk breaking the bond of trust they'd formed by gauging if there was more between them.

It wasn't just Ella she was worried about though; it was herself too. Ella did things to her she couldn't explain, and it wasn't that easy to set her feelings aside anymore. Cam didn't want to be an experiment because she knew that with Ella, it would be impossible to go back to the way they were once they'd crossed the line. But now that she was alone, it proved even harder not to imagine what it would feel like to kiss her and to brush her lips along Ella's delicate neck. *Don't think about it, Cam. It's never going to happen.*

23

"You look super-hot, Ella," Tyler Kane said with a smirk before taking a bite of his gourmet burger. "I was hoping they'd pick you," he continued with his mouth full of food.

"Thank you. You look..." Ella racked her brain, searching for the right words. "You look pretty interesting yourself." The seventy-dollar gold-dusted buns at *Gold Burger* were ridiculous, and so was Tyler's outfit, Ella noted as she studied his triple-denim ensemble. His shirt, pants and jacket were all covered in studs, the material looking way too hot for the high temperatures. He'd kept his shades on inside and Ella could see her own reflection in them each time he looked up.

Her make-up was itching, her heels were uncomfortable, and her black dress was too tight and revealing for her liking, but her stylist had insisted it was a perfect look for a first date. She'd been so happy wearing her yoga clothes lately that she'd almost forgotten what it felt like to be dressed up like a Christmas tree. *What am I doing?* She was annoyed to be wasting her free afternoon with

Tyler, but she comforted herself with the knowledge that she was due to finish filming in two weeks. Then, she'd have all the time in the world for her new favorite pastime. *Cam.*

There had been a strange tension between them, after she'd come out to her. The way Cam had looked at her was different now as if she realized the opportunity was there, yet Ella knew she'd never make a move unless she made it very clear that she wanted it and that she was ready. Ella tried to analyze the attraction between them. It wasn't just a deep kind of caring, combined with mutual physical attraction; she was sure of that. It was also highly sexual too. She could feel it in every nerve ending, and if she were honest with herself, she'd felt it for weeks. It was hard to stay focused on anything when she couldn't stop fantasizing about what it would be like to kiss Cam, to see her naked, to touch her...

"Ella?" Tyler's voice woke her up from her erotic thoughts.

"Sorry." Ella faked a warm smile, conscious of the photographers who were watching them from outside the window. It had been over two-and-a-half years since she'd last done this, and she was a little out of practice. *Or maybe I'm just distracted.* "What did you say?" She attempted to dust the gold off her salmon burger bun, then cursed when it stuck to her fingers instead.

"I said my new movie will be out soon. It's awesome," Tyler boasted. "I'm sure you've seen the trailer."

"No, I haven't. Is it that Marvel movie?" Ella asked, vaguely recalling Tom saying something about it during their pre-date meeting in which she'd signed an NDA, preventing her from publicly speaking about Tyler without his management's permission. She reached into her purse for some hand sanitizer to clean her fingers and noticed Tyler now had gold dust in his eyebrows.

"Yeah," he whispered; his eyes wide with excitement. "I did most of the stunts myself. Not many actors do that, you know."

"I know, that's pretty impressive." Ella tried her best to come across as interested.

"Yeah. They nicknamed me Thunder Boy on set." Tyler smirked and took another enormous bite of his burger. "So, my manager and I were thinking that it would be good if you came to the premiere with me. It's in two months."

"Two months from now?" Ella sounded shocked. "That's a bit long to be going out together, don't you think?" She waved a finger in between Tyler and herself before wiping her hands. She thought about handing him the sanitizer too and telling him to clean his face but devilishly decided not to.

"Nah. Two months is over before you know it, especially if we're having fun." Tyler spotted one of the other diners filming them and took her hand. "Why don't you come over to my house tonight? Bring your bikini so we can sample my new Jacuzzi." Ella had to stop herself from instinctively pulling her hand back. The thought of sitting in a Jacuzzi with Tyler disgusted her no end, and she wondered if she would have been attracted to him if she was straight. *No chance.*

"Listen, Tyler. This is strictly business," she said, keeping her voice down. She waited for a couple of seconds before she retracted her hand and picked up her cutlery. She'd make sure to have something in her hands at all times from now on. "I'm not interested in anything more, and I have no idea why you thought that I would be. We only met once before, and we barely spoke."

Tyler gave her a sweet smile, pretending they were having a romantic conversation as he lowered his voice too and whispered. "Are you serious? You don't even want to bang? What's in it for me, then?"

Ella gasped at his words, almost choking on the piece of burger she was chewing. "Seriously? Shit like that is never part of the plan," she whispered back as she leaned in and painted on another smile. "It's exposure, for both of us. That's what's in it for you. We're in the top ten lists of the most desirable singles in the US, and it's just a fucking game to get into the tabloids and grow our following. Not that I care about how many followers I have; I don't even know why I'm here." She sighed. "I'm sorry; this was a mistake. I shouldn't have come."

"Do you have any idea of all the A-listers who would give an arm to date me?" Tyler huffed, unable to hide his frustration any longer. He sat back, crossing his arms.

"Then go date them instead." Ella leaned back too, mimicking his body language.

"I will." Tyler looked like a stubborn child who was about to throw a tantrum. "I'm getting action tonight whether you're a part of it or not. There are thousands of chicks who are dying for a piece of this." He patted his chest, then narrowed his eyes. "Hey, wait a minute. Weren't you papped being all snuggly with your yoga teacher or something?" He scrolled through his phone, searching for the latest gossip on Ella Temperley. He smiled when he found the pictures and discreetly turned his phone around for Ella to see. "Is she the reason you're doing this dating thing?" he whispered. "Did she turn you? I bet she came on to you during one of your private lessons and you just jumped at the opportunity to try it. I can't imagine you as a lesbian but since..."

"Since what?" Ella cut him off. "Since I don't want to sleep with you? Jesus, are you really that full of yourself? It's none of your fucking business who I sleep with. But I'll tell you one thing, Tyler, it's certainly not going to be you." She stood up and pointed a finger at him. "And don't you dare drag Cam into this. She's too good to be part of this ridiculous charade."

"So, I was right. You *are* a lesbian." Tyler shot her a smug smirk. "Why else would you be so defensive?"

"Fuck you, Tyler." Ella felt like she was about to explode with rage, and she needed an outlet. She looked at her half-eaten burger, picked it up and flung it toward Tyler without thinking it through. Then she walked out, leaving him at the table with green wasabi mayo dripping down his face.

24

'ELLA TEMPERLEY DUMPS TYLER KANE AT GOLD BURGER'*. Ella sighed as she read the headline. She should really stop looking at those celebrity gossip websites, but she couldn't help herself. The article was accompanied by a picture of them smiling at each other over lunch, then another picture of Ella in action with a face like thunder. She didn't like seeing herself like that, but she immediately felt a little better when she turned the page and saw a picture of Tyler's mayo-covered face. *I dumped him?* That meant that the media assumed they'd been dating already and after only half an hour with him, she couldn't think of anything worse. Well, it could get worse, of course. It could always get worse. Tyler would be furious now and was probably looking for revenge.

Even though Tyler had signed an NDA too, she'd behaved inappropriately, meaning their contract could be broken. Being outed by Tyler was Ella's worst nightmare, and she felt dirty and ashamed for even having taken part in the arrangement. No one had forced her; she'd agreed to Tom's plan, and she had no one but herself to blame for this mess. She hadn't done anything as dumb as this in a long time because she'd been keeping to herself.

Lately, something had breathed life back into her, though. Or rather someone. She could laugh again at times, eat, engage with people and have fun. She even liked venturing out of her house now, but with that glimpse of freedom came the media and they were always there, wherever she went. She knew the reason for her new lease of life was Cam, and she had no idea what to do with that. As Tom had mentioned, she was still getting the roles she wanted, but that wasn't going to last forever if she didn't step back into the spotlight. That meant interviews, talk shows, parties, award nights… What would happen if she came out to the world? She certainly wouldn't get the romantic comedy roles that paid so well. People wanted believable couples on screen. But did she really need the money? And did she really still want those types of roles? It was a decision she'd have to make sooner rather than later. Her phone buzzed, and her heart skipped a beat when she saw it was a message from Cam.

'Hey, how did the 'date' go?'

'Not according to plan,' Ella replied. Then she added: *'Check the latest gossip. Tyler is going to make my life a living hell, I think I might have to go away for a while after we wrap up the movie. Do you want to come along to my place in Palm Springs for a couple of days? It's blissfully private there.'* She waited for a message back but instead, her phone rang.

"Are you okay, Ella?" Cam sounded worried.

"Yeah. Just reading some shitty articles about myself, that's all. It took them no more than forty minutes to get it online. Tyler was such an asshole. I can't believe I actually willingly went along with that crap."

"I'm so sorry about that." Cam paused. "What happened?"

"He assumed I'd sleep with him. When I made it clear that wasn't going to happen, he mentioned you as the reason, and that made me furious. I then threw a burger in his face and walked out." Cam laughed, and Ella could imagine what she looked like at that moment. Glowing, sweaty and sexy after her class, and all she wanted was to be near her.

"I'm sorry, I didn't mean to laugh, but I salute you for doing that and I'll kill him if he ever crosses my path."

"Thank you, but I might beat you to it." Ella hesitated for a moment. "So, about Palm Springs... do you want to come?"

"Yeah, I'd like that," Cam said. "But I have private clients on the weekend, and I can't cancel on them. I can do Monday to Thursday though, if I can get someone to take over my classes. Vanya will be back soon, so I'm sure she'll be able to sort it out."

"Really? That would be amazing." Ella couldn't stop smiling as she felt her heart warm, and her frustrations melt away. "I can pick you up on Monday morning, the week after next? I probably won't see you until then. We're doing extra-long days on set as it's the final push, so we're starting at seven each morning and finishing late."

"That sounds exhausting, make sure you take care of yourself."

"I will. I'm looking forward to seeing you soon."

"Yeah, me too." There was a short pause. "And Ella? Call me if you want to talk, okay? I know you must have been through this over a hundred times, and I might sound naïve if I say we can fight these fuckers, but I'm here for you and always on your side."

"I know. Thank you, and I miss you and..." Ella hesitated. "I can't wait to see you again." She was grinning from ear to ear after she'd hung up. Apparently, just hearing Cam's voice was enough to lift her mood. Besides that, four days with Cam was a thrilling prospect, and she hoped she'd be able to get through the last scenes without being too distracted. Their recent conversation kept playing over and over in her head and all she was able to think about now, was Cam's darkened expression when she'd told her she liked women. They were both clearly aware that the mutual attraction was there, but they were also aware of how special their friendship was and to Ella, finally having someone that she trusted wholeheartedly again was everything.

It was becoming harder and harder to keep her distance, and the more time they spent together, the closer she felt to Cam. She was desperate to kiss her, touch her... Hell, she wanted to rip her clothes off and have her way with her, even though she'd have no idea what to do. Well, that wasn't entirely true. She'd watched more female on female love scenes than she cared to admit, and in her fantasies, she always knew exactly what to do. Years of craving for a woman's touch had taken its toll, and Ella felt like she was about to explode each time she thought of her and Cam as more than friends. Just thinking of her had made her last love scene with Neil Messenger so convincing that they'd wrapped it up in two takes, which was likely to be a record in her industry. Even the director had given her a curious look at one point, probably assuming she was madly in love with Neil. Ella closed her laptop and turned back to the script on the small desk in her trailer. *Back to work, Ella. Concentrate.*

25

Ella looked at her phone for the tenth time that hour. The five days in which she hadn't seen or spoken to Cam had felt like an eternity. She missed her like crazy, and so she'd invited her on set today. Cam had immediately replied:

'Really? I'd love to come on set. Are you sure that's okay? I can come in between my classes. See you later X C'

Ella wasn't supposed to invite people over here, there were strict rules about it, but she'd finally managed to get hold of the director's assistant, who was often busier than the director himself, and he'd printed her a non-disclosure agreement for Cam to sign when she arrived. Ella had a three-hour break in between scenes, and although it wasn't much, it was better than not seeing her at all. She felt addicted to her, and five days cold-turkey had made her shifty and even a little sad.

Now, she was tapping her fingers on her desk, nervously waiting for someone to bring Cam over so she could give her a tour on set. The long evening gown she was wearing after shooting that morning's scene felt slightly uncomfortable, but she hadn't bothered changing, knowing she would have to go back into dress, hair and make-up again this afternoon. There was a knock on the door, and Ella quickly checked herself in the mirror one last time.

"Ella, your twelve o'clock is here. Cam Saunders?" Raphael called.

"Hey." Ella's lips pulled into a smile when she opened the door and saw Cam there, next to Raphael. Cam was wearing tight, blue jeans and a casual blue and white striped linen shirt. The top four buttons were undone, giving Ella a nice view of her cleavage. "I'm so glad you could make it. Do you want to come into my trailer?" She batted her eyelashes.

Cam shot her a playful look, leaning against the doorway. "No woman has ever asked me that before so I'm certainly not going to decline. You look amazing by the way. I assume that's got something to do with the movie?"

"Who knows?" Ella teased. "Maybe I just dressed up for my stunningly hot yoga teacher who's about to get a tour of the studio grounds." She felt her cheeks flush when Cam's eyes burned into hers.

"Are you flirting with me, Ella?" Cam tilted her head to one side, a teasing grin spreading across her face. "Because if you flirt with me, you're going to get as good as you give. I'm only human, and there's only so much self-restraint I can practice before I start pouring my charms all over you."

"Try me." Ella caught her stare and held it.

Cam let out a chuckle and stepped inside, reminding herself to stop taking the bait. Whatever it was what they were doing now, it was bringing them closer and closer to the point of no return, and she cared too much about Ella to let their relationship be ruined by a fling that was sure to change all dynamics between them. *God help me. I'm in so much trouble.* She left a baffled Raphael, who had witnessed their flirtations, outside and waved at him. "Thank you, Raphael, it was really nice to meet you."

"Thanks, Raphael, you can go if you want. I'll see you tomorrow for our breakfast meeting," Ella called after him before he left. "He's a good guy," she said when he was out of sight. "And loyal. It's hard to find people like that."

"I saw a picture of you two in a magazine. The article speculated you guys were dating."

"Yeah well, I'd tell you not to believe everything you read, but I guess you know that by now." Ella followed Cam with her eyes as she walked past her. She hadn't meant to flirt with her, but it was hard not to, the way Cam was looking today. She loved seeing Cam in her yoga wear, but this was a whole new level of indulgence.

"Jesus, this thing's like a mansion." Cam looked around the trailer that was padded with white leather and housed a long couch, stretching along one side. There was a dining table seating four and a swanky kitchenette with modern appliances, including an industrial juicer, a coffee maker and an ice machine. The door at the back was closed, but she imagined an equally fresh and stylish bedroom behind it. "I love it."

"Yeah, it's not bad, right?" Ella opened the fridge. "Want anything? Coffee, tea, juice, water, Champagne? I'm not done shooting yet, so I'm going to make myself a coffee."

"Coffee sounds good." Cam sat down on the couch and stroked the soft leather. "You've got a good thing going on here, Ella. Thanks for inviting me, I've never been on a movie set before."

"So you're excited to see it?" Ella smiled as she put a Nespresso capsule into the machine and placed a take-out cup underneath.

"Yeah, totally. I didn't even know it was possible to get in here as an outsider. My mom always told me it was strictly prohibited on her set."

Ella added almond milk to Cam's cup – pleased she'd asked Raphael to get some that morning – and handed it to her. "You're right. We're not really allowed to let people in, but I'm important to the movie, so I knew they weren't going to say no." She grinned as she made herself a coffee too. "I rarely make demands, but I've missed you. Sorry, that sounds silly, I..."

"No... It's not silly, I've missed you too," Cam said as she stood up and followed Ella out of the door and into the open-air studio with dozens of indoor and outdoor sets. She was surprised when Ella led them to a golf cart, parked behind the trailer. "This is so cool. I've always wanted to try one of these."

"Oh yeah? Do you want to drive?" Ella walked around to the passenger seat and waited for Cam to climb behind the wheel, then handed her the key. Cam grinned as she inspected it.

"Is it electric? How does it work?"

"Electric, forty-eight volts," Ella said. "There's nothing to it, it drives just like an automatic car." She pointed to the two pedals and laughed when Cam turned the key and stepped on the pedal, launching them forward. She then laughed even harder at seeing Cam's perplexed expression. "Yeah, more or less like that. I think you've got the basic idea."

"Right... I thought it would be a little more subtle, but obviously, it's not. Never mind, I've got it now." Cam winked at her and smiled. "So, where are we going, boss?"

"Straight on, then take a left at the next junction." Ella waved at a group of colleagues who walked past and shot curious glances their way. She hadn't expected any different, being seen driving around with Cam after all the recent gossip, but the reality was that they really were just friends, and she wasn't going to refrain from seeing her just because people wanted to speculate. "First stop is that building over there." She pointed to a tall concrete warehouse about half a mile ahead of them after Cam had turned the corner. Part of the long street looked like a small town, with a church, storefronts and sweet little houses. Farther down was a more suburban layout with pristine yards and real trees.

Cam found it surreal to drive through the set, passing a mixture of different architectural styles and half buildings, some of them even lacking side walls. It had seemed like a maze when Raphael had walked her over here and by the looks of the many streets they passed now, the studio covered more ground than a small town.

"Is all of this for the movie you're working on?" she asked.

"No, we shoot indoors mainly. The sets in that warehouse over there have been built specifically for this movie. We finished shooting the outdoor scenes in the Hollywood Hills two months ago, and now we only have the indoor scenes left. One of the reasons I chose to be on this movie was because I didn't feel like travelling last year, but for my next one, I'll think about what kind of project I want to do, rather than narrowing down the selection because of location. I'm thinking about doing a couple of indie movies, maybe. Something a bit more substantial than a rom-com."

"That's quite a change from what you're doing now." Cam waved a hand. "Not that I think the movies you've done are lame, although I have to admit, I've only watched a few of them."

"Exactly, that's my point. I wouldn't watch them either. I'd like to play a character who forces me to really challenge myself for once and to work on a movie that I'd like to watch myself. All this... this is easy for me. I've done it forever, and I feel like now is the point where I have to make a change. Otherwise, the only way to stay current will be through fake dates with idiots and attending stupid parties."

"Sounds like you've done some thinking," Cam said. "I think it's a brave decision. How does your manager feel about it?"

"Tom?" Ella shot her a mischievous look. "He doesn't know yet, and neither does my booking agent." She waved at a young guy who was walking in the same direction with a clipboard, and he waved back at her. "That's one of the director's assistants. We have two on this set. The director's assistants oversee a crew of production assistants, or PAs as we call them. They're like the eyes and ears on set, and they make sure things are where they need to be at all times. It's probably the most stressful job within the movie industry; the poor PAs get fired all the time for forgetting stuff or being unable to find things others have misplaced. It's not fair, but it's how you've got to start if you want to make a living in the movies. That over there is the charging station for the walkie talkies everyone carries around," she continued when she saw Cam studying the white tent.

"Do you have one of those?"

"Yeah, I do, but I only start carrying it around an hour before I'm on call."

"It's not at all what I expected." Cam noted there weren't many people around in general. She'd expected chaos, but instead, it seemed highly organized. "At least I won't have to watch out for traffic here," she joked as she drove slowly so she could take in everything that was going on. Rails of clothing were being rolled from one building to another, make-up artists were dragging cases behind them, their toolbelts stuffed with make-up brushes and other paraphernalia. There was a large gazebo with an outdoor cooking station filled with long tables and benches, where groups of people dressed in formal period clothing were eating. A man and a woman in black PA shirts were hanging decorations in a tree in one of the fake suburban yards, taking great care in how the props were positioned. "Hey, isn't that Neil Messenger?" She narrowed her eyes as she looked over her shoulder while passing a man in formal evening attire.

Ella looked over her shoulder too. "Well spotted, pull over. Would you like to meet him?"

"I'm sure Neil's got better things to do than talk to me." Cam parked the cart next to the building and handed the key back to Ella.

"I don't think he has. He's on a three-hour break, just like me and he usually just sits in his trailer and plays video games with his assistant." Ella turned around and shouted: "Hey, Neil! Come over here for a second."

Cam watched the handsome man in his mid-thirties turn around and eye Ella in surprise. Then he started walking back toward them as they got out of the cart.

"Ella. What's up?" He smiled as he looked from Ella to Cam and back. "What are you doing driving around on your break? You usually disappear."

"I know, but not today." Ella gave him a beaming smile. "This is my friend Cam. I'm showing her around the set."

"Ah, Cam..." Neil shook Cam's hand. "It's nice to meet the infamous yoga instructor."

Cam laughed. "Don't believe everything you read."

"Oh, I never read anything but it's been hard to miss," Neil joked. "So, is there going to be a steamy yoga session happening on today's break? Can I join?"

Ella rolled her eyes and shook her head. "Sorry to disappoint you. There's no yoga session, just sightseeing. Do you know if studio thirteen is free?" She gestured to the warehouse.

"The last people just left for lunch, so go knock yourself out." Neil grinned, holding up a burger. "The buffet for the extras is still up if you want some carbs. I'm not really into that superfood they feed us."

"Is that why you were lurking around when we broke for lunch?" Ella chuckled and pointed at him. "For the extras' buffet?"

"Where else am I going to be fed?" Neil shrugged. "I've got no girlfriend to bring me fast-food and my assistant quit yesterday because he got a better offer from some oil sheikh in Abu Dhabi." He turned to Cam. "So, you're the reason Ella won't go out on a date with me, huh?"

Cam grinned, not sure how to reply to that. "Hey, I'm sure it's nothing personal. Maybe I'm just a better cook."

"Yeah, but does she buy you socks, though?" Neil arched a brow suggestively as he lifted the hem of his pants, revealing a pair of beige socks with brown bacon strips all over them. He'd pulled the crazy socks up high, and they looked so ridiculous that Cam and Ella both cracked up.

"No, I haven't been so lucky, so you win, I guess," Cam said.

"If only I had someone to admire them on my muscular calves." Neil pulled a dramatic face.

"I doubt you have a shortage of girlfriends, Neil," Ella interrupted them. "But if you ever get super lonely or super hungry, let me know, and we might let you join us. For dinner only," she clarified. Her so-called lesbian affair was already the talk of the town, so she decided she might as well have a little fun with it. Neil knew just as well as she did that there was rarely truth to the gossip, but at the same time, she was pretty sure he wondered why she had zero interest in him.

"Sounds good, I'll hold you to that, guys." He gave them a wave, adjusted his tuxedo jacket and turned on his heel, whistling as he walked off.

"Thank you, I had an amazing time." Cam grabbed her bag from Ella's trailer and stepped back outside.

"I'm glad you enjoyed it." Ella checked the time on her phone and sighed. "Well, I'd better get back into hair and make-up. We're rehearsing and shooting again soon."

"Oh yeah? What are you wearing this afternoon?" *Here we go again.* Cam didn't want the flirting to stop, now that they'd started. It was too much fun, and besides, it was innocent, wasn't it? *No, Cam, it's far from innocent.*

"A negligée," Ella teased.

"Hmm... Too bad I'm going to miss that."

"I could keep it on and come over to yours later?" A rush of heat coursed through Ella at the thought of showing up on Cam's doorstep in a negligée and having Cam's eyes on her. She loved the way Cam looked at her. *What am I doing?* "I could bring some take-out, and we could just hang out," she quickly added in an attempt to hide her desire.

"Really? What time do you finish?" Cam asked, looking positively surprised.

"Around seven, I think. I can't stay long because I have to get up again at five, but I'd love to meet up, it's been boring without you. Unless you've got plans?" Ella grabbed her purse, her walkie-talkie and her phone and closed the trailer door behind her.

"No, no plans," Cam said, reminding herself to finish the staff schedules as soon as she got home so she'd have the evening off. "You could always stay over. It will save you the drive, and I have a spare bedroom." She half expected Ella to turn down her offer, but instead, Ella nodded and smiled.

"Are you sure? I'd love that."

"Great." Cam waved and got in the car with Raphael, who had just pulled up at the trailer to take her back to the exit. "I'll see you later then."

26

"Where's that negligée you promised me?" Cam joked as she opened the door to Ella, who was wearing denim shorts and a peach colored T-shirt with Japanese writing on it.

"Sorry, no luck on the nightshirt. I had to hand it back in, we're re-shooting the same scene tomorrow morning, so you'll have to make do with this." Ella held out her arms and looked down at herself.

"This will do just fine," Cam said, casting a not so subtle glance over Ella's bare legs. By now, she wasn't sure if she was kidding herself anymore because she really, really liked the look of her tanned legs in the short shorts. "Do you want wine?" She opened the fridge, then closed it again. "I have cold gin and tonic, or lukewarm wine because I forgot to put it in the fridge." She shot Ella an apologetic look. "Or fresh mint tea, I have that too."

Ella smiled. "I think I'll have a mint tea. Do you want me to get some from the porch?" She'd spotted the various pots of herbs on her previous visit and therefore opened the doors without waiting for an answer, walked outside and came back with a big bunch of mint from the terracotta pot under the window. "You want one too?"

"Sure. There's honey in the basket over there." Cam pointed in the general direction of the condiments, then opened the take-out bag Ella had brought along. "Yum, falafel. Good choice." She turned back to Ella. "Do you want to watch a movie?"

"A movie?" Ella arched a brow as if she had no idea what she was talking about.

"Yeah. You know, a motion picture. Like the ones you work on every day."

Ella shook her head and snickered. "I know what a movie is, I just don't think I've ever watched a movie with someone else for fun." Her smile widened. "I'd love to, as long as it's not one of my own."

Cam laughed too. "I'm glad mundane things excite you. At least you won't get bored of me." Her eyes twinkled, clearly amused. "Don't worry; I won't put any of your movies on. They're not really my thing." She opened the doors to the porch further, then moved the TV outside, untangling the string of cables before she placed it on the porch table. It was a nice evening and she liked enjoying the sea breeze while she wound down from her hectic day. It had been busy without Vanya there and Cam realized more than ever how much she needed her.

"You hate my movies, don't you?" Ella scrunched her nose. "You can tell me, I won't be offended." She took hold of the couch's armrest and helped Cam move it into the doorway before settling down on it.

"No, it's not that, but you know... a romantic comedy involving a man and a woman; it just doesn't do anything for me." Cam joined her with the tea, a blanket and the food. She divided the pittas, salad, humous, mint sauce and falafels over two plates and handed one to Ella. "I've watched a couple though, with Vanya. She's got a total girl-crush on you, and I can't blame her. You looked so hot in that Hawaiian-themed movie." She covered her face with her hands when she realized what she'd said. "Oh God, now I totally sound like a man."

Ella laughed. "Hey, it's okay, I'm flattered. Besides, I won't deny I like looking at you too. You look like a fluid sculpture when you do yoga. It's beautiful." She grinned as she watched Cam's cheeks take on a darker shade of pink and decided to change the subject.

"Anyway, what are we watching?" she asked, taking a bite of her falafel.

"Whatever you want." Cam turned to her, still a little flustered. "What do you like?"

"What do I like..." Ella repeated suggestively. "I'm not sure what I like because I lack experience... in the movie-watching department," she added. She thought about it for a moment, then shook her head. "I have no idea. I haven't watched anything in a long time, but my co-stars are all raving about that new detective series at the moment. *Swamps?* How about we watch that? At least I'll be able to join in on the conversations on set." She smiled. "And it will give me an excuse to come back to watch the rest."

"Sounds good, I haven't seen it yet either." Cam switched on the TV and looked up the series on her on-demand channel. "I have to warn you though; you might be spending a lot of time here. I've heard it's addictive." She arched a brow. "And you have to promise me not to watch any episodes without me. It's an unspoken rule."

"Of course. What would be the fun in that?" Ella pulled her legs underneath her, half-facing Cam. When their eyes locked, her breath caught. The darkness in Cam's gaze, her tanned skin, her lips, her sculpted shoulders... *So strong*. She could smell Cam's shampoo and her unique citrusy scent, and fought the urge to reach out and run a hand through her hair. There was a moment in which she was almost sure that Cam felt the need to touch her too, but instead, Cam turned her attention back to the remote and pressed play.

"You were right. This is so addictive," Ella said after the third episode.

"Yeah, it's pretty good." Cam turned to her. "You look sleepy. Do you want to continue another time?"

"Maybe that's best. I don't want to fall asleep in the middle of it, and we've both got an early start tomorrow."

"Well, the bed is made, and there's a towel on the dressing table if you want to have a shower." Cam turned the TV off.

"A shower would be great." Ella pulled the blanket further over them. The sea breeze was cooler now, but she loved the view and simply sitting next to Cam felt so good that she didn't want to get up just yet. "Can we stay here for a little while longer?"

"Sure." Cam sank further down on the couch and put her feet up on the footstool. If she was being entirely honest with herself, she could have stayed there for days. It was fun and easy with Ella, and she felt so comfortable around her that she didn't even have to try. The only thing stopping her from relaxing entirely was the constant pull between them that made her stomach flutter like a swarm of bees. *If only she weren't so damn beautiful.*

They sat there in silence, listening to the sounds of the ocean. After a while, Ella's eyes fell shut as she leaned into Cam. Cam could feel by her slow and steady breathing that she was falling asleep. Her heart started racing at the sensation of Ella's warm body against her own as she turned to look at her. Ella's bare arm was resting against hers, her head tilted toward Cam on the backrest of the couch, causing soft breaths to tickle the skin of her neck. Cam carefully lifted her arm and put it around Ella to make it a little more comfortable for her. As a result, Ella's weight shifted, and her head moved down to Cam's chest. It wasn't intentional and entirely innocent, but still, it did something to Cam that she hadn't felt in a very long time.

The closeness of Ella, who she was starting to see in a whole new light, filled her with warmth. They'd become very close in only five weeks, and although she'd tried hard not to think of Ella in a sexual way, it wasn't easy. She was simply smoking hot, and her smile – her real smile even more so than her on-screen smile – was mesmerizing. She'd smiled more in the past weeks, and knowing Ella was starting to enjoy life again meant everything to Cam.

Every day, she told herself to be careful, to not get too close. Getting hurt was easy in a situation like this. Ella was unstable, and if anyone was familiar with how unpredictable depression could be, it was Cam. Ella needed her friendship right now, and Cam needed her presence, for no other reason than that it made her happy. She knew the flirting was getting out of hand, and she reminded herself again to be careful, to keep more distance. As Ella snuggled closer against her, though, Cam found herself doing the opposite, tightening her grip around her. She half expected Ella to wake up, but she didn't, so she inhaled against the tousled blonde hair and cursed herself. *What's she going to think when she wakes up? It looks like I'm trying to make a move on her.* The idea of putting an arm around Ella had felt so natural that she hadn't given it a second thought, but now that they were sitting so intimately a whole string of other thoughts were racing through her mind, and they were far from pure. *Fuck. I'm so attracted to her.*

It took a little while for Ella to analyze the situation when she woke up. Adrenaline started racing through her when she felt a warm body against hers, and Cam's slow and steady breaths against her hair. She was lying half on top of Cam, who was still sleeping. Her head was resting on Cam's chest and Cam had an arm around her. Ella's heart pounded so hard she was afraid it might wake her up. She had no idea what time it was, but she didn't want to reach for her phone on the table. It felt safe, wonderful and exciting to be so close to her, and she was pleasantly shocked by how her body reacted to the closeness. Heat spread between her legs when she realized the softness she felt against her ear was Cam's breast. Then she looked down at her hand on Cam's bare midriff. *Fuck...* Cam's T-shirt had crept up and apparently Ella had made herself more than comfortable while she snoozed. She lay very still, trying to keep her breathing under control as fantasies threatened to take over her headspace.

Time passed in a delightful haze as she watched the dark sky outside turn a paler blue. Her neck hurt from being curled up in the same position for hours though, and after a while she had no choice but to shift a little. Cam stirred, then gasped as she woke up and looked down at her.

"Oh God, I'm so sorry Ella. I didn't mean to..."

"What?" Ella pretended to wake up and turned to look up at her through sleepy eyes. Worried Cam could feel her hand trembling on her skin, she retracted it and sat up, stretching. "No, *I'm* sorry. I shouldn't have fallen asleep on top of you." She managed a smile despite her nervous state. "You must have been so uncomfortable. What time is it?"

"I don't know." Cam looked flustered as she reached for her phone. "It's four-thirty." She sighed. "I was going to wake you up so you could go to bed, but I dozed off and slept so deep."

"I slept like a baby too." Ella missed the contact already. All she wanted to do was go back in time and snuggle against Cam's warm body, but instead, she faked a yawn. "It's time to leave soon anyway so I might as well have a shower and stay up."

"Okay. I'll make you a coffee." Cam was about to get up, but Ella stopped her.

"No, really there's no need," she insisted, worried she wouldn't be able to act normal around Cam with all the feelings that were currently coursing through her in that moment. "Go back to sleep for another hour. I'll see you next week."

27

"You look different today." Theresa took a sip of her coffee and crossed her legs.

"Different? How so?" Ella unconsciously ran a hand through her hair, unsure if she was referring to her physical appearance.

"You look like you have other things on your mind. Good things."

"Oh right..." Ella's cheeks reddened. Could Theresa really tell she was experiencing a crush?

"Don't be embarrassed. I'm a therapist. I'm trained to read people." Theresa paused. "Have you seen Cam again since we last spoke about her?" She continued when Ella nodded. "Would you like to talk about her? I feel that Cam might be playing an important role in your life right now."

"Yes... I'd like to talk about Cam." Ella grinned. She could talk about Cam all day and night. "I've seen her quite a few times, actually. We've become friends." She hesitated. "I don't know if you read gossip, but there's been some speculation that we're dating. It's not true, but we have spent a lot of time together."

"I wasn't aware of the speculation. I don't read those kinds of articles, especially not when it concerns one of my clients," Theresa said. "Does it bother you?"

"No, not really," Ella admitted. "It bothers me in the sense that I don't want Cam to suffer from it."

Theresa nodded and jotted something down on her notepad. "You mentioned last time when we spoke that you had sexual feelings for her. Has that changed since?"

"It hasn't gone away if that's what you mean," Ella said. "If anything, it's grown way stronger." She sighed. "I feel this urge to kiss her every time I see her, and last time I was at her house, I fell asleep half on top of her. I can't even begin to describe how I felt when I woke up. It felt so amazing that I pretended to be asleep for God knows how long after that." She continued to blush, not quite believing she was being so open about it.

"And do you think Cam shares those feelings?" Theresa asked.

"I know she finds me attractive. She makes flirty remarks, and the way she looks at me makes me think she does like me in that way. Ever since she told me she was gay, I haven't been able to stop analyzing her behavior." Ella cleared her throat. "And I don't know if I'm imagining things, but I could swear we have off-the-scale chemistry when we're together."

"Have you thought of asking her about it?"

"Yeah, I have, but it's a difficult thing to bring up. We talk about everything apart from that. I tried but she danced around the subject. I did come out to her, though."

"You did?" Theresa seemed positively surprised. "And how did that make you feel? Coming out to a friend for the first time?"

"It felt good. I'm at ease around Cam and the conversation just naturally headed in that direction. I was nervous, sure, but afterwards, it wasn't a big deal, and now I've started wondering why I've been so terrified of people knowing I like women all these years." She bit her lip. "I was hoping that conversation might lead to more, but she just offered me her support, and we left it at that. I've invited her to come to Palm Springs with me for a couple of days, so we'll see what happens."

"So, you'd like to take the friendship further?"

"Yes," Ella said, barely in a whisper. "But I'm also scared of ruining the first real friendship I've had since Helena." She shook her head. "I don't even know if I'm ready for something like that. I'm still not myself, and I'm not sure if it would be smart of me to even go there. Do you think I'm ready?"

"I think you're doing fine, Ella. But the question is – do *you* feel ready? I can't answer that for you."

"I feel ready. I mean, it's on my mind all day and night. Being with her is literally all I can think of."

Theresa smiled. "Then I hope it works out for you."

"Really?" Ella frowned. "Is that all? You're not going to tell me that I might be attracted to her because she rescued me or because she's the only lesbian I know? Or that I'm just interested in experimenting with a woman and that I shouldn't do that with a friend?"

"Is that the case? Do you think you're attracted to her because she's the only lesbian you know?"

"No." Ella shook her head. "Absolutely not."

"Or because she rescued you and you feel safe with her?" Theresa shot her a questioning look. "You've clearly given this a lot of thought."

"No. I mean, I do feel safe with her but that's not the reason."

"And you're not just using her to experiment?"

"No, I'd never, ever do that to her."

"Well, then, your intentions are good."

"Oh." Ella studied the woman who she'd expected to get a stream of probing questions from, but Theresa remained silent and waited for her to talk instead. "So you don't even think I'm looking for a distraction because I've been going through a hard time or that I should come out to the world first?"

"That's up to you. If you prefer to come out first, then you should do that. Do you feel like you owe it to the world?"

"No." Ella chuckled. "It's nobody's business."

Theresa nodded. "Being in therapy or dealing with loss doesn't mean your life has to be on hold, Ella. A lot of people deal with difficulties their whole lives. And we can talk about this for hours, but it's not going to change how you feel or what you really want. I'd say the fact that you're having these feelings again is a very positive sign and I can imagine it's scary for you, but love is unpredictable. It comes when it comes, and you can take it or leave it. And when you take the leap, it can only go two ways: right or wrong, and you have to be prepared for both. You've been through a lot, but you're strong and the fact that you want this doesn't have to mean you're looking for a distraction because she makes you feel good. It can simply mean that you want it, so don't overthink it too much."

"Hmm." Ella smiled at her as her doubts slowly melted away. She wanted it more than anything. She just hoped Cam felt the same.

28

"Are you excited for our little break?" Ella opened the trunk of her car so Cam could throw her duffel bag in.

"Yeah. I can't wait to see your hometown." Cam smiled and closed the trunk, before she gave Ella a long hug. "Come here, it's good to see you again." Ella looked almost angelic, she thought, dressed in linen shorts and a crocheted white top. Her tan was deep, and her blonde hair was blowing in the wind. How she longed to run a hand through that hair, pull her toward her and kiss her...

Ella held onto her tight. "It's so good to see you too." She inhaled against Cam's neck and had to force herself to let go. She'd missed her more than she'd expected, and she'd been counting down the days they'd been apart. They hadn't seen each other since waking up on the couch together, and despite the smiles and the casual vibe, Ella knew they would have to talk at some point. She hadn't been able to think of anything else other than Cam all week, and now that she was sitting next to her in the car, her stomach wouldn't stop fluttering.

"I love your car," Cam said, running a finger over the smooth leather of her seat. The bright yellow convertible was the total opposite of the black SUV Ella usually drove. "But I suppose I didn't expect any different from a gorgeous, world-famous movie star." She waggled her eyebrows, sending more flutters through Ella's core.

"Thanks." Ella felt herself blush. "Technically, it's not mine. Maserati lets me drive it to promote their brand. I wouldn't have chosen a yellow car myself, but as it was free and drives like heaven on speed, I was obviously delighted to have it." She shrugged. "Let's be honest, I don't think many people would say no to it."

"What? You got this car for free?" Cam stared at her. "Do you get a lot of freebies?"

Ella nodded. "I do. Clothes, mainly. Designers send them to me, and I get gadgets too. Phones, laptops... I usually send stuff back that I don't use, or I'll give it away so just let me know if you need anything." She shot Cam a grin. "I'm expecting a heap of yoga apparel, now that the world knows I'm into that, so I'll let you know when the first package arrives."

"That sounds amazing, count me in." Cam closed her eyes as they turned onto the freeway. It was nice to get out of town for a couple of days. She hadn't allowed herself much time off since she'd opened the studio. Not that she needed time off, her job was about as relaxing as it could get, but still, a change of scenery was never a bad thing. She'd looked forward to seeing Ella again, and she'd thought about her a lot. In fact, their last night on the couch hadn't left her for a second, and even though she knew it was a bad idea to picture her mouth on Ella's, she was unable to push the thought from her mind. Now that she knew Ella was into women, and that the attraction was mutual, well, it was hard to carry on as if there was no elephant in the room.

"Did you bring your bikini?" Ella asked.

"Yeah, I did. Do you have a pool?"

Ella arched a brow and gave her a smile. "I have a bad-ass pool *and* a Jacuzzi."

"Of course you do." Cam bit her lip. God, now all she could picture was her and Ella in a pool together. "Do you go to Palm Springs often?" she asked. "I don't recall you talking about going there."

"I haven't been there since Helena died," Ella confessed. "It was our shared second home. We grew up in Palm Springs, but our childhood home wasn't nearly as fancy as this place. I've been renting it out, but I decided that it's time to face the past and make use of it again and besides, it's a great hideaway. The paparazzi tend to stay in LA, so I'll have more privacy there when fucking Tyler Kane does his Late Night interview tomorrow."

"Asshole," Cam grunted. "What do you think he's going to say?"

"I don't know, and frankly, I don't care. If Tyler claims our date was a decoy to keep my sexuality quiet, he'll practically admit to being a fraud himself. And if he simply tells them I'm gay, he'll be lying too in a way, as I never admitted it to him. I could probably sue him for that, but that would only draw more attention to the situation." Ella sighed. "If he does it though, I'd rather be away from LA. By now, I'm so tired of worrying about what Tyler's going to do that I'm thinking I might as well get it over with and just let him say it."

"Just let him say it?" Cam repeated. "Coming out should be your choice, not Tyler's. It's a big thing and you should be able to do it your way."

"I know..." Ella accelerated, pushing them both back in their seats. "But in my business, nothing is sacred, and sometimes we just have to accept things for how they play out and deal with them as they come. It is what it is and right now, going to Palm Springs is the right way to deal with that creepy little self-absorbed shit. Hopefully a change of scenery will stop me getting all worked up about it."

Cam huffed. "I'm still going to kill him if I ever see him." She turned to Ella, who seemed surprisingly calm about the situation. "Do you feel ready to go back there? To the house you shared with Helena?"

"I don't know. I guess I'll never know if I don't try. And I feel like I can handle anything when I'm with you. I'm really looking forward to having a break, and I don't feel the dread that I usually do when I contemplate going there." Ella smiled, and Cam found it hard to believe that this was the same woman who had tried to drown herself only eight months ago. She seemed so together now, as if she'd decided it was time to move on and take on life again.

"You seem happy," she said.

"I am happy." Ella's eyes met Cam's for a moment, and Cam could swear she saw a flirty glimmer in them." Not always, of course," she added. "But lately I've had more good days than bad ones, and this is definitely a good day." She paused as she indicated and turned onto the San Bernardino freeway. "I've stopped feeling guilty when I'm happy. I'm still on anti-depressants, but I feel ready to start lowering the dose." Ella shrugged. "So yeah, I'm doing good."

"I'm so glad you're feeling better." Cam put a hand on Ella's thigh. "I've noticed that you're smiling more. And you're certainly eating a lot more, so that's a good sign, right?"

"With your cooking? How could I not?" Ella grinned. "So what about your house? Why didn't you sell it? Why did you move in?"

"I'm not really sure," Cam admitted. "I couldn't be there at first, and I thought about selling it, sure. But when the realtor was over, and he talked about it as if it was purely a business transaction, which it was for him of course and I can't blame him for that..." She paused for a moment. "Well, I just couldn't go through with it. I wanted to hold on to it, but I couldn't live there either, so I rented it out until I felt strong enough to move in. I think I expected to be miserable there at first, but I wasn't. And as time passed, I started to understand that my mother had bought the place on a good day. She saw the beauty of it that I see, and I know she was happy there for periods of time. I really don't think she bought it with the intention of drowning herself one day, or that's what I tell myself, anyway."

"It's a beautiful place," Ella said. "I'm glad you moved in. Otherwise, you wouldn't have been there when I was at my lowest." She swallowed hard, pushing the memory away. "I love your house; it feels so homey and warm and personal. I've always wanted a home that reflected who I was, but I was always too busy and never really sure of who I was either, I suppose. But I'm starting to get to know myself now, and I've got a feeling you know me too, that you see me for who I am."

Cam turned in her seat to look at Ella, overwhelmed with feelings she wasn't supposed to have. "I'll tell you who you are," she said. "You're kind, smart, funny, driven, generous, strong and..." She paused. "And beautiful." She smiled as she watched Ella's cheeks flush. "You're all of that and way, way more but I'm not going to go on because you might get too full of yourself."

Ella laughed at that. “Thank you for making me feel like a million dollars, it does my ego good.”

As they drove farther over the freeway, hills came into sight, then bare mountains to their right, their tops still covered in a little snow. Leaving the city behind, and passing through the barren landscape, Ella’s excitement grew, knowing they would have four whole days together. After the exit to Palm Springs, palm trees were lining both sides of the road, and it started to become a little greener.

The first sign of life was the Palm Springs Visitor Centre before villas, restaurants and businesses appeared; all painted in muted colors until they drove into the town center where most buildings were white. Hibiscus, aloe Vera and yellow and purple wildflowers were lining the road, making for a spectacularly bright color scheme.

“Spring is the best time of the year to be here,” Ella said. “In late summer, there’s very little color left.” She took a right turn and drove up into the hills, where small roads were lined with grand gates, surrounding big houses. Passing them all, she drove higher up until there was nothing but a narrow, dusty road. She was coming home.

29

"This is it." Ella steered the car through the white gates and waved at her caretaker who opened them for them. "Hey, Sid."

"Welcome back, Ella." When Ella got out of the car, Sid held his hand out to her, but she surprised him by giving him a hug instead. "It's good to see you again." She let go and turned to Cam. "Sid, this is my friend Cam. Cam, this is Sid. He looks after Flamingo House." Ella looked around the big landscaped garden, where a perfect, bright green lawn stretched around the one-storey, white building, only broken up by a long, beautifully maintained pond. She felt a sting for a moment when memories of her and Helena came flooding back, but she took a deep breath and painted on a smile. "You've done a great job, Sid, the lawn looks fantastic."

"Thanks, Ella. I think you'll be pleased with the back yard too." He picked up Ella's baggage and walked up toward the house.

"Flamingo House?" Cam shot Ella an amused look.

"Yeah, it was already named Flamingo House when we

bought it because they used to have flamingos in the front yard." Ella pointed to the door. "When the previous owners moved and took the flamingos with them, Helena and I painted the door a pinky-orange shade instead so the name would at least make some kind of sense."

"I see." Cam smiled at the sight of the brightly colored door in the middle of the white building. "It's beautiful here. It feels like an oasis, it's so private..."

"That's exactly why we bought it." Ella took Cam's hand. "Come on, I can't wait to show you the rest."

The front door opened into a simple, modern hallway. It looked like a show house, Cam thought, as there were no shoes or coats, or any clutter lying around in the sleek space that ran into another corridor with three doors to their left. It was beautiful though, with bright paintings on the walls and fresh flowers on a cabinet underneath an ornate, silver mirror.

"All my personal stuff is in the basement storage," Ella explained when she saw Cam looking for any signs that tied the house to her as she followed her into the living room. "I didn't want the tenants to know it was mine, so I kept it pretty minimal on the decoration."

They wandered into a long living room with a sunken seating area at the back where a bright green velvet half-circle couch stood in front of a wide pillar with a built-in fireplace. The entire space overlooked the mountains through tall, glass walls. Despite its modern appearance, the house felt very vintage. The couch looked like it was a reproduction or perhaps even an original from the seventies, and the rest of the furniture was clearly inspired by the seventies too. A cocktail bar, cleaned and polished to perfection, was built against the other side of the pillar where the floor was higher. There were big plants and fresh flowers everywhere, in brightly colored ceramic pots and glass vases. The cream, yellow and green rugs that were scattered over the full length of the living area were thick and luxurious.

Cam's jaw dropped when she looked up toward the ceiling, where a fancy crystal chandelier covered most of the space above the seating area.

"Did we just step back in time?"

Ella joined her underneath the chandelier and smiled. "This house was built in nineteen sixty-nine. Helena managed to find enough original furniture from that time to decorate the whole house with. It was one of her many passions."

"It's incredible." Cam walked through the room, peering outside through the glass walls. On both sides of the floor to ceiling windows, velvet curtains were drawn back, their forest green color matching the couch. The windows offered a breathtaking view over the desert, the mountains in the far distance and the town center of Palm Springs below. They turned when they heard Sid's voice echoing through the room.

"Where would you like me to put your cases?"

Ella shook her head and waved a hand. "Don't worry, Sid, we'll take care of that. Thank you for calling the florist for me and please take the rest of the day off, we'll be fine from here."

"Thank you, Ella. It was nice seeing you again. I'll keep my phone on, so just let me know if you change your mind and need anything."

"I will, thanks Sid." Ella gave him a smile, then pulled Cam along with her. "Let me show you to your bedroom so you can put your things away." She walked back through the hallway and opened the second door on the right. "This will be yours." The room they stepped into was decorated in a mixture of cream and gold tones. The large bed, covered in gold colored bedding stood in front of a velvet, heart-shaped buttoned headboard, and was adorned with luxurious pillows. On the nightstand stood a corded vintage dial phone, next to a floral printed box of tissues that seemed to have come from the same era.

"It's beyond amazing." Cam sat down on the bed and bounced on the mattress.

"This room has actually never been used while I've lived here, so I think it's about time," Ella said, walking around it as if she was taking everything in for the first time. "My bedroom is to your left and Helena's old bedroom is to your right." Her expression saddened for a moment, but she quickly pulled herself together. "I don't think I'm ready to go in there yet."

"You don't have to, just take your time," Cam said in a reassuring tone. "Show me your room instead."

"Okay." Ella beckoned Cam to follow her and Cam's eyes went wide in amazement when she opened the door to her own bedroom.

"This is crazy." Cam ran a hand over the sizeable pink velvet couch that stood opposite a big box-spring bed in the same fabric. The wall behind the bed was covered in pink, green and white flamingo-patterned wallpaper that would have been totally camp if it didn't look so perfect and original, combined with the rest of the furniture. On the floor was a thick, light-pink rug and on the white sidewalls were enormous framed photographs of flamingos, matching the rug. The color pink was carried through in the smallest of details, from the hairbrushes on the mid-century wooden dressing table to the lightbulbs in the table lamps currently residing on the fuchsia-pink nightstands.

"I know it's crazy and very over the top, but I like it." Ella smiled. "It's nothing like me, but it suits the house, don't you think?" She drew the pink curtains aside, revealing a beautiful view over the private yard. "And this is the back yard." She opened the sliding doors and stepped onto the wide, slate deck running across the back. It was almost level with a pool that ran along the entire length of the house, with a separate section at one end where the Jacuzzi was situated. There were bright yellow deckchairs on the lawn behind the pool, and white and yellow striped seventies parasols shading them. The bright pink bougainvillea along the outer edge of the garden stood in beautiful contrast to the green lawn, the blue pool and the yellow chairs, giving the outside space a happy vibe. "I see Sid's already put the furniture out for us. Helena wanted the yard to look like a setting from a Slim Aarons photograph, and I'd say she succeeded."

"No doubt." Cam turned to Ella. She looked like she belonged here, in her white outfit and Cam could picture her, swimming and sunbathing with her twin sister. She could see a hint of sadness in Ella's eyes as she looked at the pool. "Are you okay?"

"I'm okay. I just need to get used to being here without Helena. But she'd want me to be here, to use the house that she curated with so much care."

"So you guys bought it together?"

"Yeah, we bought it for our twenty-first birthday. We'd made quite a lot of money by then from the sitcoms and movies we'd done. Helena wanted to invest. She was already thinking about quitting the movie industry and studying architecture back then, and she was afraid she'd burn through her savings if she didn't invest in real estate. We had a will made up so that if anything happened to either of us, the other would get sole ownership of the property, protecting it from our mother's greedy hands." Ella kicked off her sandals, sat down at the edge of the pool and lowered her feet into the cool water. Cam sat down next to her and did the same. "I'll never sell it," she continued, this time with a small smile on her face. "And from now on, I'm going to make more use of it. Will you help me get some of my stuff out of the basement tomorrow?"

"Of course." Cam put an arm around her, and Ella leaned into her, resting her head on Cam's shoulder.

"Thank you for being here with me, Cam. It makes everything a little easier." She hesitated. "Do you mind going for a walk with me? There's something I'd like to do first."

30

"This is her." There was a tremble in Ella's voice as she spoke. She let go of Cam's hand and placed the bunch of wildflowers she was carrying on the grave in front of them. She'd picked them on their walk to the cemetery, crossing fields to assemble the brightest flowers she could find.

Cam watched her kneel down and remove the overgrown weeds from around the headstone that read: *'Helena Temperley. Beloved daughter and sister. 1990-2016'.*

The cemetery on the outskirts of Palm Springs was beautiful and quiet. There were old trees, a small, modern church, a big, well-kept lawn and an abundance of flowers blooming along the paths. The lightest of breezes whistled in the trees and wisps of clouds floated above them, the fluffy white almost translucent against the blue sky. The smell was different to LA, Cam noticed. It was sweeter; the dry, earthy smell of heat and desert blending with the flora.

"I haven't been here since the funeral," Ella said, keeping her gaze fixed on the ground as she tried to swallow down the lump in her throat. “I wanted to, but I just couldn't. It's too…”

Cam sat down next to her and pulled Ella in close when she started crying. The soft whimpering noises turned into heavier sobs as Ella shook in her arms and buried her face against her chest. Cam stroked her back and held her tight. It tore her apart, seeing Ella like this, but there was nothing more she could do.

“Helena just wanted to be like everyone else, so she took the bus.” Ella continued to sob. “Once she'd moved to New York, she loved doing normal things with her new friends like grocery shopping, hanging in the park and taking the bus or subway. She said it was more relaxed there, that people didn't care as much and that it was easier for her to blend in. I guess she was trying to make up for living in a bubble all those years, and so that day, she was on a bus with her friend when a truck drove into them, right where she was sitting. The doctors believe she died immediately on impact. She wouldn't have known what was happening and she didn't suffer. She was just there one moment and the next, she wasn't.” Ella took deep breaths but was unable to stop her tears from streaming down her face.

“Was it the truck driver's fault?”

“I'm not sure, it's still not clear. There was something wrong with the signals. He didn't drive through red, and neither did the bus, but he might have been going too fast. The truck was just so heavy that the driver couldn't brake on time. There are ongoing court cases, but I stopped getting involved because it was draining me, and whatever the outcome, it's not going to bring her back.”

“What about her friend? Have you spoken to her?”

“Yeah. I spoke to her a month after the accident. She was badly injured, and she doesn't remember much from that day. She told me they were on their way to a party." Ella was silent then, running her fingers over the flowers she'd picked, breathing deeply in an attempt to stop herself from crying. "Helena loved wildflowers," she said after a while when she'd composed herself enough to speak again.

"Oh yeah? What else did she love?" Cam asked in a soft voice.

Ella sniffed again. "She loved so many things. The desert, art, design, music, animals, cookies, dancing..." She let out a soft chuckle. "Women... She was a good person, and she was passionate about so many things. She'd just started living her life the way she wanted. It's so unfair."

"I know it's unfair."

"I'm sorry." Ella took off her shades, wiped her eyes that felt like they were full of grit, and put them back on. "I thought I'd be all out of tears by now, but clearly I'm not." She placed her hand on Cam's that was resting on her shoulder.

"Don't apologize. It's okay to cry."

"I wish she could have met you."

"Maybe she knows I'm here with you. Maybe she knows everything," Cam said.

"Or maybe she knows nothing."

"Maybe." Cam swallowed hard, at a loss for words of comfort. "But I like to think that people we've lost still have some kind of presence in our lives and that they know we miss them." She placed a tender kiss on Ella's cheek. "Do you want to be alone for a while?"

Ella shook her head. "No, I'd like you to stay if you don't mind." She pulled Cam's hand down over her shoulder and pressed her face against it.

"Of course." Cam ran her other hand through Ella's hair and felt her shiver. "What's your best memory of her?"

"I have so many." Ella let out a deep sigh. "But I hardly ever dare to think of her." She paused. "My best memories are from the time that we were here together. On our breaks from shooting, and the times she was here during her vacations. After she moved to New York, she always came to Palm Springs during her breaks, and I tried to be here as much as I could, too. It was just me and her in that big house. We communicated without speaking, we finished each other's sentences during conversations and always made the same observations when it came to other people, or things that happened around us. We rarely had people over, because quality time had become so rare then. We went on hikes, and indulged in long lunches. We even camped out in the desert one night." She chuckled through her tears. "We had to sleep in the car in the end because I got scared. Helena was always the brave one."

"I don't blame you. I don't think I'd want to sleep in the desert either, with all the coyotes and rattlesnakes."

"Yeah." Ella sighed. "Despite being so alike, we differed in that aspect. Helena was a desert child; she loved the desert. I was always more drawn to the ocean, and that's why I like LA. But Palm Springs has its charms too. I think I see that now more than ever."

"I like it too," Cam said. "It's not even far from LA, but I feel like we've crossed a border. The smell, the dry air, the landscape, the vegetation and the light..." She let go of Ella and lay down on her back in the grass, looking up at the sky.

Ella immediately missed the contact and lay down next to her, so their arms touched, wondering why even here, in front of Helena's grave, she still needed the physical closeness. Cam took her hand as if she could read her mind, and Ella let out a soft sigh, feeling a little better.

"We used to have two red-tailed hawks in the yard," she

said. "They nested in one of the trees and one of them was pretty tame, which is rare. I don't know if they're still there, they might be. I've read they can live up to twenty-five years." She turned her head to look at Cam. "Helena used to talk to the female, which was the larger one. She'd lie on her lounge chair and stare up at the hawk who would sometimes sit on the edge of the roof and look down at her in return. It was weird, like they had some kind of bond. Helena had read that in Native American history, the birds were considered highly symbolic – it was believed that they acted as messengers between heaven and earth – and she was fascinated by that. She never fed her, but the hawk kept coming back until eventually one day, she landed on the terrace table, right in front of her. I was watching them from the living room, and I was surprised that Helena wasn't scared. The bird could have taken her eyes out, but instead she just sat there, as if she was simply enjoying her company. That was the last time Helena was home. I've always wondered what would have happened if she'd still been here. If the hawk would have just hopped inside or if she would have joined her on the table for breakfast each morning." She sighed. "I guess I'll never know."

"No, you won't, but that's a beautiful memory." Cam tightened her grip on Ella's hand, entwining their fingers as they lay there, facing each other.

Something passed between them then, some kind of deep understanding. A force that was invisible yet so present that Cam felt like she should grab it and hold onto it. At that moment, they both knew that they weren't just friends anymore.

31

It was late in the afternoon by the time they returned. Their long walk had been quiet at first, but Ella had started talking again when they neared the house. She seemed better now, relieved even, Cam thought. She remembered she'd felt like that herself, after visiting her mother's grave for the first time.

They'd walked hand in hand the whole way back, neither of them commenting on it. Cam had stopped telling herself it was just a comforting gesture because even though that was a part of it, it was so much more. The way Ella ran a thumb over the back of her hand, and the way Cam tightened her grip each time she looked at her... They both craved it. Cam reluctantly let go when they were in front of the gates. She needed distraction, a little afraid to be alone with Ella.

"Hey, can I take you out for dinner in town?" Ella asked, as if she was thinking the same thing. "Then I can finally return the favor after your fabulous cooking."

"Sure. But aren't you worried you'll be recognized? We can order take-out if you prefer to stay here."

"No, I'd love to go out for dinner." Ella smiled as she typed in the security code to the gate. "I don't often get the chance in LA, there's too many paparazzi hanging around. I've brought a great disguise with me, just to be on the safe side." She stopped as they waited for the gate to close again, hesitating for a moment before she looked up at Cam. "So is this a..." She sighed in frustration as she shuffled on the spot. "Is this a date?"

Cam could see the nervousness in her eyes and didn't know what to say at first. The question was so direct, and she simply hadn't expected it. Excitement welled up as she tugged at the neckline of her T-shirt, needing to cool down.

"I'm sorry. Forget I ever asked," Ella continued, rambling now. "I thought maybe you and me, well, there's been this... this thing between us but I might have imagined it and..."

"No," Cam interrupted her, taking her hand again. "You haven't imagined anything." She smiled and held her gaze. "I'd like it to be a date so if you want that too..."

"Okay." Ella looked relieved as she nodded. "Then it's a date."

"You weren't exaggerating when you said you had a great disguise. Is that your go-to outfit for dates?" Cam joked as she nibbled on a breadstick. She wouldn't have recognized Ella if she hadn't seen her transform. Her oversized brown seventies style shades covered the top half of her face, and the long, light pink Coachella hippie-chick wig made her look like some kind of new-age tourist. Her look was completed with a white summer dress, leather sandals and a big, white, floppy hat that kept threatening to blow off her head. Cam had put on a baseball cap and a pair of shades, just in case someone recognized her too, although she doubted people would pay much attention to her when she was with Ella.

Ella kicked her playfully under the table. “Don’t make fun of me, I tried really hard to make this wig look good.” She took a sip of her wine. “I’ve actually never been on a real date before. Only fake ones.”

“I figured as much.” Cam leaned in and tilted her head with a smile. “Well, if this is a real date, I’m sure you’ll allow me to tell you that you look stunning.”

Ella gave her a quizzical look. “Thank you, but the wig and...”

“No, Ella. You look beautiful. You always do.” Cam held her gaze, knowing there was no going back from this. Now that they had established that they were on a date, she wanted Ella to feel special, and she wanted her to know exactly what was on her mind.

“Thank you, so do you,” Ella said as more color rose to her cheeks. She felt the hairs on her arms rise as Cam brushed her fingertips over the table. The light touch left a warm, lingering sensation on her hand that spread throughout her entire body and settled between her thighs. Knowing it was intentional left her wanting so much more, and she was unable to stop a stream of steamy thoughts from racing through her mind. She almost jumped up when she heard the waiter beside her, pulling her out of her fantasy.

“Welcome back, Miss Temperley,” he whispered as he placed two small salads in front of them. “Enjoy your appetizers.” He took the wine bottle out of the standing cooler next to their table and topped up their glasses.

“Oh God, can you really tell it’s me?” Ella looked up at him and kept her voice down as she spoke. She’d always been a regular at the Palm Garden, but it had been years since she'd been here, and it came as a total surprise that the man she vaguely recognized had already figured it out. "I'm sorry, I don't remember your name..."

"Jamie," the waiter said. "I doubt anyone else knows you're here, so don't worry." He gave her a conspiratorial smile. "To be honest, it was your order that gave you away. We don't get many people here who ask for a Caesar salad with raisins instead of anchovies."

Cam laughed at Ella's perplexed expression. "I know, that's weird, right?" she agreed with him. "No wonder the kitchen remembers that. You should really reconsider your food choices, Ella. I mean raisins on a Caesar salad? Come on, that's just wrong. How did you even come up with that?"

Ella giggled. "Just wait. You're going to eat your words once you've tasted it because it's actually delicious." Cam and the waiter exchanged comical glances as he let his professional guard down for a brief moment. Then he composed himself again and cleared his throat.

"Anything else I can get for you?"

"That will be all, Jamie." Ella handed him a fifty dollar bill. "And thank you for keeping this between us."

Jamie gave her the money back. "No need for that, Miss Temperley. We've never revealed your unusual food choices, and we certainly won't spill about you being here now." He smiled at them before he walked off.

"What a nice guy." Ella stared after him in surprise.

"Yeah. You've clearly been here a lot, and they appreciate you, despite your questionable food choices," Cam said. "But you know, there are a lot of nice people in this world, Ella. You might have had some bad experiences, but not everyone is insincere."

"I know." Ella let her eyes roam over Cam. She looked so sexy tonight. She'd changed into a white shirt and a pair of low-cut jeans that hung snug around her hips. Her tanned skin against the white fabric of her shirt, and her tousled dark hair, made her look irresistible, and Ella couldn't stop looking at her mouth. Behind Cam was a beautiful backdrop of mountains and a garden full of exotic plants, cacti, flowers and palm trees. It was getting dark now, and for the first time, she noticed how romantic the Palm Garden really was. The flickering candles on the tables, the stringed lights glistening in the trees and the soft classical music, playing in the background. "Do you think he's read the articles? Do you think he assumes we're on a date?"

"I don't know. We are on a date, aren't we?" Cam licked her lips, knowing Ella's eyes were fixed on them. "Would you mind if he knew?"

"No." Ella held her gaze and fire burned deep in her belly. "I'd be quite honored if he thought you were my girlfriend. I'd say I'd hit the jackpot if that were the case."

"You would?" Cam shuffled in her seat as she allowed feelings she'd suppressed for weeks to come rushing back in a heartbeat. *Here we go again.* "I'd be pretty honored too if he thought I was dating you." *Maybe we should take it slow. Maybe this is a bad idea. This can never end well. Am I just an experiment to her? Is she serious about this?* A lot of things went through her mind it that moment, but what came out of her mouth was something else entirely. "I've been fantasizing about kissing you for weeks," she said, dropping her gaze to Ella's mouth. She watched Ella take in a quick breath as her lips parted and a look of raging desire settled over her. Seconds went by with neither of them speaking. The air between them was charged with sexual energy as they both held their breath, waiting for the other to speak.

"Everything okay with the food?" Jamie interrupted

them. He looked down at their salads that were still untouched.

"Thank you, everything is great," Ella said, looking completely flustered as she started poking her fork into a lettuce leaf.

"Would you like some extra parmesan with your..."

"No, no, I'm good, thank you, Jamie." She hadn't even heard what he'd said, unable to tear her eyes away from Cam's. This was the moment she'd been waiting for. She'd hoped, and maybe expected something would happen between them while they were here, but hearing Cam say she wanted to kiss her simply shook her to the core. She felt a rush of excitement as she took a sip from her water, never breaking eye contact.

"Me too," she whispered, finally acknowledging Cam's bold statement. It was all she could manage to say.

32

The cab drive back to Ella's house had been filled with unspoken thoughts. Cam hadn't kissed her after their long dinner – which hadn't been uncomfortable but not entirely natural either after their mutual confession – and Ella hadn't brought it up. They'd changed the topic to food and travel, nervous about continuing the heated subject when the restaurant got busier. As a result, their conversation was left unfinished, and when they got home, Ella had taken a shower while Cam settled on the couch to read a book she'd brought with her. She didn't take in a word she was reading, though. All she could think of was Ella, standing naked under the shower. *Does she want me to join her? Should I have made a move on her?*

Cam wasn't usually this confused when it came to women, but she'd never been in a position where she cared so much about the other person that she was terrified of ruining a good thing before it even started. And a lot of things could happen if they took it further. A lot of good things, but also a lot of bad things.

"Do you want to join me in the Jacuzzi?" Cam almost

jumped up from the couch at hearing Ella's sultry voice. She turned and let her eyes roam over Ella, who was standing in the doorway in a skimpy, bright blue bikini with a mischievously flirty look on her face. *God, she looks sexy.*

"Ehm... yeah, sure." Cam felt a flutter of anticipation as she held her gaze. Ella licked her lips suggestively and didn't shy away. "Give me two minutes. I just need to get changed."

The two minutes turned into ten minutes, as Cam tried on three different bikinis she'd brought along, inspecting herself in the mirror from all angles. She wasn't usually self-conscious about how she looked but seeing Ella just now had made her heart race, and she knew something was about to happen. The chemistry between them was off the charts, and with each day they spent together, Cam had more and more trouble stopping herself from acting on her physical cravings. However she wanted Ella to make the first move because she wanted her to be sure. And right now, Ella seemed as sure as she could be. Eventually, Cam opted for a simple, black triangle bikini which didn't leave much to the imagination. The hairs on her arms rose as she imagined sitting next to Ella in the Jacuzzi, their arms and legs touching...

"You sure took your time," Ella said as Cam stepped into the tub. The warm water felt heavenly on her skin, and Ella's arm brushing hers made her shiver. "Were you dressing up for me?" Ella poured two glasses of Champagne from the bottle on the edge of the tub and handed one to Cam. The Jacuzzi was the only source of light in the dark garden. Above them, the sky was littered with stars, and it almost felt like they were in their own little universe. Cam gave her a smirk, took a sip of her drink and moved a little closer, placing her glass next to the bottle.

"Maybe. But I'd say you've been dressing up for me too.

Or should I say dressing down?" She could have sworn she saw Ella shudder when their thighs touched, and she inched even closer to gauge her reaction. Ella's chest was heaving up and down fast, her small breasts rising above the water each time she breathed in. "What's wrong? Is the great Ella Temperley nervous?" Cam's tone was teasing and playful.

"Why would I be nervous?" Ella's light-blue eyes were darker now, as she turned to her. There was no doubt about what she wanted. She looked down at Cam's lips, then back up, meeting her eyes again.

"I don't know." Cam gave her an innocent look. "You tell me." She took Ella's glass and placed it next to her own.

Ella bit her lip as she smiled, then sighed in frustration and nudged Cam with her shoulder. "Stop teasing me, Cam." She took a deep breath, looking more hesitant than Cam had ever seen her. "Okay, I'm just going to ask you outright. Why haven't you made a move on me already? I've been waiting for you to do something, anything, forever but you never do. You said you wanted to kiss me..." Ella turned to straddle Cam's lap.

Cam let out a quiet moan when she felt Ella's weight on top of her, and her hands immediately reached behind Ella's back to pull her closer. She stared up at Ella's pleading eyes, breathing fast too, now. Her self-control had already crumbled the moment she'd seen Ella in a bikini. Cam couldn't remember ever wanting anything as badly as she wanted Ella right now.

"Don't you know how much I want this?" Ella continued, reflecting Cam's thoughts. Her voice was shaky with arousal from Cam's strong arms around her, and their bodies pressed so closely together. "I'm not fragile, okay? I'm ready, and I need you to kiss me, Cam. I'd make the first move myself if I were braver but…" Her words were dampened by Cam's lips on hers.

She kissed her softly at first, searching for signs that Ella might be uncomfortable. It felt so right and so good that she had to force herself to hold back. When Cam heard a soft moan and felt Ella shiver, she parted her lips and deepened the kiss as she moved her hands up and ran them through her hair. Even though she'd known what was coming, and she'd fantasized about it countless times, nothing could have prepared her for the storm that started brewing inside her. Ella's soft, full lips, her tongue dancing with her own, her hands that were now making their way up Cam's arms toward her neck and nestled in her hair… Ella was rocking her hips on her lap so sensually, her moans so deep, that Cam almost came, just from the sensation of her. There were more moans, louder this time, and Cam wasn't sure if they came from herself or from Ella. Before she lost herself entirely, she pulled out of the kiss and looked up at Ella.

"Are you okay?"

"Yeah… That was amazing." Ella's chest was heaving up and down so fast that it made Cam tremble. Her lips were still moist from their heated kiss as she lowered her gaze to Cam's mouth. "And I want more," she whispered, leaning in to kiss her again.

"Then let me make you feel even more amazing," Cam mumbled against her lips before they sank back into another earth-shattering kiss with even more urgency, more need. She lowered her hands to Ella's ass and ran them over her firm cheeks, drawing another moan from her mouth. Switching positions, Cam lifted Ella from her lap, pushed her down on the mosaic Jacuzzi bench and straddled her. Ella's eyes were full of longing, sparkling with excitement and need. She didn't seem nervous anymore, just desperate to be touched. Her hands were on Cam's back again as they fell into another kiss, her nails scratching her skin as she traced her spine down to her ass. Cam pushed Ella against the wall and moved her mouth toward her neck, placing a trail of kisses down to her collarbone, one hand firmly in Ella's hair, pulling her head back.

"Fuck!" Ella gasped at the touch and instinctively pushed her hips up, a rush of heat spreading between her legs. Her head started spinning when she realized what they were doing, and what else was about to happen. She'd been longing to be with a woman for so long and in the past weeks, being with Cam was all she'd been able to think of. Now that her fantasy was finally coming true, it was almost too much to handle. Cam's light kisses and the touch of her tongue on her skin sent electric jolts to every nerve ending in her body. "That feels so good..." She took in a quick breath when Cam's hand grazed her breast while she ran it down to her stomach and back up.

"You have no idea how much I've been longing to kiss you." Cam trailed her tongue over Ella's lips, making her shudder. The physical need to have Ella fought against her brain, telling her to take it slow. It would be Ella's first time with a woman, her first real time, and she was worried it was too soon.

Ella seemed to have other ideas, though. "Please," she begged against Cam's mouth, running her hands through her hair. "I really need you to release me from this burning ache. I feel like I'm about to explode." She pulled away and looked at Cam, earnestly. "Please, touch me."

Cam's eyes met Ella's, torn between hesitation and lust. "Are you sure? I don't want you to rush into something you're not ready for."

"I've never been more ready." The tremble in Ella's voice almost sounded like a moan. "I want you so badly."

"I want you too." Cam bit her lip and swallowed hard. It was impossible to think straight while her whole body screamed for Ella and her mind was in turmoil. "Let's move inside," she finally said. "Is that okay with you? I want this to be special."

"Anything." Ella took Cam's hand and stepped out of the Jacuzzi, marveling at her body, only covered in a skimpy bikini that she was dying to take off. She handed Cam a big, white towel.

"Wait." Cam stopped her when she was about to reach for her own towel and pulled her into hers instead, wrapping it tightly around the both of them. A soft moan escaped Ella's mouth when their bodies came together again. Cam could feel her feverish body heat now, without the water surrounding them, and the burning desire to touch her again only grew stronger when Ella pressed herself closer against her.

"Jesus," Ella muttered. "This feels..."

"I know." Cam held her and kissed her when neither of them moved, too consumed with simply standing there close together, breathing in each other's need. She felt Ella go limp in her arms and was barely able to stand herself. "Your bedroom or mine?"

"Mine." Ella released herself from Cam's grip and walked ahead into the house, her hips swaying seductively as she led the way to her bedroom, where she turned on the two nightstand lamps. Standing next to the bed, her hands trembled as she pulled at the strings of her bikini top until it fell to the floor. She was nervous and excited and seemed to have no control over her body anymore. She moved down to the strings on her hips, pulling them simultaneously, causing her bikini bottoms to fall down too while facing Cam, who was watching her from the doorway.

"You're so beautiful." Cam's lips parted as she stared at her small breasts, then met her eyes. Ella's bedroom was bathed in a soft light, the harmonious shades of pink pouring over her satin sheets. The seductive glow of the nightstand lamps made her silky hair look peach-colored, and her skin dark and luminous. She untied her own bikini and took it off, then crossed the room, closing the distance between them. Raising a hand to Ella's face, she traced her cheek down to her neck, then slowly let her fingers run over Ella's breasts. "Are you okay?" she asked again.

Ella nodded slowly, a small smile playing around her lips. She gasped when Cam's fingers grazed her nipple, then followed the curve of her waist down to her hips. She was aching to touch her too, but her sudden insecurities and lack of experience with women sent her mind into overdrive. *What do I do now? What if I do it all wrong?* As if Cam could read her thoughts, she took Ella's hands in her own and placed them onto her breasts. Ella saw goose bumps appear on Cam's arms and felt her nipples harden under her touch. It was the most wonderful feeling. "God, you feel so good."

"Just relax," Cam said in a soft voice. "Relax and enjoy it. That's all you need to do."

Ella let out the breath she'd been holding as she let her hands roam over Cam's breasts, stroking her soft, smooth skin. It felt surreal to finally touch a woman's breasts and the fact that they were Cam's only heightened her excitement.

. . .

"You're perfect." Ella trailed her fingers down Cam's tight stomach. "So soft and feminine, yet so strong at the same time..."

Cam walked them toward the bed, took Ella in her arms and lay her down. She kissed her, softly, then with more determination as Ella pulled her in and deepened the kiss.

Ella gasped when Cam wedged a leg between her thighs and kissed her in the most urgent, yet tender way – as if making Ella feel good was her only goal in life. She could feel herself getting wet, her center aching to be touched again, and she spread her legs as her hands traced Cam's waist and her shapely behind. Feeling Cam's body under her fingers while they kissed, was wondrous and so incredibly sexy.

"You're amazing, Ella," Cam said as she kissed her way down Ella's neck and over her breasts. She bit down softly on her nipple, then twirled her tongue around it, making Ella moan and buckle with pleasure.

"Fuck!" Ella cursed. Watching Cam do that to her was one of the most arousing sights she'd ever witnessed, not to mention the most pleasurable thing she'd ever felt. "Fuck..." she cried again as she raised her chest, craving more. "You have no idea what you're doing to me..."

Cam took her time to cover every inch of her upper body in kisses, listening to the sounds Ella made while she tasted her.

Ella closed her eyes, gave into the moment and let go of her insecurities, riding the ecstatic waves of pleasure as they explored each other. After many years of longing for a woman, she was amazed by how natural it felt, and how right, as if everything had fallen into place the moment Cam had first kissed her. When Cam moved her hand between her legs and ran a single finger over her folds, Ella cried out, clutching her fist into Cam's hair. "Oh, God..." She tilted her head back, her body almost exploding from overstimulation. "Please don't stop whatever it is you're doing."

"You mean this?" Cam moved a teasingly slow finger toward Ella's clit, then let it linger as she watched Ella buckle in ecstasy. She moved it back down, taking in a quick breath at the silky wetness she felt. Ella wrapped her legs around her hips and pulled her in closer, then nodded, letting Cam know what she wanted. Slowly, Cam entered her then, carefully pushing two fingers inside Ella while she lowered herself over her again and kissed her.

The moan that escaped Ella's mouth was loud and throaty, the result of years of pent-up sexual frustration finally being released. Her body was shaking with pleasure at the feeling of Cam's fingers inside her, filling her up and slowly penetrating her, her soft warmth, and Cam's tender lips crushed against hers. She put a hand on Cam's cheek and pulled out of the kiss. "Wait...I want to..." She hesitated, before boldly looking Cam in the eye. "I want to feel you too."

Cam's eyes darkened as she looked down at her, a small smile playing around her lips. She steadied herself on her elbow and her knees and lifted her hips, then pulled out of Ella and took her hand in hers, guiding it down between her legs.

"You're so wet," Ella whispered as she slid her fingers through Cam's folds. It felt magical to touch Cam like this, to see and feel her reaction and to hear her soft moans.

"It's what you do to me." Cam, whispered. She could tell by the look in Ella's eyes that touching her had turned her on too. "You make me crazy." She took in a quick breath when

Ella slowly dipped a finger inside her, then another. She moaned louder and started rocking back and forth on Ella's hand as her fingers went deeper, then slowly started thrusting into Ella again. A fiery heat spread through her body, igniting a spark that turned into an untamable wildfire. She hadn't been intimate with anyone in over a year, and having Ella's fingers inside her sent her body into a state of delirious pleasure. Now that she'd had a taste of her, she knew she would never get enough. They fell into a passionate kiss, moving together as one, still slow but with more urgency now. Cam lifted her head and watched Ella's lips part in a smile. She brought her mouth close to Ella's ear. "Is that good?"

"Uhuh. So good." Ella's other hand was in Cam's hair as they both moaned with each thrust. Cam could tell Ella was close, so she pushed the palm of her hand down over her center, making slow circling motions as she moved in and out of her.

Ella reveled in Cam's movements and sensual kiss as she felt a satisfying glow spread out from her core. She held Cam close as she tensed in her grip, her legs wrapping even tighter around her. Her walls started contracting around Cam's fingers, and she could sense that Cam was close too. She was shaking, surprised at the intensity of what she was feeling as she cried out again, digging her nails into Cam's skin. The sensation of Cam's core, tightening against her own made Ella force herself to keep her eyes open and look at Cam as she came too. It was a beautiful sight, watching her face pull into an expression so primal and raw. Every wave of Cam's climax washed over her too, as if they were nothing but their bodies, together. Ella finally buried her face in Cam's neck, exhaling deep when her breathing steadied, and she slowly came back to her senses. Their connection at that moment felt unbreakable, and she knew it hadn't been a mistake.

Cam collapsed, lying there while she regained control over her body that was still glowing and limp. Their hearts were beating in sync, fast and rhythmically, the fingers of their free hands now entwined. She lifted her head and looked at Ella before placing a soft kiss on her lips. Ella's eyes were glazy when their eyes met. The lust had faded from her gaze, but had been replaced by calm and wonderment.

"It's... it's so beautifully intimate," she whispered. "It's like you're inside my head, inside my soul... It feels like we're one."

Cam was unsure of what to say because she couldn't have phrased it more perfectly than Ella just had. "Yeah, it is," she finally said in a soft voice. She stroked Ella's cheek, then traced her jawline and the side of her neck. She felt her pulse that was still faster than normal. "But it's not like this with everyone. This is just as special for me as it is for you."

"I know." Ella smiled. "I can feel it."

"So this is what it's like to be with a woman." Ella lay on her side, her head resting on Cam's pillow after hours of making love and talking. Her bare skin felt amazing against Cam's. She was so warm, and now that they were dry, the sensation of her softness was only heightened. "If I had known, I probably wouldn't have waited this long." She looked up at Cam. "But I'm glad I waited, that you were my first." She still didn't feel like sleeping, somehow afraid that she'd wake up to find the magic had faded.

Cam wrapped her arms around her and pulled her closer, inching the comforter further over them. "I'm relieved I didn't disappoint you." She smiled and noted she was getting aroused again, just at the feeling of Ella, naked against her.

Ella laughed. "Are you kidding me? Do I look disappointed to you?"

"No, you don't," Cam admitted. She leaned in and slowly ran her tongue over Ella's upper lip. Ella trembled and moaned softly, parting her lips as their mouths melted together in a feverish kiss that turned wild and heated when Cam turned them over and wedged herself in between her legs. Ella bucked her hips and pulled her in as tight as she could, wrapping her legs around Cam's waist. Cam pulled out of the kiss and looked down at Ella, whose eyes were fiery and full of longing. "I want to taste you," she whispered.

"Please," Ella whimpered, covering her face with her hand when Cam started kissing her way down her breasts and her belly. She felt as if she was about to explode and wasn't sure if she could handle all the overstimulation, but still, she wanted nothing more. She bit her knuckle when Cam kissed the patch of hair between her legs, then turned to the inside of her thighs, trailing her tongue up to her center. "Fuck!" Ella gasped when she felt Cam's warm tongue on her folds, slipping between them, tracing her sex up and down in delicious slow-motion. It felt insanely, mind-blowingly good. Her hand reached under the covers for Cam's hair, and she grabbed a handful, pushing herself harder against her mouth.

Cam moaned and licked her length up to her clit. She loved how Ella tasted, loved how she reacted to her touch, and she felt light-headed from knowing she made her feel like she'd never felt before.

"Turn around," Ella panted.

Cam stopped for a moment, not quite sure what she meant.

"Turn around," she said again, with more urgency in her voice. "I want to taste you too."

Cam pushed the covers off her and met Ella's eyes. A spark of excitement shot through her, turning her on even more if that was possible. She hadn't done this since her college days. Not since she first started experimenting with women. But Ella wanted it all, and she needed to make up for lost time and experiences. She smiled and turned around, placing a knee on each side of Ella's shoulders, before she dove back down to consume her again.

Ella's hands trembled as she reached up to stroke Cam's ass, then lifted her head toward her wet center, trying everything in her power not to get distracted by the warm tingle that started building up in her lower abdomen each time Cam flicked her tongue against her clit. She kissed the moist skin of Cam's inner thighs and moved up between her legs, feeling braver when Cam moaned and pushed back against her face. Ella licked her, carefully at first, then more persistent when she'd had a taste of her. Cam tasted sweet and tangy and so, so good... She wanted to make it last but was unable to fight the orgasm that threatened to take over. Desperate to give Cam what she wanted, she sucked her clit into her mouth, the way Cam was now doing to her. The throaty sounds coming from Cam made her hazy and a little crazy inside as she balanced on the edge of her own climax, not willing to tip over yet. She repeated the movement, over and over again, even as tiny explosions filled her, spreading in waves as they increased in intensity. She moaned as she continued to bring Cam to orgasm, still shaking as her own subsided. Soon, more glorious sounds echoed through the bedroom. She closed her eyes as Cam's release came in a cry of joy, and she buried her face in her wetness, wanting it all.

Ella let her head fall back into the pillows, drained and relaxed. Cam collapsed on top of her and let out a satisfied sigh. She took Ella's foot and kissed it before she turned around and crawled back up, then pulled the covers over them.

"Come here." She pulled Ella into an embrace and snuggled close against her as she kissed her forehead and stroked her hair, knowing she was a lost cause.

33

The first thing Cam saw when she opened her eyes was pink. She blinked a couple of times, frowning when she was confronted with an enormous portrait of a flamingo that was looking right at her. She chuckled to herself and turned to Ella, who was steadily breathing against her shoulder, still fast asleep. She looked so peaceful and sweet, curled up in the sheets.

It had been a while since Cam had woken up next to a woman, and she realized it would be a first for Ella. *Is she going to be okay?* She thought so. Ella hadn't exactly seemed shy last night, and she certainly hadn't given Cam the impression that she might change her mind in the morning. Softly, she stroked Ella's cheek, pulling loose strands of hair away from her face. Ella stirred for a moment, then smiled in her sleep. Cam watched her for a while, feeling blissfully happy as flashbacks flooded her memory. Despite their late night, her internal clock had woken her up at six, and she was wide awake. They hadn't closed the curtains last night, as there was no one on the premises, but she suspected Sid would be here soon to tend to the yard before it got too warm. Early desert light was streaming in through the glass doors, flooding the room in a yellowish, almost sepia looking glow. *Where do we go from here?* That thought scared her a little. Ella was a famous closeted actress, and she was well… she was falling for her. Hard.

"Good morning," Ella said in a soft voice.

"Hey. I'm sorry, I didn't mean to wake you." Cam wrapped an arm around her and kissed her forehead.

"No, I'm glad you did." Ella blinked a couple of times and sighed as she scooted closer. "What time is it? I never sleep through the entire night."

"It's early. Six, I think. Do you have coffee in the house? I can wake you up in a couple of hours if you want to sleep a bit more."

"There's coffee in the right kitchen cupboard, and there should be almond milk in the fridge. I asked Sid to get some groceries before we came. But I don't want to sleep, and I don't want you to get up. I want you to stay in bed with me." Ella shot Cam a mischievous smile as she ran a hand over her back down to her ass, still marveling at how soft her skin was.

She felt amazing, like a new woman. It was as if the world was different today but at the same time, exactly how it should be. She'd worried she'd panic, but there was nothing but happiness and giddy excitement, mixed with a raging desire that had taken hostage of her entire body. Every nerve ending was deliciously responsive, and every touch felt like sensory overload. Waking up next to Cam was quite possibly one of the best things that had ever happened to her. Well, apart from last night, of course. She shivered as she remembered their steamy lovemaking and looked up at

Cam to meet her dark eyes that told her she had similar thoughts. "I want you, Cam," she whispered, kissing her softly.

"I want you too." Cam smiled against her lips and ran a hand through Ella's hair, slowly combing her fingers through it. Then she pulled away, hesitating for a moment. "But we probably need to talk first because I really like you, Ella. No..." She shook her head. "Liking is a big understatement because it's so much more than that. I'm falling for you, and I need to know where this is heading. I'm not normally like this but with you..." her voice trailed away. "I'm not sure if I can continue this without knowing where I stand or how you feel."

"You're right." Ella's voice was soft and sweet. "We do need to talk. I've had feelings for you for a while, and after last night, it feels like they've multiplied tenfold." She watched relief wash over Cam's face as she said it. "I want to be with you, but I don't really know how to be with someone. I've never done the dating thing, and I'm not even out."

"You're doing just fine." Cam smiled. "We can take it slow, and no one needs to know about us."

"That somehow doesn't seem fair on you," Ella said. "You're so comfortable in yourself and for you to be dating a closeted woman..."

"I don't care. It's not like it will be any different from the way we used to hang out, apart from that we might be spending a lot of nights together." Cam took Ella's hand and kissed it. "Listen, I don't want to pressure you into anything. That's not why I wanted to talk. Knowing that you feel the same way about me is enough for me, and if that means we see each other once or twice a week in the privacy of our own homes, I'm happy with that as long as I get to wake up with you."

“Really?”

“Yeah, really. You need to take your time and this...” Cam gestured between herself and Ella. “This doesn’t mean I expect you to come out.”

“I know you don’t, but I want to, eventually. Everything’s changed. I feel different. I feel amazing.” Ella sighed. “I’m worried about you, mostly. Life in the spotlight isn’t easy. Not for me but especially not for someone new to it. It can break people.”

“Don’t worry about me,” Cam said, placing another kiss on her forehead. “Before any of that happens, you’ll have to deal with coming out first. Nothing will happen until you do, in your own time, when you want it. And if you don’t, that’s your choice too, and that’s fine with me. In the meantime, my lips are sealed.” She chuckled. “And after that too, because I have nothing to say to those fuckers. And let’s face it. No one’s interested in a yoga teacher anyway. They’ll get bored of writing about me soon.”

Ella giggled, the seriousness fading from her face. “I don’t know about that, you’re pretty damned attractive.”

Cam grinned. “I’m glad you think so, but I don’t think that’s enough to start stalking me long-term.”

“Maybe not, but we won’t have a moment to ourselves if we’re in a public place together, that’s the reality. You told me you enjoyed your privacy, so I just want you to know what you’re possibly getting yourself into.”

“We’ll face those challenges when we get there.” Cam pulled Ella on top of her and sighed, the feeling of Ella’s warm and willing body and her smile taking away any lingering doubts. “As long as I know that you feel the same, I don’t care. Let’s just take this as it comes and deal with it together, okay?”

“Okay.” Ella kissed her and wedged a leg between her

thighs. “Now please do that thing again that you did last night.” She teasingly brushed her lips over Cam’s. “You know, that thing you do with your tongue.”

34

"Do you want to get out of here for a bit?" Ella leaned over Cam, who was reading on one of the lounge chairs by the pool. They'd spent the morning unpacking Ella's personal belongings, and Sid had helped them put her old pictures back up on the walls. Inside, boxes were still stacked up in the hallway, but there was no rush and Ella didn't want to spend too much of their precious time on it.

Cam looked up at her and smiled as she shielded her eyes from the sun. "Sure. Are you getting cabin fever?"

"Not when you're in my cabin," Ella joked. "But I want to show you something. It's a bit of a drive. Do you mind?"

"I don't mind a drive." Cam sat up and pulled Ella onto her lap. "Besides, I need some distraction from you in a bikini. I can't even read when you're walking around looking like that. Not that I particularly want to read," she added. "Has Sid left yet? Because I can think of way better things to do." She wedged a hand under Ella's moss green bikini top and ran her tongue up her neck, to her earlobe. "I'm sure you'll agree," she whispered in her ear while sliding her other hand into Ella's bikini bottoms, cupping her center hard. Ella let out a moan as her head fell back against Cam's shoulder.

"Jesus, Cam," she panted, closing her eyes while Cam worked two fingers inside her, caressing her breasts with her other hand. Cam's mouth was on Ella's neck and on her ear, biting gently as she ran her tongue over her sensitive skin. Her firm grip and skillful fingers made Ella weak in the knees. "I think he left to get some stuff, but he'll be back soon and..." Ella moaned, failing to finish her sentence.

"That's okay. I only need two minutes," Cam whispered in her ear. She grinned when Ella's moans became louder. "Or maybe I just need one."

There was nothing for miles, except for bare desert to their left and the Salton Sea to their right, still and shimmering in the afternoon sun. Apart from some trucks and RVs, it was quiet on the road. The land became even more barren after they'd passed the Salton Sea, with only a little bit of vegetation and a couple of trees scattered around on both sides of the road, the earth cracked like dry clay. There was an old train track with a rusty train that looked like it had been there for decades and there were a few homes that had clearly been deserted long ago.

"Somehow this doesn't seem like your scene," Cam joked, casting a sideways glance at Ella. "But I'm keeping an open mind."

"Honestly, I wouldn't have come here if Helena hadn't insisted I go with her years ago." Ella turned to Cam and smiled. "But I'm glad I did. You'll see."

The vegetation started getting slightly denser, with more bushes and patches of grass as they neared a small town called Niland, where they passed farms, homes, some small businesses and a couple of worn-out motels. Cam laughed when Ella took a right turn, into a dusty desert road.

"Are you serious? Do you even know where you're going?"

Ella laughed too. "I hope so. I think I still remember."

They were both quiet as they passed motor homes and tents along the road, where small travelling communities had set up camp. About a mile ahead, Cam saw something massive and colorful. She couldn't make out what it was until they neared, and Ella stopped in front of what seemed to be an enormous Christian shrine, painted on a mountain.

"We're here. Salvation Mountain." Ella stopped the car along the road. "Come on, we'll have to walk the rest of the way." She put on her cap, and her shades – her standard disguise when she wasn't home or in the car – and they walked over the hard desert floor toward the mountain. A small sign in the ground, held up by two rocks that said 'welcome', and a blue chemical toilet, were the only indications of life on the quiet patch of land initially, but as they came closer, they heard voices coming from one of the many dome-shaped buildings on the premises that were also painted brightly. Cam stopped in her stride as she stared at the surreal display.

"It's quite amazing, don't you think?" Ella lowered her cap over her forehead as she turned to Cam.

"Totally. What is this?" Cam looked over the mountain range that was covered in slogans and illustrations in vibrant colors. The words 'God is love' stood out as the largest and most significant text, underneath a huge red heart and next to a blue and white striped painted waterfall that cascaded down the mountain. On the top of the hill stood a white cross, casting its shadow over the land. "It looks like a massive Christian shrine. How many people worked on this?"

"Mostly, only one man for thirty years," Ella said. "His name was Leonard Knight. I've never had the pleasure of meeting him, but Helena met him once, and she said he was an amazing man. He lived in that old fire truck over there." She pointed to a truck that was also covered in paint and bible verses, the word 'love' repeated over and over. There were more painted cars and motor homes dotted over the land, blending in seamlessly with the larger than life artscape in the background. The sun intensified the colors, making it almost overwhelming to look at. "He built the actual mountain too," Ella continued. "It was all flat here until he started stacking up hay bales that he covered with adobe clay and latex paint. And now it's..." She paused, searching for the right words. "A place of worship, I guess."

"And love," Cam added, reading the word over and over again everywhere she looked. There were hundreds of red hearts too.

"And love," Ella repeated, taking her hand. "That over there," she said, pointing to a dome-shaped building, "is a home he built for himself, but he never moved in because he preferred his truck in the end. There's also a museum." She led them to a couple of larger dome-shaped structures. "Everything is made of dead trees, old tires and other stuff he found in the desert. Again, the buildings were covered with clay and painted with flowers, trees, birds and biblical scriptures."

They wandered around, taking in the land-art. There were five other tourists, posing for pictures in front of the museum but everyone respectfully kept their voices down. They went into the makeshift building that was painted brightly on the inside too. There were notes and small personal objects that visitors had left behind, and a family of birds was nesting in the rafters.

"Leonard died in 2014," Ella said, "but his supporters still carry on his work. The paint is bought from donations, and volunteers work on expanding it. I made a donation in Helena's name last year."

"I bet that will keep them going for a while," Cam joked. She shielded her eyes as they walked back outside, almost blinded by the sunlight after being in the dark cave-like structure. The brightness of the spectrum of color overwhelmed her once again and she took a moment. "How come I live in LA, and I didn't know about this place?" she asked, snapping some pictures of the mountain against the blue sky. It really did look stunning with its neutral, sand-colored surroundings.

"I bet there are a lot of places out here you don't know about." Ella pointed east. "There's something else a little farther down I want to show you. Let's get back in the car, I'm frying out here."

After a short drive, they got out of the car again. Ella covered up her shoulders with a scarf she found on the back seat, her skin burning despite the many layers of sunscreen.

"Come on." She pulled Cam with her over the dusty terrain. "This whole area is called Slab City," she said, gesturing to the surrounding area where trailers were set up amongst tents and makeshift homes. Shelters were built from old palettes, cloth and other recycled things and it seemed like a giant, old water tank functioned as a home too. "It's the last decommissioned and uncontrolled area in the US and on paper, it doesn't exist. Most of the residents are permanent around this time of year. The snowbirds come to stay here during the winter months only. Some have moved here because of poverty, and some have moved here because they simply want to live off the grid. It started out as super basic, but now some habitants have solar power and fully functioning homes. They grow stuff and are self-sustainable, apart from water, which is delivered."

"I'm trying to understand how people can live in this heat but it's hard," Cam said, already boiling after their two-minute walk. "I assume Helena was the one who took you here too?"

"Yeah. She was curious like that. I was nervous to come here because there's no law enforcement. But most people don't want trouble; they just want to be left alone." Ella shrugged. "Even though I probably stand for everything they hate."

"Yeah, I guess there's no denying that you are a walking billboard for capitalism." Cam smiled and grinned at a big man with a beard, who waved at them. He was wearing a cape and a cowboy hat that was decorated with pins, feathers, bows and badges. "It feels a little post-apocalyptic here. It's completely surreal and fascinating, but surely we can't just go snooping around people's homes?"

"Of course not," Ella said as they neared a piece of land with something that, from a distance, looked like a collection of trash. "But we can have a look over there. It's the *East Jesus Art Installation*, and it's open to the public."

From up close, Cam could see that the piles of 'trash' were actually art installations now, as they walked underneath the sculpture garden's entry, constructed from old water tanks, wire, wind chimes, bikes and a car door. They wandered around, taking in the sculptures: a mammoth made out of blown-out tires, a bottle wall, a whale made out of plastic bags, a 'sinking' house and a huge wall of old TV's on which cynical slogans were painted.

"I'd never thought I'd see something like this out here in the desert." Cam took a couple of pictures, then turned her phone to Ella, who smiled for the camera.

"Yeah, it's cool, right?" Ella looked up at her. "Let's take one together." She wrapped an arm around Cam's waist and kissed her cheek as she held up her phone to take a picture of them in front of the bottle wall. "Our first picture together," she said, color rising to her cheeks when she looked at it.

Cam kissed her back and shot her an endearing look. "You're blushing."

"I know! I just realized as I said it how sappy I sounded."

"No, not at all. It's cute, and that picture's going up on my bedroom wall."

"Talking about sappy," Ella joked. She nudged her as they walked back to the car. "Are you tired yet? We didn't exactly get much sleep last night."

"Are you kidding me?" Cam swept her hand in front of her. "I love this. I had no idea you were such an insider on the desert."

"I know a place or two." Ella said as she got into the car. "I suggest we get some food and make a detour through Joshua Tree National Park on our way home. It's pretty amazing at night."

"Okay, let's do it." Cam got into the passenger seat and handed Ella a bottle of water from her bag. "I'd love to see more, and I can drive home if you want."

The desert had never been Cam's thing, but she had to admit that it was growing on her. Even the most barren strips of land they passed were beautiful. There was something about the way the light hit the sand-colored earth and the slight shimmer of the heat above the ground that made everything look intriguing and mysterious.

They entered Joshua Tree National Park at the south entrance after stopping off to buy more water and some food to eat on the way. Ella drove them to Cottonwood Spring; an oasis against the dry desert, lined with fan-palms and cottonwood trees, then continued through the park, where extensive flats were filled with spikey, eccentric looking Joshua trees. The landscape was like nothing Cam had ever seen; the trees concentrated in certain areas where it looked like they had congregated for a strike, their branches raised like protestor's arms waving in the air.

Then they drove to the Cholla Cactus Garden, where they made a stop and got out of the car just as the sun was beginning to set. The spiky, hairy plants rose from the surface as far as the eye could see, some of them as high as five feet tall.

“They also call the chollas teddy bears, because they're so furry, at least they appear so from a distance,” Ella said. “This is where the Colorado Desert merges into the Mojave Desert. You can clearly see the landscape changing here, where the Joshua trees are replaced by cholla cacti, and the Little San Bernardino Mountains smooth out into rolling hills instead of large boulders. It's quite spectacular, right?”

“It sure is.” Backlit by the low sun, the plants did look like creatures, now that it was darkening around them. The last bit of sunlight was pouring over the valley, and the sky turned a reddish gold before fading into a darker pink and purple gradient. Cam put an arm around Ella when they sat down on a rock to watch the striking display and didn't let go until the early night had covered them, bringing a chill to the air.

"It cools down really quickly at night." Ella crossed her arms as they walked back to the car. "It can be as high as a hundred degrees during the day and then drop to sixty-five at night. Are you cold, or are you okay to make one more stop? The stars will be visible soon. It's clear and moonless tonight so it should be good."

"No, I'm not cold. But I wish I had a jacket to give you." Cam wasn't lying; she seemed to be burning whenever Ella was near. After the sunset, a deep sense of calm had settled within her and it was one of those rare days she never wanted to end.

"You're so gallant," Ella joked, batting her eyelashes. "Don't worry; I have a blanket in the trunk."

"Very smart."

"Hey, it's just experience. I lived out here for years, so I always put tons of water and a blanket in my trunk before I venture out of Palm Springs. Helena and I used to come here early mornings or late at night when it would be quiet and too dark for anyone to recognize us. I've always been pretty good at blending in, but when we were together, it was a whole different thing; twins rarely go unnoticed, especially not famous twins." She smiled and shook her head. "I wasn't sure how I'd feel, coming out here without her, but I'm having a really great day."

"I'm having a great time too." Cam pulled her in and kissed her temple. She felt a peaceful kind of happy, but at the same time, almost a little crazy from all the new feelings that had taken control of her. *Oh God, I'm in so deep.* "I can't say I've ever actively sought out a place to go stargazing. It's kind of romantic, don't you think?" She tilted her head to meet Ella's eyes and shot her a teasing look. "Are you secretly a hopeless romantic?"

"I don't know, I think I might be." Ella gently ran her fingers over her hand and grinned as she got in the car. "Are you?"

Cam blushed, not expecting the question back. "I guess I am too," she admitted as Ella drove off. "I wasn't really before, but with you, the idea of candlelight and stars excite me. Is that cheesy?"

"No. It's sweet," Ella said in a soft voice. "I never understood why people loved my movies so much, especially the ones that were full of over-romantic clichés. But I'm not ashamed to say that I get it now."

They drove back in the direction of Cottonwood in comfortable silence, both sucked into the landscape that looked entirely different now in the dark. The black silhouettes of the Joshua trees looked eerie, the tall ones resembling angry monsters and the shorter ones dead bodies rising from their graves, their arms linked together. Ella stopped at a roadside rest area and took the blanket out of her trunk.

"Let's get warm," she said as they sat down on the hood of the car. She draped the blanket around them and snuggled close against Cam as they faced the flats of the park. The starry sky above them was the kind of sky Cam had only ever seen in photographs; millions of tiny white pinpricks twinkling against the endless midnight-blue.

"I feel so small right now," she whispered as if she was afraid of disturbing the peace.

"Me too." Ella let out a deep sigh. "It seems impossible to be here without thinking about the universe – life and death – and wondering why the hell we're here, right? I used to think about that a lot when I was really low. I suppose I was desperately trying to come up with a reason to carry on and I knew that looking at the stars was the closest to the truth I'd ever find. It all seemed so pointless back then." She paused. "I still think about it, but not in a melodramatic way. It's more a sensation of awe I feel now."

"Awe is a good way to describe it. It's like the most beautiful art, waiting to be understood," Cam said. She turned to Ella, amazed by how beautiful she looked tonight. The wind from the drive had blown her hair into a tousled mane, and her infectious smile lit up her whole face each time their eyes met. She looked back up when she realized she was staring. "Is that the Milky Way?" she asked, pointing to a blob of concentrated light that faded out into an uneven ellipse at both sides.

"It is." Ella looked impressed. "It's not as bright as it usually is at the very height of summer, but it's pretty visible tonight. We get meteor showers out here too; I think August is a good month for it. I've only seen it once, but I'll never forget it. Helena and I decided to have a midnight swim once after we heard on the news that a big one was expected. We didn't think we'd see much as we were at the house, but we switched off all the lights an hour before anyway. We were floating around on our pool floats when it started, and it went on for hours. It was breathtaking."

"Did you make a wish?"

"I did."

"And did it come true?" Cam lay back, resting her head against the car's window.

Ella did the same and thought for a moment before she answered the question. "Yeah, I think it has." She appeared a little embarrassed at her confession as she took her phone out of her purse and scrolled through it, clearly attempting to veer away from the topic. "As I'm being all hopelessly romantic anyway, I might as well put on some music." She connected her phone to the car's speakers and put on a cover of the song Vincent by Don McLean.

"Now *that* is cheesy," Cam teased her.

"Hey, it was the first thing that sprung to mind." Ella chuckled. "You know, the stars and all... Besides, I like the melody."

"Yeah, I actually like it too, just don't tell anyone I said that." Cam opened her arm so Ella could rest her head on her chest. She ran her fingers through Ella's hair, savoring the moment while they listened to an acoustic version of the song, performed by an artist Cam didn't know. The more she explored Ella, the more she found, and what she found made her like her even more. By now, she knew there was a whole lot more to Ella than what the media had led her to believe, and she hoped wholeheartedly that somehow, this could work. Because even though Ella was famous, rich and loved by millions – and she was an anonymous yoga teacher who knew nothing about her world – in the end, they were just two people who had found each other under the strangest of circumstances. What were the odds that Ella had attempted to end her life right in front of her house? And what were the odds that Cam had seen her and managed to save her? And what were the odds that after everything, they were now lying here on top of Ella's car hood in the middle of a desert, watching the stars together? When she turned her head to tell her that, Ella's lips brushed hers, warm and with tenderness. Desire immediately welled up inside her and poured out like a broken dam as she sank into the kiss. And in that precious moment, through the desire and something that felt pretty close to love, she was a little sad, knowing there would never be a moment like this again.

35

"I could get used to this place." Cam took the menu the waiter handed her and sank back in her comfortable chair. "And I especially like the 'leave your phone by the front desk' policy. People are actually talking to each other here, instead of just looking at their phones the whole time."

Ella nodded. "I like the Palm Garden too. It's a bit boring to go to the same place two days in a row, but at least it's safe here. It's nice knowing that nobody will be snapping pictures of us." She opened her own menu, which was kind of unnecessary as she already knew what she was going to order. Cam had noticed she wasn't really reading and laughed.

"Please tell me you're not going to ask for raisins on your Caesar salad again."

"Of course, I am." Ella rolled her eyes for comical effect, then closed her menu and leaned in, giving Cam a flirty look. "Once I find something I like, I'm all over it. Haven't you noticed?"

"Oh, I've noticed alright." Cam brushed her foot against Ella's under the table. "You're insatiable."

"I could say the same for you." Ella's smile dropped as she spotted two people following a waiter into the garden to a table in the back. "Fuck," she whispered. "Fuck, fuck, fuck."

"What?" Cam looked at Ella, then over her shoulder in the direction Ella was staring at, wide-eyed. Ella pulled her sun hat further over her forehead and sunk lower in her chair, hiding behind Cam.

"It's my Mom. What the hell is she doing here?"

"Your mom?" Cam cast another glance over her shoulder. "The one in the long, green dress with the blonde bob? She doesn't look nearly old enough to be your mom." The man she was with looked younger than Ella, but from their body language, she concluded they were on a date. She quickly turned back when the woman looked in their direction.

"Yeah, that's her. Don't be fooled, she's had some work done. That, and she had me, or rather us, when she was only eighteen."

"Hey, don't worry. We could leave quietly and go somewhere else?"

Ella nodded. "Yeah, I really want to leave; I don't want her to see me. She finally stopped trying to contact me after I blocked her number and I..." She looked at her cucumber juice, then searched for her credit card in her purse, taking it out with a trembling hand.

"Don't worry, just get out of here and wait in the car. I'll pay for the drinks." As Cam said it, the sun was blocked by someone behind her, casting a shadow over their table. She could tell by Ella's face that it was too late.

"Ella... It's so good to see you again," a female voice said with an emotional quiver.

Ella looked up with panic written all over her face. "No, Mom. I told you I don't want to talk to you." She composed herself and lowered her voice. "Go back to your toy boy over there. He looks bored and I have nothing to say to you."

"But honey, I've missed you so much. I've tried calling you hundreds of times and if you'd just let me explain..."

"There's nothing to explain." Ella's voice was devoid of emotion as she cut her mother off. "Please leave."

Cam turned around and came face to face with the spitting image of Ella. People unaware of the situation would have probably guessed she was her older sister. She looked flamboyant, and way too overdressed for a weekday lunch. Her green kaftan dress was hanging off one shoulder, matching her beaded sandals and her shades with green mirrored glasses she was holding in her hand. Now that she was closer, Cam could see that the sheen on her forehead was evidence of subjection to a substantial amount of Botox. Her lips were plumper than Ella's and clearly artificial but other than that, the resemblance was remarkable. The heart-shaped face, the big, light blue eyes, the dark, sharply arched eyebrows and the slightly pouty lips... Ella's mother looked at her then, as if she'd only just realized her daughter wasn't alone. Her face pulled into a nervous smile when their eyes met.

"Hi. You must be Camila Saunders. I read about you in the tabloids," she said. "So, is it true? Are you two dating?" She put a hand on Cam's shoulder when she didn't answer. "I'm Bernice Temperley, Ella's mother. It's nice to meet you."

"Her name is not Bernice, it's Betty," Ella sneered, cutting her mother off before Cam had the chance to answer. "And who I date is none of your business, Mom," she continued. "Now, it's really straightforward. Either you leave, or we leave. I don't care either way as long as you don't make a scene."

"Fine." Bernice collected herself and took a deep breath. "I won't make a scene if you'll hear me out for two minutes. Two minutes, that's all I need." She didn't wait for an answer as she pulled a vacant chair from underneath another table and sat down next to Cam, facing Ella.

"I'll leave you guys to it," Cam said, about to get up.

"No, please don't go." Ella pleaded, reaching for her hand. "I'd really like you to stay; we can go somewhere else after my mother's finished her two-minute speech." She looked at her mother. "How did you know I was here, anyway? Did you follow me?"

Bernice shook her head. "No, I live here so I come here all the time. I moved back to Palm Springs a while ago. It's not like I've got anything left to keep me in LA."

"Don't play the victim. You did that yourself."

"I know." Bernice seemed defeated, but she carried on anyway. "I miss you so much, Ella. I wish we could be friends again."

"We were never friends." A frown appeared between Ella's brows as if she couldn't quite believe what her mother was saying. "You were always my manager first, and my mother second. Friendship was never part of the deal."

"You're right. I was always your manager first, and that was wrong; I see that now. But not having you in my life has been incredibly difficult. I've had a lot of time to think and I'm so sorry for what I did to you."

"You mean stealing from me?" The fierceness in Ella's eyes almost frightened Cam. She was always so softly spoken, timid even at times, but right now, the anger was radiating from her every pore. "Just say it like it is, Mom. You stole from me, it's as simple as that." She held up a hand when her mother was about to answer. "You know what? I would have forgiven you for all the times you did that to me. Moving my management to Tom was the best decision ever, but maybe, just maybe, our personal relationship could have come back from those stunts you pulled. Not the trust, but I really believed part of our relationship could have been salvaged. I mean, you're my mother after all, and I didn't have anyone else..." Tears welled up in Ella's eyes. "But Helena's diaries... I can't forgive you for that. To do that, to publish extracts from her diaries for the whole world to read... It was disgusting."

"I know I always pushed her to be someone she wasn't," Bernice said in a broken voice. "I knew she had no interest in the entertainment industry, and still, for years, I had her going to auditions, I put her through makeovers and drove her to talk shows and interviews, just like I did with you. I created a persona out of her, out of both of you. I know it was my fault that she never figured out what she really wanted to do with her life until she was in her early twenties but I loved her, and her death broke me, just like it broke you, and I felt terribly guilty that she had so little time living her life the way she wanted." A look of regret settled over her face. "From the pictures I've seen, and from what I've read, her university years were the happiest, and I wanted to make it right somehow. I wanted the world to know who she really was. Not the successful movie star who attended A-list parties, posed for glamour magazines and dated handsome boy-band singers in her teens. But the Helena who loved architecture, music and festivals. The Helena who was smart, creative and compassionate. The Helena who loved who she loved and didn't care what other people thought of her. I never asked you what you wanted either. And now that I've lost both of you, I've realized I made a big mistake." She paused, lowering her voice: "I was just trying to make right what I'd done wrong."

"Well, you couldn't have done it more wrong if you tried. You had no right to break in and steal those diaries, and you had no right to put them out there. How much did you make from the book, huh? One or two million? Or was it more than that? Was it worth it?"

Bernice didn't answer as color rose to her cheeks.

"We're leaving." Ella stood up and took Cam's hand. "You should go back to your date. That boy doesn't look like he's old enough to order for himself." Ella made sure to emphasize the word 'boy'. "How old is he anyway? Twenty-two?" She huffed. "What the fuck are you doing dating someone half your age?"

Bernice looked down, her eyes glazy now. "I'm just lonely. I'm so lonely, Ella."

Ella winced for a moment as her mother said it, but she turned her back to her anyway and left.

36

"I didn't mean to drag you out here to get thrown into all this drama." Ella helped Cam unpack the take-out they'd picked up on their way back to the house. "I'm sure you could do without it."

"Don't say that. I'm here for you." Cam started arranging the sushi on two plates and poured them both a glass of bourbon she found in one of the kitchen cabinets, sensing Ella needed a drink. Not that drinking was a solution, but the way she'd been shaking on their way back told Cam that seeing her mother again had upset Ella and maybe it would calm her down a bit. "Do you want to talk about it?"

"No, not really." Ella took a sip of her drink and let out a long sigh. "I said everything I wanted to say to her, and I think we're done." She turned to Cam. "Did you see that guy she was with? I mean, what the hell? He was in his early twenties, younger than me."

"She probably really is lonely."

"She'll never be lonely. She likes her own company best. And even if she were lonely, it's not like I care."

"You do care, Ella. I saw it in your eyes."

"You have no idea what I feel." Ella's eyes widened as she spoke. She wasn't used to people going against her. It rarely happened, and on the rare occasions that it did, it usually came from Tom, who would dance around the subject carefully, never this directly. "I'm sorry, I didn't mean it like that," she immediately continued. "But surely you must understand that there's no way I can forgive her."

"You're right, Ella. I have no idea how you really feel. But you're also kind of an open book to me. I can tell when something affects you." Cam's voice was calm and sweet as she focused on the plate. "I understand that you can't forgive her, but there's no shame in admitting that seeing your mother again, after so long and after everything that's happened, has upset you." She turned to Ella and met her gaze. "I'm on your side, but that doesn't mean I have to agree with you all the time."

"I know." Ella's stern expression slowly softened as she looked into Cam's eyes. It amazed her how Cam could make her forget about things just by looking at her. When she reached out to touch her cheek, Cam caught her hand with her own and kissed it so tenderly that Ella felt a lump settle in her throat. "You're right," she whispered. "I think she's lonely. That doesn't change anything, though."

"No, it doesn't, but people can change when they've been at their lowest. I'm not saying you should forgive her, just don't discard her entirely because you might regret it one day." Cam let go of Ella's hand and handed her the plate. "Let's take this outside, shall we? We don't need to talk about your mother right now. Just think about it."

Ella stared down at the sushi for a moment before she chuckled. The food was arranged into a smiley face, with a California roll mouth, a wasabi nose, tuna maki roll eyes, pickled ginger eyebrows and salmon sashimi hair. "You're amazing," she said, putting the plate back down. She wrapped her arms around Cam's neck and stood on her tiptoes as she gave her a long and lingering kiss.

"Come on in, the water's really nice." Cam splashed water at Ella who was watching her swim from the sun lounger.

"I don't know. I want to but I kind of freaked out last time I thought about going in my pool in LA ..." Ella bit her lip. "I'm not so comfortable with deep water anymore."

"I get that, but I'm here. You'll be fine once you're in." Cam smiled. "Just hold onto me."

Ella stared at Cam's toned shoulders as she hung onto the edge of the pool. She didn't feel the panic she'd felt that night at home. In fact, she felt quite the opposite, drawn to Cam's bikini-clad body like it was all she could think about. She'd finally pushed the confrontation with her mother to the background, still a little irritated that it had cast a shadow on their perfect vacation.

"Promise me you'll hold me?" she asked.

Cam grinned. "What... do you seriously think I'm not going to have my hands all over you as soon as you get in here, looking like that?"

"Alright, then." Ella laughed as she got up from the lounge chair, walked toward the edge of the pool in a white and navy striped bikini and sat down, dangling her legs in the water. Cam's arm was around her waist as soon as she lowered herself. She sighed at the cool water and Cam's skin against her own.

"See? That wasn't so bad, right?" Cam's hand reached for her butt and squeezed it as she held onto the edge of the pool with her other hand. Ella wrapped her arms around her neck and kissed her.

"No, it wasn't. In fact, this feels really, really good." Ella's heart started beating faster, but it had nothing to do with fear. Every time she was close to Cam, every time Cam looked at her the way she did now; as if she wanted her more than anything, adrenaline shot through her, and she longed for her with every fiber in her body. "You're so beautiful," She whispered. "And when you hold me, nothing else seems to matter and I love that. I wish we could stay here forever. Just you and me, away from everything..." She shook her head. "I'm sorry, I know you have a life and friends and a business you have to get back to, but I haven't felt like this in a long time. I feel happy here. *You* make me happy."

Cam's mouth pulled into a wide smile as she inched even closer. "You make me happy too and believe me, there's nothing I'd rather do than stay here with you. But the reality is, you're still Ella Temperley, and the whole world knows you. It might seem enticing to hide out here in the desert, but it's not a long-term solution."

"I know." Ella bit her lip and locked her eyes with Cam's. "I just need to figure out how to be myself again. My new self, out in the open."

"But you haven't changed, Ella." Cam put a hand on her cheek. "You're still the same, amazing woman you always were and if you decide to come out, I promise you, it won't be as scary as it seems right now."

37

"Any news on the Tyler Kane situation yet?" Cam asked. They'd decided to go hiking today and were preparing a picnic in the kitchen. After an early yoga session, a swim and a coffee by the pool, they were both wearing fluffy robes. Ella's was pink, matching her bedroom, and Cam's was a cream and gold one that she'd found in hers.

"Yeah, I just got a message from Tom. He promised to send me a recap as I didn't care to watch it last night." Ella moved the fruit Cam was chopping into plastic containers and placed it into her backpack. "Tyler basically said in the interview that he was cheating on me and that I totally freaked out when he confessed." She rolled her eyes. "I didn't see that one coming, but I guess he was terrified of people knowing there was someone in this world who wasn't into him. He publicly apologized to me for being unfaithful, apparently. Tom says the phone's been ringing all morning, but he's letting the tabloids know I'm not commenting on it so a least I won't have to confirm or deny the story."

"That's good, right? That he made up some stupid story?" Cam moved onto making couscous, pouring hot water over the wheat semolina.

"Yeah, I suppose it's good. It's a little embarrassing for me, now seemingly having been cheated on by Tyler Kane." Ella pulled a face and laughed.

"Imagine that." Cam laughed too and handed Ella a cucumber and two tomatoes. "Can you chop these for me? I promise it won't sting."

"Ha ha, very funny." Ella gave Cam a quick slap on her butt and started chopping them while Cam seasoned and stirred the couscous, adding in a handful of herbs. "So have you done a lot of hiking?"

Cam shrugged. "Only a little. I go into the Hollywood Hills sometimes. Does that count?"

"Of course that counts. Those trails are long and hard." Ella tilted her head. "Never mind, they're probably really easy to you, so at least you'll be able to carry me if I get tired."

"No one's getting carried, princess." Cam grinned as she lifted Ella up on the cooking island and stepped in between her legs. She stroked her thighs and leaned in to kiss her. "But I can give you a warm-up if that helps."

"You keep on surprising me, Ella. I honestly thought we were going on a shopping mall hike," Cam joked as she parked Ella's car at the Whitewater Preserve Visitor's Center after half an hour's drive. She could hardly believe how green it was here, after driving through the barren landscape up to the Canyon for the last five miles. "No offence, you just don't seem like the type to come out here."

"And I didn't take you for a crazy driver." Ella was finger-combing her hair that had turned into an untamable mess after the drive with the convertible's top down. "How fast did you go out there?"

"Hey, I don't get the chance to drive a beast like this every day, and it wasn't like there were many cars on the road." Cam tapped the hood of the car as if giving it a compliment for good behavior.

Ella laughed. "Well, you can borrow it anytime, Ms. Indy 500. But to answer your question, no, I'm not much of a hiker, I'll happily admit that. I just figured that if there's one thing my mother doesn't do, it's hiking so at least I won't have to worry about bumping into her. I don't even think she owns a pair of sneakers."

Cam nodded. "Right. I get it now. But you've been here before, right? Do you know the trail?"

"Yeah, I've been here a couple of times. It's been years since I've been here, but it's kind of nice to be back." Ella put on her backpack, her cap, and her shades and Cam did the same. "And seeing you in those tiny shorts is a bonus." Ella let her eyes roam over Cam's toned and sun-kissed legs in the tiny gray jersey shorts, then back up at her loose, white T-shirt that was so thin that is was almost transparent, showing the outline of a black bikini underneath. "Do you need me to put some more sunscreen on you?"

Cam chuckled. "I think those three layers you put on me earlier will be more than enough but thank you for the offer. Do you need another rub?"

Ella shot her a flirty look. "Always. But I think it can wait until we're somewhere more private." She kept her voice down so she wouldn't draw attention to herself. "It should be fairly quiet on the Canyon View Loop Trail. We might even find a spot all to ourselves." She took Cam's hand as they passed a small campsite with grass, huge trees and an emerald-green pond behind the center. Dragonflies were circling over the water, and a garter snake was lazily basking on a rock right in the middle of the pond, attracting attention from tourists and local visitors. They took the opportunity to pass through unnoticed and walked the stretch along the valley floor next to a river, enjoying the sound of the water spilling over the rocks and the scent of greenery. It was peacefully quiet and the wind was still; the river valley protected by the enormous rock formations that formed the canyon walls. The crisp, clear water was in stark contrast to the sweltering desert heat, and they were relieved to find a little beach where they put down their bags before wading into the river to cool down.

"God, this feels nice." Ella closed her eyes as she carefully walked farther into the shallow river, then splashed some water on her face. It wasn't even midday and she felt like she was steaming alive. Cam kicked water her way, and Ella screamed when the cold drops hit her all over.

"Hey, stop that!" She laughed and splashed back at Cam, moving closer as she kept attacking her. Cam chuckled and took hold of her in an attempt to stop her, but she tripped on a slippery rock and tumbled over into the water with Ella on top of her. "Fuck, that's cold!" Two passersby stopped for a moment to check if they were okay, then continued their walk when they heard them laughing.

"Look what you've done, now we're both wet," Ella said in a giggle as she straddled Cam and kissed her. Cam kissed her back, hungrily, as she pulled her closer against her. Suddenly remembering where they were, she tore her mouth away from Ella's and looked around.

"I don't think this is what you had in mind when you

said you didn't want to attract attention to yourself. Two women kissing in the river next to a popular trail..." She smiled and brushed her lips over Ella's, unable to resist one last kiss.

"Yeah... not the best idea," Ella agreed, her eyes full of longing now. She reluctantly got up and helped Cam up too, then looked down at her tank top. "I'm glad I wore black today," she joked, pointing at Cam's white T-shirt that now left nothing to the imagination. It clung to her breasts and stomach, showing her bikini top and even her abs underneath. "Not that I mind, it will certainly motivate me to get to that quiet ridge faster."

Cam laughed as she rolled the short sleeves up to her shoulders, squeezed out some of the water and tied the hem into a knot, baring her midriff. "I'm glad to be of service."

They crossed the river a little farther down and followed the trail upwards. The path narrowed at some parts with a steep drop to one side, looking down at the river. On their way, they spotted wild cows and farther up, bighorn sheep on the canyon's ridgeline. They were both out of breath by the time they reached the top. The view from the ridge was stunningly beautiful, with a flat, dry landscape and jumbled rock formations to the east, and low mountains covered in rich vegetation to the west. A picnic table amid a large patch of yellow and purple wildflowers seemed like the perfect place for a break.

"Nature is beautiful out here," Cam said, sitting down next to Ella. She took a sip of her water and handed the bottle to her.

"Yeah, I'm glad we came here." Ella scooted closer to her. "However it's a shame your T-shirt dried so quickly."

Cam arched a brow and grinned. “You couldn’t be any gayer if you tried.”

“I know.” Ella gave her a smirk as she unpacked their lunch. “I’m starting to realize what I’ve been missing all these years.” She put the fruit and the couscous on the table and handed Cam a fork.

“I bet you are. So, I take it from your wet T-shirt reaction that you’re officially a boob-woman now?”

Ella looked amused as she thought about that. “Yeah, I guess I am. Although when it comes to you, I’m pretty much obsessed with every part of your body.”

“The feeling is entirely mutual.” Cam put an arm around Ella, pulled her in and kissed her cheek. She turned to look over her shoulder when she heard something rustling behind her. “Oh my God, look.”

Ella turned too, slowly. “It’s a bobcat,” she whispered. “I’ve never seen one in the wild before.”

“Me neither,” Cam said, keeping her voice down. “It’s much bigger than I expected. Are they dangerous?” The large cat with a tawny-gray and brown coat stood still on the path, his big, pointy ears shifting in different directions as he looked straight at them.

“I’m not sure. Aren’t they supposed to be scared of us?” Ella didn’t sound too sure of herself. She let out a sigh of relief when the cat spotted a group of hikers who had reached the ridge. It ran off, disappearing out of sight within seconds.

Cam looked relieved too. “I can see why you didn’t like to camp out in the desert now; it wouldn’t be my thing either. It’s beautiful though. I had no idea there were bobcats here; it’s not like we’re entirely in the middle of nowhere.”

“Apparently there are lots of them, but they rarely come near people. Maybe he was after our lunch.” Ella pulled her cap further over her head when the group passed them, and when Cam waved at them, she gave them a polite nod too. "There are rattlesnakes and bears here too, you know." She chuckled when she saw Cam's eyes widen. "And here I was, thinking you were tough."

"Hey, I never claimed I was tough." Cam opened her lunchbox and stirred her fork through the couscous. "I'm just a skinny yoga teacher. If a bear crosses our path, it's every woman for herself." She grinned. "Just kidding. I'll totally fight a bear for you."

Ella laughed. "Oh yeah? And what about a snake?"

"Hmm... a snake is questionable. I'm actually terrified of snakes. What's your phobia?"

"I don't know..." Ella thought about it. "I get pretty skittish around centipedes, actually. I won't faint or anything, but if they're really big, I'll run out of the room, and I might even scream."

Cam shot her a goofy grin. "Okay, a centipede I could definitely save you from so you're safe with me."

"Then I'll save you from snakes." Ella confirmed. "I've seen Sid remove them from the yard a couple of times; I think I'd know what to do. Have you ever been bitten?"

"Only once, in Goa. I was afraid of them long before that, so it only made my phobia worse," Cam said. "It wasn't a deadly one, but I got bitten on my ankle, and my leg was really swollen and stiff for a good three or four days. Vanya had to roll me around on an office chair we borrowed from reception."

Ella laughed again. "I can imagine that scene. What was India like?"

"It was great. I've only been to Goa because that's where my yoga course was, but it was beautiful and colorful. The night markets are amazing, they have the most gorgeous churches, and everything is vivid and vibrant. The yoga school was in a small village along a quiet strip of beach. We had classes on the beach every morning and evening, meditation in the afternoon and delicious food all day long. It was physically challenging but life was really simple at the same time, and I liked that. Vanya and I arrived on the same day, and we became friends almost immediately. Greg joined two weeks later; he's Vanya's fiancé now. He only stayed for a month because he was in between jobs. Greg wasn't there with the intention of perfecting his yoga skills like Vanya and myself. He simply needed a break from corporate life and technology, so he skipped the advanced classes in the evening, and they put him to work in the kitchen instead." Cam laughed. "I suppose the stay didn't exactly meet his expectations but it was immensely entertaining to watch him hide each time they called him in for cooking duty in the first week. Even funnier was seeing him sneak around to look at his phone every hour. The resort had a no-phone policy, so we were only allowed to use them after 9 pm, and I don't think he'd ever gone a day in his life without it. But in the end, he gave up fighting it and had fun with the cooking and clearing his mind. We all fell into this comfortable rhythm, and I think it chilled him out more, made him take life less seriously. The same counts for me, I suppose."

"I could do with a break like that. I've always wanted to go to a place where nobody knows who I am. Somewhere I can just strike up a conversation with strangers, eat local food and explore without people whispering my name."

"I don't think there are many places in the world left where people don't know you. Maybe somewhere in the Amazon rainforest, or perhaps Inner Mongolia?" Cam chuckled. "Alaska?"

"That sounds good to me. Maybe after my next movie. Will you come with me?" Ella said it as a joke, but Cam sensed that she meant it.

She smiled, pulled Ella in and kissed her. "Sure. I'd love to come with you."

38

"Do you mind staying in tonight?" Ella asked after they'd returned and showered together. "I'd like to go for dinner, but I'm just worried about seeing my mom again. I don't know where she hangs out these days apart from in the Palm Garden, and I don't really want to risk it." She dried her hair, then twisted it into a large white towel and secured it onto her head. Cam came up behind her and shot her a flirty look in the mirror. She was still naked when she wrapped her arms around Ella's waist and kissed her neck. Ella stared at their reflection and smiled at how strange and wonderful it was to see herself like this, with another woman.

"Sure, let's stay in. Why don't you relax while I get some groceries or a take-out?"

"You just want to borrow my car," Ella teased.

"Maybe." Cam moved her mouth to Ella's ear, and Ella moaned when she bit her earlobe. "But borrowing your car isn't the first thing on my mind right now."

"Oh yeah? What's on your mind?" Ella whispered. She watched Cam untie her robe and open it. When she looked up, their eyes locked in their reflection as Cam ran her fingertips over her breasts, making her nipples harden.

"I want you to watch," Cam whispered back, her breath heavy against Ella's ear.

Ella nodded slowly; her eyes still locked with Cam's. Her body trembled with arousal as she lowered her gaze to Cam's hand on her breasts, clamping her tight against her chest. Cam's other hand traced her belly, down to the small patch of hair between her legs. Ella gasped when she grazed it with her fingers. She was so turned on that she didn't know what to say. Not that it mattered; Cam's hand running down through her swollen sex took away any logical thought in her brain, and she wouldn't be able to speak if she tried. Ella gazed at herself as Cam's hand cupped her center. "You drive me wild," she whispered, her breath catching at every word.

Slowly, Cam started massaging her, making circles with her fingers, right where Ella needed it. Her movements were so sensual and suggestive that Ella immediately felt tension building up between her legs. A carnal desire coursed through her as she rotated her hips, increasing the friction. Watching Cam do that to her was so sexy and erotic that she suddenly understood why people had mirrors in their bedrooms. Cam's eyes were dark and wild, and Ella could feel her breaths quicken against her neck and her ear as she shamelessly stared at their reflection. Cam's strong arm was still around her, caressing her breasts. Her other hand spread her open, before her fingers moved further down. Ella gasped and cried out, whimpering when Cam entered her. She bucked her hips, needing to feel her deeper. Her eyes focused on Cam's hand as she watched her fingers disappear inside her over and over until she fell over the edge, shuddering against her naked body. She let out a deep, delicious sigh, fell forward and steadied herself against the sink. A smile spread across her face when her eyes locked with Cam's in the mirror again.

Cam bent over her and smiled back. "Did you like that?"

Ella shook her head and chuckled. "Are you kidding me? I think I might be addicted to you."

Ella flattened the last cardboard box and shoved it behind the couch. She'd finished unpacking while Cam was shopping and cooking, and she'd found a lot of things she thought she'd lost; props from movies she'd done, her collection of favorite T-shirts, the water bottle she used to carry around everywhere, her old denim jacket, photo albums and dozens of pairs of shoes. It hadn't been easy when she'd stumbled upon some of Helena's boxes, but the more Ella unpacked, the easier it got, and she was glad she was finally able to face her belongings without being overwhelmed by sadness at the memories.

She looked around, trying to figure out why the house seemed so different tonight. There were pictures up on the walls now, and some of her awards were on display on the shelves. There were shoes in the hallway, coats on the hangers and throws and pillows on the chairs and the couch, and candleholders on the tables. But even though it looked a lot homelier now, that wasn't what made the difference. She turned to the dining table, where Cam had lit the candles she'd bought today. Music was playing softly in the background and there was a delicious smell in and around the kitchen.

"I see you found my Bluetooth speakers," she said, smiling at Cam who was singing along to a bossa nova style song.

"I did. I hope you don't mind." Cam didn't wait for an answer and handed her a glass of wine she'd just poured. "Here you go, princess."

"Thank you." Ella took a sip and her body flooded with warmth as she realized that Cam had brought the house back to life. The kitchen counter was full of plates filled with different tapas, and Cam moved around like she knew the space inside out already. Ella smiled at the sound of Cam's knife against the chopping board and the sizzling sound of garlic in the pan. When she looked outside, she saw something shimmering. "What's all this?" She walked out to the poolside, where Cam had set the terrace table. It was covered by a white cloth and decorated with more candles and a big vase filled with pink roses. She'd also found the switch to the tree lights, their soft light casting a romantic atmosphere over the back yard. "Cam, this is amazing."

"Did you say something?" Cam stuck her head around the door, then rushed to Ella when she saw tears trickling down her cheeks. "Hey, what's wrong?"

"Nothing's wrong." Ella flew around her neck and hugged her. "It's just so perfect and so sweet..."

Cam hugged her back, then lifted her up and spun her around, making Ella laugh again. "I just wanted to cook you a nice dinner," she said when she put her back down. She was pretty sure from Ella's reaction that she hadn't been wined and dined much in her life, at least not in the romantic sense. "And you deserve the world so please don't cry."

Ella wiped her cheeks and sat down when Cam pulled out a chair for her. "These past days have been the best and most exciting days of my life," she said, looking up at her. "So forgive me if I'm a little overwhelmed."

"I've really enjoyed them too," Cam said, as she kneeled down and kissed her. "And I can honestly say that no one's ever made me feel the way you do."

Ella swallowed hard and fell into Cam's embrace again. "I didn't even know this existed until two days ago. The feeling of being together, of being part of this wonderful intimate thing that two people share... I know I might sound naïve, but I had no idea how great it could feel."

"You're not naïve. You're far from naïve." Cam brushed fingers through Ella's hair. "I'm so lucky to have you."

Ella smiled. "You know, I was thinking that it's okay if you want to tell Vanya about us. Maybe not about how we met, but she's your best friend and I don't want you to feel like you have to lie to her."

"Are you sure about that?"

"Yeah. Vanya seems solid. If I were that close to someone, I'd want to tell them too, so go ahead."

"Okay. That will make things easier, I suppose. I was wondering about what I'd say to her when I get back tomorrow; I didn't give a reason for my vacation, so she'll have been brewing over it for days."

Ella laughed. "Then release her from her curious chains."

Cam nodded, relieved that Ella had brought it up. "I will." She looked over her shoulder and waggled her eyebrows at Ella as she walked back into the house. "Wait there. I'll bring the food out."

"That was the best meal I've had in years." Ella put her fork down and sat back, full and satisfied after hours of talking, eating, laughing and drinking. "I'm so glad we came here." She had a twinkle in her eyes as she said it.

"Me too." Cam smiled as she got up and walked around the table, then stood behind her, running her fingers through her hair. Ella's eyelashes fluttered at the touch. Everything was so intense with Cam; every touch so sensuous and tempting. She felt it everywhere; from her head to her toes as the light touch of her fingers spread out through her entire body. Cam's sultry voice echoed in her ear. "Do you want to go for a swim?"

"Yes." Ella stood up too, turned to face her and took off her dress. She watched Cam let out the breath she'd been holding, clearly excited at seeing her near-naked body. Ella unclipped her bra and let it fall to the ground too, then slowly lowered her panties, revealing her body that was glistening with sensual sweat. It was warm tonight, the temperatures reflecting the feverishness Ella felt inside. "You go in first. I'm still a little nervous around water," she whispered.

"Okay." Cam took off her T-shirt, equally slow before pulling down her shorts. Ella stared at her as she removed her underwear and gracefully dove into the water. When Cam resurfaced and swam toward her, her hair was slicked back and water was dripping down her face. She looked effortlessly sexy and totally irresistible as she steadied her elbows on the pool's edge and held out her hand. "Come here."

Ella lowered herself into the water while Cam's arms embraced her. She spun them around, pinned Cam against the pool wall and pressed herself against her body. She moaned softly, then gave her a seductive smile.

"Let's make the most of our last night, shall we?" Their moment was interrupted by a loud, raspy screech that made them turn around and look up at the house. Ella's heart started beating in her throat when she saw a red-tailed hawk, perched on the edge of the roof. "That's her," she whispered. "It must be her, she's about the same size and she's sitting in the same spot. So strange... she shouldn't even be active at night."

Cam followed Ella's gaze and felt a shiver run down her spine at seeing the majestic bird, her silhouette morphing when she spread her wings, as if announcing her return. There was another screech, before she settled and just sat there, looking at them.

"She's beautiful," Cam whispered. She expected the bird to fly away any minute, but it didn't. Ella put an arm around her neck and leaned on the edge of the pool next to her, resting her head on her shoulder, still and quiet.

39

"Do you want to go for a coffee before I drop you off at the yoga studio?" Ella asked as they were driving back into town. On their way home from Palm Springs, she'd been trying to come up with excuses to spend more time with Cam, feeling reluctant to say goodbye, and now she found herself slowing down as she neared a coffee shop close to Cam's studio.

Cam smiled as she looked at her watch and put a hand on Ella's thigh. "Sure. I've still got forty minutes; my class isn't until two." She was surprised Ella wanted to sit down somewhere public with her, but she suspected she was still on a high from the mostly private time they'd had in the past four days.

"Great." Ella turned into the small parking lot and skillfully maneuvered them into a shady spot before putting on her usual disguise, consisting of her cap and shades.

Cam put on her cap too, even though it was more out of habit now. "Why don't you sit down, and I'll get the coffees," she suggested.

"No, it's fine, I'll get them. Iced?" Ella shot Cam a sweet

smile when she nodded and walked in with a stride in her step while Cam found them a table. A trio of moms with prams at a nearby table whispered behind hands as they followed Ella with their eyes, then looked at Cam curiously. Cam pretended she hadn't seen them when she sat down, turning her gaze toward the sidewalk instead.

"Here you go." Ella put down two large iced coffees and sat down next to her. "That wasn't so bad. I don't think anyone recognized me," she whispered.

"Thanks." Cam decided not to tell her about the moms, who were looking at both of them now, not wanting to ruin Ella's good mood. She took a sip from her coffee and turned to her. "Thank you for a great break, Ella." She knew she had a goofy smile on her face but was unable to wipe it off. "And thank you for bringing me breakfast in bed," she added in a whisper. "That was super sweet."

"You're welcome." Ella's eyes sparkled with amusement. "And it was lovely of you to eat the scrambled eggs that tasted and looked like burnt rubber." She giggled quietly. "I'll get better, I promise."

"Are you kidding me? Those eggs were amazing. It was like you took cooking to a whole new level," Cam joked, keeping her voice down.

"Yeah, I think I might have invented a new building material." Ella sat back and sipped from her coffee. "So, what now? When will I see you again?" She looked at Cam, still mystified as to how she could make her feel this good. Her eyes shifted from the slight dimples in Cam's cheeks to her dark eyes and eyebrows, thinking she'd never seen anyone as gorgeous as her. She fought the urge to reach out and trace her sharp jawline and her mouth and imagined how Cam's lips would part if she brushed her thumb along her lower lip.

Cam chewed her straw, not sure if she should say what she was about to say. But she'd noticed the way Ella looked at her, and she was pretty sure she felt the same. "How about tonight? Do you want to come to my place?" She hesitated. "Unless you need some time to yourself or course..."

"No." Ella's face pulled into an even bigger smirk as she shook her head. "No, I don't need time to myself, and now that I'm not working, it's perfect timing."

"Alright then, I'll see you tonight. We can watch another episode of that series we started." Cam stopped Ella, as she was about to put a hand on her knee. "Don't, Ella. I think those women behind us might be talking about us."

"Oh." Ella retracted her hand and pulled her cap further down over her face instead. "Are you sure?"

"No, I'm not sure, but if they are, you might not want to do that."

"You're right. They probably are talking about me. I'd be surprised if I wasn't all over the tabloids today because of Tyler Kane's interview and being here with you is only adding to the general confusion. But you know what? I don't care all that much anymore. If people see us together, then so be it. There's nothing to talk about if we don't smooch each other's faces off." She rolled her eyes. "Well, that's not entirely true because they'll talk anyway but what I mean is that I don't care if they speculate."

"Good attitude," Cam agreed.

"Yeah, right? Do you think I should talk to Tom? Tell him about us?"

Cam shrugged. "That's up to you. Do you want to tell him?"

Ella sighed. "Jesus, now you sound like Theresa."

"Really? Fuck, I do sound like Theresa, don't I?" Cam laughed. "I meant it, though. You should only tell him if you're ready to tell him. But keep in mind that nothing is ever as bad as you think it is and he might be surprisingly supportive."

"Tom? Yeah, right." Ella let out a sarcastic chuckle, stood up and grabbed her coffee. "It's not exactly in his best financial interest if I tell him I'm gay." She hooked her arm into Cam's as they walked back to the car. "But you know what? I think I'm going to tell him anyway."

40

"Are you comfortable with the current situation?" Theresa asked after Ella had told her about her trip to Palm Springs and what had happened between her and Cam. She'd talked non-stop for twenty minutes, leaving very little out, including the run-in with her mother.

"Do you mean with Cam or with my mother?"

"Let's start with Cam." Theresa smiled.

"Okay... Yes, I'm comfortable with it." Ella shrugged. "I guess I've had my whole life to prepare myself for accepting my sexuality, it's not like I didn't know I was into women. But it was always only ever in my fantasies, and now that it's real, everything makes sense. *I* make sense. I feel..." she paused, taking a moment. "I feel so alive."

Theresa made a note, then looked up at her. "That's fantastic, Ella."

"Yeah. I feel like I was out of gas and someone filled my tank up and took me for a really fast spin. I'm still buzzing with adrenaline. I know it's very early days, and that anything could happen, but just the fact that I'm able to feel this much emotion gives me so much hope." Ella smiled. "I also feel like I finally need to make some decisions, although that thought's a little scary."

"Are you referring to coming out?"

"Yes."

"Does Cam want you to come out?"

"No." Ella waved a hand dismissively. "It's not like that. Cam's not pressuring me in any way, but I feel proud to be with her, so yeah, of course she has something to do with my change of heart. It felt so nice to be out in public with her. I think Helena's death has made me realize that life is unpredictable and that it can be over within a blink of an eye. I don't want to waste any more time living a lie." She took a deep breath. "I've decided I'm going to tell my manager."

"That's a big step. Good for you, Ella." Theresa glanced at Ella over the rim of her glasses. "You're doing well."

"Thank you. I think so too."

"And moving onto your mother; do you feel some issues have been resolved after your conversation with her? We agreed in one of our previous sessions that it might be good to talk to her so you could try to let go of some of your anger, but it doesn't sound like it was a very adult conversation."

"It wasn't; I was unprepared and furious."

"Do you blame her for Helena's death?"

"Is that what you think?" Ella asked, defensively. She realized her hands were balled into fists and her nails were digging into her skin.

"No, I'm asking you a question." Theresa wrote something down while she waited for Ella to answer.

"I want to blame her. Our mother just kept pushing Helena further and further toward something she didn't want and eventually, she pushed her away. If Helena hadn't been in New York at the time, she wouldn't have been in the bus accident, and everything would have been fine. Helena was in the wrong place at the wrong time, and our mother drove her there. She chose New York because she wanted to be far away from her and from LA." Ella sighed. "But at the same time, I know that in the end, it was a freak accident and of course my mother had nothing to do with it. If Helena hadn't chosen the front seat in that bus, she would still be here." She hesitated. "I also know that my mother is devastated and that she would do anything to turn back time, so no, as much as I want to blame her, I don't."

"Are you sure about that?"

"Yes." Ella hesitated, then let out a resolved sigh. "No, I'm not sure. Maybe some part of me does blame her, deep down."

Theresa simply nodded as if she already knew that.

41

"What's my girl been up to?" Vanya asked in a teasing tone. "I haven't seen you in forever, Cam." She spun around on her chair and rolled over to Cam's desk when Cam came in with a wide grin plastered over her face.

"It's been four days, Vanya. That's hardly forever." She rolled her eyes and laughed, then wiped her face with the towel that was hanging around her neck. She'd been so full of energy that she suspected she might have worked her students too hard. She didn't bother asking Vanya if she wanted coffee and put two cups under the machine. Vanya always wanted coffee, but for some reason, she hated making it herself.

"Whatever. Your phone was switched off, and you'd taken your mystery time off, so I want to know what you were up to. Unless you want me to guess?"

"No, I don't want you to guess." Cam couldn't suppress another smile as she handed Vanya a cup of black coffee and stirred some almond milk into her own brew. "Can we keep this between us?"

"This? The coffee, you mean?" Vanya faked ignorance as

she took a careful sip from her coffee. "It's good but not top-secret good."

Cam laughed. "This conversation."

"Of course, I'm sorry. Just excited that you're back, I've been talking to myself in here." Vanya's expression turned more serious now. "Well?"

"I was with Ella." Cam sat down behind her desk and put her feet up on the stool underneath as she switched on her laptop.

"I knew it." Vanya let out a little shriek of excitement and gave Cam a fist bump. "I knew it, I knew it, I knew it. You two did dirty things together, didn't you? Don't even answer that, I can tell by that look on your face."

"It's not like that. Ella's not a conquest. She's... really great and I care about her a lot. That's why this needs to stay between us."

Vanya nodded. "My lips are sealed." She sighed. "God, she's so beautiful. I bet she looks amazing naked."

Cam looked at Vanya and raised a brow. "How many times do I have to remind you that you're not gay?"

"You're right, I'm not. Just a little for Ella Temperley," she added with a cheeky grin. "So... what happened? I want the juicy details."

"We went to her place in Palm Springs, and we had an amazing time there." Cam felt like a teenager; her thoughts and feelings were all over the place, and she was restless and full of energy. She hadn't stopped thinking of Ella for a second since she'd dropped her off and she couldn't wait to see her again tonight.

Vanya studied her. "And? Details?"

"You're not getting any details, babe. That's it."

"Oh, come on. That's not fair. You have to give me something." Vanya rolled back to her own desk, hoping the distance might persuade Cam to spill a bit more. "What type of lingerie does she wear? Or does she even wear any? Did you have sex? You did, didn't you? How many times?"

Cam scrunched up a piece of paper from her notepad and threw it at Vanya. "Enough. Like I said, that's all you're getting. Now let's get back to work. I have another class to teach after I've checked my messages."

"Boring," Vanya protested. She managed to keep silent for a brief moment, then turned back to Cam again, her eyes widening as a thought struck her. "Oh my God, will you bring her to my wedding as a plus-one? That would be like the best wedding gift you could ever give me."

"No." Cam shot her an amused look. "Of course I'm not going to bring her to your wedding. Ella needs her privacy, especially after all the stuff they've been writing about her. How do you think she'll feel at a massive wedding where five-hundred people are trying to get a snapshot of her? Your mother-in-law would probably make her pose in between you and Greg in your wedding photos just so she can have a celebrity on her mantelpiece."

"But we're not having a massive wedding anymore," Vanya said, looking more than a little smug. "I took your advice and managed to secure a vineyard that I love, and they only take a hundred-and-twenty people for events, so we've disinvited everyone we don't know and told them the wedding was off. Same date, though." She rummaged through her bag, then walked over to Cam and handed her an envelope.

Cam was surprised as she opened it and studied the beautiful and simple new invitation with a black and white picture of Vanya and Greg on the front. It had a completely different look and feel from the original garish gold-rimmed invite inlaid with a picture that Vanya hated herself in. "This is really pretty. So you disinvited people? I bet Sour-Face wants to kill you right now."

"Uhuh. She does, but Greg and I both agreed that this is what we want, and I won't let her boss me around ever again. We've transferred the wedding fund back to his parents, then sent them the new invite." Vanya shrugged. "I know they'll come, regardless. He's their only son and I think Greg's father's realized that Sour-Face has been a little too intrusive in the past months. It's chaos, of course. No one's speaking to anyone right now, but I'm positive it will all work out in the end and that everyone we've invited will be there." She smiled. "And you know what? I'm not even dreading it anymore. In fact, I'm looking forward to it."

Cam stood up and gave Vanya a hug. "Good for you, babe. I'm proud of you for standing up for yourself." She grinned. "And I'm really excited to be there as your witness."

Vanya hugged her, then took a step back and gave her an intent stare. "So, will you bring her?"

Cam laughed and shook her head. "I don't know. I'll ask her but we haven't known each other for that long, and I don't know where this is heading."

"Oh, I can see where it's heading," Vanya was quick to say. "It's heading right into the sunset, surrounded by rose petals, rainbows, unicorns and pink Champagne. So, is she really gay? Who would have thought, huh?"

"I don't know," Cam lied. Telling Vanya about their status was one thing but talking about Ella's sexuality was another. "We have a special connection, but as I said, I don't know where it's heading." She grabbed a water bottle from under her desk and took a long gulp.

"Sure," Vanya grunted. "I'll try not to be too nosey." She lowered her voice as she picked up a magazine from her desk and waved it at Cam. "So, what about that Tyler Kane interview? Did she even date him at all, or did he make that up?"

"Of course he made it up. Ella would never go out with an idiot like him, but this is between us."

"Hmm... I thought so. I told Greg I didn't believe Ella Temperley would lower herself to date such a self-absorbed pig. She's too smart for that." Vanya looked up when someone knocked on the door. "Come in."

"Hey ladies!" Jason, from the juice bar, stuck his head around the corner and looked at Cam. "There's a man here to see you, Cam. Says he's interested in private lessons. I told him you're fully booked and that there's a waiting list, but he wouldn't give up. Do you have a minute for him?"

"Yeah, I'm coming." Cam stood up and followed Jason to the reception area, where a big, bearded man was waiting for her. He didn't look like a yoga enthusiast or someone who could even reach his toes, but Cam didn't care if he was a beginner. Everyone had to start somewhere, and she liked a challenge.

"Hi, I'm Cam Saunders," she said, shaking his hand as she sat down at his table.

"George Christopher." The man looked nervous as he shot her a quick glance before turning to his phone.

"Nice to meet you, George. I believe my colleague Jason already told you we have quite the waiting list here, but I'm happy to go over the program with you. Perhaps you'd like to know a little bit about the group classes instead? We'll be opening a second studio soon, so there will be spaces available again." Cam took a sip of her water.

"That would be great, Cam Saunders." George seemed like he was only half-listening, still focused on his phone. "Is it okay if I ask you a couple of questions first?"

"Sure, go ahead," Cam said, a little confused as to why he was addressing her with her full name.

"Thank you." George tilted his phone up toward Cam, then asked: "Are you in a sexual relationship with Ella Temperley?"

"What?" Cam frowned, not grasping the question at first as it was so unexpected. Then her eyes widened as she realized he was filming her.

"Are you in a sexual relationship with Ella Temperley?" George asked again.

"How dare you." Cam stood up and attempted to snatch the phone out of his hand, but George stood up too and held it over his head, taking a step back. Cam felt raging anger well up and had to force herself not to get physical with him because right now, she really wanted to punch him. *Not here, Cam. This is your yoga studio. No fighting here.* "Jason, will you please help me escort George out?" she yelled. "Although I doubt that's his real name." She took George's arm and pushed him toward the door.

Jason was there within seconds and took his other arm. "Is there a problem here?"

"Yes, there is. George is not welcome here. Not now, not ever."

"Hey, let me go, I can let myself out." George tried to wiggle himself out of their grip as they took him outside to the parking lot. "This is harassment, I was only making conversation, and you haven't even answered my question yet."

"No, what *you're* doing is harassment, George. Now give me that phone." Cam made sure to tighten her grip on him as much as she could while she tried to pull down his arm. He was not going to get away without at least a couple of bruises. She wanted to kick him in the balls, but by now, people were watching them from the reception area, and she knew it was best not to make a scene.

"Do you want me to floor him?" Jason asked, equally aware of their clients staring at them.

"No need, you can have my phone, George shouted. "I'll let you erase it if you just let me go. Please let me go. You're hurting me, dude." Then he turned to their audience and yelled: "Help me! They're hurting me!"

"It's fine, let him go," Cam finally said, hoping George would calm down. As soon as Jason let go of his arm though, George turned around and elbowed Cam in her shoulder. When she let go of his arm to grab her painful shoulder, he ran off.

"Fucker," Jason muttered before sprinting after him. Despite his size, George was fast and made it to his car before Jason could get a hold of him. He shot him a grin before he slammed the door shut and drove off with screeching tires.

"Are you okay?" Jason asked when he came back, panting.

"Yeah, I'm okay," Cam said, still shaken from the incident.

"I swear, I will track him down and kill him." Jason's hands were balled into fists.

"Don't bother, Jason. He might be the first, but I've got a feeling he won't be the last. From now on, send any new people to Vanya or tell them they'll have to wait for our second studio to open downtown."

"Okay." Jason hesitated as they walked back inside. "Was he here because of you and Ella Temperley?"

"Yeah." Cam decided to say no more.

42

"More headlines, Ella." Tom slammed the magazine down on his desk, frustration oozing from his every pore. "Is it really so hard to find another yoga teacher?" He pointed to the picture of Cam getting out of Ella's car in front of the studio. There were more pictures of them, one of them taken when they were having coffee together after returning from Palm Springs. It had been relatively quiet for two days, but the latest publications were full of new pictures and further speculations.

Ella looked at the picture taken outside the coffee shop and realized one of the women sitting behind them must have taken it and sold it. From the way Cam was whispering in her ear, it looked like she was about to kiss her. The picture didn't upset her; it looked sweet. But her anger rose when she turned the page and saw a shot of Cam on her own, walking into Pure Studio, clearly oblivious to whomever was shadowing her. *'THE WOMAN WHO SEDUCED ELLA TEMPERLEY'*, the headline said.

"Assholes," she muttered, furious that they'd been following Cam too.

"Assholes that can make or break your career," Tom said sharply. "I don't know why everyone is so obsessed with this lesbian storyline. Even Tyler Kane's interview didn't help much." He sighed. "And your booking agent called me this morning. He needs to know what the deal is because he wants to – and I quote – make sure he matches you with more 'appropriate projects'. Frankly, I think some people might find it riskier to sign you after this drama. Now, I know you don't want to hear this, but I'd really like to set you up with someone again, and I'd appreciate it if you didn't cause a scene this time."

"No." Ella shook her head and sat back, ignoring the rest of the magazines Tom shoved in her direction. "That's enough, Tom. I'm done playing games, and I'm certainly not going to find myself another yoga teacher."

Tom gave her a long, hard stare. "Ella, you're currently being considered for the leading role in one of the biggest movies on the production planning this year. Why on earth would you sabotage yourself like this?"

"Because it's true." Ella closed her eyes for a moment and rubbed her temple, bracing herself. "They're right. Cam and I are together. We weren't when they first started speculating about us, but we are now. She's the best thing that's happened to me in a long time, and I'm not going to disrespect her or myself by pretending I'm dating someone I'm not." She swallowed hard during the long silence that followed. "So yeah, I *am* gay. I always have been."

"What the hell..." Tom's face went pale, and his eyes started shifting in every direction but Ella's. She could almost hear him panicking, thinking about ways to solve the problem. "So you two are an item." Tom had always been a great problem solver, but of course, there was no solution this time. He couldn't wave his magic wand and un-gay her, and even if he could, Ella didn't want him to. He looked deflated as he sat back and fiddled with his pen. "Why didn't you tell me sooner?" he finally asked, his voice a little less harsh now.

"Would it have made a difference?"

"No," he admitted.

"I never told you because I've never met anyone special before." Ella wedged her shaking hands between her thighs. She was coming out to her manager of all people. "And now I have."

"Can you trust her?" Tom asked.

"With my life." Ella bit her lip as she realized the irony in that.

"Okay, in that case, we can buy some time. Keep it quiet until you've signed for that movie and then keep it quiet some more. We don't want to look like we only waited for the ink to dry until we make the announcement. In the meantime, I'll think about the best way for you to tell your fans. Maybe it's an interview, maybe it's social media, or maybe it's better to be discreet about it and let them speculate further." He sighed. "Or maybe it's best if you decide on the how and what yourself. It's your life after all and coming out is a very personal thing."

"You mean you don't think I should hide it?" Ella frowned. She wasn't sure what she'd expected, but it wasn't this.

"Hey, I might not like what you've just told me... purely from a commercial perspective," Tom added. "But I've worked for you for seven years, Ella, and I kind of consider you a friend, regardless of what you may think of me. I want you to be happy, and I certainly don't have a problem with the fact that you're gay, that would be absurd. I can't deny I expect it to affect your income though."

"I don't care if it affects my income," Ella said. "But I want to keep working, of course, and I feel like I'm ready to take some risks on film roles now and do something different. That blockbuster you keep mentioning… I'm not really interested in it. I know it pays well, and I know a lot of people will want to see it, but it's just another one in a long row of identical movies on my filmography. I've always wanted to try some more challenging roles and moving away from romantic comedy would give me the chance to prove that I can do that."

"Are you serious right now, Ella?" Tom looked even paler now. "Are you telling me you're gay *and* that you'd like to move away from romantic comedy, all at the same time?"

"I am," Ella simply said. "It feels like the right time. It only makes sense to move away from the kind of roles I've been playing. Soon, the whole world will know I'm into women, and if the general audience has a problem with me playing happily-ever-after-straight, and if I don't even care that much about playing those roles anymore, then why shouldn't I try something else?"

Tom sighed. "I suppose you have a point. But for that to happen, someone will have to offer you a serious role first." He thought about it for a moment. "You might be a star but casting you for any other kind of role is still a risk for indie filmmakers. And don't forget they'll assume they can't afford you."

"Then let them know I'm open to negotiations." Ella slammed her hand on the desk. "I'll go to auditions, just like everyone else. I'll sit in the long queue all day, every day, if I have to. I don't care."

Tom nodded as he studied Ella. "And you're sure about this?"

"Yeah, I'm sure." She reached into her purse and handed

him a file. "I've shortlisted some scripts that I'm interested in. If one of their casting teams wants me to audition, I'll drop everything and be there in a heartbeat."

"Very well." Tom cleared his throat. "You know, as your manager, I will always have your best interests at heart, and if this is what you truly want, then I'll do everything in my power to make it happen for you. I'll call your agent and I'll have a long, good talk with him." He sighed and shook his head. "It's not going to be easy for you, but please know that I'm always here if you want to talk. And if you want my advice... just live your life the way you want to and don't comment on anything until you're ready. When you are, then let me know if you need help."

"Thank you, Tom." Ella had been dreading this conversation, but now she felt as if a weight had been lifted from her shoulders. Maybe she had misjudged Tom after all. "It's good to know you're on my side."

"Hey, I'm your manager. What other side would I be on?" He stood up and walked Ella to the door. "I'll take a look at that list of yours and find out what I can about the projects. Expect a call back from me in a couple of days." He flinched when Ella flung her arms around his neck and gave him a hug as she stood on her tiptoes. He hugged her back, clearly a little uncomfortable with the sudden intimacy. There weren't many real hugs going around these days, especially not in Hollywood. But he smiled anyway as he tightened his grip around her. "You take care now, Ella. It's going to be fine."

43

"I'm sorry he harassed you." Ella studied the video, in which Cam was filmed close-up in her studio. They were looking at her phone in Cam's kitchen, both grimacing in disgust when she played it.

"Are you in a sexual relationship with Ella Temperley?" George's voice was loud and clear. After the question, there was a half-shot of Cam's face, taken from above. "Yes," Cam said, angrily. Then the clip was cut, before she finished her completely unrelated sentence.

By now, it had gone viral and even though Cam had tried to ignore it, she still kept getting messages from friends and family, asking her if she'd seen it and if it was true. Even cousins she hadn't spoken to in years suddenly seemed to have her number now.

"Don't be sorry, it's not your fault." Cam ran a hand through Ella's hair. "I'll just refrain from talking to strangers for a while."

Ella sighed. "They do this all the time. I never thought they would directly go after you like that... are you sure you're still okay with this?"

"Okay with what? With being in a sexual relationship with you?" Cam joked as she walked them toward the fridge and pushed Ella against it. "Yes," she said, pulling the same angry face she had in the video.

Ella laughed. "I'm glad you still find this funny. What I meant was, do you want to keep some distance for a couple of days, to let things cool down in the media? I'm afraid they might start tracking you too, now."

Cam ran her tongue over Ella's upper lip, then kissed her, long and slow. "No," she said when she pulled out of the kiss. "I don't want to keep any distance whatsoever. Do you?"

"Absolutely not." Ella's breathing was ragged now, and Cam could tell her actions had aroused her no end.

"Good. I like that answer." Cam gave her a mischievous smile. "Now, more importantly... have you ever been fucked hard against a fridge?"

"No..." Ella took in a quick breath when Cam lifted her dress and ran a hand over her waist before skimming her breasts. "I can't say I have." She paused, moaning when Cam unclipped her bra and pushed a hand underneath it. "But I'm open to new experiences."

Cam smiled against her lips as her thumb grazed Ella's nipple. "Turn around," she whispered.

Ella bit her lip and stared at her for a moment, a hazy look of desire burning in her gaze before she turned to face the fridge. Cam lifted her dress again and Ella gasped at the cold stainless steel surface against her belly and her breasts. Fridge magnets were poking into her skin, but she didn't care. Her body had processed the demand before her brain had, and she could feel the wetness spreading from her center. Cam's breath was heavy in her ear as she wrapped an arm around Ella's waist and slid her hand into the front of her panties. Her other hand disappeared into the back, caressing her ass before she slid it further down between her legs and pushed two fingers inside her.

"Oh God... yes..." Ella reached behind her and grabbed hold of Cam's hair as Cam filled her up while her other hand rubbed her clit, hard and fast. Cam retracted, then penetrated her deeper as Ella pushed back against her hand, letting her know she wanted more. "Faster," she panted. "Please take me, Cam." She braced herself for the storm of delight she knew was coming and tried to stay steady on her legs when Cam moved in and out of her faster, fucking her while she ran her fingers up and down through her folds, kissing and biting her neck and her earlobe until Ella turned into a moaning heap of pleasure.

Magnets, cards and paperwork fell to the floor, the sounds dampened by her whimpers. When she was close to climaxing, Cam cupped Ella's center hard and kept her fingers inside her while Ella thrust back on her hand. She cried out loudly and threw her head back against Cam's shoulder, shuddering in her strong grip. She fell forward, resting her forehead against the fridge as she recovered, taking long and deep breaths. "Shit, Cam, you're..." she fell silent when she failed to find the right word to describe how Cam made her feel and chuckled instead.

"What, was it bad?" Cam asked, smiling against her ear. She knew it wasn't bad; Cam was pretty confident with her women-pleasing skills, but Ella's reaction surprised her.

"No, no..." Ella laughed. "You certainly know how to cool a girl down, you're so amazing that I don't even have words for it. I just wish I could do that to you too. I don't have that much experience when it comes to sex and..."

Cam turned her around to face her. "But that's exactly what you do to me, Ella. You drive me insane. You blow my mind when you touch me. No one has ever come close to how my body reacts when we make love."

"Really?" Ella looked at her as her mouth pulled into a smile.

"Yeah, really. Haven't you noticed?" Ella's smile widened, and she was suddenly feeling a bit more confident. Yes, she'd noticed Cam's expression when they'd made love, and she'd felt her climax as if it was her own but hearing her say it was a different thing entirely. Deciding she was going to take charge, she put a hand on Cam's chest and pushed them in the direction of the couch.

"I guess I've noticed you like me touching you," she said as she took off Cam's T-shirt, as always, marveling at her tight abs.

Cam fell back into the pillows and groaned when Ella draped herself over her and tore off her sports bra. Within seconds, Ella's mouth was on her breasts, her tongue circling her nipples before she sucked and bit them softly. Cam fought the urge to close her eyes as euphoria washed over her, because she wanted to watch Ella. Ella's ponytail had come loose, and strands of hair were dangling in front of her face as her mouth travelled down Cam's stomach now. The spaghetti strap of her summer dress was hanging off her tanned shoulder, and she looked stunning as she kissed her way down Cam's body until she kneeled onto the floor and pulled down her yoga pants and panties. Cam swallowed hard. The excited glimmer in Ella's crystal blue eyes evoked her need even more as Ella put both hands on her knees, spread them apart and settled in between her legs.

"What are you..." Cam gasped when Ella's tongue traced her folds in a teasingly slow and seductive manner, then settled on her clit. She had to force herself not to let go yet, because the pleasure was almost more than she could take, and she wanted it to last. "Fuck, Ella..." She ran her hand through Ella's hair as her core tightened. Moaning louder, Cam bucked her hips against her mouth as endorphins rushed through her bloodstream. It felt so good that she was unable to keep her eyes open any longer, the pulsing ache between her legs begging for release. Closing them, she threw her head back against the couch's armrest and bit her knuckle, hot waves taking over.

When she came down from her climax, Ella's mouth was still on her center, kissing her. Cam looked down at her and chuckled.

"Believe me, you have nothing to be insecure about." She lifted Ella's chin to look at her, knowing she'd never get enough of those blue eyes.

"Good." Ella crawled up and straddled her, her dress barely clinging to her body now. "Because you're stuck with me." She shot Cam a grin and took her hands. "I told Tom about us."

"You did?"

"Yeah. He was trying to set me up again and I just couldn't take it anymore."

"Wow. I didn't expect you to do it so fast, but I'm proud of you." Cam laced her fingers through Ella's. "How did he react?"

"He was shocked, of course, but also surprisingly supportive as you already said he might be. I may have underestimated him; he was actually really nice about it once the panic settled. He told me to take my time and that he'd support me when I was ready." She paused for a moment. "The past weeks have been a rollercoaster and after my first night with you, I feel like a bomb has exploded. I have no choice now; I have to be honest with myself. Going on living the way I did just isn't an option anymore. I want to be open and free to do whatever I want."

"And what is it that you want?" Cam asked.

Ella didn't have to think about that because the answer was simple. "I want you," she whispered.

"And I want you too." Cam felt emotional as she pulled Ella into a tight hug and buried her face in her neck. It felt like the turning point she'd hoped for, but never expected to come.

"Let me clean up this mess." Ella bent down and picked up the magnets that had fallen and placed them back on the fridge door before gathering the other items that had found their way to the floor. "It's so cute that you have magnets."

"Really? A lot of people have magnets."

"No one that I know."

Cam laughed. "But I'm guessing the people you know take their private jets to exotic places whenever they want. You can't compare it to normal people getting excited about going somewhere."

Ella laughed too. "True. But you should know that I don't have a private jet and that I haven't actually travelled much at all. I mean, I've been to places, sure. But it was always for work and I never had much time to explore. It's something I'd really like to do more, make time for it, you know?" She narrowed her eyes as she noticed something on the top of the pile in her hands. "Hey, isn't this your friend Vanya?" She studied Vanya's wedding invitation as she put it back on Cam's fridge and secured it with a 'Paris' magnet. The invite was big and lavish, with gold foil boarders surrounding Vanya and Greg's engagement picture.

"Yeah, she's getting married next month. Her mother-in-law designed that invite. Their wedding was supposed to be a big deal with five-hundred people, but they've changed their minds about it and now they're having a more intimate one." Cam searched for the new invitation in her bag and handed it to Ella.

"Oh, that's a lot nicer." Ella chuckled. "I'm sorry, is it wrong to say that?"

Cam poured them both a glass of white wine and handed her one. "No, not at all, Vanya would agree with you. Greg is a great guy but she's a little less excited about her future mother-in-law, who picked that picture."

Ella laughed. "That bad, huh?"

"I don't know. Vanya tends to be a bit dramatic, but I've met the lady in question twice. She had me running around doing chores for her all afternoon on both occasions and I didn't dare say no, so I think she might have a point."

Ella opened the invite and read the details. "Who's your plus-one?"

"No one. I'm her witness and I'm going by myself." Cam leaned against the cooking island and took a sip of her wine. "Unless you would like to come? I mean, I don't want you to feel like you have to," she quickly added. "I'm just saying the invitation is open if you'd like to be my plus one."

"Really?" Ella bit her lip, a flush creeping onto her cheeks. "It looks like it will be an amazing wedding and... Well, since you and I are dating..." She hesitated. "Are we dating?"

Cam chuckled. "Do you want me to make it official?" She put her glass down and pulled Ella close. "Because I'd be very happy to call you my girlfriend."

Ella blushed even harder now as she brushed her lips against Cam's. "I like girlfriend."

"I like it too. And of course I'd love for you to come with me. I just assumed you wouldn't be comfortable with it. It's not a big wedding but it's still a crowd and people will take pictures."

"I'll be fine." Ella winced. "Unless Vanya doesn't want me to come, of course. I don't want to take the attention away from her on her big day." She shook her head. "I'm sorry, I should have thought of that before."

"Don't worry about Vanya. She's your biggest fan and she'd be over the moon to have you there. In fact, she practically begged me to bring you."

"Really?"

"Yeah. I was meaning to ask you, but you beat me to it. Vanya's got a pretty good poker face but still, it must have cost her at least five years of her life to contain her excitement when you walked into our office that morning." Cam laughed. "So yes, she'll be delighted if you come."

Ella reached up and ran a hand through Cam's hair. "Okay, in that case, I'd love to come with you."

"Great. I'll book a room for both of us, then." Cam picked up her phone and messaged Vanya, letting her know she was bringing a plus-one.

44

"Damn it. They're here." Ella looked out through the sliding doors. Down on the beach were two photographers with huge cameras, shamelessly staring up at her. One of them was scratching his crotch in the process. "Assholes."

"Who's here?" Cam brought her coffee over and followed Ella's gaze to the bottom steps leading up to the porch. "Oh... those guys. Didn't take them long to figure out where I lived, huh?"

"They're quite resourceful. I'm sorry."

"Don't be, it's not your fault." Cam closed her robe and adjusted Ella's robe too. "They won't be able to get any shots through the glass but it's annoying we can't just sit outside and have our coffee in peace."

"Welcome to my life." Ella turned to her. "I'm used to this, but you're not. And sure, they'll get bored of us eventually, but it will take weeks and that can seem like a lifetime when you're being watched twenty-four seven." She paused. "And believe me, when I come out, there will be twenty of them instead of two. It's only going to get worse."

Cam nodded as she thought it through. "You're right," she said as she wrapped her arms around Ella's waist from behind and kissed her on the cheek. "It is going to get worse, but nothing is going to keep me away from you, certainly not those rats. She hesitated for a moment, then let go of Ella, walked over to the kitchen and grabbed a dish towel. "You know what? Those pictures are worth nothing if our faces aren't in them." She cut out two small holes and placed it over her face, securing it with a piece of string. "We're going to attack them right back; see how they like it." She handed Ella another dish towel and mumbled behind the cloth: "Here. Make one for yourself too."

"Are you serious? What's the plan? We can't exactly hurt them."

"No, but we can hurt their cameras. And plain old simple water is perfect for that."

"Okay... It's unconventional and a little extreme." Ella laughed. "But it sounds entertaining to me." She took the dish towel and measured where her eyes would be. When their faces were covered and their disguise secured, Cam filled two large buckets of water and gave one to Ella.

"Remember," she said, "hold the bucket low. They won't see it until it's too late. They'll try to get a snapshot of us no matter what, even with our faces covered so they'll be looking up through their lens, not noticing what else is going on."

"Sure, let's do this." Ella laughed even harder now, feeling giddy at the prospect of finally getting back at the people who had made her life miserable over and over again. She loved how Cam was able to have fun with it, and even she herself was having fun with it now.

"We're not hurting anyone," Cam whispered as she opened the sliding doors. "It's just water but it will damage their precious cameras and besides, they're trespassing. That bottom step is mine and its within my rights to pour water over it whenever I please, wearing whatever the hell I want on my face. And I feel like right now is a great time to give the steps a good clean." Ella followed her as they walked toward the edge of the porch, right above where the two men were sitting. "Are you ready?"

Ella nodded. "I'm ready." They leaned over the railing, looking down at the confused photographers. They'd heard the sliding doors open and were now standing on the bottom steps, their lenses pointed skyward. One of the men frowned as he briefly looked over his camera and saw their dish towel covered faces, but by then it was too late to run, and two bucketloads of water came pouring down on them.

"Fucking bitches!" one of them cursed. The other one was too panicked to speak, frantically shaking his camera before he took off his T-shirt to wipe it dry.

Ella chuckled and snapped a picture of them on her phone. "I know I shouldn't lower myself to their game, but this is just too good not to go on Twitter. It's about time I got back on social media anyway; it's been over two-and-a-half years and I'm slowly losing followers."

They went inside to grab their coffees, then sat down on the porch and watched them leave. Ella uploaded the picture with the caption: '*Two down, thirty-eight more to go. #bringiton.*' Then she took a selfie of herself and Cam, their faces still covered by the dish towels, and uploaded that too before they took them off. '*#waterwarriors,*' she added.

"Are there really forty of them?" Cam asked, reading the post.

"More or less. The ones who work for magazines anyway. The freelancers are the worst and I have no idea how many of them are around. New faces keep popping up and I barely recognize them anymore. The freelancers are fearless because they have nothing to lose and everything to gain. They work for themselves so they can't get fired and they often wear a disguise so they can't get sued either. But the two down there just now have been pestering me for years and I can honestly say that I haven't felt this exhilarated in a long time." She put a hand on Cam's thigh. "Thank you, that was an excellent idea."

Cam smiled, leaned in and kissed her. "I'm glad I could be of help." She took a sip from her coffee and chuckled. "You know, there's more where that came from. We could order water guns, maybe even a water cannon if such a thing exists?"

Ella's eyes widened as she reached for her phone again. "Cam Saunders, you are a genius." She looked up water guns and they laughed as they searched for the most powerful ones they could buy.

Ella sighed when she put her phone away two hours later, after putting in her order. "I might as well have a bit of fun with it, right? Besides, my followers seem to love the tweet. It's gone viral already so hopefully the tabloids will have something else to write about other than my sexuality."

"I hate that it's so twisted in your business," Cam said, putting down two fresh cups of coffee.

"Yeah, me too. I want to be judged on my ability to act, not on who I sleep with. It shouldn't make a difference."

"But unfortunately, it does. Are you worried about your career?"

"A little. But a career means nothing if I can't be who I am and date who I want. I'm excited to try some new stuff, to venture into unknown territories. I want to play strong and exciting characters and to work on movies that make a difference. But above all that, I want to be with you, Cam. I'm crazy about you, so overall, I care a lot less about my career than I did before because it's not the only thing in my life anymore."

Cam felt a warmth spread through her at Ella's words. "I'm crazy about you too," she said in a whisper as their eyes locked. "But I don't want this to be a romanticized or spur of the moment idea because of the way we met. I want this to be real and lasting, uncontaminated by the fact that you're famous and that we're both women. We're stronger than anything together, and I know we can make this work, no matter what happens." She watched Ella's eyes fill with tears and smiled. "I'm here for you and it's going to be fine, I promise."

45

"Cam!" Vanya was shouting as she rang the doorbell three times before Cam had the chance to answer.

"Hey babe, what are you doing here?"

"I'm sorry, I know it's your day off." Vanya opened the door wider, letting herself in. "I just had to speak to you face to face, consider it a long lunch break."

"I don't care about when and how long your lunch breaks are, you know that." Cam glanced at her curiously. "Are you okay?"

"Yeah, I'm fine." Vanya looked around the room and lowered her voice. "Are you alone?"

"Yeah, why?" Cam studied her, mildly amused. She could tell it wasn't anything serious and besides, Vanya barged in like this on a regular basis. "Coffee?" She walked over to the coffee machine and made them both one.

"Thank you." Vanya took the mug and leaned over the kitchen counter, sighing dramatically as if she couldn't stand on her legs. "I'm really stressed right now, Cam. It's bad."

Cam took a sip of her coffee. "Stressed about what? Is it the wedding?"

"No. Actually, yes." Vanya looked up with mock-panic in her eyes. "Ella Temperley is coming to our wedding."

"I know. I thought you wanted me to bring her."

"I do!" Vanya's voice went up a notch. "But I never expected it to happen and now that you're actually bringing her, I'm terrified she won't have a good time."

Cam chuckled and gave her friend a hug. "Vanya, it's *your* day, not Ella's. She's just tagging along and if you don't feel comfortable with her being there, I'll tell her, and she'll understand."

"Nooo..." Vanya shook her head. "No, no, no, no, no. I want her to come but I feel this terrible pressure that I need to impress her. Do you not get that?"

Cam stared at her, trying really hard to put herself in Vanya's shoes. She realized that although Ella was just Ella to her, Vanya clearly had her on a pedestal, just like millions of other people in the world. "Would it make you feel better if you got to know her first? We could have dinner here, and you could bring Greg?"

"Really? Do you think she'll be up for that?"

"Yeah. Ella's at my place most nights anyway. I'm sure she'd love to get to know you both."

Vanya nodded slowly, as if she couldn't quite believe it. "That would help, I suppose..." She bit her lip and fiddled with her nose ring. "Okay. So, when are we going to do this? What do I wear? What do we bring?"

"How about Friday?" Cam suggested. "Ella isn't working but I'll check with her just in case and I'll let you know by tonight. No need to bring anything."

"Friday works for us." They both turned to the door as it opened.

"Honey, I'm home," Ella sang as she walked in with an enormous cardboard box. "The webstore we ordered from couldn't deliver this week, so Raphael and I went to pick up the toys at the store. I can't wait for you to see them." She plonked down her goods, then looked up in surprise when she saw Vanya. "Oh, hi there. It's Vanya, right?" She walked over to Vanya, who stood nailed to the ground, and gave her a kiss on each cheek. "It's nice to see you again. I hope Cam told you I borrowed some of your yoga clothes. Did you get them back? I really hope you didn't mind."

Vanya pulled herself together and smiled, suddenly remembering Ella had asked her a question and she was supposed to answer back. "No, I didn't mind at all. Did you enjoy the class?"

"Yeah, I did. Cam put me on the waiting list, so I'll be able to join once all the craziness goes away." Ella shrugged. "You know what I mean."

"I just invited Vanya and Greg over for dinner on Friday," Cam interrupted them, noting that Vanya was about to faint, although she was pretty good at hiding her excitement. "Are you free, Ella?"

"Yes, I'm free. That sounds like fun." Ella gave Vanya a big smile as she tugged at the neckline of her T-shirt while fanning her face with her other hand. "It's so warm outside. I've been sweating like a pig trying to get that box out of the car and I really need a shower. So I'll see you on Friday then?" She walked off toward the bathroom, leaving a baffled Vanya behind. "Looking forward to it!"

"Me too!" Vanya yelled after her, then turned to Cam. "Oh my God, she's really nice... just like a real person."

"Vanya, she *is* a real person." Cam laughed and finished the last of her coffee as she walked Vanya back to the door, subtly sending her on her way so she could get under the shower with Ella. "So, Friday, let's say seven-thirty? Oh, and needless to say, tell Greg to keep this between us."

"We'll be here, and I'll tell him." Vanya frowned as she glanced at the box in the kitchen and wiggled her finger at it, her face and neck covered in red blotches. "Are those... sex toys?" she whispered.

"What?" Cam fell silent for a moment, processing the question as it suddenly clicked that Ella had used the word 'toys'. The box was big enough to hold a small fridge and the thought of it being filled with sex toys amused her to no end. "Oh those," she said, shooting Vanya a playful wink as she opened the door. "Yes, they are. Lots and lots of sex toys."

46

"How do I look?" Ella straightened her black cocktail dress in front of the mirror in Cam's bedroom. "I feel like it's too formal."

Cam closed the drawer she was looking through and turned to her. "You look gorgeous, as always."

"Are you sure? Should I wear something more casual?"

"It doesn't matter." Cam sat down on the bed and pulled Ella onto her lap. "You're you and you're beautiful. It makes no difference what you wear."

"Yeah, but I'm about to meet your best friend and her future husband properly for the first time and I have zero experience with private, social interactions. I'm fucking nervous Cam, so help me out here." Ella sighed. "I've never been to a small dinner party and I've never met a best friend."

Cam kissed Ella and ran a hand through her hair. "Believe me, if you could see Vanya right now, you wouldn't feel nervous. My guess is she's already had two panic attacks just at the thought of having dinner with you tonight."

"Well, the feeling is mutual." Ella pouted her lips and

sighed in defeat. "I think I might change into something else anyway. Give me a shout if you need help with dinner."

"Thank you so much for having us over." Vanya walked into Cam's living room with Greg on her arm, scanned the room for Ella and lowered her voice. "Where is she? I felt like a celebrity walking in here. There are three paparazzi parked out front."

Cam shrugged and gave Vanya a kiss on her cheek. "Yeah, there are two down on the beach too, so I thought it best if we ate inside. Ella's just getting dressed." She didn't mention that Ella had already changed her outfit five times and turned to Greg instead. "Greg, my man. How are you?"

"Always good seeing you, Cam." He gave her a hug. "And it smells amazing as always."

"Thanks. Hope it will taste good too." Cam pulled out a seat for him and Vanya at the dining table and handed Greg a bottle of cool white wine to open and pour. He was dressed casually, in jeans and a white linen shirt. Vanya looked casual too in a denim dress, but Cam could tell she'd put a lot of effort into her hair and make-up. She'd put on a pair of jeans and a white shirt herself. It was still hanging half-open from her last make-out session with Ella, so she quickly buttoned it up. She turned at the sound of the bedroom door closing. "There you are." Her heart skipped a beat as Ella walked in and smiled at her. She'd gotten changed again, into a knee length white cotton dress and a gray cardigan this time. She was barefoot and looked angelic with her hair loose, only a thin silver chain with a pearl droplet framing her neck.

"Hi Vanya, it's nice to see you again." Ella walked over to

Vanya and gave her a hug. “And you must be Greg, it’s great to meet you.”

“Likewise.” Greg looked a little taken aback. “I honestly thought it was some practical joke at first when Vanya told me we were going to have dinner with you, and I certainly didn’t believe her when she told me you were Cam’s plus one at our wedding.” He frowned and looked from Cam to Ella and back. “But I guess I was wrong. So, you two really are together?”

“Off the record....” Ella put an arm around Cam. “Yes, we are.” She shot Cam a sweet smile as she looked up at her. “Do you need help with the food?”

“No, I’ve got everything under control. Why don’t you sit down? I’ll be five minutes.” Cam walked back to her cooking island, feeling happy at the instant chatter she heard. Ella seemed to have no problem finding things to talk about and Vanya had managed to keep her cool yet again.

She started plating vegetarian antipasti onto a big, wooden tray: chunky pieces of marinated mozzarella, big slices of ripe tomato, fresh basil, meaty Kalamata olives and grilled artichokes with parmesan oil and black pepper. She placed it on the table alongside fresh rosemary ciabatta and a bottle of olive oil. Then she opened the doors to the porch, letting in the sea breeze, put on some bossa nova music and placed the speaker outside.

“Why did you just put that outside?” Greg asked.

“So the paps down on the beach won’t be able to overhear our conversations.” Cam explained. “We’ve become quite inventive over the past week and we’re even having fun with it now.”

“Oh my God, I saw your tweet and it made me laugh so hard,” Vanya said turning to Ella. “Did you guys really throw water over them?”

"We did. And they haven't been back. But there are new ones, of course. There are always new ones." Ella pointed to the porch. "We've also covered the porch railing with a Goodwill banner so even if they do manage to get a snapshot, at least a charity will get some visibility. We can change it to something else next week if you have a cause that you're passionate about."

"Clever." Vanya laughed. "Perhaps you could put our wedding announcement up there?" she joked. "I've always wanted to be famous." She shook her head and composed herself when Greg nudged her. "Just kidding, it must be really annoying having them there all the time."

Ella laughed too. "I'm used to it, but Cam's not, so we're trying to keep our privacy as much as we can. They don't know anything apart from that we're spending a lot of time together and it's best if we keep it that way, just for now. But you know, a little prank now and then never hurt anyone." Her mouth pulled into a smirk. "Were you serious about the wedding announcement? Because we could totally do that."

"Ella?!" Cam, who had sat down next to her, almost choked on an olive as she broke into laughter. "That's just weird."

Ella shrugged. "Who cares? Vanya wants to be famous, if only for a day or two and believe me, that's more than enough," she added, taking a sip of her wine. "Why not mess with them a little more? They'll be totally confused down there." She pointed in the general direction of the beach where the paparazzi was holding up.

"I'm in," Vanya said, barely able to contain her excitement. "And so is Greg."

Greg rolled his eyes. "Since when do you speak for me?"

"Since we're getting married in three weeks. I'll be stuck

with your mother for the rest of my life, so it's the very least you can do." Vanya batted her eyelashes at him.

"Fair enough. Can't argue with that," Greg said, holding up a hand.

"Alright then," Cam chuckled, pleasantly surprised with the amusing turn the conversation had taken. "A banner it is. Our wedding gift to you. But I can't promise you it will reach the tabloids; I'm not sure if there will be much general interest in the wedding announcement of a yoga studio manager."

"Maybe not, but I have an idea for some after dinner entertainment that might help on that front," Ella said with a mischievous look on her face. "First, food though. I love Cam's cooking, don't you?"

Vanya and Greg both nodded. "The best," they said in unison.

"Save some room for the main course." Cam passed the board around and sliced the bread. She'd been a little nervous for tonight, but she was having fun now, and she could tell Ella was too. She put a hand on her thigh and Ella covered it with her own as she shot her a loving look.

Vanya, who had witnessed the moment of affection, was intrigued. "So how did you guys meet, Ella? Cam told me you met on the beach but surely there must be more to the story than just that? I mean, you guys run in different circles entirely and the chances of you two striking up a conversation and staying in contact, well, I'd say they're quite small, right?"

Ella thought carefully about her answer. She didn't want to ruin the good vibe by telling Vanya the truth, but she didn't want to lie either. So, she stuck with the story Cam had already told Vanya.

"There really isn't much to say. It started raining, I got

wet and Cam offered me a towel and some dry clothes to go home in. That's all, nothing romantic. I brought them back the next day and we had a nice talk, so I gave her my number. Then we became friends and eventually, we discovered we had feelings for each other." It didn't feel right to reduce the complex and beautiful relationship they had to a couple of sentences, but it would have to do, at least for now. "What about you guys?" she asked with genuine interest, changing the subject. "I heard you met in Goa. Tell me about it."

"Are you ready for some fun?" Ella handed Cam and Greg cut-outs of Vanya's face that she'd printed out after dinner. She'd poked the eyes out and stuck rubber bands to the sides.

"I can't believe I'm doing this," Greg said as he covered his face with the DIY mask and secured the bands behind his ears. "I'm a grown-ass man with a very grown-ass job and this is seriously juvenile."

"Oh come on Greg, it will be fun." Vanya, who was the only one not wearing a mask, studied the selection of NERF Super Soaker guns in the big box. "Christ Ella, you must have spent a fortune on these. They even have..." She looked over the box again, then broke into laughter. "I get it now. The toys, huh?"

Cam nodded and shot her a cheeky smile. "Best toys in the world."

"Amazing air pressure too," Greg added as he tested one of them in the sink, suddenly a little more interested in the plan. "And a battery powered pump, that's insane."

"Yep. They weren't cheap." Ella winked. "But they do have a hundred-foot reach." She gave Greg an approving nod when he took his pick, a little giddy and tipsy from the wine. “Good choice. Excellent grip, powerful blast and it looks pretty cool too,” she joked as she handed him the gun. She chose a smaller gun for herself so she could film during the attack. Then she put her phone on a selfie stick and took a picture of them with their masks and multicolored weapons. ‘*Ready for battle. #bringiton,*’ she tweeted along with their picture.

“Wait, we’ll need this too,” Greg said, feeling all riled up now and ready for a fight. He had a boyish grin on his face as he scrolled through Cam’s phone and put on the Ghostbusters theme song, causing all three photographers to look up as they crossed the porch and leaned over the railing, blasting water at them. There was cursing and screaming as they threw themselves over their cameras to protect them and crawled around the corner. A couple of teenagers on the beach were filming the photographers. When they were out of sight, they pointed their phones up to the four people on the porch who all looked like Vanya, including the real Vanya, waving their water guns in the air and celebrating the victory.

It was after midnight by the time Vanya and Greg had left. Cam couldn’t recall a night she’d ever laughed so much, and Ella was still grinning too as she closed the door after saying their goodbyes.

“That was so much fun.” Ella wrapped her arms around Cam’s waist and kissed her. “Is this what normal people do? Eat, talk and laugh without showing off or trying to outdo each another?”

“Pretty much.” Cam kissed her back. “I’m glad you had a good time.”

"Yeah, we should totally do this again and I'm really looking forward to the wedding now." They walked back to the couch, a little drunk from all the wine they'd consumed. Cam fell back into the pillows and Ella lay down with her head on Cam's lap, her legs dangling over the couch's armrest. She reached for her phone on the coffee table, curious as it kept lighting up. "Oh my God. I've got over half a million likes already." She sat up and frowned, scrolling through her notifications. "This is crazy. Look."

Cam took her phone and studied the tweet, of which the re-tweets were growing by the second. "Looks like people think it's funny and *#waterwarriors* is actually a thing now." She chuckled as she scrolled further down. "Here's a video one of those kids took, down on the beach." She showed it to Ella, and they laughed as they watched themselves, holding their water guns up with Vanya masks on. "Everyone is asking who the woman in the video is. I think Vanya might be getting more attention than she bargained for."

"I'm sorry, it's my fault." Ella winced. "I didn't expect it to go viral and I may have gotten a bit carried away."

"Don't worry about it, it's fine." Cam chuckled as she bent over and placed a kiss on Ella's forehead. "Thank you for giving my friend the best night of her life. I don't think Vanya will ever stop talking about this."

47

"I have three words for you. Best. Night. Ever." Vanya put a gift bag on Cam's desk and shot her a smirk. "And thank you to you both for making me go viral on Twitter."

"Oh yeah, how is that going?"

"Still trending." Vanya grinned. "I actually feel a little famous now. Anyway, I got you and Ella a present."

"Babe, you shouldn't have." Cam blew her a kiss. "You know you and Greg are always welcome, and yes, it was fun. Ella had a great time too."

"I'm glad she did. She's really lovely." Vanya pointed to the bag. "Open it."

Cam smiled as she took out two beautiful white cotton robes with her and Ella's initials embroidered on the pocket. "Thank you. They're lovely, it's so sweet of you." She frowned at the thoughtful gift. "When did you have them made?"

"Yesterday, after work. There's this amazing shop in Santa Monica that customizes on the spot. They even give you a glass of bubbly while you wait."

"They look expensive. You didn't have to do that."

"Of course I did. I had such a wonderful night and besides, you both need something to wear when you get dolled up for all those public events you'll be attending together. You can't possibly let Ella wear your tatty old robe?" Vanya lowered her voice. "I saw this really amazing hairbrush in the bathroom and an eyelash curler I've been coveting up for a while now, so I know Ella has good taste." She lifted a finger, stopping Cam from getting a word in. "By the way, has she moved in with you? I figured she had, since I saw your whole bathroom cabinet was full of her stuff. Oh, and let's not forget the huge pile of clothes and lingerie on your bed because they were definitely not yours."

"Why were you in our... I mean, *my* bedroom?" Cam asked, correcting herself.

"Sorry. Just gave myself a tour of the house after I'd been to the bathroom." Vanya shrugged. "I was a little tipsy, so I got nosey."

"Tipsy has nothing to do with it, you're always nosey."

"Okay fair enough, I'll admit, I am nosey. But you still haven't answered my question."

"Of course she hasn't moved in," Cam said, putting her feet up on the desk. "We've only been together for three weeks, it's early days. Besides, Ella's got a bad-ass penthouse in Hollywood and a villa in Palm Springs. Why the hell would she want to move in with me?" She realized it was actually nice to be able to discuss her relationship with Vanya, now that she didn't have to lie to her.

"Yeah, that's a good point." Vanya thought about it for a moment. "So will you be moving in with *her*?"

Cam rolled her eyes. "Give it up, Vanya. No one is moving in with anyone yet. And if or when it gets to that point, we'll figure something out. Ella usually stays at my place because she loves the view and she likes to do yoga with me in the mornings and right now, we're happy the way we are."

"Yeah, but you must have thought about what's going to happen long-term."

"Not really, Cam admitted." She'd been so caught up in their little bubble that she was simply enjoying spending time with Ella.

"Seriously?" Vanya pulled her dramatic face again. "Well then you need to start thinking about it, babe. If Ella comes out and makes it official, and you're going to be living together, your life is going to change big time. You'll have staff; cleaners and maybe even a driver, and don't forget, most people will know your name and you might even get crazy fans of your own. Your privacy will be out of the window and you'll be way more isolated in your relationship with her than you would if you'd just been dating some anonymous woman. You may never be able to go shopping together or go for a walk along the beach or have lunch in a popular restaurant, so you can say goodbye to your favorite taco stand, at least when you're with her." Her voice went up a notch as she continued: You'll be publicly scrutinized over everything you do while you're at Ella's side, not to mention, you'll have to cope with all the women who will throw themselves at her. Then, there will be the tabloids of course, selling stories implying one or both of you are cheating on the other... I could go on and on."

"You've obviously given this much more thought than me." Cam let out a deep sigh and sank further down in her chair. "Well, Ella doesn't have a driver and I actually wouldn't mind having a cleaner. Besides that, no one will be interested in me. I'm just her girlfriend and if crazy fans are throwing themselves at her, I've got nothing to be jealous about. Ella's been in the business her whole life, she knows how to deal with them." She hesitated. "I suppose I've had to make some small changes, like moving my morning yoga session to the porch and keeping my sidewalk-facing blinds down but that's hardly a sacrifice and as far as the tabloids are concerned, I don't read them. And about the tacos..." She smiled. "If it's Ella or tacos, I'll quite happily never eat another taco in my life."

Vanya sat down on Cam's desk and took her hand. "You're right. I didn't mean to sound negative; you know I'm the biggest advocate for your relationship. I'm just super protective of you. Not in relation to Ella of course, I worship the ground she walks on... but from everything that comes with her."

"I know and that's sweet, but you don't need to worry about me. I can handle it. I'm here most days anyway and with the new key-card system, no one who isn't welcome will be able to get in."

"True, but there will be more drastic changes than that here, too." Vanya switched to her business voice now. "And I mean that in a good way. We'll get more famous clients in here as well as in our new studio, just by association, which means we'll need more security. And I haven't even told you yet that our waiting list has tripled within a week. It's crazy."

"Tripled?" Cam gasped. "Jesus, we'd better get on with the new studio and make a decision then." She opened the file on her desk, containing the details of the potential spaces they'd looked at. "I know the lease is high, but I really like the one with the roof terrace. You?"

"Me too." Vanya agreed. "And with so much traction, we

should put the membership price up for this one and make it a little smarter, so people get what they pay for. That will cover the higher rent and maybe give us a buffer to start a third one down the line."

"A third one? Jesus, you're on fire, Vanya." Cam held up the brochure and smiled. "Okay, let's do it. Are you up for being my business partner?"

"Business partner?" Vanya stared at her. "You mean as in official partner?"

"Yeah. You told me last year that you wanted in financially and now that we're opening a second studio and as you just said, maybe even a third down the line, you won't be able to manage all of them." Cam's smile widened, knowing she was going to make Vanya very happy. "So, we'll need new managers, which will give you the opportunity to deal with the bigger picture and, as discussed, I'll sell you twenty percent of the company before we expand so you can enjoy the fruits of your labor. I'll even throw in five percent for free on top which you can consider a bonus for being so amazing all these years. How's that? Is Greg still okay with lending you the money?" Her chair almost tipped over when Vanya flew around her neck. "I take it that's a yes?"

"Yes! Of course it's a yes." Vanya bit her lip, for once lost for words. "Oh my God, this is so exciting, I can't wait to tell Greg. Thank you, Cam, I really needed a challenge."

"I know you did. And I've been wanting to offer you this for a while, but I was waiting to see what our options were in terms of expansion first. I'm sorry it took so long." She tore herself away from Vanya, who was almost strangling her with her hug. "You said you were bored. Is going viral on social media and having your own business in one week enough excitement for you?"

"Definitely enough excitement." Vanya was beaming. "Oh my God, I'm getting a new job title now, right?"

"Yeah, take your pick." Cam laughed at her friend's enthusiasm. "As long as it's not princess president or global chairwoman or something crazy like that, I'm open to suggestions."

48

Ella walked out of the audition with a stride in her step. She'd been terribly nervous today but the fact that it had all happened very last-minute had made it a little easier. She hadn't auditioned in so long that she'd forgotten what it felt like to have sleepless nights over a part. And she really wanted this one.

The leading role was based on a recovering heroin addict who tries to redeem herself by devoting her life to helping other addicts get clean. The part was both challenging and exciting. She had to hand it to Tom – he had really gone to great lengths to get this audition for her. Audition requests regarding the scripts that Ella had shortlisted had started to come in only a week after their conversation and here she was, twelve days later.

She got into her SUV and turned the music up as she drove away from the hotel in Bel-Air where she'd just given the performance of her life. Despite the heavy traffic, she enjoyed driving through LA today. She rolled down her window to let the sun in and took a deep, long breath. Just the thought of seeing Cam soon made her smile. She'd spent the night in her own apartment, preparing for the audition and she'd missed not only Cam, but also the cozy beach house, and waking up to the smell and the sound of the ocean.

It was strange to have a break from work, but she liked it. She was looking forward to checking out the mental-health facility she'd recently sponsored and talking to the therapists and the volunteers who were due to come together for the pre-opening meeting at the new walk-in center tomorrow. She dialed Raphael's number and he immediately picked up.

"Hey there. Are we all set for tomorrow?"

"Hey Ella. Yes, all done. Are you still okay for me to pick you up at ten?"

"Absolutely. Thank you for sorting out the rest of the computers and phones. Do they have everything they need?"

"Everything they need and more. So, am I picking you up from your apartment or will you be at your friend's house?" For the first time, Raphael's tone was a little teasing as he said it.

"I'll be at Cam's. And she's my girlfriend," Ella added with a grin.

"Oh, okay." Raphael chuckled. "I had a feeling she was, but I didn't want to make assumptions."

"It's fine. Thank you for being so discreet about it." Ella smiled, color creeping to her cheeks. "Sorry, I forgot to text you her address, I'll do that now." Her phone lit up, showing an incoming call from Tom. "I've got to go, Tom's calling. See you tomorrow!" Ella accepted the phone call and waited for Tom to speak.

"Ella."

"Tom." She mimicked his serious business tone, feeling a little giddy.

Tom cleared his throat. "Are you making fun of me?"

"Never. What's up?"

"Well, I have good news for you." Tom didn't sound too excited, but then he never did. "I just got off the phone from the casting director of *Reva's Battle*. He didn't want to tell you until he'd given everyone a fair chance, but he said they knew the moment you auditioned that you were the right one for the role. They want you for the movie, Ella. Apparently, you make a convincing Reva."

Ella didn't say anything, too baffled to speak. Her hands were trembling on the steering wheel and her heart was beating out of her chest.

"Ella? Are you still there?"

"Yeah, I'm here. I just can't believe it." She let out a loud victory cry, releasing all the pent-up energy she'd been carrying around today, then laughed out loud. "Oh my God, I am so happy right now."

"Don't celebrate just yet. They have a couple of conditions before you sign." Tom paused. "They want to cut your hair. Short-ish and choppy, they said, whatever that means. I don't expect it to be pretty. They also want you to put on weight for the final scenes."

"Sure, no problem," Ella was quick to say. "Anything else?"

"No, that's it. So... you're okay with doing that?" Tom sounded surprised at how easy she had accepted the deal after pestering her for months about other roles.

"Of course. Sounds to me like you're the one who's got a problem with it."

"No, I don't have a problem. I'm happy you got the role you wanted." Tom sighed in defeat, clearly realizing he was fighting a losing battle. His American sweetheart was slowly evaporating before him, morphing into something far less predictable and commercial. "Congratulations, Ella. I'll forward you the details. Enjoy the celebrations."

49

"Hey. How did your audition go?" Cam looked up from her laptop when Ella came home.

Ella threw her purse on the couch, walked over to Cam and kissed her neck and her cheek until Cam turned around in her chair and pulled her onto her lap.

"It went well, actually." Ella brushed her lips against Cam's, then kissed her slow and deep. "Really well," she continued.

"Really? That's great." Cam ran a hand through her hair.

"Yeah. I was so nervous. As I told you, I haven't auditioned in years, but I was well prepared, and they liked it. The casting director said she was surprised that I pulled it off."

"That means you stand a good chance of getting the role, right?"

Ella grinned as she waved her phone in the air. "Tom called me when I was on my way back. I've got the role!"

Cam gasped. "Congratulations! That was your first choice, right? The one playing a recovering heroin addict?"

"Yeah." Ella chuckled. "Never thought I'd be playing one but here I am."

"I'm so proud of you!" Cam stood up, lifted Ella up in the process, and spun her around a couple of times before sitting back down. "When do you start filming?"

"In three months, which should give me more than enough time to prepare. We're filming in LA mostly and a couple of weeks in Mexico. I'm so excited. The director is really talented and there's a mix of some super interesting and upcoming actors who have already signed up for it." Ella stood up, walked to the fridge and pulled out a bottle of Champagne that they'd brought back from their Palm Springs break. "We should celebrate." Her smile was giddy as she opened it, poured two glasses and handed one to Cam before sitting back down on her lap.

"Cheers to you." Cam clinked her glass with Ella's and took a sip, then kissed her again.

"Cheers to me." Ella turned to Cam's laptop. "So, what are you up to?"

"I'm just finalizing some paperwork with my lawyer. Vanya's now officially co-owner of Pure Studio and we signed the lease for our second location today." Cam pressed send on her email and closed her laptop, grinning from ear to ear. She was happy with the arrangement, and even happier that she was finally able to reward Vanya for all her hard work.

"Oh God, I forgot that was today. That means congratulations to you too, hot yoga teacher, slash multiple business owner, girlfriend." Ella shot her a flirty look. "We should definitely celebrate now."

"What did you have in mind?" Cam lifted the hem of Ella's navy silk top and ran a hand over her back. "Do you want to go out?"

Ella shivered at the touch. "No..." Her eyes were filled with desire as she leaned in and brushed her lips over Cam's. "I want to go to bed."

"Here you go." Cam closed her robe before she walked out onto the porch with two mugs of chamomile tea. It was almost midnight and the beach was deserted. The paparazzi hadn't been there in two days, which had enabled them to sit outside more. The night was dark, and the calm crashing sound of the waves was so soothing that she hadn't bothered putting music on. She loved it here, and she loved having Ella here too. By now, it felt so natural that she couldn't imagine her life without her anymore. They hadn't spoken about formal arrangements. Instead, Ella had slowly brought more and more of her clothes, shoes and toiletries over, discreetly placing them on one of the less overfull shelves in Cam's closet. Cam put her feet up on the porch railing, blissfully relaxed and happy after two hours of 'celebrating' in bed.

"Thank you," Ella said in a sweet voice. She took a careful sip of her tea. "You know, I forgot to mention that the premiere of *Spring's Promise* is in three weeks' time."

Cam furrowed her brows, mentally scrolling through the projects Ella had told her about. "Is that the one you finished last year? The seriously soppy one about the undercover princess?"

Ella chuckled. "Yeah. It's not my proudest work but I expect it to be a success and I was wondering if you'd like to be my plus-one?"

"Your plus-one? As in your date?" Cam stared at Ella in surprise. "It's a massive event, Ella. You know that bringing me as your date would confirm the gossip, right?"

"I know." Ella took Cam's hand and kissed it. "But it's time."

"Okay… in that case, of course I'll come with you. It would be my honor." She grinned. "But I'm not wearing a dress."

"You don't have to wear a dress. I can ask one of the stylists I work with to arrange a really nice tux for you if you want?" Ella suggested. "But you have to stop giving me that sexy smile because it just makes me want to jump you all over again and I can't even think straight." She felt another surge of arousal at the sparkle in Cam's eyes when she reached out and put a hand on her thigh. "What's this?" she asked when she felt something in the pocket of Cam's robe.

"Oh, I forgot. This was on the doormat just now." Cam fished an envelope out of her pocket and handed it to her.

Ella frowned. "That's strange. My post usually goes to my apartment, or to Tom."

"I didn't see it earlier and there's no stamp. Someone must have dropped it off."

"Hmm…" Ella tore it open and folded out the handwritten letter. Her smile immediately faded when she realized who it was from. "Damn it, it's from my mom. She must have figured out where you live and that I was here." She contemplated tearing it up, then changed her mind and read it. After she finished, the sadness Cam hadn't seen in a while returned to her gaze.

"Is everything okay?"

"Yeah, I suppose so." Ella handed her the letter and Cam read it.

. . .

Dear Ella,

I don't know what to do anymore. For a year I've been hoping and praying that I'd see you again but after we ran into each other in the Palm Garden, I've felt lonelier than ever. Losing one daughter was, and still is, hell but having lost you too now, is something I can't cope with.

I understand why you don't want to see me anymore. I've betrayed your trust more than once and I've been a terrible mother and manager. I also understand you're angry about Helena's diaries, but I need you to know that I never took them for the money, which I donated to Helena's friend who survived the crash and is still rehabilitating. You and Helena were always the center of my universe and all I ever wanted was for the world to see how special you both were. I know now that I went too far, it was wrong not to allow you both to make your own career choices and to follow your own paths. I didn't feel like I got to know the real Helena until I read her diaries. She was always close to you, but since she moved to New York, she avoided me mostly and although I can't blame her for that, I just wanted to get to know her. When I saw you with that woman, who I presume is your girlfriend, looking like you were in love and happy together, it hit me that I didn't really know you either. I always told you what to do, instead of asking you what you wanted. So I'm asking you now, please let me get to know you, just as your mother. If you don't want to see me again, I'll respect your decision. I hope you've been able get back on your feet after losing your sister and I hope you'll find happiness with this woman who you seem crazy about.

I'll always be here for you and I love you,

Mom.

Cam handed Ella back the letter but didn't say anything.

Ella took it with a faraway look in her eyes and put it in her pocket, her jaw clenched tightly as she stared into nothing.

"I can't deal with this right now," she said in a shaky voice. "And I don't want to talk about it. Can we please go to bed?"

"Of course." Cam didn't argue. Ella was clearly upset, and she assumed the letter had dragged up all kinds of memories she'd been trying to give a place to or forget about. She closed up while Ella went to bed. When she slipped off her robe and got in next to her, she saw Ella was crying, curled up on her side. It tore her apart seeing her like that and all she wanted was to make everything better but there was nothing she could do to take the pain away. She wrapped an arm around Ella and pulled her against her, softly stroking her hair. After a while, the soft whimpers stopped, and Ella's breathing became steady as she fell into a restless sleep.

50

Ella straightened her shoulders and painted on a smile while she waited for Raphael to reverse into Cam's small drive. She still felt a little gloomy after reading her mother's letter and she wasn't sure why it had affected her so much. She'd always been able to shut her mother out emotionally but maybe Theresa had been right in telling her it would catch up with her sooner rather than later if she didn't deal with it.

Today, nothing was going to get in her way, though, so she pulled herself together and got ready to meet the team of wonderful specialists and volunteers who were dedicated to making young people's lives better. She'd supplied the funds, and Raphael had been coordinating the project together with the clinic manager, with Ella becoming more involved over the past two weeks. Ella and Raphael had been shopping for furniture, computers and phones for the call center and the meeting rooms, musical instruments and art paraphernalia for the workshop, and anything else they needed to get the clinic up and running. She'd paid the lease three years upfront too, after learning about the financial struggles of the organization.

It was amazing how fast something could come together when everyone joined forces. Just like their other two walk-in clinics, the new *Help LA* center would house two qualified therapists and a team of volunteers who provided support, a listening ear and music and art therapy – all working together to build confidence in the kids and fight loneliness and isolation. It felt good to finally do something that wasn't centered around herself, and she'd enjoyed seeing the positive results and the happy faces of the volunteers as the work progressed.

"Morning Raphael." Ella slapped his shoulder as she got in the car.

"Morning Ella. Congratulations on the role, I got your text." He studied her intently. "Have you been partying? You look tired."

"No, just a late night." Ella reached into her bag and handed him a wrapped gift. "I got you a little present for your nephew on my way back from the audition yesterday."

"Ella... that's so sweet. You didn't need to do that."

"Of course I did. I wasn't sure what he needed so I put a gift voucher in the sippy cup; I'm sure your sister would love to pick something out for him herself."

"Thank you, that's really thoughtful." He grinned. "My sister won't believe it if I tell her it's from you."

"Well, I'd love to meet them one day. You can always bring them over for one of our morning meetings."

Raphael's grin widened. "Okay, I'll do that." He turned to her as he stopped for a red signal. "You know, I hardly recognize you from when I first started this job. You were always friendly and sweet, but so vacant and sad at the same time. Do you mind me saying that?"

"No, not at all. You're right; I do feel like a different person. It's not always easy but I'm enjoying life and that's something I hadn't expected to happen ever again," Ella said. "I wouldn't say it's necessarily because of Cam. I've worked hard on myself to get to where I am, but I'm not going to deny that it helps to meet someone special." She paused. "Do you have a girlfriend?"

"I'm seeing someone casually." Raphael grinned shyly. "A guy I met at the gym. But it's been casual for a while now and I'd like to take it further. I'm not sure how he feels about it, though."

"Oh, you're gay too." Ella frowned. "Isn't it crazy how little we know about each other?"

Raphael nodded. "The agency you hired me through told me not to overstep personal boundaries. Both ways. But I think we've already crossed that line."

"Yeah, we have." Ella shrugged. "They told me the same, but I don't really care anymore if you don't." She smiled, suddenly feeling an urge to know everything there was to know about the wonderful guy who'd been so loyal, kind and patient with her over the past months. "So, are you going to talk to him?"

"I don't know. Do you think I should?"

"Yeah, talk to him, tell him how you feel. He's a lucky guy to have you and honesty is the best way. If he doesn't feel the same, at least you'll know where you stand."

"It's scary to have honest conversations." Raphael shrugged. "And I'm not very good at the whole talking thing."

"Yeah, I know it's scary." Ella let out a long sigh. "I'm not very good at it either."

. . .

"I must say, we were surprised that you wanted to help out," Nancy, the chairwoman of *Help LA,* said. Ella and Raphael were sitting in the recreational room with twenty-five volunteers, two therapists, the head of recruitment, the facilities manager and the funding manager. "No offence," she added, "but we're a very small organization and we're not getting much exposure. It's unusual for celebrities to get involved with small charities as they don't get much out of it themselves. I'm by no means claiming that's the only reason celebrities do charity work," she quickly added. "But I'm sure you'll agree it often plays a big role in their decision."

"You're right, that's often the case," Ella said. "Big organizations are in a position to help on a big scale, and I'm sure that a lot of people choose them for that very reason, most of them purely from the goodness of their hearts. But local charities are essential too, especially when it comes to something as delicate as mental health. To have an open door with friendly faces and professionals who can help turn someone's life around is invaluable. You guys do great work and I wanted to do something in my own community." She took a moment and cleared her throat. "I also wanted to help because I've suffered from severe depression myself. I'm in a privileged position where I can afford a whole team of therapists. Not that I have a whole team, I have just one," she said, letting out a nervous chuckle. "She's helped me a great deal and I honestly don't think I'd be here today if it wasn't for her." Ella wasn't used to talking about herself so openly and it felt a little daunting, but she carried on, knowing a lot of the volunteers had been through the same. "But a lot of people are not so lucky to afford help, especially young people who may be homeless, or in a bad situation at home. If it wasn't for you guys, they would have nowhere to go. Believe it or not, I know what loneliness feels like. Sometimes just having someone to talk to can be enough and sometimes people need help on a deeper level. It's great that you provide both." She looked around the group, locking her eyes with every single one of them. It was a safe space, she knew that. "I'm telling you this in confidence, but I promise you I'll speak up about my personal experiences in the near future, when the time is right, because as I'm sure we all agree, it's important to talk about the topic, especially since there's still a stigma attached to mental health issues."

"Thank you for sharing that." Nancy stared at Ella for a moment, then shot her a warm smile, seeming equally surprised and touched by her confession. "And we're truly grateful for your help with the new center."

"You're welcome." Ella smiled. "I know money can make things happen but I'm not the one working here day in, day out. You do that. That's why I shouldn't be the one speaking to the press this afternoon." She looked at Donna, a young woman who had been volunteering since she'd sought help from the organization herself, five years ago. After their meet and greet earlier this morning, she knew a lot of volunteers were here because of that same reason. "Let Donna speak." Ella pointed to Donna, whose whole face lit up. "She's personally benefitted from your organization and I think people should hear her story. Unless you don't want to be on camera of course," she added, giving Donna an opportunity to decline. "If you do, I'll announce you and stand next to you if that makes it easier." There was a knock on the door and Raphael patted her on the shoulder.

"That will be the cake," he whispered, as one of the volunteers let in the delivery man carrying five giant boxes.

"Ah, the cake. Thank you, Raphael." Ella stood up and made her way to the kitchen. "Raphael has arranged lots of cake for us all to celebrate. We'll make some more coffee so just help yourselves."

51

"Ready for the big day?" Cam asked Vanya after her class. Vanya was still lying on her yoga mat, tired after a heavy session.

"I have no idea." She sat up and shrugged, looking defeated. "I keep on thinking I've forgotten something, but I've double checked the venue, the band, the DJ, the decorations, the bridesmaids' dresses, my dress, my mother's sari, Greg's tux, the limo, the cake and I think everything's arranged. My mom's taking care of the food and I know she'll do an amazing job at that, so I obviously had to give Sour-Face something to do too. I asked her to do the flowers since she always claims to be such an expert with arrangements. Not that that means anything; the woman says she's an expert at everything. But yeah, we're good. I even asked Greg to go over the table plan again last night and it's all fine... I think," she added. "Oh Cam, I'm so nervous."

"Why are you nervous?"

"I don't know. It's a big thing, committing to someone for life."

Cam smiled. "Well, thankfully, in this day and age it's possible to change your mind down the line but that's not going to happen. Greg's a wonderful guy and you two are very happy together. Why would marriage change that?"

"You're right." Vanya sighed and rubbed her temple. "I just hope his mother behaves. Apart from our flower conversations, she's been more or less blanking me ever since I told her I was planning the wedding myself and she was appalled when I told her that it wasn't going to have a 'white' theme; I don't think she trusts me to pull it off."

"And you're going to prove the mighty Sour-Face wrong." Cam held out her hand and helped her up. "Any last-minute things I can help you with? Ella said she could help too if needed."

"Really? Ella said that?" As always, Vanya's face broke into a huge smile just at the mention of her. "That's so sweet but I can't think of anything right now. How is she anyway?"

"It's calmed down a little with the paparazzi. They're not parked in front of the house or hanging out on the beach anymore, so that's nice. She's been busy working with that mental health charity she told you about over dinner the other night; they're opening a new center in East LA." Cam smiled. "Oh, and she came out to her manager."

Vanya gasped. "No, she did not."

"Uhuh." Cam didn't mention the new movie role as it was still a confidential matter.

"So... are you guys official now or something?"

"Not yet, but I'm going to be her date at the premiere of *Spring's Promise*." Cam laughed when Vanya looked like she was about to faint as they walked into their office. "And you're only telling me this now?"

"When else was I supposed to tell you?" Cam let Vanya in, then closed the door behind them.

"Duh." Vanya rolled her eyes. "How about the moment you found out you were going? Oh no, wait. I forgot you're Cam Saunders and you don't care about that stuff." She picked up a newspaper from her desk and held it up. "You're going to be all over these. Aren't you at least a little nervous about it? Come on, you're only human, Cam."

"Of course I'm a little nervous. I don't like being in the spotlight but I'm going along to support her. Besides, I'm proud to be her date."

"You'd better be proud, Cam. She's the most talented and beautiful actress in the world if you ask me, and everyone's going to be batshit jealous of you for being not only her girlfriend, but her first-ever girlfriend." Vanya looked at her intently. "You've thought about that, right?"

"No, I can't say I have." Cam sat down at her desk, looking a little deflated. "But you seem to be more informed about the ins and outs of Hollywood than I am, so I'll take your word for it."

Vanya nodded. "Informed is an understatement and I'm going to help you through this. So, what are you going to wear?"

"A tux."

"That's it? A tux?"

"Yeah, a really nice tux, what's wrong with that? One of the designers Ella works with has ordered me a fancy one, so I'm sure it'll look good." Cam shrugged. "I expect it will be a bit crazy for a while but there's no point worrying about the aftermath until we get there."

"Sure." Vanya rolled her eyes. "If only I could be as calm as you. You're about to be exposed to the world and I'm having a breakdown just thinking about my wedding."

"Hey, don't worry about it so much. Knowing you, your wedding will be great. Ella and I are really looking forward to Saturday." Cam shot her an assuring look. "Go home, get some rest and we'll see you in two days."

52

"Are you sure about this?" Cam knew there was little point in asking because Ella's driver was already pulling up at the venue. Ella looked beautiful in a bohemian peach-colored dress, her face sparkling with something shiny her make-up artist had applied. The top half of her hair was pulled back into a loose braid and the rest of her long blonde locks hung over her shoulders like a golden waterfall. Cam had dressed up for the occasion too and was wearing formal black satin trousers with a matching cummerbund and a white shirt.

"I'm sure." Ella gave her a sexy wink, letting her know she was excited to do something normal, even if 'normal' meant attending a wedding with her first girlfriend ever.

They stepped out of the car as it stopped in front of the gates of a big white mansion in Malibu. Ella waited for Cam to walk around and help her out.

"Thank you." She tightened her grip on Cam's hand. "Please don't let go today," she said in a near whisper. "We're together, I don't care what people think."

Cam nodded and smiled at her. "Don't worry, I won't let go."

They were greeted by one of the groomsmen, who was checking the guest list and letting everyone in. He looked at Cam, then at Ella and held his gaze in a wildly confused stare.

"Cam Saunders plus one. Yes, I've got you here," he stammered, never taking his eyes off Ella. "But you're..."

"Thank you," they both said in unison, swiftly walking on as they heard whispers and gasps behind them.

"They'll be fine once they get over the first shock," Cam reassured Ella, when she saw more people staring at them. They were led into a grand reception room with a beautiful hand-painted ceiling and crystal chandeliers, where glasses of Champagne were being handed out. The back of the room looked out over vineyards, as far as the eye could see. Fields in different shades of green stretched out over the hilly landscape behind a big yard with long tables, set with white linen, crystal glasses, white china, pink roses and vine leaves.

"It's so pretty," Ella said, in awe of the decorations.

"Yeah, she really pulled it off." Cam turned around when she heard a sneering voice behind her.

"Hey, young lady, where do you think you're going with that? You are far too young to drink." The woman who spoke was towering menacingly over one of the bridesmaids, who Cam recognized to be Shruti, Vanya's cousin.

"It's not for me, it's for Vanya," Shruti stammered.

"Give that to me. Vanya is not having alcohol before the ceremony. It's only 3 pm for God's sake!" The woman stomped her foot twice to make her point, then grunted to herself as she rubbed her temple and turned away from the girl, who sloped off after handing her the glass.

Ella stared at the woman too, lowering her voice. "That must be Sour-Face."

"That's her alright," Cam whispered back as she quietly pulled Ella along with her, keeping her head down to avoid Greg's mother. "I'll say hi to her later. First things first." She took another glass of Champagne from the tray a waiter was carrying, and followed Shruti through the hallway with Ella at her heels. She knocked twice on the door the girl had just disappeared through. "Hey, pssst, it's me."

"Thank God you're here!" Vanya pulled them both inside the suite where she was getting ready. "I've been waiting for a drink for an hour." She gratefully accepted the glass Cam handed her and took a long gulp, then sighed in relief. "That's better. Why is it so hard to get a drink around here?"

"It's Greg's mom," Shruti said with a shrug, before staring at Ella, wide-eyed. It was clear that the girl was in awe.

"She's right. Sour-Face is on form today." Cam laughed as she spun Vanya around. "But who cares? You look absolutely stunning, babe."

"You do," Ella said, giving Vanya a hug. "And your hair with the flowers... it's so adorably cute."

"Thanks." Vanya beamed. "Shruti did it. She wants to be a hairdresser and she's great with a curling wand already."

"You did a great job, Shruti." Ella gave her a warm smile, sensing Shruti might be fangirling on her.

"Thanks." Shruti's cheeks flushed and she nervously fiddled with her corsage. "I think she looks pretty too."

"I did my own make-up because I didn't want to walk around with a caked-on face the whole day and I'm pretty stoked with how I look." Vanya ran a henna-covered hand through her long, dark hair that had been curled into nonchalant waves. She wore a headband of pale pink flowers that matched her pink satin, off the shoulder, dress – her upper arms covered by a wide, asymmetrical ruffle. It was long and flowy, and the fabric shimmered in the light as she moved. A thin gold chain, attached to her nose ring, reached up to the shell of her ear, where it was secured with a gold stud, and she had more gold chains around her neck, adorned with pink, precious stones. "The jewelry is just a little nod to my Indian heritage. I think my mom will like it," she said with a happy smile. "She hasn't even seen me yet; she's been too busy directing the kitchen staff."

"Well, I think you look like a rock star. I've never seen such a cool bride in my life." Ella reassuringly patted her arm. "Are you ready?"

Vanya took a deep breath. "I'm ready. I haven't seen Greg since yesterday and I really miss him, so yeah, I'm excited." She downed the rest of her Champagne. "How is the venue looking? They were still setting up when I got here."

"It's fabulous. You're going to love it." Cam told her. "Everything seems like it's under control but I won't deny that I'm, a little nervous. I've never been a witness before."

"Don't you dare say that." Vanya gave her a playful nudge. "All you need to do is remember your name when you sign on the dotted line. I'm the one under pressure here, so get your act together."

"You're right. I think I can manage to remember my name." Cam chuckled and took Ella's hand. "Well, we'd better get back out there. Greg will be waiting for you soon."

"Okay. I'll see you out there. Oh, and Cam?" Vanya chuckled and lifted her dress, looking down at her feet as she wiggled her toes painted with a bright pink nail polish.

"Guess what? Sour-Face is going to have a total meltdown because I'm going barefoot."

Cam burst out in laughter, followed by Ella and Shruti. "I can't wait to see her face."

Cam and Ella took a seat in the front row facing the gazebo at the edge of the yard where the ceremony was due to take place. It was covered in white linen and the ornate wooden columns were adorned with vine leaves and pink peonies. A photographer was taking pictures of guests while the marriage officiant, who was dressed in a sharp, black suit, got ready under the gazebo. A cellist in a long, pink gown was sitting behind him, tuning her instrument.

"Do you mind if I take a picture?"

Ella tensed up for a moment, when the photographer turned his lens in their direction, but she smiled and nodded. "Sure, go ahead." She almost fell off her chair when Greg's mother sat down and pushed herself against them, photobombing the picture with a wide grin.

"Oh, just one more," she said, leaning in further for another shot. Then she turned to Ella and held out her hand. "Hi Ella. It's so nice to meet you. I'm Aubrey, Greg's mother."

"Hi Aubrey, it's very nice to meet you too."

Cam leaned in too and shook her hand. "Hi Aubrey, it's lovely to see you again." When she failed to notice a sparkle of recognition in Aubrey's eyes, she continued: "I'm Cam, Vanya's witness and business partner."

"Oh, of course. Hi, Cam." Aubrey gave her a friendly nod and immediately focused on Ella again. She clearly had very little interest in anything other than the famous actress, who was apparently the only silver lining in the whole wedding fiasco.

"It's gorgeous, isn't it?" Ella said to her. "So romantic. Vanya really did an amazing job." She could tell Aubrey was trying everything in her power not to pout at the comment.

"Yes, well, it's not how we normally do weddings in *our* family. It's a little small and unconventional but I suppose she's done her best."

Their conversation was interrupted by murmurs and clapping when Greg walked to the front and took his place by the minister. He waved at Cam and Ella then grinned at a couple of his friends who were making fun of his pink tie. Cam was joined by Vanya's mother, who sat down next to her and gave her a kiss on her cheek.

"Hi Cam. You look gorgeous, sweetheart."

"Thank you. So do you, Mrs. Singh. This is really pretty." Cam ran a hand over the gold embroidered fabric of her sari. "How's the food coming along.?"

Mrs. Singh sat back and let out a deep sigh. "I think it's under control," she said, a little nervously. It better be; I've been up for the past two nights doing the preparations."

"Well, I've eaten your food before so I have no doubt it will be amazing," Cam reassured her.

They were hushed by the minister, who then gave a sign to the cellist. She played beautifully; softly at first, then louder as Vanya walked down the rose-petal covered isle with her father. Cam felt overwhelmed with emotion as she watched her best friend join Greg and take his hands. Then the cello music subsided, and the minister started reading a passage from 'Captain Corelli's Mandolin' by Louis De Bernières.

"Love is a temporary madness, it erupts like volcanoes and then subsides. And when it subsides, you have to make a decision.

You have to work out whether your roots have so entwined together that it is inconceivable that you should ever part. Because this is what love is. Love is not breathlessness, it is not excitement, it is not the promulgation of promises of eternal passion..."

Cam took Ella's hand in hers while he continued, and entwined their fingers. She could sense Ella was getting emotional too from the way she kept squeezing her hand and leaning into her. Mrs. Singh reached for her other hand, almost crushing it as she sobbed throughout the rest of the ceremony.

"Who says wine and Indian food don't go together?" Vanya held up her glass in a toast as they dined at the long tables in the yard. She'd been beside herself after the ceremony and was possibly the most chilled out bride Ella had ever seen. On the terrace behind them, a blues band was playing old classics and in front of them, the vineyards were golden now, caressed by the lowering sun.

She'd had fun meeting new people, after they'd gotten over the shock of meeting a real life movie star, and she didn't feel uncomfortable at all. The fact that it was an intimate wedding helped of course. People were here for Vanya and Greg, not to be seen and make new contacts. It was simply a wonderfully social affair with nice guests, fantastic food, a romantic atmosphere and great music, and she couldn't have been happier, sitting next to Cam who was totally cute when she was a little tipsy. Greg's old college friends were hilarious, and his family was a little stiff but very friendly, nevertheless.

Ella had finally managed to escape his mother, who had dragged her into several pictures since the ceremony, politely yet firmly directing her where and how to pose. Vanya's family was lovely and chatty, most of the women dressed in colorful, flowing saris and the men in kurtas or suits. The table was laid out with even more delicious food after the samosas and pakoras had been eaten, and now they were passing around fragrant rice, salads, yoghurt dips, paneer in spinach, spicy stuffed breads, curries and other vegetarian dishes. To Ella, it felt great to be a part of something, rather than being the center of attention, but Vanya clearly loved that it was 'her' day and she was the loudest of them all, much to everyone's amusement. Greg looked happy too; all loved-up with his new wife.

"This food is so good," she said to Cam, passing her a bowl of salad.

"Yeah, right? I've only been to dinner at Vanya's parents twice but it's the best food I've ever eaten." She grinned. "And I agree with Vanya; it goes well with wine, no matter what people say."

"You're super cute when you're a little drunk," Ella whispered, squeezing her thigh.

"So you still want to dance with me later, even if I'm going to be a tad wobbly on my feet?"

Ella turned when she heard Shruti giggling next to her. "Hey, what's so funny little one?" Vanya had asked everyone to move over a little so that Shruti, who was desperate to sit next to Ella, could join them on the long bench.

Shruti blushed and looked from Ella to Cam and back. "Are you two really dating?" she asked, a little too loud.

Ella almost choked on her food at the question and noted that about ten pairs of eyes were focused on her now. But they weren't the judgmental stares she was usually subjected to, and no one looked like they were about to cash in over her answer. They were rather looks of amusement and endearment at a thirteen-year-old's innocent lack of subtlety. Not that it would make any difference what she said now, she was here as Cam's date and it was pretty obvious what was going on between them. She shot Shruti a conspiratorial look and leaned in.

"Promise you won't tell anyone?" She whispered in her ear.

Shruti nodded, wide-eyed. "I promise."

"Okay then." Ella winked. "Yes, we're dating."

Shruti gasped and covered her hand with her mouth. "You're a lesbian," she said, again too loud, making the other guests laugh.

"Yes, I am." Ella took a bite from her food as if it was nothing, but inside she was a little shaken up from admitting it in front of a table full of people. It felt liberating though, and so she shrugged and turned to Shruti with a smile. "What about you?"

Shruti blushed again, even harder this time. She glanced over at her parents, who were sitting at the far end of the table and decided it was safe to answer. "I think I am too," she whispered, covering Ella's ear. "But I'm not sure because I like Ben in my class too."

"That's okay." Ella rubbed her shoulder. "You don't have to pick a side. Just go out with whoever makes your heart sing." She arched a brow. "Although you might be a little young to date just yet."

"Does Cam make your heart sing?" Shruti asked in a teasing tone.

Ella took Cam's hand under the table and gently caressed it. Cam, who had overheard the conversation shot her a sweet smile and gave her a kiss on the cheek, making Ella grin from ear to ear. "Yes, she does, sweetie."

53

"It's so beautiful here." Ella sat down in the grass at the end of the yard, overlooking the vineyards. The sky was pitch-dark, but the full moon was bright tonight, shining a mysterious light over the hills. The backyard of the mansion was quiet, with only a couple of people smoking on the terrace. "I really should get out more. There's so much to see outside Hollywood and that was one amazing wedding. Do you think Vanya and Greg had a good time?"

Cam sat down too and put an arm around her. "I think they had a great day. Did you?"

"Yeah." Ella took her hand and pulled it further down over her shoulder. "I've been to many extravagant celebrity weddings, but I've never had so much fun as today. And you can see that they clearly love each other, it's not just some kind of publicity stunt or a crazy idea that seems great in the moment but doesn't work long-term." She took a deep breath, cherishing the strong wind that swept through her hair. "Have you ever thought of getting married?"

"No, never," Cam admitted. "I've never been with

someone long-term who I was sure I wanted to spend the rest of my life with." She hesitated. "Actually, maybe I thought I wanted to spend the rest of my life with Sam, my first girlfriend, but that's what everyone thinks of their first love, right? And even then, getting married wasn't on my mind; I was way too young for that. But now that I've met you, I can't say it didn't cross my mind today." She chuckled. "Oh God, I'm blushing. What about you?"

"I never thought about it either. Until today," Ella added, her face flushing too. She'd thought about it many times today, picturing herself and Cam under the gazebo where Vanya and Greg had stood that afternoon. She knew it was silly, as they hadn't known each other for very long, but what she felt for Cam was so strong that she couldn't imagine being without her anymore. Was it love? She wasn't sure. All she knew was that it was pure and beautiful and that it made her feel strong. "It wasn't something I ever saw in my future," she continued. "Dreaming about getting married one day meant I had to come out first and I hadn't even started thinking about that until recently." She shrugged. "It's not like I was brought up on the values of marriage anyway. My dad was never in the picture and my mom's been single for most of her life, apart from fleeting boyfriends who moved in for a couple of months at a time. She wasn't short of action, but she didn't care much for them either. I think they were just a convenience. Her life always evolved around Helena and me. It's strange that she never got that obsessive with men until now."

"It can't have been easy for her though, as a single mom," Cam said. "No husband, no job and then imagine the panic when you find out you're having twins."

"No, I suppose not."

"What about her family?" Cam asked.

"My mom ran away from home when she was sixteen. She never talked about my grandparents. I don't even know if they're still around. She mentioned her brother once, who's been in and out of prison for the past twenty-five years, but they're not in contact. My guess is that she didn't have it great, growing up. I've been thinking about it, lately. Maybe it wasn't all selfish. Maybe she was just determined to give us everything she never had." Ella shrugged. "She just didn't know when to stop and no matter how much money we earned, it was ever enough."

"Maybe. Nothing is ever all black and white."

"Yeah. I've been thinking about the letter too." Ella buried her head in the crook of Cam's arm and looked down.

"I know you have." Cam pulled her closer. "Do you want to go and see her?"

"I think so. I know I'm entitled to be furious, but I can't help feeling sorry for her. I believed her when she said she was lonely because I've been there too, and I don't wish it upon anyone." She turned to Cam. "You were right about that, but I was so upset that I didn't want to think about it. Besides, I don't deal well with confrontation and I didn't want to feel responsible for her after everything she put me through, yet she's all I've got. Apart from you," she added with a smile.

Cam kissed her temple softly. "Then you should go and see her."

"Really?"

"Yeah. Not just because she's your mom but because deep down, you want to. I know you do. And she..."

"Hey lovebirds!" Vanya came up behind them, interrupting their conversation. She drunkenly sank down next to Cam, almost tripping in the process. "Wow, isn't this a view, huh?"

"It's beautiful. You did so well, babe. How are you feeling?" Cam, asked.

"Happy." Vanya's answer was short and honest. "I did the right thing. I honestly don't know what I was so nervous about. Because guess what? Greg's the love of my life. And guess what else? Sour-Face is dancing in there." She fell back and pointed to the mansion behind her. "The woman is actually having a good time for once, even though she'll never admit it to my face. But... I don't care; I've got video evidence."

Cam laughed. "I bet you made sure of that." She pulled Vanya back into a sitting position and put an arm around her too, feeling lucky to have the two most amazing women in her life by her side.

"It's wonderful to know that someone's always got your back, you know? That someone's always there for you," Vanya said, slurring her words a little. "I love him. I love him so much."

"We know you do." Ella squeezed Cam's hand and Cam squeezed hers back. "Hey, do you want some water?" She asked when she noticed Vanya's eyes were drooping. "I know it's nice out here, but you don't want to miss the end of your party, right? And I'm sure Greg is dying to have another dance with you."

"You're right." Vanya took the water bottle Ella handed her and downed the contents in one go. "Oh God. I think I might need some very strong coffee too." She started to hiccup as Cam helped her to her feet and quickly rearranged her dress. Cam then hooked her arm into

Vanya's and Ella took her other arm. "They didn't harass you too much, did they, Ella? Our guests?"

Ella chuckled. "No, not at all. Everyone's been really lovely, even Sour-Face." She deadpanned. "Come on, I could use a coffee too."

54

Ella had been quiet during the drive to Palm Springs. She was absently twirling a lock of hair around her finger over and over as she leaned her head on her arm over the car door. Cam shot her quiet glances as she drove, knowing Ella was nervous to see her mother again. They hadn't called ahead but Ella had been certain her mother would be home as it wasn't lunchtime yet. Apparently, Bernice Temperley only ventured out if there were drinks involved. After Raphael had managed to find out where she lived, she'd tried to convince Ella to let her mother know they were coming but Ella was having none of it. Perhaps she was hoping she'd find her mother with one of her toy boys, giving her an excuse to leave again if she changed her mind.

"I don't think I should come in with you," she said, taking Ella's hand. "This is between you and your mom."

"Yeah, you're right." Ella swallowed hard. "Will you stay close, in case I want to leave?" She was surprised to find the GPS indicated they were almost there as they were in the town center now. She'd expected her mother to live in a grand villa in the hills but instead, they were guided toward a modest townhouse, next to a retro diner.

"I'll wait in there, okay?" Cam parked the car in front of the sleek white diner as there was no space in front of the house.

"Okay." Ella took a deep breath and nodded. "I won't be long."

"Take as long as you need."

Ella rang the doorbell and straightened her mint-green summer dress. Her hair was pulled back into a long braid and she wore small pearl earrings with a matching necklace. She wasn't sure why she'd felt the need to dress so conservatively. Maybe she was subconsciously rebelling. Her mother had always encouraged her to dress according to the latest trends and this was far from it. She glanced at the windows, noted the curtains were drawn and checked the time on her phone. *10 am.* She rang again and waited until finally the door opened.

"Ella..." Bernice wiped the sleep from her eyes and closed her robe. She blinked a couple of times as if processing what was happening, then stepped outside and pulled Ella into a tight hug. "You're here. I can't believe you're here." She started sobbing against Ella's shoulder, leaving Ella in an awkward position where she had no idea what to do with her arms. Her mother had never been physical with her and she couldn't remember ever being hugged by her. She felt for her, but still pushed her back a little, needing some distance.

"Hi."

Bernice tried to compose herself as she smiled through her tears. "Hi. Come in." She opened the door further and led the way through a narrow hallway, into a dark living room. It wasn't big but it looked homey, with pictures and paintings on the pale-lemon colored walls. The curtains were white with a gray floral pattern and on the tiled floor lay a cozy off-white rug.

Ella had a feeling the interior had come with the house, as it was far from her mother's usual flashy style. She held her breath when her eyes rested on a big framed picture of her and Helena on the wall behind the cream colored sofa. It was taken the day before Helena moved to New York, in their home in Palm Springs. Ella had thrown a farewell party for her and despite their rusty relationship with their mother, she'd been there too. Had her mother taken this picture? Ella couldn't remember. They looked happy in the close-up, both with an arm around each other's shoulders. Apart from their hair and make-up, they looked identical. Helena had dyed her shoulder-length hair dark brown and she had a sharp fringe. Ella's hair was blonde and loose, like she usually wore it. Her near make-up free face made her look like the boring good girl, next to Helena whose eyes were emphasized by thick, black eye-liner and lots of mascara.

"Please, sit down. Can I get you a drink?" Bernice rushed over to the windows and opened the curtains, wincing for a moment when the bright light washed in.

Ella sat down on the couch. A pillow was lying on its side and a blanket was thrown over the couch's armrest, as if her mother had been sleeping there. It stung to see the empty wine bottle on the coffee table in front of her and a coffee mug next to it. She hadn't even bothered pouring it into a wineglass. As if her mother knew what she was thinking, she quickly cleared the coffee table.

"Coffee if you have." Ella shifted in her seat, avoiding eye contact.

"Of course." Her mother shot a quick glance at the clock on the wall and took everything into the kitchen. She came back five minutes later with two mugs of coffee, and looked from the couch to the chair and then back again, finally deciding to sit on the chair.

"Thank you so much for coming, Ella, it means everything to me."

Ella fell silent for a moment as she finally met her mother's eyes, that were tired and red-rimmed. "I don't really know why I came..." She hesitated. "But I got your letter and I'm here now, so let's talk."

"Okay." Bernice's face lit up just a little. "How are you?" she asked, perching on the edge of her chair, resting her elbows on her knees.

"I'm good." Ella gave her a small smile. "I'm much better. I was a complete mess for a long time but I'm getting there. I've had help and I can see the light at the end of the tunnel now. I may not get out of the tunnel entirely, but I can enjoy life without Helena and I know that's what she would have wanted for me." She noticed her mother was fiddling with her nails, just like she always did herself when she was nervous. "How are you?"

Bernice almost looked shocked to hear the question, but then maybe no one had asked her that in a long time.

"I'm going to be honest with you, Ella. I've been sad, very sad. Sometimes I don't know why I get out of bed or why I'm here at all." She paused. "There's a guy sleeping in my bed and I don't even remember his name, so I apologize in advance if he wakes up and walks in. It's the nights, you know. The nights are the worst and I can't sleep because I can't stop thinking, so

I need company to stay sane. Despite that, I still couldn't sleep last night, so I came out here and tried drinking myself to sleep instead. I've tried sleeping pills of course, but the doctor stopped prescribing them because I was taking too many."

Ella nodded. "I've stopped taking them too. It will get better, eventually."

"Yeah. I'm sure it will." Bernice didn't sound convinced as she said it. "So, was that your girlfriend? Cam Saunders, the woman you were with at the Palm Garden? I'm sorry I posted the letter through her door, but I know you've told Tom to cut out my correspondence and I didn't know where you lived now. Her name was in the tabloids, so it wasn't hard to find her."

"Cam, yes. She's a yoga teacher and she's got her own studio in West Hollywood. But I guess you read about that too. She's waiting for me at the diner next door."

"Are you happy together?"

"Yeah, I'm crazy about her."

Bernice sighed. "And there I was trying to set you up with famous boys all those years. Why didn't you tell me?"

"How could I tell you?" Ella tried not to raise her voice, so she balled her hands into fists instead. "I had to be a star. I had to be famous and pretty and talented and popular and all those things you pushed me to be. I was taught from an early age that it was important to be seen with influential people and that dating handsome male co-stars was a smart move, so tell me honestly Mom; what would you have done if I'd told you I was gay?" She continued when her mother didn't answer. "You would have told me to keep it to myself, grit my teeth and pretend to have a crush on whoever was the most eligible boy-star in Hollywood at the time. You would have told me that sometimes you have to make sacrifices to get what you really want. Isn't that what you always said?"

"You're right." Bernice looked beaten as she slowly nodded. "I probably would have said that." She shook her head. "Oh God, I've been such a bad mother."

Ella watched her cry but didn't reach out to comfort her. Too much had happened for that. But against all expectations, she did feel something. Something that made her want to stay and talk more. "You did what you thought was right," she finally said. "Well, maybe not all the time," she added, thinking back to the occasions big sums of money had disappeared from her account. "And don't think I can forgive you for the book, no matter what your motives were... but I have good memories of you too, and I loved you. I think I still do, I mean, you're my mother after all."

Bernice looked up, a sparkle of hope twinkling in her eyes. "Really?"

"Yeah, of course. I remember how proud you were of me when I got a new role, or when I won an award. I remember you put all your time and energy into us and that your whole life revolved around us. I know you meant well, it just got out of hand."

"I got greedy," Bernice said in a weak voice. "I didn't need the money; I already took twenty percent as your and Helena's manager and I was living a very comfortable life. But I wanted more. Another house, another car ... I had nothing growing up and suddenly having access to all those luxuries made me lose all perspective. Material things used to be important to me, I even believed they made me happy. I didn't realize the only thing that mattered had been right in front of me until it was too late." She sniffed and cleared her throat. "There are no excuses for what I did, and I don't expect you to forgive me, but if we could see each other now and then... maybe we could build some kind of relationship."

Ella studied her mother as she thought about what she'd said. Her mother seemed like a different person and she wasn't sure if she was being manipulative or that the loss of her daughter had changed her. It didn't sound like her at all.

"Maybe we could try that," she heard herself say. "I can't promise you anything but I'll unblock your number so you can call me when you're in LA and maybe we could go for a coffee or lunch together if I'm free."

"I'd really like that." Her mother's relief was almost palpable as she let out the breath she'd been holding and shot Ella a warm smile.

Their conversation was interrupted by the door opening and they both looked up to find a young man in the doorway, only covered by a towel wrapped around his waist. It wasn't the same man Ella had seen in the Palm Garden, but he might as well have been because he was just as young and had the same blonde hair and muscular build.

"Do you have anything to eat in the house, B?" he asked. Then his eyes widened as he saw Ella. "Fuck..." he whispered. "You're Ella Temperley." His gaze shifted to Bernice. "Temperley," he mumbled to himself as it clicked. "You must be..."

"I think it's time for you to go now," Bernice said, looking more than a little embarrassed. "I don't have any food in the house, and I'd like to be alone..." She winced. "I'm sorry, what's your name again?"

"Dewey." Dewey shot Ella another look. "Sure, I'll go. But can I just quickly have one picture before I go? My phone's in the bedroom, give me a minute to get it."

"No, Dewey. No pictures," Bernice said coldly as she got

up and opened the hallway door, then pointed to the bedroom. "And get dressed, please, I have company."

"It's okay, I need to go anyway." Ella stood up too, glad the interruption had given her a reason to leave. It was the first time in years they'd talked without arguing and she thought it best to leave in case she got angry again.

"Oh, but you don't need to..." Bernice was about to protest but changed her mind, sensing too that parting ways right now was the sensible thing to do. She nodded. "Fine. Thank you so much for coming to see me, I'd love to see you again soon."

Ella walked into the hallway, trying to dodge another hug. "Take care of yourself," she said as she opened the door. "And get some help. Drinking is not a solution. Believe me, I speak from experience."

"I know." Bernice grasped Ella's hand. "I'll see you soon, right?"

"Yeah. Call me." Ella quickly pressed her hand and left.

55

"I'm pleased to hear you decided to see your mother." Theresa looked up from her notepad and gave Ella a warm smile. "Do you feel better for it?"

"Yes, I do." Ella sank further back in her chair and put her feet up on the footstool. It was so comfortable that she'd ordered one for herself. "It was really strange, sitting down with her, but I'm glad I went. We didn't talk about Helena much, like you suggested. It was only a short visit, but we're meeting up again and we can take it from there. I don't know how it's going to play out but I'm willing to put in the effort and try to start fresh rather than dwell on the past."

"Excellent." Theresa seemed unusually chirpy today, as if she was more than pleased with Ella's progress. "And do you feel ready for your big night tomorrow?"

Ella laughed. "No. I'm terrified."

"That's only natural. Coming out by bringing your first girlfriend to a big event is a bold move."

"I wasn't going for the bold move," Ella said. "It's an important event for me and I want Cam to be a part of it. I'm so proud to be with her and honestly, I can't imagine her not being there. I'll talk to the press in the days after the premiere, at some point. At first, I felt like it was nobody's business, but now I'm thinking it would be good for me to be more open about it. It might encourage any of my LGBTQ+ fans, who are struggling, to come out too. I met this young girl at a wedding, and I don't think she's told her parents that she's bisexual. Maybe she doesn't want to tell them but if she does, and if I can give someone like her a little courage to talk about it, then I'd be able to use my influence in a positive way."

"That's a wonderful insight." Theresa put her feet up too, and Ella noted it was the first time she'd seen her so relaxed. "I'm going to share something personal with you, I hope you don't mind."

"No, please do." Ella tilted her head, curious about the strange turn their conversation was taking.

"My wife was reading a tabloid the other day. As I told you, I don't read them myself, but she'd left it open on a random page as she ran to the door to sign for a package. I saw a picture of you and Cam, and it made me smile. It suddenly clicked who the devilishly attractive yoga instructor was and how you'd ended up here in my practice."

"Yes." Ella grinned. "She was the one who referred me to you. She told me you'd been a great help to her."

"I'm glad. I can't talk about it of course, but please give her my regards."

"I will. So, your wife, you said?"

"Yes. Therapists can be gay too, you know." Theresa gave Ella a playful wink and they both laughed. "As I'm sharing anyway," she continued, "I'm afraid I will have to tell you that I'll be closing my practice in three months' time, but I have a handful of really great therapists that I can refer you to."

"You're closing the practice?" Ella was baffled. Seeing Theresa each week had become such an integrated part of her life that she couldn't imagine her not being there anymore. "Why?" She shook her head. "I'm sorry. That's private, I shouldn't have..."

"No, it's fine, I'm happy to tell you. My wife has accepted a job offer in Tel Aviv and I'm going with her. I'm taking some time off to finally write a book, which is something I've been wanting to do for a couple of years."

"Wow, that sounds amazing."

"It is. I like the idea of immersing myself in a different culture for a while, to travel a bit and see more of the world."

"I can tell you're excited." Ella studied her. "You're different today."

"I'm excited, yes, but not just for personal reasons. It brings me joy to see my clients happy after struggling for so long." Theresa handed Ella a file. "Here is some information on the therapists I recommend. They're all great in my opinion. We can continue our sessions as usual over the coming twelve weeks but in the meantime, you'll need to let me know if you're interested in either of these therapists so I can refer you sooner rather than later."

"Do you think I need a new therapist?" Ella asked.

Theresa thought about it for a while, then shook her head. "I think you can manage on your own now, and I think you know that too. But if you're more comfortable with continuing, then that's fine, of course. Some people go through therapy for years, or even decades, simply because it gives them a sense of direction and clarity."

Ella chewed her lip as she flicked through the pages. "I think I'm fine," she said, handing Theresa back the file. "It feels like the end of a very dark period of time, or as if a new chapter in my life is starting. Not because you're leaving but because exciting changes are about to happen. Life-altering changes. I feel strong and although I'm scared, I'm ready for whatever the future holds." She paused. "And I have Cam, of course. I think I love her. No," she corrected herself. "I know I love her."

Theresa's smile widened. "Love is a beautiful thing. It's fascinating and complex and the most important emotion in human experience. You're lucky."

"I know." Ella felt a strange sensation after saying it out loud. She was all warm and fuzzy inside at finally being able to admit what she'd felt for weeks. "I haven't thanked you, for what you've done for me. I'm very grateful."

"No need to thank me, it's my job." Theresa looked up when someone knocked on the door. "Thank you, Bree!" she said, loud enough for her receptionist to hear it. She checked her watch, then shook her head in confusion. "God, look at that. I didn't realize we were over time, that's never happened to me before. My next appointment will be waiting."

Ella chuckled, stood up and picked up her purse. "I'll see you next week, then."

"Yes, I'll see you next week. Good luck tomorrow." Theresa shook her hand. "Let the new chapter begin."

56

"How's married life, Mrs. Singh-Watson?" Cam asked when Vanya came into work half an hour late.

"It's great." Vanya beamed as she sat down behind her desk. "Not much different from before really, but still, it feels nice to be a team on paper." She bit her lip and grinned. "Sorry I'm late. We were having sex. Actual morning sex. That hasn't happened since we first started dating."

"Good for you." Cam arched a brow curiously. "So, the honeymoon has reignited the spark, huh? How was your week in paradise?"

"Hawaii was great. Amazing, obviously. But it wasn't that." Vanya glanced at the door and lowered her voice. "Remember I told you I caught Greg watching porn? The video with the vibrator?"

"Ehm, yes, but I don't really want to think about that. Greg's my friend too, and it took me weeks to get that image out of my head."

Vanya continued, ignoring her. "Well, I ordered one. A vibrator, to bring on our honeymoon. I figured it was his thing, and so I thought why not give it a go, right?" She whistled, fanning her face in an exaggerated gesture. “Well, let me tell you something, it’s been eye-opening for both of us. We’ve been at it all week and even last night when we came back and this morning. He likes to watch...”

“No, no, no, no!” Cam covered her ears, closed her eyes and started humming. “I’m really happy for you but you’re seriously oversharing right now,” she said when she opened her eyes again and noted Vanya had stopped talking. “I don’t want to know.”

Vanya shrugged, a wide grin spreading across her face. “Whatever. I’m just saying, maybe you should get one.” She turned on her laptop, opened a file on her desk and turned back to Cam. “Are you excited about tonight? How’s the tux?”

“I’m not sure if excited is the right way to describe my feelings.” Cam laughed. “I’m a little scared, actually. It’s a big thing.” She sighed. “I’m trying to mentally prepare myself for the storm that will come with our first public appearance together, but other than that, the tux looks great.” She opened a picture on her phone and showed it to Vanya, who rolled over to her on her chair. “I had a fitting three days ago, but it was so perfect for me that it didn’t really need any alterations. Ella’s dress is stunning too, I’m not sure how I’m going to keep my hands off her.”

“Fuck, Cam. You sexy beast!” Vanya stared at the picture of Cam in the suit and whistled again. “I know I wasn’t too keen on the tuxedo idea, but this is...” She looked up at Cam and laughed. “If I wasn’t married...”

“Gross, don’t say that.” Cam laughed too as she snatched the phone out of Vanya’s hand. “So, you approve?”

“Duh.” Vanya rubbed Cam’s shoulder. “Hey, I know it’s a big thing and I want you to know that Greg and I are here for you both, Cam. And you guys can always stay with us if you need to escape. I know you like our spare bedroom."

"I do like your spare bedroom and I especially like the Jacuzzi bath in the en suite bathroom."

"Perks of a rich husband." Vanya waved her hand, showing off her wedding band.

"A very cool, kind and awesome rich husband." Cam shot Vanya a grateful smile. "We might take you up on the offer, if worse comes to worse."

"Anytime, babe. So, you two are good, huh?"

"Yeah, we're more than good. I..." Cam hesitated. "I love her."

Vanya's eyes widened as she bounced up and down on her chair. "You love her!" she repeated in an excited cry. "I knew it, I knew it, I knew it." Her enthusiasm made Cam laugh again. "Didn't I tell you? Huh? About the unicorns and rainbows and pink Champagne? Have you told her yet?"

"No." Cam knew her face was turning red and quickly covered it with her hands. She had no idea why she was oversharing her emotions now, but she felt good for saying it out loud. "I haven't told her yet, I only just realized it myself."

Vanya stood up and draped herself over Cam, covering her face in kisses. "You need to tell her. Believe me, she feels the same. I even told Greg the night after the dinner at your house that I was convinced you guys were meant to be together. It's like fate somehow decided you were right for each other. The way she looks at you..."

"You really think so?"

"Yeah, I really do. And tonight is going to be great." Vanya took her hand and gave Cam a quick hug. "I'll get the room ready, just in case."

57

"You look so incredibly hot." Ella let her eyes roam over Cam, who was wearing her brand-new black tuxedo. She adjusted Cam's bow tie and ran a hand through her dark hair while they waited for Ella's driver to pull into her drive. "And you wear it like no other woman ever could."

"Thank you, but you're the one who looks hot here." Cam reached for Ella's ass and squeezed it, just before they got into the limo. Ella's hair was pinned up in a glamorous up-do and she wore subtle make-up and a pair of simple, diamond earrings. Ella's black, backless dress left little to the imagination, and Cam couldn't keep her eyes off the side of her ribcage where the curves of her breasts were visible as the dress cut into a low V at the back.

Ella chuckled when she caught her staring. "I thought you might appreciate a bit of side-boob."

"Is that what it's called? Side-boob?" Cam laughed too. "In that case, I'm definitely a fan of side-boob." She ran a finger down from just below Ella's armpit to her waist, causing Ella to shiver. "Are you nervous?"

"Yes," Ella took a deep breath, then slowly exhaled. "It's

the first time I've brought a real date to a premiere. After tonight, there won't be any doubt as to whether we're together or not. Especially not with you looking so sexy and well... let's be honest... gay." She giggled as she pushed the button to close up the privacy wall between them and the driver, then seemed to ponder over something for a beat. "You know what I've always wanted to do?" A smile played around her lips as she hiked her dress up and straddled Cam. Her eyes were fiery when she looked down at her and traced her jawline. There was no doubt about what Ella wanted; Cam knew that look all too well by now.

"If it involves doing naughty things in the back of a limo, I'm not going to say no to that." Cam moaned softly when Ella brushed her lips against hers, then claimed her mouth in a passionate kiss.

"Good. Then we're on the same page here," Ella whispered.

"You're killing me, Ella." Cam could feel Ella's rapid heartbeat against her own and knowing she was turning her on only flared up her desire. She pulled Ella's head back by her hair and kissed her neck. The nails of her other hand dug into Ella's back, then made their way down and slipped under her dress, cupping her ass. Ella moaned and slid the spaghetti straps off her shoulders, revealing her breasts when her dress fell down to her waist. She gasped when Cam's mouth moved down to them, taking a hard, pink nipple into her mouth. She started bucking her hips, grinding her center against Cam's abdomen when Cam bit down, just hard enough to make her balance on that delicious edge of pain and pleasure. She didn't care that they were on their way to her first public event of the year, and she didn't care that her hair was getting tousled or her dress creased. She wanted Cam, needed her more than anything right now.

"Oh God. Please fuck me, Cam."

Cam looked up at her, a carnal craving oozing through her gaze. "Can he hear us?" she asked in a raspy voice, referring to the driver.

"No, only if I push the intercom b..." The rest of Ella's words were dampened by another deep and passionate kiss as Cam slid one strong arm around her waist. Her other hand moved from her ass over her thigh and in between Ella's legs. Their kiss deepened when she felt the pool of arousal through Ella's panties.

"I'm going to make you come so hard," she mumbled against Ella's mouth as she slid her hand inside Ella's panties and ran her fingers through her wetness. She kissed Ella's breasts again, ran her tongue over her nipples and scraped her teeth over her ribcage, desperate to have all of her at once.

"Jesus." Ella covered her mouth with her hand to stifle a loud moan when Cam pushed two fingers inside her.

Cam watched Ella's eyelids flutter as she moved her hips on her hand, giving herself over to her. Ella looked more beautiful than Cam had ever seen her and once again, she had to remind herself that this was real. That the worst moment in Ella's life had led to something so good, so real and honest between them that it was hard to imagine her life without her now. Their bond felt unbreakable, their connection seamless and intuitive and God, how she needed her.

She turned them over, lay Ella down on the long black leather seats and lowered herself on top of her, still inside her. A black stilettoed heel fell off Ella's foot when she wrapped her legs around Cam's waist and pulled her down into a kiss, moaning louder now while Cam continued to fuck her, teasingly slow. Ella was always a delight to watch but when she was aroused and gave herself wholly to Cam, nothing compared to that look of desire in her eyes. Cam was transfixed on her face, unable to look away. She felt Ella's walls contract around her fingers, as she shuddered and gasped, covering her mouth with her hand once again to hold back a long and throaty cry. She was trembling, breathing fast as she opened her eyes and looked at Cam, wide-eyed.

"You certainly made good on your promise," she said in between breaths, trying her hardest to compose herself. Then they both laughed as Ella wiped traces of lip gloss from Cam's mouth. She kept her thumb on her lips, stroking them, and when their eyes locked, she softly ran her other hand through Cam's hair.

Cam's smile faded and her expression turned serious when she felt her heart swell with emotion. "I love you," she whispered.

Ella looked surprised at first. The silence between them seemed to last forever but the tear running down her cheek said more than a thousand words ever could. She placed a tender kiss on Cam's mouth, lingering for a long moment as if working up the courage to speak.

"I love you too." Ella's voice was soft and sweet. "No one has ever said that to me before. No one." She tried her hardest to hold back her tears, conscious of her mascara that would soon turn into a black mess on her cheeks, but she failed. "And I'm glad you're the first." She pulled Cam against her and realized that in that moment, she almost felt whole again, as if the chunk that had been ripped out of her soul after Helena's death had been partially replaced, somehow. It wasn't the same and it would never be the same. It was a different kind of love, but it was beautiful, passionate, overwhelming at times and enough to make her heart sing with joy. Cam looked emotional too, smiling through her tears. Their eyes shifted to the front of the car when the limo came to a sudden halt and the driver's voice sounded through the intercom.

"We're here, Miss Temperley."

"Damn it, so soon?" Ella muttered. They sat up, and she let out a soft moan when Cam pulled her fingers out of her, then brought them to her mouth and licked them clean in a way that caused another rush of arousal to course through her. Ella couldn't think straight after what they'd just said to each other, but she was on a high and felt like she could handle just about anything. Outside, she saw hordes of journalists and photographers waiting for her along the red carpet. She pressed the intercom button. "Thank you. Could you give us five minutes please?" She frantically wiped her cheeks in an attempt to remove any mascara stains.

"I'm afraid I can't do that, Miss Temperley. There are twelve other limos waiting behind us." Ella sighed and pulled the straps of her dress back over her shoulders before securing the loose strands of hair behind her ears, then put her heels back on.

"I understand, we'll be ready in a minute." She turned to Cam. "How do I look?"

"Like you've just been fucked. I think it might be better without this but other than that, you look beautiful." Cam laughed as she pulled out the loose hairpins that were now sticking out the back of Ella's head, releasing her hair that had settled in a messy lump at the base of her neck. She laced her fingers through it, then brushed the last bit of mascara from underneath Ella's eyes. "I'm sorry, I should have thought about that before I..."

Ella silenced her with a kiss and smiled. "Don't be sorry." She pressed her forehead against Cam's and whispered: "I love you so much and I'm so proud to be here with you."

"Me too." Cam shot a sideways glance at the crowd outside and felt nerves bubble up now, despite the happy glow that had her in a blissful haze. She ran a hand through her hair, attempting to tame it after Ella's hands had been all over it. "Wait... How do *I* look?"

Ella blew her a kiss when she realized there was no time left as the driver had walked around the car and was now opening the door for them. "You look perfect, as always." She stepped out, waited for Cam to get out of the limo and took her hand, then gave her a reassuring nod. "It will be fine, Cam." She leaned in and whispered: "And don't worry; I know it looks intimidating but they're just cameras and you can ignore any questions they yell at you."

"Sure." Cam had the feeling Ella said it to put herself at ease more than anything, but she nodded anyway and gave her a confident smile. "Ignore everyone," she mumbled to herself as they walked onto the red carpet, holding hands. She blinked a couple of times, unprepared for the flashes that almost blinded her, and she felt a little foolish for having underestimated the overwhelming impact of that short walk. Blocking out the noise and the questions directed their way, she tried to steady her nerves as she continued to smile.

She'd never experienced Ella as the famous actress that she was. To Cam, she was her friend, a wonderful, beautiful, sweet person and now, also her lover. Being here with fans screaming at Ella brought the reality home and she felt immensely proud of her. *Pull yourself together, Cam. You're here to support Ella, not the other way around.* The embrace Ella gave her was enough to relax her a little when they arrived at the end of the carpet, in front of the theatre entrance, where the pictures were being taken. Ella looked up at her and giggled, adjusting Cam's bow tie that was hanging at a weird angle.

"I guess we both look a little roughed up." She ran her fingers through Cam's hair, then wiped the last bit of lip gloss from the corners of her mouth. Cam laughed too and removed a hairpin she'd missed from Ella's hair. When she put it in her pocket, she realized people were laughing.

"I think it's fairly obvious what we've been up to," she whispered in Ella's ear.

Ella took her face in her hands and locked her eyes with hers. "Then we might as well confirm their suspicions." She leaned in and kissed her softly, then smiled against Cam's lips as Cam put her arms around her waist and tugged her closer. The yelling became louder and photographers elbowed each other out of the way to get a shot of them. Ella pulled out of the kiss and grinned. "I'm sorry, I wasn't planning on doing that." She turned back to the crowd and put an arm around Cam's waist while she waved at her fans who were yelling her name.

58

"Wow, that was intense," Cam said as they were on their way home from the premiere. They'd skipped the after-party as Ella had decided it might be a little too much considering the amount of journalists who were there. She put a hand on Ella's thigh and turned to her. "How do you feel? I mean, the whole world knows you're gay now, I don't think you need to spell it out anymore."

Ella smiled. She hadn't stopped smiling all night. "I feel good," she said. "I feel lighter. It's like there's been this dark cloud hanging over me for years and I've been worrying it was going to rain. And then, when it finally started raining, it was just water and I realized it couldn't hurt me. So yeah, I'm fine. Better than fine, even."

"I'm glad you don't regret it." Cam put an arm around Ella and pulled her against her. "So now what? You're going to be the center of attention over the coming weeks."

Ella nodded as she rested her head on Cam's chest. "Yeah, it's going to get crazy, but I'll deal with it. Not tonight, though. Tonight, I want it to be just you and me. Are you still okay with me staying over? There might be a lot of paparazzi down on the beach tomorrow."

"Of course. I want to spend every free minute with you, Ella."

"Me too." Ella hesitated for a moment. "You know, I've been thinking of selling my apartment. I'm hardly there and I never really loved it anyway. It doesn't feel like home. Not like your place feels like home."

"Really?" Cam's heart started beating faster. "You could always move in with me while you look for another place." She placed a kiss on the top of Ella's head and inhaled the scent of her shampoo. She'd never cared much for honeysuckle or coconut before but since she'd gotten used to Ella's hair products, they were her favorite now. "I mean, you could move in permanently of course. I'd love that, but it might be too soon for you and it's not exactly luxury living."

Ella looked up at her. "So you're saying you'd like it if I moved in with you?"

"Of course I'd like that. I can't think of anything better than waking up with you each morning." Cam paused for a moment. "But I'm also conscious that my house is nothing compared to the swanky places you're used to living in."

Ella's face broke into a huge smile. "I love your place, Cam. I don't need space or walk-in closets or outrageous luxury. All I ever wanted was a real home with someone I want to spend the rest of my life with. So yes, if you want me to move in, I'll be delighted to move in." She smiled. "And if you change your mind and decide it's too soon, well, it's not like I'm short of funds. I could always rent something close by. I can be a bit messy and I'm a terrible cook as you well know and..." She was silenced by Cam's lips on hers. When she pulled away and looked at Cam, her eyes welled up for the second time that day.

"I don't care about any of that, Ella. I just want to be with you, as much as possible, night and day, so let's do this. You and me."

Ella nodded and smiled as she sniffed. "Okay. You and me."

59

Ella opened the sliding doors to the porch and was shocked to see a film crew, a dozen photographers and about fifty people waiting on the beach with their phones, ready to get a snapshot of them. The crowd moved as one when she came out, hands reaching up, their lenses pointing at her while they shouted her name. Her heart started beating in her throat when she realized how big of a deal this was. Kissing Cam last night had seemed the natural and right thing to do, but now she'd have to handle the consequences. She slowly retreated back to the living room, leaving the door open as she joined Cam, who was making coffee.

"Morning princess. They've been there since six," Cam said without looking up, stirring almond milk into her coffee. "It's a good thing I took the day off because their cars are blocking my drive." She didn't seem agitated by it, Ella noted. In fact, Cam was smiling as she pulled her in for a kiss.

Ella took a deep breath as she let go and took a sip of her coffee. "I think it's time to talk," she said, turning to Cam.

"There are too many of them out there, we can't keep on fighting them off forever. Will you come with me?"

"Of course." Cam ran a hand through her hair and smiled when a lock of Ella's blond bedhead bounced right back up. "You're right, there's no other way to get rid of them. Should we get changed?" They were both wearing the white robes Vanya had bought them, their eyes still sleepy.

Ella shrugged. "I'm fine like this, they've already seen me. Do you want to get changed?"

"No, let's get it over with." Cam took Ella's hand in hers as they walked out onto the porch and descended the steps. "Squeeze my hand twice if you want out."

Ella nodded. "You do the same."

They sat down next to each other halfway down the steps, both with their coffees in their hands. The sudden silence told them their action was totally unexpected. A couple of photographers looked up, anticipating a cascade of water to pour down on them any minute.

"Don't worry, this is not an attack." Ella gave the crowd a smile as she looked at them. "Besides, I see you've all got your waterproof lenses and covers by now, so there wouldn't be much point." There was a chuckle from the crowd and Ella told herself she was safe here. Anyone who got to them physically would be trespassing and could be arrested. "I assume you're here because you want answers to questions, so go ahead," she said, taking Cam's hand. Despite the confusion amongst their audience, it only took a split second for the first person to ask a question.

"Ella, why did you keep your sexuality hidden? Were you ashamed? Or were you afraid it might limit the movie roles you were being offered?"

Ella shook her head as she looked at the woman who had asked the question. "I'm not ashamed of anything. My life is private, that's all. I choose to disclose what I want, where I want and when I want to do it." She gave her a polite smile. "Saying that, the situation in Hollywood did influence my decision to stay quiet about it until now. A good actor should be able to play any role, not just the ones people identify them with but unfortunately that's not how it currently works in my business. Besides that, I never met anyone before who I was willing to risk my career or turn my life upside down for. That changed when I met Cam." She couldn't help but grin as she said her name.

"So you're admitting that you're in a sexual relationship with Camila Saunders?"

Ella laughed at the obscenity of the question. "Yeah, I totally am. Isn't it obvious?" She looked down at her and Cam's entwined hands as her smile widened, then turned back to the cameras. "This is my girlfriend. Her name is Cam and I love her."

Cam felt a goofy smile creep up on her face, and she kissed Ella on the cheek in an attempt to hide it. In that moment, a frenzy of camera flashes broke out as Ella was bombarded with more questions.

"Where did you guys meet?" one of the journalists at the front asked. Ella bit her lip and looked at Cam, who shot her a reassuring look.

"Whatever you say, I'm with you," she whispered. "But you don't have to share anything you don't want to." Ella nodded, took a deep breath and turned back to the crowd, that turned silent now, waiting for her answer.

"We met right here, at the beach," Ella said. "Or rather by the shore from what I can remember. I tried to drown myself, almost nine months ago, and Cam risked her own life saving me." She paused, a little nervous at the eerie silence that followed after the expected gasps and murmurs.

"It was on my birthday. Mine and Helena's birthday," she continued. "I've been very depressed since my sister died. I felt incredibly alone and I saw no way out. There was a storm that morning and as soon as I walked into the sea, I was swept away by the current. I didn't realize how badly I wanted to live until I got sucked under and there was no way back." She tightened her grip on Cam's hand as a tear rolled down her cheek. "Cam dove in and saved me. She could have drowned herself but somehow, she managed to get us both out. We didn't see each other for a long time after that, and I got help. When I felt a little stronger, I looked her up again, and we became friends." She shrugged. "And I can't deny that I was attracted to her of course, I mean look at her." There was chuckling coming from the crowd, then more camera flashes followed.

"How are you now, Ella?" another woman behind a film camera asked.

"I'm... much better." Ella smiled as Cam wiped away a tear from her cheek and held her close. "I've learned to deal with my sister's death and although I miss her every day, I can laugh again, enjoy the little things and most importantly, I can love. But I'm lucky that I've had an amazing therapist and that I've had medication to help me. Many young people don't have that luxury because they simply can't afford it, or they may be frightened to talk to their friends or family about it." She turned her gaze to the biggest camera she could see, seizing the moment. "That's why I got involved with *Help LA*. It's a small charity and they do great work in the local community. Physical health is important, but mental health is important too, and sometimes therapy, medication or even something as small as having someone listen to your problems or fears can make the difference between life and death." She held up her hand when someone was about to throw in another question and raised her voice. "Wait, let me finish while I've got your attention, I'm not done answering the question yet. Worldwide, between ten and twenty percent of children and adolescents experience depression or mental disorders. This can influence their development, their confidence and their potential to live fulfilling lives. Unfortunately, there's still a major stigma attached to mental disorders, which can sometimes simply be solved with talking and, or medication. *Help LA* aims to break down the barrier of isolation by opening up their doors and inviting young people in the community to talk about their problems and by providing comprehensive and responsive services in a safe setting." She smiled, content that everyone was listening now. "Needless to say, *Help LA* needs donations, but they also need volunteers, so check out their website for details and find out how you can make a difference by helping out."

"Thank you, Ella." Someone said. "Now onto the next question, which I'm sure is on everyone's mind. What do you expect to happen career-wise now that you've come out?"

Ella managed to suppress an eye-roll at how short-lived their attention span was. "I don't know. I honestly don't know." She shrugged and smiled, leaning into Cam. "I have a very exciting project coming up which I can't wait to be a part of. That's all I can say right now."

"Cam, are you going to propose to Ella?" someone else shouted.

Cam winced, surprised that a question was directed at her rather than at Ella. She felt a cold sweat break out when everyone's attention was turned to her, then remembered that she was here to support Ella and that she should just be herself.

"I'm sure I will at some point," she said, placing another kiss on Ella's cheek. "I love her and yeah, of course I'd like to marry my girlfriend one day. Maybe she'd even like to marry me back." She chuckled when a symphony of sighs and cheers sounded from the beach. Ella squeezed her hand twice, and she continued. "But for now, it would be great if we could have some privacy so we can enjoy our time together." She stood up and put her arm around Ella. They were surprised to notice the chaos of questions had subsided and that some journalists and onlookers had even decided to leave.

Ella shot her a smile as they walked back up the steps. "I think they're leaving," she whispered.

"I think they are."

EPILOGUE

Ella noticed the fire pit on the porch was burning when she came home. The soft, flickering shadows of the flames and the smell of burning wood made her smile as she crossed the room and went outside. Although November nights were chilly in LA, Cam was usually out here when she got home. It had been a long day on set, and she was glad the most emotionally draining scenes were wrapped up.

"Hey princess." Cam spun around on her chair and opened the blanket.

"Hey." Ella sat down on her lap sideways and kissed her as Cam wrapped the blanket around them both. "I've missed you. How was your day?"

"It was good. Nice and chilled."

Ella laughed. "Nice and chilled, huh? Says the woman who runs the two, and soon to be three, most popular yoga studios in LA."

"Hey, it's all about delegation and good people. Vanya's the one with the burning ambition. I just teach and develop the programs." She smiled. "How was your day?"

"It was good. Pretty intense, but in a good way. We shot that scene I was worried about. It went well."

"I wouldn't expect any different from you." Cam massaged her thigh. "And now that you have three weeks off to put on some weight, I've made you a nice full-fat vegetarian lasagna with extra cheese. It's in the oven, it should still be warm." She winked. "There's some praline ice-cream in the freezer too."

Ella chuckled. "Thank you; I've been looking forward to this break. Food, food, food and more food. Did you manage to get some time off by the way? I was thinking that maybe we could go to Palm Springs for a couple of days. My mom wants to see me again, and I thought we could meet up at the Palm Garden for my birthday." Ella rolled her eyes. "And with 'we', I mean you, me, mom and her latest toy boy. This one's called Chris, if I remember right."

Cam laughed. "Okay... so Chris now, huh? Well, I've managed to find a replacement for five days, so I'd love to meet up with your mom." She brushed a lock of hair away from Ella's face. It was shorter now, but if anything, she looked even more stunning. The choppy bob with fringe made her look effortlessly sexy and incredibly cute at the same time, and Cam just couldn't stop herself from running her hands through it at any opportunity. "So, you want to celebrate your birthday?" She felt a spark of excitement, thinking of the two kittens she'd be picking up from her colleague Jason's house, to surprise Ella with. A stray cat had given birth to a litter in his yard and the two adorable ginger brothers had immediately melted Cam's heart when he'd shown her the picture. She knew Ella would be over the moon.

Ella nodded. "Yeah, I do. Nothing big, just a lunch. I feel ready."

"That's great. I bet your mom will be happy too. I'm glad you're speaking to her again and I hardly dare to say it, but I think I might even like her a little." Cam raised a brow when Ella grimaced. "Hey, she's actually pretty entertaining and who knows? Chris might be the knight in shining armor she's been waiting for."

At that, they both burst into uncontrollable laughter, knowing all too well that Chris would be a buff workout enthusiast half Bernice's age with a very limited vocabulary and even more limited table manners.

"I just wish she would learn from her mistakes." Ella got up and fetched a bottle of red wine and two glasses from the kitchen. "Anyway, I'll let her know we're coming and that we're looking forward to meeting Chris. Oh, and Vanya and Greg are coming for dinner tomorrow in case you forgot." She sat back on Cam's lap, pouring the wine.

"I know." Cam took the glass and clinked it against Ella's. "I spoke to Vanya about it today, she's bringing dessert." She hesitated. "I hope you don't mind but I invited Neil too."

"Neil?" Ella frowned. "As in Neil Messenger?" She chuckled. "Jesus, you guys really hit it off at that reunion dinner last week, didn't you?"

"Yeah, I like him, he's funny. I told him he could bring a date, but he said he'd rather come alone and that he was looking forward to adult conversation. Looks like he's got the same problem as your mother."

Ella giggled as she sank back against Cam. She took a sip of her wine and watched the flames before them dance in the wind. The gusts were getting stronger by the minute and the sound of the swirling waves turned into powerful crashes as they hit the shore. She liked sitting here with Cam, and they'd spent many nights like this, simply enjoying the view.

"I think there's a storm coming," Cam said.

"Yeah, I can feel it too." Ella sighed and took Cam's hand, thinking back to that morning, almost a year ago now. "What a difference a year can make, huh?"

"I was just thinking the same thing." Cam tightened her grip on Ella's hand and placed a soft kiss on her cheek. "And how bizarre that we're here now, together."

A serious expression now fell over Ella's face. "If you hadn't saved me, well..." She shrugged. "Out of all the beaches I could have driven to last year, I drove here. Do you think it was fate?"

"I don't know." Cam closed her eyes as she inhaled deep against Ella's hair. "But I do know that I love you more than anything and it means the world to me to see you happy."

"I love you too." Ella turned to Cam, tears shimmering in her eyes. They were happy tears, she realized as she wiped her cheeks. There hadn't been many sad tears lately. She'd moved in with Cam and cherished every moment with her. The days were a gift, rather than a challenge and every morning she woke up in Cam's arms felt like coming home. "You know," she continued, "my sister's death to me was pain in its purest, most confrontational form. The grief was like a high-resolution photograph, so sharp that there was no escaping reality, and the only way to soften the edges was to keep looking at it until it numbed me." She smiled. "But as just as photographs fade over time, blurred by a soft, sun-bleached filter, the memories have become bearable again, and even beautiful at times."

"I know what you mean." Cam took a sip of her wine, then placed her glass on the table, staring out over the ocean. "It doesn't go away but it changes into some kind of strange acceptance."

"Yeah." Ella paused for a moment. "I never knew loss

before, but I never knew a love like this either. And you know what? You've been my warmth, my light and the filter that makes everything look just a little prettier and a little more hopeful. And God, Cam, I love you more than words could ever express."

Cam felt herself well up too at Ella's words. "You're everything to me, Ella. You're..." Her voice trailed away as she looked up when she noticed something from the corner of her eye. A dark shadow moved toward them, swaying through the sky. "Wait... what is that?"

Ella's gaze turned skyward too, and her eyes widened when she saw it was a red-tailed hawk. It was hovering over them, leaning on the wind, its majestic wings static until it dove down and settled on the porch railing, right in front of them. The impact of its landing was hard and sudden, and Ella's heart was almost beating out of her chest as it screeched and looked right at her.

"Hey," she whispered, after the first shock had settled, then smiled when it cocked its head as if greeting her back. Despite its size, and the flames reflected from the fire pit in the bird's fierce eyes, it had a soft, almost sweet demeanor as it simply sat there, curiously studying her. Ella was surprised by the words that came from her lips then. "How did you find me?" Of course, she didn't expect an answer, but she still found herself waiting for one.

"Is it..." Cam frowned and fell silent, equally shocked. "Do you really think it's the same one?" She felt Ella shiver against her as her hand fisted her hair. A lot of things went through her mind at that moment, but she didn't voice them. It was crazy to think the hawk from Ella's yard in Palm Springs had flown all the way here, just to see her but something deep down in her gut went against all logic and told her that was exactly what it had done.

"I think so." Ella continued to lock eyes with the bird as if hypnotized. "It doesn't make any sense, but yes, I think it's her." She wasn't quite sure if by 'her', she meant the hawk, or something on a higher, spiritual level. Whatever it was, it was weird and wonderful and almost magical. She smiled at the bird and nodded, tears streaming down her face now. "Thank you for coming to see me. I..." Before she could finish her sentence, the bird cocked its head again, then flapped its wings before taking off into the night. "I miss you," she whispered, more to herself this time. The hawk was gone as fast as it had come, and neither Ella nor Cam knew what to say in the minutes that followed. Ella stayed in the warmth of Cam's embrace and felt a strange sense of peace settle over her. She was happy, she was moving on but above all, she was so grateful to be alive.

ACKNOWLEDGMENTS

I'm so incredibly grateful to have an amazing team of people I work with on a regular basis. Working with friends is the best thing in the world!

First and foremost, thank you Claire Jarrett, my beloved editor! You've stuck by me even though I'm probably the messiest person in the world to work with and I hope we're going to work on many more books together. *Living* was a difficult one and I appreciate all the time and effort you put into it.

Thank you to Laure Dherbècourt, my main beta reader, for always giving honest and specific feedback, and to Ro Fetterman for hunting my Britishisms (glad there weren't any this time hehe).

Also, Miira Ikiviita, Emily Browning Cromer and Debs Armishaw, I really appreciated your last-minute help. Thank you so much, guys!

Most importantly, I'd like to give a huge thank you to the wonderful people who have opened up to me about their struggles with depression, and helped me understand the situation from different perspectives. It was a humbling experience, and I wish you all the love and happiness in the world. Thank you, truly.

ABOUT THE AUTHOR

Lise Gold is an author of lesbian romance. Her romantic attitude, enthusiasm for travel and love for feel good stories form the heartland of her writing. Born in London to a Norwegian mother and English father, and growing up between the UK, Norway, Zambia and the Netherlands, she feels at home pretty much everywhere and has an unending curiosity for new destinations. She goes by 'write what you know' and is often found in exotic locations doing research or getting inspired for her next novel.

Working as a designer for fifteen years and singing semi-professionally, Lise has always been a creative at heart. Her novels are the result of a quest for a new passion after resigning from her design job in 2018. Since the launch of Lily's Fire in 2017, she has written several romantic novels and is currently working on 'The Compass Series'.

When not writing from her kitchen table, Lise can be found cooking, at the gym or singing her heart out somewhere, preferably country or blues. After living in Amsterdam and Hong Kong together and getting married in Spain, she and her wife have finally settled in the UK with their dogs El Comandante and Bubba, and their cats Kanye and Tittie (who also has his own clothing line).

ALSO BY LISE GOLD

Lily's Fire

Beyond the Skyline

The Cruise

French Summer

Fireflies

Northern Lights

Southern Roots

Eastern Nights

Manufactured by Amazon.ca
Bolton, ON